SECRET VALOR

SECRET VALOR

Emanuele F. Portolese

Copyright © 2007 by Emanuele F. Portolese.

Cover Illustrator: Thomas McAteer

Library of Congress Control Number: 2007900022
ISBN: Hardcover   978-1-4257-4606-3
           Softcover   978-1-4257-4605-6

All rights reserved. No part of this book may be reproduced or transmitted in any form or by any means, electronic or mechanical, including photocopying, recording, or by any information storage and retrieval system, without permission in writing from the copyright owner.

This is a work of fiction. Names, characters, places and incidents either are the product of the author's imagination or are used fictitiously, and any resemblance to any actual persons, living or dead, events, or locales is entirely coincidental.

This book was printed in the United States of America.

To order additional copies of this book, contact:
Xlibris Corporation
1-888-795-4274
www.Xlibris.com
Orders@Xlibris.com

37538

To Contrive
Thank you for your
support. Hope you
enjoy this story.
Emanuele

Acknowledgements

Secret Valor could never have materialized without vital support from my loving wife and partner, JoAnn. Her patience over time, help with editing and encouragement at my lowest moments were vital to me. I am deeply grateful for the many hours she spent reading and rereading this novel and the sacrifices she made along the way. The continuous love and encouragement from my daughters Lisa and Laura, my sons-in-law Rob and Alain, and my granddaughters, Victoria and Veronica, have meant more to me than I can ever express. It is also important to convey my appreciation to others among my family and friends who took the time to read and comment on the initial draft of this novel: my mother, Palma Portolese; my mother in law, Edith Abney; my sister Patt Coyle; my brothers and their wives, Don and Penny, Pat and Carol, Joe and Jean; and to my very good friends, Joe and Lola Sample. I want you to know that your input is very much appreciated and contributed greatly to this novel. Thank you all so very much.

January 28, Washington, DC

Well past midnight, it began to rain, which was a good thing. The water fell shimmering against the orange light of the arc lamps they set up on the site. It was hard, grim work. The recovery teams had brought in listening gear to probe the rubble for survivors. The deadly clicking of Geiger counters was everywhere. The interior of the dome had been an inner and outer shell of solid cast iron; it now lay in jagged shards the size of small houses, steaming from the lingering heat of the blast, piled among the shattered marble. In their protective suits, the men moved slowly across the devastation like pale ghosts among the ruins of some ancient temple. Only this time the ruins were less than ten days old. One fireman, tapping for possible signals from buried victims, struck something metallic with his pry bar. It rang differently than the iron, like a bell. Bracing himself, he levered aside a broken slab, kicked away more debris, and stood very still. "Here she is," he said over his radio, and then, against all orders, pulled his mask from his face so he could see her more clearly. When they swung the portable light into place, the rest of them could see he had been crying, his eyes red with exhaustion. At his feet, they could see the face and massive length of the goddess of freedom triumphant—Thomas Crawford's great bronze statue that had topped the Capitol since the Civil War. Undamaged as if by a miracle, shining in the harsh spotlight, she smiled serenely up at them in the pouring rain.

Prologue

October 1973
Port Said, Egypt

*I*t was still dark when Fajil al-Said moved silently down the bleak concrete steps of his Soviet-built flat in the Qahirah section of Port Said. He was a quiet young man from an extremely poor family of dockworkers; tall and slender with sad gray eyes and deep brown, almost black hair. Fajil had been long in training as a Moslem cleric, and this was to be his first day as a muezzin, calling the city to morning prayers from the tower of the Central Mosque on Shari Safiya. His wife, Alla, had been up with his baby daughter, Kamira, most of the night, but she had let him sleep because she knew he would be singing for the first time over the great loudspeakers, his rich voice would bring the entire city to worship. She had carefully washed and ironed his white cotton robe the day before in readiness for this proud day.

As he rode his bicycle into the city center along el-Gunhuriya Avenue, Fajil breathed in deeply. In the early morning light, the streets were nearly empty. Later he knew they would be choked with the foul fumes of trucks and motorcycles and donkey carts, the flotsam traffic that suffocated this crowded port city at the mouth of the Suez. But for now, before dawn, the air was pure and fresh and Fajil could taste its innocence. The morning. The creation. As innocent as a child's first hours, Fajil thought. A good idea for a religious tract, a lesson of innocence. Fajil steered his bicycle around the corner of the central market square and glanced north to the sea. It would be a clear day, with the summer's oppressive heat finally broken by the lazy autumn breezes moving in from the eastern Mediterranean.

As he turned onto Shari Safiya, the morning sun broke over the outer harbor and painted soft pastel colors on the rows of white stucco office buildings and flats with their ornate carved shutters. The palms standing in rows along the boulevards of the business district swayed gently in the cool morning air. To Fajil, their fronds looked like the fingers of the faithful reaching to the sky. He laughed at himself, murmuring a prayer. He knew he was a hopelessly sentimental man.

He noticed everything, tasted the air, felt the grandeur of Allah's gifts working through him. How he loved this grimy, sweating port with its traders, its grand offices of French, Greek, and Lebanese entrepreneurs, the dusty warehouses where he had worked with his father and brothers loading pallets crammed with jute, cotton, and tea. It felt to him like the crossroads of the world.

Turning onto Shari Abbas, Fajil saw that the shopkeepers had already begun to set up their stalls in the central market. He could smell the bread coming fresh from the ovens near the Central Square, and realized he was hungry. But he never ate or drank, not even tea, until his prayers were complete.

Fajil arrived at the Central Mosque and climbed the stairs in the high tower overlooking the city. The view was magnificent out over the harbor and shipyards, with the early morning ferry approaching from the Port Fuad suburbs across the bay. The sun now was rising brilliant red in the sky, and the light was everywhere, shining as if to cleanse the sins of the city. Fajil raised his hands to the sky and sang into the microphone with his high tenor voice, singing to Allah the song of praise.

When the morning prayers came in, high and haunting, the faithful of the city leaned over their prayer rugs, singing with the muezzin. But then, suddenly the air raid sirens went off, at first a low moan, then a piercing, cycling howl that woke the city into panic.

Just above the water, far in the distance, Fajil barely made out the dirty gray shapes growing larger and larger. There was no sound from the flight of Israeli F-4 fighter-bombers. There were at least twenty of them. He recalled the city had been bombed before, in 1956 and 1967. Before, there had been bulletins from the military authorities, special civil defense drills for all districts; but this was a complete surprise.

Fajil watched from the tower. Even the cursed Israelis would never hit a mosque, so he felt confident he was safe. They also never hit the residential areas, therefore he knew his family was safe. A row of angry black puffs appeared near the first of the planes as flak guns along the shipyard harbor began firing. It was funny, he thought, how you never knew where the guns were until they fired.

To Fajil it was a kind of beautiful, deadly dance in the air, the planes looking like hunting falcons as they rose up in their bombing runs to dive in on their targets along the commercial harbor and shipyard. The bombs could never be seen falling; only after they hit the ground did the bright orange blossom to indicate where the deadly missiles had landed, sending plumes of dust and flames spiraling gently into the morning sky.

Fajil watched one plane in particular out on the edge of the harbor. It seemed the tracers were converging on it. The plane trembled slightly as the wavering contrails reached it. It began to trail a thin line of gray smoke, and broke from its formation, bursting into flames, slowed over the Qahirah residential section, then rolled over in an agonizingly slow dive straight down into a row of apartment houses. There were multiple explosions and the smoke and flame rose into the sky in an ugly black streak.

Only then did Fajil notice it was his neighborhood; the section of flats a little more than two miles away was familiar to him. Then he realized what had happened. Moaning softly, he rushed down the steps of the tower, found his bicycle, and rode off into the burning city. It took him nearly thirty minutes to fight his way through the ambulances and fire trucks, the stalled cars and the vendors' carts, which had overturned in the attack. The water mains had been destroyed and the city's precious lifeblood flowed through the streets unchecked, running red with the reflection of the burning buildings.

When he found his flat he knew he was too late. His building had taken the full force of the bombs released by the wounded pilot. It was a series of collapsed walls and ceilings tossed together like great gray cards of concrete, utterly engulfed in the flames fed by broken gas mains.

Fajil ran around to the back of the building. A staircase, held firm by a few steel-reinforcing rods, led to the second story where his flat had been. Bomb fragments had peppered the walls with holes the size of a man's hand. He found the door to his family's flat blown in half. Screaming, he kicked through a pile of rubble and plaster and smashed furniture. The bedroom where he had left his wife and daughter had been sheared away as the building had collapsed and now lay under tons of wrecked concrete. He looked in vain for his mother, his brother, and his sister. He knew that every member of his family had been killed. Like his wailing from the tower moments earlier, his voice rose again in a pitiful shriek as he fell into the dust, moaning, and tearing at his robe in total frustration and anger.

He didn't move for nearly an hour, crying now and again uncontrollably, until the fires had burned themselves out and the survivors were picking through the ruins of the apartment house like wretched birds, salvaging scraps to make shelters in the streets.

That evening, as it was growing dark, Fajil noticed a charred panel of aluminum with rivets in it, a piece of an airplane, wedged into the wall of his *kitchen. It was curved remarkably like a sword and had strange markings on it, probably a technical diagram of some sort. Then he noticed the writing. He had studied English in school, and could not help but try to read what it said. He brushed away the plaster dust, and pulled the piece out of the wall, cutting his hand.*

On a small brass plate riveted into the panel it read, "McDonnell Douglas Aircraft Corporation, St. Louis, Missouri."

September 16, 1975
Dirksen Senate Building, Hearing Room B-236
Washington DC

The crowd, larger than usual, was gathering for the afternoon hearing. The Senate Select Committee on Energy and Natural Resources was convening to hear testimony on the fluctuations of the gasoline prices during the 1974 oil crisis. Senator Ira Glasser, Democratic Chair of the Committee for Energy and Natural Resources, was reveling in the considerable media coverage his hearings had generated. A Brandeis law professor and former Attorney General for the state of Massachusetts, he was a short, arrogant man with a wild shock of white hair who could use all the exposure he could get. Nothing was wrong with probing a sensitive public issue for a future attorney general of the United States. Following a couple of day's testimony by the usual droning consultants and frightened oil company executives, Glasser had reserved the afternoon's proceedings for a real star, the kind of man who could pack them in and not cause much trouble in terms of detailed testimony: Wade Pike, of the Pike family of Chicago.

It was still hot in Washington for the early fall, and the air in the windowless hearing room grew stale and close. First, Sen. Nancy Hodge from Nebraska had begun her questioning of Pike, and he had graciously handled her polite queries with just the right blend of confidence and humility. Since the Pike family controlled several thousand railroad jobs in Nebraska, Senator Hodge was careful not to probe too deeply. Sen. Langley Crawford from North Carolina then weighed in with his slow drawl, each question taking an eternity. Sen. Don Pulaski from Michigan picked up the questioning, hitting hard on the damage that oil price rises had done to the auto industry. He closed his remarks, and Pike said with great charm, "A great many businesses were hit badly by the oil shock. If you saw my balance sheet for the last two years, you'd wish you were in the auto industry."

The crowd murmured appreciatively. Senator Glasser glanced at his watch and stifled a yawn. He perused his order of testimony. As it was nearing four o'clock, he motioned for the junior senator from Colorado, David Bergstrom, to start his questions. It was understood the member of the committee with the least seniority would just ask a few cursory questions for the news crews and they would all pack it up for the cocktail hour.

Bergstrom, a tall man with sandy blonde hair and lean, tanned face of a skier, cleared his throat.

"First of all, Mr. Pike, exactly where were you on January 10, 1974," he asked. The room went dead silent; all the questions up to now had been quite friendly. The committee wasn't interested in going into details. Bergstrom

had waited two days for a chance to have any input with the proceedings. Many of the reporters in fact had already left. One of the few remaining was Ben Burke of the Baltimore Sun who had stayed idly to watch. What he witnessed, and wrote later in his best seller, "The Immigrant's Son" won him the Pulitzer Prize.

With the television lights on him, Bergstrom became a different man. His jaw hardened, and his voice had the tone of a district attorney protecting the law. He was no longer diffident. After a few seconds of silence, he repeated his question to the surprised Pike.

"I say, sir, again, what were your whereabouts on January 10, 1974?"

Wade Pike looked puzzled. Who was this guy anyway?

"I'm sorry, Senator Bergstrom, I'm a busy man, and like most successful businessmen, I have only a short term memory. Which, in past negotiations, has proved quite useful."

A ripple of laughter moved through the sparse crowd at the insouciance of Pike's reply. He seemed very much like a fisherman lazily playing a fish on a line.

Pike noticed no change in Bergstrom's stare, and continued, "May I respectfully request the committee for a moment to consult my appointment book? My attorney has thoughtfully brought it with him. The man thinks of everything."

Again, slight laughter moved through the crowd. An assistant pulled the thick cordovan leather day diary from a briefcase. After casually flipping through a few pages, Pike answered.

"I remember it now, Senator Bergstrom. I was in Reno and Lake Tahoe over a three-day weekend visiting with family friends and business associates. You see, the Pike family trust has business interests in the Golden Spur Casino in Tahoe. Now and again we go to inspect the premises and receive a briefing from its general manager, a Mr. Wilt Derringer. Wilt is generous enough to let us play poker with him on the house, which we own of course. It's remarkably similar to what we do at the Commodities Exchange in Chicago."

Again the audience and even some members of the committee laughed.

Bergstrom did not change his expression. Looking down to his notes, he continued. "On the night of January 10 you were seen by witnesses leaving the Golden Spur at 9:05 PM in a limousine. These witnesses have sworn to this in an affidavit, so we can accept their authenticity." Turning his eyes once again to Pike, "Sir, where did you go in the car?"

Pike felt the heat of the lights now. He wondered if he showed any stress to the television cameras.

Bergstrom shifted impatiently in his chair. His voice was low in the microphone, remarkably calm.

"Sir, do you deny to this committee the fact that you left the casino at 9:05? I wish to remind you that you are under oath."

Pike turned and whispered something to his attorney.

"Senator Bergstrom I do not deny that I left the casino that evening. In the interests of personal discretion, I do not wish to reveal where I went."

Senator Glasser sat bolt upright, his face flush with anger. The situation was growing tense for no reason, and he was not in control. Pike's testimony was supposed to be window dressing anyway for the press. Still worse, the cameras were focused on Bergstrom, a young man with eyes the color of steel.

"Mr. Pike, does your—" Bergstrom started but was quickly interrupted.

"Senator Bergstrom, as the hour is late I recommend we break for the day so we can begin fresh in the morning," Glasser's booming voice slammed against the high ceilings and echoed around the walls. "It has been a long afternoon, and I trust the committee and Mr. Pike can pick up where we leave off."

As he spoke, quickly returning to his characteristically unhurried tone, Glasser was thinking of how he would cut this freshman straight off at the knees once they were out of the chambers. He knew how sensitive new senators were to fitting in; after all, it was the only way they could gather any meager attention on the voting floor. He didn't in any way anticipate Bergstrom's reply.

"It is only 4:15, Mr. Chairman, and Mr. Pike has testified for less than an hour," noted Bergstrom politely, a cool steady voice. "I will be brief if Mr. Pike will be forthcoming in his responses to the Committee. Just a few minutes more, Mr. Chairman, and I will be finished with my questions so as not to take any of Mr. Pike's time in the morning."

Glasser sighed softly, rapping his thick Waterman pen on the table impatiently. It seemed like things were well in hand again. "All right, Senator Bergstrom. Kindly continue."

Bergstrom paused, wrote a note on a legal pad before him. He leaned forward to his microphone, and asked, "Mr. Pike, does your need to maintain personal discretion obviate the need for the American people to know why you left the casino at 9:05 PM, January 10, 1974?"

"No, it does not, Senator. But I must—"

"Then again, why did you leave the casino at such an early hour?"

"I had a business meeting."

"A meeting with whom, Mr. Pike?"

"I cannot recollect, Senator. It could have be—"

"Sir, do you deny the following persons met you at a lake estate owned by the Pike family trust located at the north shore of Lake Tahoe on High Point Road, at Incline Village?" Looking at his notes, Bergstrom continued, "Mr. Carlton

Gladding, CEO of North American Oil? Mr. J. T. Williamson of Ranger Petroleum Resources Corporation? Mr. Farley Johnston, international chairman of British Petroleum? Or do you, under oath, wish to deny the signed affidavit listing the persons at this secret meeting, and that the purpose of this meeting was to arrange for a massive price-fixing plan for gasoline following the fall outbreak of hostilities in the Middle East."

Pike's face whitened visibly. He did not seem to have an answer, and the press photographers caught him for the papers the next day, head down, as if his spirit had been broken. He put his hand over his microphone and turned to confer with his lawyer, and the delay seemed to be a statement in itself.

Glasser had to do something. The situation was out of control. He hadn't expected anything substantial to come out of these hearings. Worse yet, he was not the one with the inside information. Where the hell did Bergstrom get this stuff?

To fill the silence, Glasser lifted his gavel and looked at his watch. "I believe the Committee is prepared to carry on this line of questioning at 9:00 tomorrow morning, Senator Bergstrom. If my distinguished colleague would—"

"Respectfully, Mr. Chairman, . . ." started Bergstrom.

"Mr. Chairman, we object to—," Pike's attorney tried to be heard, but Bergstrom continued to hold everyone's attention.

"Does this committee wish to achieve anything useful for the taxpayers of the United States with this hearing?" demanded Bergstrom. The room was completely quiet now, and each of his words seemed to ring with the truth off the marble walls. "The angry citizens of this country rightly expect this committee to commit itself to goals and purposes beyond wasting valuable time and allowing individuals to snatch the attention of the press."

"Mr. Chairman, we object . . .," the attorney's words were invisible.

Bergstrom continued, ignoring everyone else. "I wish to speak for the good citizens of Colorado—men and women whose lives and jobs have been hurt badly by the unexplained rise in gasoline prices. Ranchers, farmers, businessmen, homemakers. The citizens of Colorado elected me to work and not to grandstand, so I will rephrase my question to please the chairman. Mr. Pike, you do not wish to say where you went?"

"We object, Mr. Chair—" It was Pike's attorney.

"You will not speak to refute the affidavits I hold in my hand concerning this meeting?" continued Bergstrom, his lips nearly touching the microphone, his voice intense. "Again, I ask you to give us your side of the story on who you met with and why the evening of January 10?"

The room instantly plunged into a riveting silence. After listening to advice from nervous counsel, Pike turned to the microphone. His words were a bombshell, and they hit the front pages of every newspaper in the nation the next morning.

"Respectfully, sir, I would like to invoke my rights under the Fifth Amendment of the Constitution."

The room exploded with gasps and murmurs from the crowd.

"Order!" *shouted Senator Glasser, pounding his gavel.* "Order! The committee will come to order!"

That night Pike flew by private plane to Veracruze, Mexico, where a car was waiting to take him through the Yucatan to a remote seaside villa in Belize. Months before, he had secreted more than one hundred million dollars to a number of banks in the Cayman Islands, Switzerland, Hong Kong, and Macao. It would take the Treasury Department's investigative team months to pick up his trail, only to loose it again.

Chapter One

Present Year
3:00 AM, Thursday, December 6
Charlotte Amalie, The Virgin Islands

It was a moonless night, utterly black. A small unmarked plane came in from the east, flying so low over the whitecaps that now and then the rising surf threw spray onto its landing gear. As it crossed over the islands off St. Croix and headed inland, it turned slightly northwest toward its destination about seven miles from the capital city of the Virgin Islands, Charlotte Amalie.

Radar from the US Coast Guard had picked up the Cessna 250 about ten miles offshore as it cruised at an altitude of less than a hundred feet and notified its station at St. Thomas. A couple months before, they would not have been able to pick it up. Even now, the signal faded in and out, frustrating the operator. Unauthorized night flights of small planes were not uncommon in the Virgin Islands. Drug running was a major industry in the area. Light planes from Venezuela or Panama found it relatively easy to drop their illegal cargo over land on numerous islands to be picked up by smugglers and transported to the mainland by diverse creative methods. Once in US territory, the drugs could be moved around with ease and eventually delivered to all fifty states. Customs agents, the coast guard, and agents of the DEA were unable to stop the numerous drops made almost nightly throughout the Virgin Islands. But the drop about to take place involved a more deadly cargo than cocaine.

A DEA spotter plane was vectored to the location of the approaching aircraft, constantly updated on its line of flight. As the unknown plane cleared the village of San Mateo, two lights appeared on a dirty roadway ahead. With landing beams now on, the plane landed quickly in the dark. A car approached as the doors of the Cessna immediately swung open and four men jumped onto the road.

Suddenly, a coast guard helicopter swung in from the south heading directly toward the plane, its lights visible on the roadway below. As the chopper flew in over the Cessna, the car sped away in the dark. A search light from somewhere on the ground focused on the plane and, as if ignited by the beams, the plane exploded in a cloud of flame and debris mushrooming two hundred feet into the air. The chopper banked hard to avoid the explosion, but was hit by debris and spun wildly, then slammed hard into the ground in a blazing inferno.

Seven miles from the city of Charlotte Amalie, two coast guard flight officers and a DEA agent died as two highly trained assassins sped to catch a morning flight to Miami.

6:10 AM
Washington DC

Barry Dipaula opened his eyes as the dark blue Mercury marquis eased to a stop in the heavy shadows in front of a matte-black steel gate at the west entrance to the White House. *Finally*, he thought.

The marquis sat for a short time, engine ticking over softly, the driver staring straight ahead into the dim lights near the guardhouse. Dipaula sat upright and reached for his briefcase, clearing his throat a bit. In the harsh glare of the headlights, he could see a uniformed Secret Service officer appear from the building. The officer waved to the driver. The metal gates jarred, then squealed in protest as both arms moved inward allowing the car to ease ahead.

The limousine proceeded up the driveway, out into an open area then stopped near the west entrance to the mansion. Dipaula stepped from the limo and glanced to the faint orange sky down Pennsylvania Avenue. In the crisp cool air, he could hear the delicate sound of several sleepless snowbirds in the trees nearby. One of the guard dogs barked unexpectedly, and the birds were quickly silenced.

He walked a few steps along the concrete path toward a marine guard standing lifeless near the door, which immediately opened from the inside.

Dipaula entered the security foyer and exchanged pleasantries with a half-dozen uniformed officers of the Secret Service. It was difficult to believe it had been over a year since he had entered this room for the first time. Dipaula crossed the green and brown carpet to the security station, passing under a Regency chandelier. Each day, upon seeing the brilliant orange-and-white color scheme in this security room, Dipaula was instantly transformed from the relatively calm world outside to the awesome, intense world inside the White House.

A veteran security officer cleared his throat and spoke just above a whisper, "Good morning, Mr. Dipaula. All's well with you today, sir?"

"I'm just fine, Mike. Glad to be inside. Running a bit late."

There were no metal detectors visible, but security was tight.

"Yes, sir, it's a bit nippy out there." The officer quickly motioned him through.

Dipaula walked briskly down the hallway and proceeded toward the Oval Office. His father had described the building to him many times. However, unlike his father, he was not perfectly at peace amid the turmoil of world power.

As he passed the Secret Service agents at the main doorway to the Oval Office, he noticed a small red light above the door was on, indicating the president was in the room. Dipaula squinted as if the light hurt his eyes. *Damn*, he thought as he stopped in front of Margaret Brint's office. "Is he on the line yet?"

Brint, who appeared much younger than her early sixties, had been a more than capable secretary to President Bergstrom over the last year. "Yes, Mr. Dipaula. He said he couldn't wait for you. Go on in. Oh, yes," she added, handing him an overstuffed manila folder, "your secretary sent this over."

Dipaula took the folder, and then entered a small lobby to his right, where another agent stood guard. He opened a door leading into the Oval Office and could see the president to the left, halfway across the room, seated behind his scrolled mahogany desk, still on the phone.

Bergstrom looked up, gave a casual smile and motioned for Dipaula to enter. He then focused back on his call as he removed his reading glasses and gently massaged his eyes. "Yes, well, before you commit your country to anything, is there a possibility that John Skinner could have a private meeting with Minister Malinkof? There are some pressing matters we must discuss regarding the loan and the sooner the better."

Dipaula moved across the presidential seal woven in the center of the carpet. In the middle of the room, opposite the president's desk sat a massive white and gold sofa, which regularly held the world's most influential people. Placed around the room were a half-dozen plush chairs with blue silk fabric and gold eagle medallions in the center of the backs. Dipaula chose to take one directly in front of the president's desk, careful to avoid unnecessary noise, knowing the conversation was being recorded.

As he waited for the president to conclude his conversation, Dipaula couldn't help but notice the emerging gray lines filtering through Bergstrom's brown hair. A side effect this high office had on the men who occupied it. Bergstrom was not only the toughest politician he had ever seen, but the most intelligent and determined as well.

"Very true, Mr. President," answered Bergstrom. "Thank you, Boris. Be vigilant, my friend."

The president slowly placed the receiver into its cradle as Dipaula opened the folder saying, "Mr. President, here are the notes for Secretary Skinner to take to Europe. I trust your conversation with Masarov went well."

"Well, good morning to you too, Barry," the president remarked. "Yes," he tapped his fingers on the notepad. "He agreed to a meeting between Malinkof and Skinner. But there was something about his voice. I imagine things are much worse inside the Kremlin than we suspect. Better get some additional data from the agency before Skinner's meeting." He paused briefly, his head lowered to the papers in front of him, then looked up and continued. "How bad do you think things really are over there, Barry?"

"Well, sir, the reports all indicate—"

"Barry, please," the president interrupted. "You got your doctorate before twenty-eight and made NSA before forty. You helped put me in this room. I trust your judgment. I've read all the reports. Now I need your personal input, what you think and feel is really going on over there. I need a hell of a lot more than layers of speculation."

"I understand, sir." Dipaula took a deep breath. "Mr. President, I have no doubt the situation is far worse than reports indicate. The agency believes the number of soldiers killed along the Chinese-Russian border is nearly twice what both sides have reported. The Chinese may have lost fourteen men during the conflict, the Russians ten. The Russian military is furious with Masarov's weak response. But the biggest thorn in their behind is the two hundred billion you've committed to Masarov for energy exploration in the Arctic and eastern Siberia. The generals view it as a golden yoke squeezing tight around the Russian president's neck and an attempt to drain them of their new oil reserves. I believe that could be a disruptive force with them."

Dipaula noticed a slight wrinkle form between the president's dark brown eyes as he sat back in his chair. The man seemed to be in deep thought, maybe regretting for a moment having committed the huge sum of money to Moscow.

"Will they move against Masarov in the next week or two?"

"I don't think so, Mr. President." Dipaula was hopeful. He knew the Russians as well as anyone in the administration. His last two books focused heavily on the Russian economy and he spent a great deal of time studying their infrastructure and their military establishment. "But they're not very predictable at this point. The rules have changed." He quickly added, "That's because the game has changed dramatically over the last few years. The sudden low price of oil has placed Russia in a difficult domestic situation. They lived well for years, but that's not the case now. The fact they are accepting money from us and not the Chinese, has intensified the problem along their border. The Chinese are incensed by the potential drop in Russian oil supply."

"Are we confident who's the calling the shots over there?"

"Yes, sir. General Obidiov is still in control of the primary opposition, their principal decision maker. However, no one believes the military will move against Masarov as long as you continue your involvement and direct support. At the present time, you're the only stabilizing force. I don't believe the Chinese will provoke the situation as long as they get some of the oil and gas from the new fields. The border clash would have triggered a much bigger response if it weren't for the energy potential for both countries."

"What if a coup is successful?"

It was Dipaula's turn to sit back and reflect. A successful coup was the one thing he feared most, and the one thing causing severe insomnia at a time he needed most to rest. "That would do it, sir. I think the Chinese wouldn't hesitate to place their military on full alert and move millions of troops to the border. With the hard-liners in control in Moscow, especially with someone like General Obidiov in control, Beijing would certainly consider that a major threat to their security.

"Mr. President, we have no choice but to help stabilize the situation in Russia, keep Masarov in power and placate the Chinese. We need to refocus their attention on the larger threat to the world. If the alliance is allowed to formalize and become a reality, the world will surely pay a very heavy price."

Neither man spoke for a long minute before Dipaula felt the need to break the silence. "You're the answer, sir; the stabilizing force. No question in my mind you need to give the Russians and the Chinese a firm message. Your State of the Union Address is still a few weeks away, but it needs a lot of work, sir. It needs to say, in a more distinct way, that the United States will remain firmly engaged during this crisis. That we will not become detached nor consent to a decline of stability and peace in the world."

The president nodded an agreement before his eyes shifted to a table near his desk. On the small table sat his favorite piece, a handsomely crafted vermeil wine cooler, its handles classical figures reaching for grapes from an arbor. Dipaula recognized the look. On a few occasions in the past, the president had focused intently on that wine cooler, as if it were a mantra or a crystal ball with an esoteric power to reveal the perfect answer to his most difficult problems.

"As we've discussed many times before, Mr. President," Dipaula's voice tightening a bit, "we've lost a lot of support and confidence over the last ten years fighting the war on terrorism. Iraq has been a constant thorn in our diplomatic side. Not many counties around the world think we can effectively act as mediator between these two superpowers, but we seem to be the only hope. While they lack perfect confidence in us, they hope some of our basic character remains. They know that if Obidiov and his people take over in Russia they'll surely blackmail a number of countries with a threat of withholding gas and oil, making things much worse for us."

The president reached for Dipaula's notes as though he had heard more than what his national security advisor had just said, his eyes appeared fixed, determined. "Skinner needs to get on this in a hurry. We can't allow either side to move too quickly or they'll set off a panic and bring everyone else down on this thing." Scanning the papers, "I want a full top-level discussion. Set that up for me, will you, Barry? We can't move too quickly ourselves; yet, we don't have the luxury of time, here. Dark clouds are forming over Moscow, and they could rain shit all over us."

December 8, 7:30 PM
New York City

The fifty-foot Christmas tree in Rockefeller Center sparkled, casting brilliant rays of light all about in the cool night air, as the ten thousand multicolored lights that adorned it swayed aimlessly about in a gentle, crisp winter breeze. Below the tree, New Yorkers of all ages, tightly bundled in their winter coats, wool hats, and scarves, glided about the enormous skating rink, which shimmered with the colorful blur of reflected lights from the surrounding buildings. A medley of Christmas carols charmed the crowd moving about the ice; puffs of steam coming from every mouth.

Across the rink, opposite the Christmas tree, was the enormous sixty-five story Citizens Bank Building of New York City. It was nearly deserted, not unusual for a Friday night, especially during the holiday season. Only a few overworked individuals were sparsely scattered in offices throughout the building.

Inside a room on the seventh floor, a faint glow could be seen flickering against the walls of the Creston Enterprise Board Room. The room was crowded with a dozen men and women clad in dark blue FBI jackets working with high-tech equipment, including monitors, recorders, and sound gear.

Special Agent Sandra Merrall focused sharply on a MultiSync monitor, which displayed in full color a fat man in a shiny suit sitting behind a desk. He was speaking in Russian with a skinny man in an even shinier suit.

Staring at the monitor, Merrall asked, rhetorically, "Why can't foreign gangsters at least dress well? The rayon in those suits is scorching my eyeballs." The other agents smiled, still focused on their screens and listening devices.

Merrall, an honors graduate from the University of Pennsylvania, was a leading member of the FBI counterterrorist intelligence team. A varsity volleyball player at Penn, she cut an imposing figure: five-eleven, lean, muscular, and extremely fit. Her auburn hair complimented her deep chocolate brown eyes. In her middle 30s, she'd already become a rising star in the bureau and was firmly in charge of this operation.

Merrall knew this was an important bust. Interpol had given the FBI an extensive dossier on the activities of Ivan Fedorak, including his somewhat obscure link to the immense Russian military underground. She had been working the fat man since his arrival from Moscow six months earlier. There was no doubt Fedorak was an enterprising big-time arms merchant with high-level connections. Her suspicions were recently confirmed that he was also a high-ranking member of the Russian Mafia. While Merrall was pretty and political, with an Ivy League brain, she also had a street cop's soul and was a worthy match for Ivan Fedorak.

Agent Haering, a nerdy linguist, pulled off his earphones, turned around and said, "Agent Merrall. Fedorak just made the sale. Heard it for sure. It's on tape; solid."

Singleton, a black female agent seated next to him, looked up from her recording equipment and confirmed the transaction. "We got it on two CDs, Sandra." Agent Linnet Singleton, physically fit, was extremely poised, intelligent, and professional. She received her bachelors from Georgetown, masters from Princeton, at the top of her class in both schools and was recently assigned to the special task force. Determined and fearless, Singleton never backed away from trouble. Merrall had insisted she be assigned to her team.

"Good." Merrall nodded, then spoke into her radio headset, "Hicks, take him down."

The other agents in the room gathered around Merrall to watch the monitor. She reached over and squeezed Singleton's shoulder. "Nice work, Linnet. My HBO doesn't come in this clean. I don't know how you hid the bugs in there with all their paranoid sweeps."

On the monitor, the two cheap suits were shaking hands. Suddenly, armed FBI agents burst into the office and aggressively pushed the gangsters to the floor.

Ivan Fedorak's fat face was smashed to the carpet; his hands were quickly cuffed behind him. His glasses fell to the floor next to his face. Special Agent Wolman walked over and deliberately stepped down hard on them, twisted his shoe, and crushed the glass into the carpet. His distorted face still flat on the floor; Fedorak's enraged eyes looked up to see a sarcastic grin on Wolman's face.

An hour later, in an FBI interrogation room in lower Manhattan, Merrall looked across a plain wooden table at Fedorak. She gave him a pedantic smile and said, "Merry Christmas, Ivan. Have I got a present for you."

Fedorak, with a heavy accent, replied, "And I have one word for you; Immunity." An ugly grin came across his face.

He was a confident man, the kind Merrall loved to kick around. She looked the mafia boss straight in the eyes and replied, "Mr. Fedorak, you sell machine guns to terrorists, how do you propose to sell immunity to the FBI?"

Fedorak's grin turned to a Cheshire smile, his tobacco-stained teeth holding more than a few ounces of gold. He sat back in his seat and casually remarked, "That will prove to be easy."

"With everything we've got on you, Mr. Fedorak," Merrall replied, "immunity will be an extremely expensive thing to buy."

The man sat up straight, put both hands flat on the table and said, "I can afford it. I have many things of great value to offer."

December 21, 11:00 AM
The Oval Office

Barry Dipaula sat on the couch next to the president. They were watching one of the four monitors sitting on a polished white cabinet against the curved wall. Both men focused intently on a specific monitor displaying the weekly program, *Eye on the District,* commonly labeled "Beltway Bigmouth," cable TV's top-rated talk show. A few piles of loose paper lay on the table in front of them.

Dipaula listened to the irritating laughter of Robert Hays, the opinionated host, and watched the face of Maj. Gen. Jake McCloud, his guest for the day. While he didn't care much for the arrogant attitude of Jake McCloud, he detested the egotistical Hays.

On the monitor, the host stopped laughing and said to the camera, "We're back with Gen. Jake McCloud. General, before the break we were talking about President Bergstrom. Our own economy is in a tailspin and rumor around Washington has it that he's gonna spend billions to bail out a Russian administration that probably won't even be around in a few months! What assurances do we have that the Russians will give us any oil or gas from their new fields in the Arctic Circle, even if we loan them billions of dollars to pump it out? Can you actually support this type of insanity?"

"Everyone knows we're faced with a potential powder keg," McCloud said. "The Alliance, which we expect to be completed any day now between Iran, Syria, Libya, Sudan, and Lebanon, would receive material support from hostile forces inside Iraq, Afghanistan, Egypt, Saudi Arabia, Pakistan, and of course, North Korea. Iran has at least four nuclear bombs and a dozen nuclear warheads; we suspect several have been shipped into Syria and elsewhere. We know North Korea has at least two dozen, maybe more. The UN may be able to contain the situation and prevent the alliance from forming, if the security council will act soon, but I wouldn't count on that happening. Israel will most likely be the Alliance's first target, which will bring us into any war. No doubt it could very well be nuclear. Russia, China, and the United States are, in reality, the only controlling forces. But we must act together and decisively. At this time, Russia, and China are facing off on their border and are focused on each other and not on the Alliance. If billions of dollars will stabilize Russia, then it's money well spent—a cheap price to pay. The three superpowers could then refocus on stopping the alliance from forming. Another fear is that if pushed too hard, Russia will dramatically raise the price of oil and gas from their new fields, putting a number of countries, including the US and China, in a very difficult position."

The camera closed in on McCloud. West Point polished and pressed, he exuded competence and control. "Of course, anything given to the Russians would be considered a loan. But it's not my call. As everyone knows, I am sworn to serve and protect the Constitution of the United States and its civilian authority," McCloud remarked. "The president is dealing with difficult issues and deserves our support."

"What Bergstrom deserves," Hayes added, "is a one way ticket back to Colorado! He barely won the electoral vote. Like Bush, he didn't even win the popular vote. Is this guy really legitimate and is there any truth to the rumor you wanna take him on in two years?"

"Robert," McCloud quickly remarked, "As a young man I spent three years in the Hanoi Hilton with bamboo shoots up my fingernails and they still couldn't make me talk about things I didn't want to. What makes you think you can?"

Hayes smiled at the general and said, "Your reticence aside, General, let's talk about your upcoming book, 'My Country, Right or Wrong.' What's it about?"

Dipaula had enough. He picked up the remote and killed the picture saying, "I'll tell you what it's about. It's about reminding the American people that Gen. Jake Thaddeus McCloud is a soldier-scholar Renaissance man who leaps tall buildings in a single bound. That man is shameless." He tossed the remote onto the table. "There are no real secrets in this town anymore. Everyone knows about the loan."

Bergstrom got up from the couch and casually remarked, "That man is a war hero, Barry, from Vietnam to Iraq." He walked toward his desk.

Dipaula stood and followed the president saying, "That man will be running against you in a few years, Mr. President."

"Well, Barry, you have to admit, he summoned up our situation as good as anyone could," Bergstrom replied.

The president took a seat behind his desk and asked, "What do you think Masarov will do with the money?"

Dipaula sat down and answered, "He has to keep his generals happy. His accepting our money won't do that. But spreading it around to the more reactionary ones will. As for China, Masarov will talk tough because it lets his people forget their once great empire couldn't beat Bulgaria in a sack race." Then, smiling, he added, "Of course, Bulgaria's tough this year. They got that kid out of Fresno State." Both men chuckled. Dipaula continued, "After Masarov's government is stabilized, he'll offer the Chinese an olive branch. He'll 'regret' or 'mourn' the loss of Chinese life—not apologize—and the Chinese will accept it, as well as a nice flow of oil and gas to settle the debt."

The president nodded. "I hope you're right. While McCloud may not be an immediate threat, his counterparts in Moscow might very well be."

Chapter Two

December 20
The Ardennes

Just two hours out of Brussels International Airport, the jet-black Mercedes sedan cut abruptly off the E5 autoroute leading to the German border and headed south toward Luxembourg through the heart of the Ardennes Forest.

It had been a damp winter day in the mountains, and the air was strangely humid. The chestnut and birch trees, saturated by a cloudburst earlier in the day, sent a ripe, sweet odor rising from the roadway.

For the last few kilometers, the driver turned on his headlights. The sedan slowed and turned left from the winding road onto an even narrower driveway overhung by a dense canopy of trees. The Mercedes proceeded on for two hundred meters then slowed to a stop in the shadows in front of a large black steel gate, which extended the width of the road. Deep in the trees to either side of the car, there was total darkness.

In the harsh glare of the headlights, a man appeared in a running suit, with a Heckler & Koch submachine gun slung over his shoulder. He waved to the driver and the iron gates moved inward allowing the car to move ahead. As the gate closed behind the limo, the driver noted with satisfaction the other men along the wall and the dogs sitting quietly next to their feet.

The limousine proceeded up the hill, then out into an open area on top of the mountain. Against the faint orange sky was the back of a stately four-story brick mansion with a red tile roof. The horizon was a bar of gold against the black shapes of the hills beyond the river.

Behind the mansion, a wide expanse of green was barely visible in the fading light: a formal rose garden, grape arbor, and lawn stretching to the edge of the sheer cliff overlooking the river valley.

The Mercedes pulled around to the front of the estate and stopped. Two men entered the mansion through a massive bronze door and walked into a large circular foyer laid with handmade Italian tiles. Three men in black jackets met the two visitors. A fourth man, an escort dressed in a formal waistcoat with tie, maroon pants, and gleaming shoes, arrived and searched the visitors expertly. He looked into their eyes briefly, then glanced away, fully aware of their reputation.

The visitors were escorted through an elegant tapestry hall discreetly observed by hidden cameras, then up a broad staircase to the main sitting room that faced the front of the mansion on the third floor, overlooking the magnificent sweep of the river valley.

Seated with his back to the door of the room was a broad shouldered gray-haired man in his middle seventies facing out the window to the valley below. He had the ample, well-fed look of an American business executive; dressed in a simple camel hair sport coat and alpaca slacks, light blue open-collared shirt; but then Wade Pike always conveyed the impression of what he was: successful and wealthy; very wealthy. A man who called the shots and always got what he wanted, he sat motionless while his visitors stood quiet, patiently waiting.

Then suddenly he clapped his hand down on the polished desk and turned to his guests. "See this son of a bitch?" he casually remarked. "Napoleon wrote his marching orders from this desk." He motioned to the crystal inkwell built into the front panel. "Dipped his pen here. I got this desk from an unscrupulous French count who had lost a few, ah, millions on a couple of untimely transactions. Since I owned him lock, stock, and barrel at the time, I took this instead of what remained of the estate. I think he later committed suicide." Wade Pike laughed softly, pleased with himself.

His visitors merely stared at him, waiting for a more intelligent and pertinent conversation. Brushing off their apparent disinterest, Pike continued, "I've always wanted the best in life. Something my grandfather drilled into me. This is why I made the agreement with you, Fajil."

Fajil al-Said motioned to his companion, a huge man wearing a black sweater and beret. "This is Kamile," he said softly. "A former major in the Syrian Special Forces; he is a trusted associate of mine for exceptional projects."

Fajil paused to let his introduction and serious disposition to take effect and then added, "We may have an agreement, Mr. Pike. Let us hope our goals remain one and the same."

Pike was a bit unnerved by the coldness, the detachment of Fajil's voice. "Will you be staying here this evening?"

"We have other engagements. Not far from here."

"Have a seat."

"No, thank you. We have been sitting for quite some time now."

Pike nodded. "When we spoke last, you were just beginning to implement things. How far along are you now?"

"Everything will be in place very soon." Fajil's eyes held firm on Pike.

The billionaire nodded again and asked, "Anything changed?"

"Nothing of consequence. However, we have been informed a certain businessman of some interest was recently interrogated by the FBI."

Pike reached into the pocket of his jacket and removed a gold-plated cigar cutter and matching lighter. Opening the humidor on his desk, he carefully selected a cigar and took a few well-orchestrated seconds to light it. After blowing a blue-gray puff of smoke into the air, he looked back at Fajil. Each man made a rapid assessment of the other. Pike was the first to blink.

"He's nothing; a nontraceable nothing."

Fajil was not fully satisfied with Pike's response.

"Will you be here long?" Pike asked.

"We will leave in the morning."

"Too bad, my stables aren't far from here. You would love my Arabians; the best stock in the world."

"We have rather important business to discuss, Mr. Pike." Fajil was anxious to be on his way.

After a brief meeting, Fajil and Kamile turned and left the room without speaking a word.

Pike went to the liquor cabinet and poured a cognac. Fajil, he would deal with later; his insolence was unsettling. He took another cigar from the humidor, cut and lit it as he walked to the window. Smoke from his first cigar rose from the ashtray near an untouched glass of brandy.

Of a more immediate concern were his partners in Libya, Sudan, Iraq, and Iran. He would need to deal with them soon, as they were moving a bit too far with this idea of an Alliance against the United States and the rest of the world. *It won't work*, thought Pike. *Can't imagine the free world allowing those renegade nations to form an alliance against them.* However, Fajil's skilled team fit his plans like a sharp scalpel in a surgeon's hand; Pike being the surgeon.

Before long, he would also have to speak with his friends inside the Kremlin walls. They were more sensible and their design was far more comprehensive. Their power would be more lasting than that of any assassin, yet, perhaps more difficult to influence.

Within the hour, a message was dispatched by telephone to the United States. Another was sent to Helsinki, transferred to contacts in St. Petersburg, and delivered to the very anxious individuals in Moscow.

As he watched Fajil's car wind its way back to the main road, Pike realized the time had finally come and felt oddly relieved. It had been a very long time and he was now well prepared to more than even the score. As Fajil's car disappeared into the trees, Pike brought the snifter up high over his head in a mock toast. "To you Mr. President. This one's—" he hesitated, and then chuckled, "I mean these two are for you." After taking a sip, he looked out the window into the darkness beyond the horizon.

December 22, 2:15 AM
Baku, Azerbaijan

Sandra Merrall detested Baku from the moment she stepped off the unmarked jet she had taken from Turkey. Located on the Caspian Sea in Azerbaijan, the oil-rich city of Baku was polluted, filthy, a far cry from New York City and Washington DC. The consolation was that she would only be here a few days. With full diplomatic support, that should be enough time to follow Fedorak's lead.

It was early morning when Merrall stood on a grimy rooftop among a number of Azerbaijani police detectives and two FBI agents watching a near-empty street below. Also huddled on the rooftop were several officers from the American Consulate in Azerbaijan.

Standing next to Merrall was Captain Talatan, who resembled the wrestler, Hulk Hogan, right down to the full mustache. She was certain his heavy leather jacket concealed an impenetrable bulletproof chest. He was looking through a pair of Cannon high-powered binoculars.

A puff of steam came from the captain's mouth, reminding Sandra Merrall how cold this part of the world could be. A moist wind blowing in from the Caspian Sea magnified the chill; threatening to freeze her exposed face.

Being this close to Iran, an arrogant, defiant enemy of the United States, made her a bit uncomfortable. She knew Iran was the architect of the new alliance and that weapons of mass destruction could easily be transferred across the border between Iran and Azerbaijan and into the city of Baku. From here, a freighter could move them to any place in the world. That thought was more chilling than the cold Caspian wind.

Below and across the road, shop lights illuminated Ayten Balayev, a sharp-dressed local businessman, as he walked out of a strip club with a curvaceous hooker under each arm.

Talatan lowered his binoculars and said, "That's Fedorak's guy, Balayev."

Merrall pulled her jacket tight around her neck. While she spent nearly her entire life in Pennsylvania, New York, and lately in the district, she never felt good in the cold. It still cut deep into her body and made her dream of someday working in the Caribbean or maybe even Hawaii. She would gladly sacrifice the four seasons for year around heat. The only four seasons that she longed for now was the one near the beach on Maui. She raised her binoculars and took a closer look at the man down below, then said, "Looks like him. If you're certain, Captain, let's take him."

Talatan spoke into his shoulder mic. A man appeared from the shadows on the sidewalk just ahead of the threesome and waved to the hookers. The women instantly begin to punch and kick Balayev. The man was totally surprised. He began to fight back as a white van suddenly screeched up, bounced over the curb onto the sidewalk, and stopped in front of the altercation. A half-dozen Azerbaijan police poured out of the van, pulled Balayev to the ground, and handcuffed him.

Later in a dreary, uninviting interrogation room, which resembled the basement of an abandoned building, Balayev, his face bruised, sat in a hard wood straight-back chair, a hot spotlight beating down on his head. Talatan stood behind him.

Merrall was seated across a table from both men, several embassy personnel at her side. Her mind wondered back a few days to when she had sat across from the fat guy, Fedorak. Unlike Fedorak, Balayev was trim, neat, but his beady eyes and sharp pointed nose soon had Merrall reflecting on a well-dressed, surreptitious weasel caught raiding the chicken yard.

Balayev's English was accented but pretty good. "CIA's no jurisdiction here," he mumbled in protest, a feigned defiant attitude was clearly visible in his eyes.

Whack! Talatan smacked Balayev hard on the head, causing the man's face to jolt sideways and his beady eyes to shut tight.

Merrall didn't protest, appearing as if she hadn't noticed. "FBI," she said calmly. "What I do have is a testimony from Ivan Fedorak who says he negotiated the sale of two Iranian nuclear artillery shells to you."

"Never heard of him," Balayev barked. Another blow from Talatan sent his head flying in the other direction.

"Have you heard of sodomy and cockroach soup?" Merrall snapped back. "Because that's what's gonna be on your agenda for the next twenty or thirty years in some Azerbaijan hellhole. Nuclear artillery shells are big business, Balayev. Even if the captain here didn't have a list as long as your skinny little arm to wrap you up tight, the nukes would be enough to put you away for the rest of your miserable life."

Merrall's words, spoken with great assurance, aided in no small way by the violent jolts to his head, caused Balayev's arrogant posture to turn to mush. "What are you selling?" he asked, half expecting another fist to fall.

"Peace of mind," Merrall replied. "We know you received a very important shipment from Iran and sold it elsewhere. With the right information, you could win protective custody in some country club prison in the Baltics for a dime of your time." She sat back in her seat, paused a moment, then added. "I don't have time for games. I'm in a very big hurry. You've got a whole ten seconds to decide; starting now!"

Chapter Three

December 24, 6:00 PM
The Sea of Cortez

The Mexican-registered fishing trawler Apiza, its tired sides streaked with rust, rolled in the gray waves as it pushed through rough seas fifty miles off the Mexican Coast in the Gulf of California and the Sea of Cortez, less than two hundred miles from Nogales and the US border. In another fourteen hours, it would turn northeast and head for land.

Eli Waseem knew he was in a tight place. A young Pakistani army officer recruited during a training visit to England, his service with British Intelligence had been interesting but never dangerous. In his identity as an engineering student earning money on a variety of Pacific fishing trawlers, he had merely been an observer; he had made radio reports now and then through a special frequency to the Royal Canadian Navy Base at Esquimalt on Vancouver Island. British Intelligence had valued his association with the drug runners and criminals that used the coastal traffic as covers. But this was the first time he sensed something was seriously wrong. In his last transmit, Esquimalt Control had asked him to press for information, something they had never done before. His companions on board had become very serious. Something big was up.

They were now sitting around the table in the belly of the ship, Waseem between Khalid and Etier. Three Mexican crewmen sat facing him across the table, including Roberto Santos, a muscular, unshaven man with thick black hair. Santos, a Mexican terrorist, was his primary focus. In Los Mochis,

Waseem had transmitted a photograph of Santos to British Intelligence, verifying he was aboard. It now appeared that Santos was not the only one he should be worried about.

In the rough seas, the trawler skidded and rolled as if it were riding a live thing; the dishes and bottles clattered constantly as the men ate and talked. The smell of rotting tuna and diesel and rank sweat filled the galley. Despite the weather, the crewmen were drinking tequila, and they laughed at the terrified mice that scurried from the food storage lockers to snatch the bits of rice that fell from the table.

Finally, Cedric, the youngest crewman, drew his fillet knife and threw it with a flick of his wrist. It flashed into the filthy deck planks, impaling a mouse, its whiskers quivering, eyes bulging with surprise. "Merry Christmas," Cedric shouted.

The crewmen roared with laughter, and the foul stench of men and tequila was everywhere. It was then that Etier placed his fork carefully down on the table, took a long pull from the bottle of cheap booze in front of him and turned to Waseem.

"Do you know what day this is, my friend?" Etier said softly.

Etier was a small, lithe man with cruel dark eyes. He drank constantly, and Waseem never knew when he was drunk and when he was serious. Waseem sensed something had gone too far. Etier was strangely quiet now. He normally spoke with a roar, full of Gallic arrogance. Now he seemed to be thinking. His eyes showing he was completely serious. In several telephone conversations, he had heard Etier use the name Fajil more than once. The name Fajil had been of intense interest to Esquimalt Control. As soon as possible, he would report directly to Cheltenham. Waseem was puzzled.

"I don't know what you mean, sir," Waseem replied.

A cruel grin spread over his face as Etier glanced at Santos for just an instant. Waseem could see his yellow teeth against the week's growth of beard.

"My friend, Waseem, we are going to visit the devil's home. It is there in Washington we will change the history of the world. Next month we shall kill the devil himself."

Santos had been staring openly at Waseem, watching his every move.

"What do you mean, joking like this?" bleated Waseem. "Surely you are making a joke with me." If it was true, he knew he would never leave the boat.

"Cut the shit," Santos grunted. "I should cut your tongue out, Etier, and feed it to the fish."

Later that night, Waseem sat on his bunk listening to the roar of an outboard and watched Santos and Khalid as they bounced over the rain-swept waves to meet a small yacht a few hundred yards away. Eli Waseem was frozen. He needed to contact British Intelligence and tell them about Washington.

But why tell me of this assassination? He thought. *Who is this Fajil?*

Waseem walked to his cabin door, and cracked it open slightly. He looked down the outside walkway through the blowing rain. No one was there.

He moved quickly toward the storage room, careful not to slip on the wet, pitching deck. The other crewmen were in the galley playing cards. He moved lightly past the galley window, holding his breath, as if they would be able to hear him with the wind whipping along the deck.

Waseem went through a steel door and down a ladder. He moved quickly now, down a narrow passageway to the storage room, entered and closed the door behind him.

Two large crates, covered by dirty, oil-soaked tarps were lying on the floor. Waseem pulled a tarp from one crate. It had Cyrillic markings on it, and the stenciled profile of a missile. The second box looked identical to the first. The other crates had Mexican markings; these he had reported earlier. Waseem stepped back, turned and left the room.

The radio room was nearby and Waseem wasted no time getting there. He entered and noticed the small halogen light above the desk would be enough. He sat at the chair, put the headphones on and examined the old console. He flipped the power switch on and dialed in the frequency, and thought about what he would give for a modern satellite phone. Sweat formed on the back of his neck and on the palms of his hands. He began to shake. He closed his eyes for a second, breathing slowly to regain control.

Why is this happening to me? He thought. *They will never allow me to step on shore. They know who I am. I've got to get this message off before they kill me.*

He began to tap out his message in code on the frequency monitored twenty-four hours a day by British and Canadian Intelligence, "U.S. hit, target One, I repeat, target One. Fajil, repeat, Fajil. Missile launchers. Repea—"

Just at that moment the door burst open. Waseem continued to broadcast. Etier entered and fired his Walther PPK 9-mm pistol rapidly, squeezing off shots as he aimed. The first shot struck Waseem in the shoulder as he shifted in his seat, throwing him forward against the equipment rack. The second and third blew him out of his chair, face down on the deck in a foam of blood flowing from his ruptured lung. Waseem struggled to turn himself; and his eyes showed him the short, smoking muzzle of the Walther, only a few inches from his forehead. Waseem's last vision was of Etier's face just above the muzzle, his eyes small, dark, vicious. There was an orange flame, and then nothing.

January 4, 1:15 PM
Washington, DC

Outside the Hoover Building, two Japanese couples bundled against the cold winter breeze, which whipped down E Street, and casually snapped pictures of the main entrance to the FBI Building. The tourists were completely oblivious to the tense meeting about to take place inside.

The small briefing room on the fifth floor was filling to capacity. As people entered, they were handed a thick bound report on Fajil and terrorists activities written by Sandra Merrall. A few staffers were forced to stand along the walls, notepads in hand.

Seated behind the long narrow tables, which filled the room were members of Homeland Security, FBI, Secret Service, CIA, NSA, ATF, Federal Marshals, and State Department security personnel. This meeting was far more significant than the periodic briefings held between intelligence and protective forces and it called for greater participation.

Bob Moore, assistant deputy director of Homeland Security, was present along with the deputy directors of three other agencies: Howard Imhoff of the CIA, Edward Clarke of the FBI, and Lucas Chandler of the Secret Service. The men sat at a rectangular table in the back of the room; their presence underscoring the significance of this special briefing. Seated near the directors were other officials, including James Donovan of the Secret Service.

Donovan appeared much younger than forty-five, muscular, with dark, slightly gray, brown hair. A former detective with the Detroit Police force, he was now head of the Secret Service presidential protective unit.

Craig Thomas, a senior White House official for national security, who worked for National Security Advisor Barry Dipaula, stood against a wall next to Linnet Singleton.

The noise level in the room was becoming somewhat unbearable when Edward Clarke stood and made his way along the wall, stepping around a few people who were carrying on some of the many minor conversations now taking place. After making his way to the front, he leaned back against a table.

"Ladies and Gentlemen, welcome to the Hoover Building. Will you please take your seats. I apologize for the temperature in this room and for the last-minute notice you received. We will try to have you out of here before four. However, there's a great deal of material to cover this afternoon and with the likelihood of a major terrorist attack scheduled in this country, we would do well to listen carefully to the very brief presentations being made and to participate fully in the questions and answers, which will follow. Over the last few weeks, the bureau has anticipated an attack by national militia forces on one of our federal buildings. We believed it to be either the State Department or the Hoover Building. However, the threat now appears to have widened to include international terrorists and the president of the United States. That's the reason each one of you was personally selected to be here. You should all have been given a report as you entered."

A few murmurs of assent broke out having to do with the report's length. Clarke gestured for quiet and then continued, "I know. Anything longer than a 'family circus' cartoon tests your concentration. But the next few weeks just may be the toughest you've ever had. Agent Sandra Merrall of the FBI will be our first speaker. Give her your attention, please." Clark motioned to Merrall.

Merrall moved to the front of the room and gestured to Singleton, who turned down the lights. She then took a deep, calming breath.

"There are two primary organizations, which constitute this immediate and very high-level threat to our domestic security and, perhaps, even to the president," Merrall said. "This afternoon, we will discuss both organizations in some detail. There are two men you will take special notes on this afternoon; Pete Christenson, head of the National Militia, and Fajil al-Said, leader of an international and somewhat rogue terrorist group."

The technician double-clicked his computer. Images moved on the large screen behind Merrall.

"In the early nineties, there were about a dozen basic contingents of local militia scattered throughout the United States. They were located in areas like Northern Idaho and Montana, as well as West Virginia, Virginia, Alabama, and Michigan. Most of the really menacing characters in those days were individual renegades and misfits like Kehoe, McVay, King, and Plettner. Small organizations of fringe groups began to sprout up like noxious weeds with names like 'The World Church of the Creator,' 'The Confederate Knights of America,' 'Covenant of the Chosen,' 'Supreme Federation,' and 'Council of Patriots,' to name a few. By the late nineties, with immeasurable help from the Internet, the labyrinth had united into a loose structure and grown to include over thirty separate units with close to fifty thousand members. It was not long before a group of men, headed by Pete Christenson, identified the common threads and began to weave a blanket of unity. They operated more freely during our focus on the war on terrorism following September eleventh. Manpower had shifted to international concerns, and fewer agents worked on domestic issues."

A map hit the screen with red dots scattered throughout the United States. Merrall, motioning with a laser pointer, continued, "Twenty-six of the thirty units have now been skillfully welded together to form the National Federation of State Militia, or NFSM, or simply the National Militia. Pete Christenson was recently elected president. He is a 'wannabe' politician who started his ambitions with the John Birch Society, then became a Republican, moved to Independent, then to the Libertarians before giving up the traditional method of gaining office."

Merrall cleared her throat and caught a glimpse of James Donovan. His eyes locked on hers; a slight distraction. *Nice-looking man*, she thought, nearly losing her place.

Donovan couldn't help but notice her lingering stare. It seemed to penetrate his thoughts, and he lost his concentration for a few seconds.

Turning her gaze away from Donovan, Merrall continued, "Pete is extremely dangerous, and has his sights clearly set on becoming president of an all-white nation or, perhaps, even becoming president of the United States."

A few chuckles around the room caused Merrall to smile. She quickly regained her serious demeanor.

"Together with a dozen men of equal distinction and hard luck in the mainstream, they formed the National Militia. They are now armed with the power of dozens of arsenals. Over the last few years, tons of explosives have been stolen from mining projects and hardware stores, enough to obliterate dozens of large targets. They are highly trained men and women, exceedingly motivated, and regardless of what some might think, most are extremely intelligent. Our tax money went to train many of them through service in the military. They have connections in places that might amaze you. We even suspect they have obtained some high placements in state and federal government. While we were focused on OBL, Al Qaeda, and other international terrorist organizations, these men were quietly forming their own organization.

"If the National Militia has joined forces with the newly forming Muslim Alliance or with international terrorists for attacks in the United States or for a hit on the president or anyone else, it's doubtful they will make any mistakes in the process and it's clear they won't stop with a single isolated attack. It will be as big or bigger than 9/11. An all-out insurrection is part of what the militia calls its Revolution Manifesto.

"We know they have already selected very specific targets throughout the country: government buildings, monuments, power stations, among others. Many in the bureau believe nationwide attacks have been well planned and could occur at any moment if the right situation presents itself. This possibility could become a real nightmare for all of us and, if it really explodes as Christenson and his people want, it could make the civil war look like a food fight at Mother Theresa's convent."

The screen went blank. Merrall leaned back against the table. Looking from eye to eye, she continued, "Take this threat seriously. If their initial hit is on the president, as we now believe it will be, their follow-through just might be in communities across the country and against a great number of public officials and buildings. Their fifteen training camps are as crammed as a Japanese subway at rush hour and keep in mind we're not talking about simple small-arms training. We may be facing handheld missiles, high explosives, biological, and chemical weapons as well. The threat is real, it is far-reaching, it is horrendous, and as indicated before, we believe it is imminent."

The room was now quiet as the significance of Merrall's final words hit home.

Ivan Fedorak's mug shot glowered on the screen.

"It gets better. While in FBI custody," Merrall began, "this man, Ivan Fedorak, a member of the Russian Mafia, revealed he facilitated the sale of two nuclear artillery shells to Anyten Balayev, an Azerbaijan national. The shells are really a new generation of tactical special weapons, designed to fit handheld missile firing devices."

Singleton clicked on the next picture. Balayev's face filled the screen. "Balayev's a known conduit for arms to various terrorist organizations. His day job is as an engineer for Caspian Petrol and Gas in Baku."

Singleton advanced the slide. It showed an organizational chart of three interconnected corporations. "The parent company of CP&G is the Kleinhoff-Mader Group, which is a wholly owned subsidiary of Dexterco Ltd., a diversified energy-holding company based in Zurich. The chairman and largest individual shareholder of Dexterco is a former American citizen named Wade Pike."

The slide advances, showing an old picture of Wade Pike, circa 1974, which fills the screen. A few murmurs passed through the room.

"He's one of the top ten richest men in the world. While he controls a business empire that has its tentacles in energy, transportation, and even media, he flies below the radar of most intelligence agencies."

George Dansie, a skeptical NSC staffer, spoke up. "Are you saying Pike may be connected to terrorists?"

Merrall turned around and said, "Well, Mr. Dansie, the FBI and CIA believe he may have employed terrorists to use them on strikes here in the United States and elsewhere."

The room instantly reacted. Some displayed surprise, others skepticism.

"You'll read the background information in the written reports."

An old photo of Kamile filled the screen. "Under intense and rather convincing Azerbaijan interrogation, Balayev revealed he sold two nukes to this man. His name is Kamile Hassan, an associate of Fajil al-Said."

An equally old photo of Fajil replaced Kamile's.

"Fajil formed his terrorist unit a number of years ago. This man has a dark history. In the midnineties, our intelligence sources began to mention Fajil often and a pattern seemed to develop. While Bin Laden was given most of the credit for terrorist attacks against US targets around the world, standing next to him in the shadows during that reign of terror was none other than Fajil al-Said. Bin Laden supplied the finances, Fajil supplied the intellect. In the late nineties, Fajil gathered up the summa cum laude graduates of Bin Laden's 'Holy War University.' Israeli intelligence has dubbed them The Viper Force. His second in command is Kamile Hassan. We don't think they were involved in the 9/11 attack, but who knows."

Merrall then advanced through a series of photographs showing various acts of destruction, including plane wreckage and bombed-out buildings. "Fajil's Viper Force may be responsible for the destruction of six commercial aircraft and twenty-three assorted bombings. CIA has linked them to the embassy bombings in Africa and Saudi Arabia, and estimates they are responsible for five hundred and seventy deaths."

Merrall relaxed a bit. "FBI believes there may be several targets. The two most likely are the White House and the Capitol, both missed on September eleventh."

"Why strike now?" Dansie questioned.

Merrall came back. "Just look around. There's a great deal of chaos in this world and the United States is right in the middle of it all. At this moment in time, our world is ready to explode. With the mounting political instability in Russia, their problems with China, our problems with Iraq, Afghanistan, Iran, Syria, and North Korea, our war on terrorism, a possible Muslim country alliance and the president's exceedingly important upcoming State of the Union Address, it's a prime time for them to make a strike in this country, against this president. Maybe even during the address. In any case, we're ramping up security along our borders and at various custom points; but, as we all know, it should not be too hard for Fajil and his men to sneak into the country."

"Assuming he's not already here," Donovan remarked.

"Where are the nukes?" asked Dansie. "Maybe they're here as well."

Everyone took a second to digest that possibility as Singleton turned off the computer.

Clarke began speaking as he walked toward the front of the room, "Thank you Sandra. Several task forces are being organized. One will be a joint task force, which will focus entirely on threats to the president from the people we have discussed today. The Secret Service Intelligence Division will coordinate that team. Others will be headed by the CIA and the FBI. Most, if not all of you in this room, will participate in one way or another. You will be getting your individual assignments following this meeting. We now have over three hundred people assigned to work on this problem worldwide. Not enough. More will be needed," he added.

"In a nutshell, we have the National Militia and the Viper Force to worry about." Clarke stood in front of the room next to Merrall. "Separately, they provide a significant menace to the United States both domestically and internationally. Working in concert with one another, on a joint project, they could spell disaster. If their anticipated hit were as much as a full year away, and no one believes it is, it would be an exhausting struggle for us to defend against. However, if it is actually planned for as early as during the State of the Union Address, as almost everyone believes is the likely case, it will very soon become a horrendous nightmare for us all. You might try to enjoy your sleep tonight, it may well be the last peaceful night you have for a long while."

Chapter Four

Thursday, January 13, 7:30 AM
Washington DC

It was five days before the State of the Union Address and a deep-chilling wind ripped hard through the district signaling a fast approaching stormy, bitter-cold season. The flood of tourists had departed months ago leaving the city relatively empty compared to the bustling, insane flurry of summer months. The brilliant autumn colors had also long ago faded, leaving behind thousands of sullen ice-encased deciduous trees, which blanketed the district. On the horizon, dark clouds were gathering, harbingers of a violent windstorm. A long, numbing winter loomed ahead.

The cold wind blew down through the trees lining University Avenue and swept over the cars moving along the busy roadway. Maneuvering carefully through the morning commute traffic, Roberto Santos, the driver of a blue Taurus, flipped a cigarette butt out the window and checking his rearview mirror, asked, "Anyone meeting us at the garage?" then turned the Taurus east onto Florida Avenue.

"No. Too many would attract attention," responded Manning from the seat next to Santos. His eyes half-closed from lack of sleep. He rubbed his cheek and added, "The feds may be assholes, but they're not blind." His voice was soft and precise, and he spoke with a light southern accent. The two men in the back seat were casually looking out the window, indifferent to a full city block of office buildings in various stages of decay, which lined both sides of the street.

The car stopped at the signal on Turner Street then turned right. Halfway down the block, Santos cut sharply into the narrow passage next to an auto repair shop with a sagging, weather-beaten sign that said in faded black paint, "Tires for Less."

Slowing to a crawl, the driver guided the sedan along the narrow rugged, oil-crusted driveway and around to the back of the shop. The ground was strewn with bits of wind-blown trash, rain-soaked leaves, cigarette butts splayed, and swollen in the mud like brown flowers, cracked batteries weeping acid, smashed headlights, spark plugs, and other discarded auto parts stretching back over forty years.

Santos parked the car next to a wooden shack locked with a rusty chain, which passed loosely through two nearly separated door handles. Its corroded hinges were loose at the top and the doors hung sadly off center. A thick brownish-green moss carpeted the damp roof.

The four men went into the bay to meet Samir, a lean olive-skinned man, and Gordon, a solid man with a neck almost as wide as his shaved head. Both were smoking and drinking tea and coffee from chipped enamel cups.

Across the shop, old tires and steel rims lay in heaps, covered with oily soot. Withered and partially collapsed cardboard boxes full of used car parts were stacked in the corners, laced delicately with cobwebs. Cigarette butts and beer cans littered the floor under a calendar of two half-naked women posing on the hood of a bright red '63 Chevy with shock absorbers between their breasts, smiling obscenely.

In the middle of the floor, there was a large steel grating, an oil sump of some kind. Samir and Gordon took crowbars and pried it up from the greasy concrete, and the others reached down into the open hole and pulled up crates by their rope handles. Inside, they found ten AK-47 assault rifles with collapsing stocks, recoil grenades with their barrel launchers, hand fragmentation grenades, five Heckler & Koch submachine guns, boxes of 9mm ammunition for the HKs, and the long gray 30-round banana clips of 7.62mm rounds for the rifles, ten apiece for each weapon. Below the crates were two long boxes, Mexican military markings stamped on all sides. Santos went down to his knees, leaned over the hole and made a cursory, visual inspection of the seals. The boxes were untouched. Only Manning and Santos knew what the boxes contained, but only Manning knew what awesome power lay just a few feet beneath them, buried under the long boxes in the cold damp earth. It made him more than a bit uncomfortable. A chill raced up his spine. He couldn't wait to be far away from this spot.

When they had finished, Manning took a few steps back and ordered in a matter-of-fact tone, "These must be checked again on the sixteenth. Samir will remain here with the equipment."

"No problem," retorted Santos with a harsh laugh. "We've made it as comfortable as possible for him." Compared to their Alexandria safe house, this was a third-world backcountry toilet.

Samir was silent. He found no humor in the big Mexican's remark. For more than a decade, he had lived in places far worse in the high mountains of Afghanistan. Sleeping on a cot in the corner of this shop with a pistol under his blanket was a luxury to him.

They lowered the crates down into the square in the concrete, piled in oily rags, and replaced the grate. With a hand-operated chain lift attached to a beam in the ceiling, Samir lifted several stripped-down engine blocks covered with grease, and lowered them onto the grate. Few search parties would look into the deep pit if they had to lift the filthy blocks out of the way.

Manning was reassured all was in order. He was anxious to leave this place.

4:45 PM
Arlington, Virginia

A very dispirited sixty-eight-year-old James Kilpatrick, secretary of the interior, buttoned his black wool coat, straightened his tie and left the doctor's office in Arlington. Kilpatrick looked a little pale during the confidential physical examination performed by his private physician. The specialist had been greatly disturbed during his review and was not at all happy when the secretary insisted the unfavorable prognosis, coronary artery disease, remain exclusively between two friends, at least for a few weeks. It was only when Kilpatrick assured him he would return before the end of January for more exhaustive tests that the physician agreed to the secrecy. After all, who was he to challenge a member of the president's cabinet and a respected friend? He insisted that Kilpatrick take with him a vial of nitroglycerin tablets in case of emergency.

Dr. Grable sat at his cluttered desk and spoke softly into his tape recorder, as if speaking to a grieving family, noting a review of his friend's visit. "Presented to me with generalized pain in chest area, advised return visit within two weeks, no later than January 30. At that time, further testing will be required." However, he failed to mention the nitroglycerin tablets and his serious concerns. He paused, took a deep breath, laid his glasses on the desk and, rubbing his tired eyes, wondered if he was doing the right thing. Kilpatrick was definitely in over his head. The stress of recent months in the president's cabinet was quickly taking its toll, one more pressure added to many burdensome years of public service and family problems. Should he have refused to go along with his friend? Did he have a duty, an obligation, to force the man to seek treatment?

After a few minutes of private confusion and frustration, Grable decided to submit to his friend's wishes. Two weeks shouldn't matter anyway. He put down the recorder and mentally prepared for his next patient.

1:50 PM
Near Lynchburg, Virginia

At the same time Kilpatrick was leaving Grable's office, the wind began blowing hard around Lynchburg, Virginia, a hundred and forty miles southwest of Arlington. The padlocked wooden gate surrounded by thick underbrush attracted no particular attention from the mostly local motorists who traveled along Route 130; a narrow, meandering country lane just outside of Lynchburg. Nor would a person notice anything unusual about the heavily rutted dirt road, which stretched a few hundred feet beyond the gate, disappearing into a thick wall of leafless trees and wild brush. From the road, the area looked like one of a thousand similar spots scattered throughout the mountains of Southwest Virginia. However, a close examination of the shiny gate hinges and the tire tracks would reveal far more than seldom use.

Beyond the gate, and down a mile of rough road, sat a completely secluded, light green single-story farmhouse. The house was discreetly tucked away behind a wall of thick trees in the rolling, pulsating hills of the Blue Ridge; a secure meeting place, a sanctuary for officers of the National Militia. It was now protected by a dozen sentries located in the surrounding hills and along the two concealed escape roads leading to safe havens.

A meeting had just concluded. Most of the participants had departed, a handful of people remained, a few in the house, five outside on the porch, including several officers.

Pete Christenson, national president, was standing with his back to the railing facing the others, an open wool overcoat keeping him warm against the chilling winter winds. His dark full head of hair gave no hint of his age. He had spent most of his sixty-five years trying to gain public recognition. A summa cum laude from Kansas State University with a frustrated political career, he had finally found his calling, his mission from God, to save the United States.

Christenson, his gloved hands out to the side clutching the railing behind him, casually said, "The explosive devices have been delivered to the garage just outside the district." Behind him was a field of weed and grass, mostly weed. Twenty feet away, a small stream cut through the property, flowing gently down from High Peak. The rocky summit could barely be seen in the distance, just visible over the barren trees and rolling hills.

Tim Bonner, minister of the guard, sat next to a glider. He fixed the button on his brown overcoat, adjusted the worn cushion beneath him, a thin trace of steam coming from his mouth, coughed lightly and agreed, "Those guys are good, real good." A drip of wet protruded from his nose. "Shit, I wouldn't work around that stuff for no amount of money; scares the hell outta me." Bonner, fifty-four, with the body of a professional wrestler, was responsible for coordinating strategic plans for the National Militia when he wasn't lifting enormous weights.

Christenson instantly cut critical eyes toward Bonner.

Two men were seated on the glider, Chad Fletcher, the minister of security, and Jerry Randal.

Randal wore a Redskin's cap, gray sweatshirt, and faded black leather jacket. He was assistant treasurer, one of the lower-level money guys. Randal shifted slightly, and asked, "What kind of stuff are you talking about, Tim?"

Bonner looked mindfully at Christenson, whose intense eyes seemed to be drilling into his skull, and then back to Randal. He shrugged, "I don't know. A type of very high explosive, I guess."

Randal wasn't satisfied with the answer; it increased his concern over why he was invited to this high-level meeting. He was an accountant, a paper-pushing bean counter, only a junior officer.

Christenson continued, his narrow, cinnamon-colored eyes brightening, "It's hard to believe we're finally gonna make things happen. There's hope my grandkids will someday live in a truly free country; not this Gestapo run police state we now have!"

About ten feet down the porch, tucked comfortably inside a warm bedroom, a heavy man in a thick wool turtleneck sweater sat listening at the window, watching the white lace curtains flap about in the icy winds blowing in a deep bite of winter. He hadn't participated in the meetings, choosing to remain a concealed observer. The eavesdropper took a long drag from his pipe, an African hickory with the face of an angry lion hand-carved on the bowl. Removing the pipe, he blew a slow puff of smoke and thought to himself, *the time has finally come. I wonder if the founding fathers felt this same stir of overwhelming excitement just before their revolution.* The feeling of oneness with the great men of history caused him to swell with pride as he compared himself with Washington, Madison, and Monroe. He touched the left side of his chest, feeling for the comfort of his military decorations, and continued to listen to the men on the porch.

Outside, Christenson looked about to confirm all was well. "Keep in mind, we're dealing with world-class professionals," he said, turning back to the men on the glider. "We're not talking about guys who fix turkey shoots over in West Virginia. Give 'em everything they need and stay as clear as possible. Our job really begins when theirs ends." Now choosing his words carefully, and glancing quickly at Randal, he said, "And that's immediately after they've leveled the damned Hoover Building."

The eavesdropper pulled the pipe from his mouth and laughed to himself, *the Hoover Building, what a joke. Christenson, you're good, real good. If the ignorant assholes only knew. The Hoover Building. That's a good one.*

After the meeting, Jerry Randal drove along the winding country road to his home in the small town of Timberlake, still concerned about why they had involved him in the discussion. Did they suspect him? He entered the house, tossed his cap on the badly worn couch and headed for the phone on the dresser next to his bed. *The bureau has to know what's about to go down,* he thought. *Damn, it sounds like they're really planning a national revolution, and the Hoover Building is gonna be the opening shot.*

After dialing his contact, Randal waited for the answer, then spoke, "Hi Carl. This is Jerry. Can we get together for a beer?"

"Who did you say this was?" asked the voice on the other end.

"Jerry, Jerry Randal; the guy who beat you two to one on the New York game."

"Yeah, right," came the reply. "What can I do for you, Randal?"

"I think we discussed your building needing some repair work, not being able to hold up sound under a major storm."

"Yeah, I remember."

"We'll need to discuss a major problem with your building."

"Can it wait?"

"Don't think so. Weather looks bad and headed your way and my schedule's kinda busy. Can't wait too long or you'll get soaked when the downpour comes."

"We wouldn't want to get wet, now would we? That beer sounds good. See you at the bar in an hour. If I remember correctly, it's your turn to pay."

"Right," answered Randal, hanging up the phone, having uttered his last word. The rounds came from behind; just a few muffled thuds and some obscure clicking sounds. It was his turn to pay.

Fletcher holstered his gun and walked back to the El Dorado parked outside. The shooter slid into the back seat, next to the man with the angry lion pipe. "Your information was correct," he said as the car pulled away and headed back to the district.

Chapter Five

January 14, 11:10 AM
The Treasury Building

The president's speech was now only four days away. Donovan tapped his fingers on the thick sheaf of Secret Service reports that indicated routine security risks near the district; deranged mental cases, dishonorable discharges, and local radical groups. He studied the report summaries for the third time, noting restrains, obstacles, transfer times, motorcade route, potential attack locations, escape plans, and numerous classified details. In the margins of the timetables, Donovan penciled in his concerns. The telephone interrupted him. He hated losing his train of thought.

"Donovan," he barked into the receiver. "What is it?"

"Mr. Donovan, I have a Sandra Merrall in the office, sir; from the FBI. She had a request from Deputy Clarke to meet with you."

Donovan was immediately annoyed. His team was under the gun with no time to waste.

Chelsea Baker's voice grew cold, and her soft Tidewater accent turned cloyingly sweet, "She said, well, she insists really that Mr. Clarke should have told you she would be coming by."

"Oh, yes, ah . . . could you ask her to wait a minute? I'll be right out."

Even though his desk was a mess, he made a routine sweep of confidential papers before stepping into the reception room where Ms. Baker was discreetly sizing up Sandra Merrall when her boss strode past.

After seeing James Donovan walk through the door, Merrall unconsciously wet her lips. No question he was strikingly handsome in his soft blue sweater; which matched perfectly his dazzling blue eyes.

"James Donovan," he murmured absently as he pumped her hand, noticing the firmness of her grip. "It's nice to see you again." His short thick hair was crumpled into a cowlick on the side where he had been unconsciously stroking through it as he studied his reports. Donovan's tie was cocked crazily to one side beneath his sweater, making him look more like a disorganized college professor than a responsible member of the Secret Service.

Donovan's throat went dry. Normally, the bureau sent over the newest generation of agents; well-spoken, bright young men with neat haircuts and modest suits, white shirts, and red ties. Even the straight-laced, spit-polished Secret Service men laughed at how obvious they looked, like illustrations out of a field manual. Merrall was different. She wore a tight black angora dress with a broad belt and a bright gold clasp in the shape of a seashell. She carried her polished shoulder bag like a weapon. Her hair was gathered tightly in an elegant French braid. She had a slim, animal grace about her, and she looked sophisticated even for a town like Washington.

"So, working weekends with the rest of us now?" asked Donovan as he escorted her into his office.

"We're all workaholics; a job requirement in this town." She took a seat next to Donovan's desk, wondering how anyone could work with such a cluttered mess.

"Right," he said in agreement, making a futile attempt to clear some of the papers from his desk. "I was in the briefing at the Hoover Building," he said, taking his seat behind the desk.

"Yes. I recognized you." *That's an understatement*, she thought.

"Very good report." *She noticed me.*

Her eyes narrowed. "How long have you known Ed Clarke?" she asked.

"He was a close friend of my uncle's; pretty much family. He's a great guy with a great sense of humor."

"I certainly agree with that," she said. "Most people I work with seem to be sitting on something sharp."

They both painted an uneasy smile as the intercom buzzed. It was Chelsea. "James, your lunch with the deputy director is coming up fast."

"Thanks." Turning to Merrall he asked, "You know Lucas Chandler?"

"Of course. Well, I know of him; never actually met him."

"Lucas is my immediate boss. He was in the meeting on the fourth. Nicely dressed black guy in the back." Donovan attempted to avoid examining her impressive figure.

Merrall nodded her head. *Sitting just behind you*, she thought.

"By the way," Donovan asked, standing from his desk, "when was the last time you had lunch in the White House?"

"The White House? Never," she said as she stood, still clutching her purse.

"When was the last time you were actually in the White House?" he asked.

"During a brief tour when I was in junior high."

"Have you had lunch yet?"

"No. Are you suggesting there's a restaurant in the White House?" she asked.

"Yeah, sort of. Let's take a walk."

"I hope it's Italian," she said with a smile.

As they passed through the reception room, Donovan stopped in front of Chelsea Baker's desk. She wore a look as rigid as granite, working very hard to appear disinterested.

"Chels, would you call desk three and tell them we're coming over and tell Lucas Ms. Merrall will be joining us for lunch."

"Certainly," replied Chelsea Baker, glancing at Merrall with a friendly smile.

"Oh, I don't want to interfere with your meeting." Merrall looked surprised. "I can come back another time."

"No, not at all. You'll enjoy meeting Lucas. He's a fascinating man. He's interested in what's happening with the militia." They turned to leave.

"Oh, Mr. Donovan," his secretary almost shouted. "Are you forgetting your jacket?"

He unconsciously rubbed his hair and looked down at his sweater.

"Oh, I'm sorry, Sandra," an embarrassed grin, "I'll . . . ah . . . I'll just be a minute."

Donovan seldom wore a jacket inside the office, even in the winter, preferring sweaters, mostly beige or light blue, with as simple a design as possible. Fortunately, Chelsea faithfully reminded him to remove his sweater and put on his jacket and the need to buff his shoes and comb his hair as he left for meetings in the White House and elsewhere. He had been in the Secret Service for many years now, but the more relaxed environment of his life as a Detroit detective was still very much a part of his personality.

After passing the security desk, they walked along the main hallway of the West Wing, through the foyer leading to the Reception Room, and then continued to the staff dining room. Tony Martinez, the White House steward, escorted them to their table. Waiting for the deputy director, they discussed the joint task force, headed by the Secret Service. It would include a half-dozen agents from the bureau and three times as many from the service.

As the waiter poured their ice tea, Lucas Chandler entered the room and stopped to speak with a few people sitting at a table near the door before catching Donovan's eyes. He immediately walked over and stood before Sandra Merrall and said, "Ms. Merrall, I'm Lucas Chandler. It's a pleasure to meet you."

"Mr. Chandler, thank you. It's certainly an honor to meet you, sir."

Chandler gave her one of his celebrated complete facial smiles before turning to Donovan. "James, how are things today?"

They shook hands.

"Not bad, Lucas."

"Well, Ms. Merrall—"

"Sandra, please."

"Of course. I understand you will be working with our intelligence division," Chandler said, placing his cloth napkin neatly across his lap.

"Yes." She waited for a young man in a bright white uniform to finish filling the water glasses before taking a quick drink, noticing the blue presidential seal neatly embossed on the glass.

"It seems the militia is poised for a major offensive," Chandler continued, his voice lowered a bit. "I understand you're the bureau's expert in that area. It's good to have you working with us."

"Thank you, Mr. Chandler."

"Lucas, please," he said, with a big smile. Chandler had no difficulty maintaining eye contact with Merrall. His problem now was to remember to include Donovan in the conversation.

Following a casual lunch and small talk mixed with a professional history and a few anecdotes, they rose from the table. Chandler departed and Donovan invited Merrall for a brief tour of the mansion.

They walked toward the heart of the White House, passed a series of doors, each with an agent standing guard. They passed the Oval Office on their right. The light above the door was lit.

Merrall was quiet as they proceeded past the office of the president's secretary, Kathleen Brint, then past the Cabinet Room on their right. The double doors of the room were open, showing the long oval table that had witnessed the innermost secrets of a nation in the papers and reports that had passed over its surface. Merrall caught a glimpse of the Rose Garden out of the Cabinet Room windows. What they could see of the grounds looked beautifully manicured for early January; even the gravel in the paths was neatly raked into scalloped patterns.

As they continued down the hall, Barry Dipaula appeared in front of them, absorbed in thought, reading a thick report as he walked. Recognizing him instantly, Merrall caught her breath.

Dipaula glanced up, "Good afternoon, James."

"Barry," Donovan casually acknowledged.

Dipaula walked by Merrall like a worried surgeon studying charts on his way to see a critically ill patient. He entered an office several doors down. Merrall followed him with her eyes and was surprised when the national security advisor stepped back into the hallway, looked directly at her and smiled, "Sandra?"

"Uh, yes. Hello, Mr. Dipaula."

Lowering his papers, Dipaula turned to face her, "Haven't seen you for a while. How've you been?"

"Fine, . . . you?"

"Well, in a word, busy," he replied with a big grin.

"I can imagine," she returned the smile.

"Good to see you again."

"Yeah," her face reddened slightly.

After a few long and awkward seconds, "Well, take care," he said, the smile had moved to his eyes.

"You, too," she said, as he turned and went through the doorway.

Donovan was a bit shocked; the uneasiness in his voice was unlike him. "You know Barry Dipaula?" he asked, as they moved down the hallway.

"Yes, casually. We met at Kathryn Lawrence's retirement party last summer. Evidently, he knew her from Colorado. We met again at a State Department reception in early October. Nice guy."

"I see," Donovan said, surprised at his own awkwardness as well. Yet, considering Sandra Merrall, it was not entirely unreasonable. Still, there was something concealed. While she projected the intensity and confidence of a ballerina, her eyes occasionally revealed something quite the contrary.

Following the brief tour, Donovan escorted Merrall to the east entrance from where she headed back to the Hoover Building.

Donovan went back to his office, removed his jacket, flipped two small gold bars, and removed his cufflinks, placing them in his shirt pocket. It was too warm for a sweater so he rolled up his sleeves and poured some coffee; black, uncorrupted coffee, not the kind with a strange exotic name and a distinctive paper cup with rippled cardboard wrapped around it. While others in the mansion conspicuously ordered Italian-sounding coffee made in a fancy gold machine, Donovan liked his from off the shelf at a local grocery and perked in his little ten-cupper, which made his trips to Seattle a bit difficult.

January 15, 8:30 AM

The garage door opened and a white Lincoln town car backed slowly down the driveway and into the quiet street, five men inside. It turned right at the first intersection, down a few blocks, and then left onto Jefferson Davis Parkway. Within minutes, it was crossing the Fourteenth Street Bridge and into the district. To its left sat the imperial white Jefferson Memorial with its tranquil lake reflecting the early morning color from the rising sun and pale white clouds from the crisp cold January sky.

They crossed over the bridge and moved slowly between the Bureau of Printing and Engraving and the US Mint, standing like concrete fortresses on both sides of the street. The driver was careful not to draw attention as he drove west down Independence Avenue, parallel to the mall and the massive buildings of the Smithsonian Institute.

A police cruiser turned onto the avenue behind them and approached the car. The driver glanced to the rearview mirror and back to the road ahead. The DC police car stayed with them as they turned right onto Seventeenth Street, cutting through the mall.

To their left, about a half mile away, was the famed reflection pool and just beyond it the Lincoln Memorial, glowing in brilliant white, taking the full rays of the rising sun. To their immediate right was the towering centerpiece, the Washington Monument and beyond it, Capitol Hill.

Every eye in the car turned to stare briefly at the Capitol, which occupied the very top of the hill and dominated the skyline. Roberto Santos looked back into his rearview mirror to see the police car turn onto Seventeenth Street behind him. He drove across the mall, careful not to break any laws nor attract attention.

"A police car," Santos remarked, trying to remain calm.

The stop light at the intersection ahead turned red. The car came to a stop. The cruiser eased in behind it. Every man in the car stared straight ahead. The light turned green and the Lincoln slowly turned to its left.

The blue and red lights of the cruiser came on and hit the driver like a high voltage zap to his heart. "They are stopping us?" he said, slight tension in his voice.

"No one panic," ordered Kamile from the backseat.

Santos pulled to the curb; the cruiser stopped a short distance behind.

Officer Terry Johnson approached the vehicle. His partner, Larry Davis, remained in the vehicle, checking its registration by computer.

Santos lowered the window, his chest pounding.

"Good morning," Johnson stood a few feet from the door. "May I see your license and vehicle registration?"

Santos was cool. He took out his wallet, handed the license to Johnson and reached for the glove box, asking, "What's wrong officer? Did I do something wrong?"

His eyes moving slowly about the car, Johnson responded, "You failed to give a signal your last two turns and you didn't seem to be wearing your seatbelt. Do you have one on?"

Santos did not. *Damnit! How stupid.* "Sorry, Officer. I wasn't thinking. I usually put it on, but . . . slipped my mind this morning."

"Carlos Rodriguez, eh?" asked the officer as he looked into the back seat. He thought to ask where they were headed but chose to leave it alone.

"This your vehicle?"

"No, sir. It's rented." Santos handed him the rental agreement. "Here are the papers."

After Johnson had taken the papers to the patrol car for a quick computer check, he decided to give Santos a warning, a few stern words regarding his personal safety.

As Johnson turned to head back to his car, Kamile whispered, "His name!"

His head half out the window, Santos called out, "May I ask your name officer? You've been very kind."

"Johnson, Terry Johnson." Looking into the rear window as he passed, the officer muttered, "You men be careful now."

Kamile breathed a slow, very controlled sigh of relief. *We certainly will be officer*, he thought. *We certainly will be.*

The Lincoln then took a circuitous route to the auto repair shop.

4:15 PM

It was getting dark as police officer Terry Johnson pulled into the driveway of his modest single-story home in Parklawn, Virginia, near the Columbia Pike and Highway 244, a few miles west of the district.

Johnson would soon be fixing his daughter's favorite, spaghetti with his special thick, sausage and mushroom sauce. He suddenly realized he had forgotten to stop for a loaf of French bread and knew he would have to go out again after taking a quick shower. Today was a fairly slow day, but he needed that shower. It was his daughter's thirteenth birthday; she had become a teenager. In honor of the occasion, Johnson had let nearly every minor traffic violator off with only a warning.

He pushed the button. In the headlights, he could see the garage door creak open and struggle upward. Johnson eased the car into the cluttered garage, stopped, set his break and turned the key. He stepped out of the car and directly into the rugged face of Roberto Santos.

"What the hell are yo—"

"You told me to be safe," Santos whispered; a grisly smile rolled across his pitted, stubble-covered face. He raised the pistol.

Johnson froze, terror swept across his face. "What—"

"Well, I decided to be," the Mexican hissed between his tobacco-stained teeth as he squeezed the trigger, exploding Officer Terry Johnson into the next life.

Within seconds, a door leading into the kitchen opened; and a young girl stepped out, a radiant smile on her face. Santos moved his weapon, looked deep into her beautiful eyes and hesitated. As the girl's eyes widened, Santos heard several dull thuds and watched the young teenager slam against the doorframe and slump to the floor. He turned to see Samir standing at the back of the car.

Chapter Six

January 16, 4:30 PM
The Treasury Building

It was two days before the State of the Union Address; time was closing in at a suffocating, overwhelming pace. The task force had met for nearly eleven hours. Most of the members had now returned to their respective offices. A few remained in the meeting room at the Treasury Building, which had been set up as command room for the joint Secret Service and FBI task force. Linnet Singleton, Joe Vornas, and Sandra Merrall sat at desks placed along the wall opposite the doorway. Another wall to the right of the door was completely lined with a dozen file cabinets. To the left of the door stood three computer tables, three printers, a facsimile machine, and a coffee table. Charlie Morrison and James Donovan were now seated at a small round table in the center of the room.

Lucas Chandler had stopped by for an update and stood in the center of the room near the table. He was asking, "So any clear thoughts on what we're facing?"

"A lot of things point to an opening shot here in the district, Mr. Chandler," Singleton noted.

Sandra Merrall sat back in her chair and said, "We've uncovered another incident. A bureau informant inside the militia was contracted to fly three people from Texas to Virginia on January twelve, just four days ago. He dropped them in Richmond. Then, immediately became bottom feed in a nearby lake.

"Another of our informants, a ranking member of the National Militia, one of their accountants, was shot to death in his home near Lynchburg, three days ago. Informants have been dropping like flies. The accountant was the fourth in three weeks. Things appear to be accelerating. Reminds me of the tremors before a major quake."

"Another thing that might be important," Morrison added. "The Mexican government reported heavy weapons may have been transported across the border into Arizona sometime around January 7."

"Weapons?" Chandler asked. "What kind of weapons?"

Charlie Morrison, eighteen years with the Secret Service, had previously worked at the Boise office. It was there he obtained a firsthand look at the National Militia. A bright, tough, hardworking agent who occasionally found the time for a quick round of golf, even if it meant getting up at five in the morning in a driving wind.

"Not certain," Morrison replied. "However, the weapons may be part of a major hit on the military arsenal near the town of . . ." glancing down at his report, "Merida in Southern Mexico. A number of handheld missile launchers were part of that heist. The description given by an operative on board ship transporting the weapons seems to match crates containing missile launchers."

"It may not be a coincidence," Merrall noted, "that one of the passengers delivered to Richmond was a Mexican fitting the general description of a man who may have been aboard that ship and may actually have accompanied the weapons into this country on the seventh of January. He used the name, Roberto Santos."

Joe Vornas broke in, "Heavy weapons could mean anything."

"The bureau's been informed a Mexican agent's on his way to the district," Merrall added, "to help with identification of Santos. If Santos is in the area, we have to find him. He could be a key. Oh, another thing, British Intelligence sent a photograph of Santos. We distributed copies to local law enforcement."

Donovan added, "Evidence still points to the president at the White House or maybe the Capitol during the State of the Union Address. A powerful statement for Fajil and a good opening shot for an all-out civil war for the militia."

Chandler stepped over to Singleton's desk, glanced casually at the situation report, then at his watch, then at Donovan, "I've got a meeting coming up. Keep me informed."

Chandler left the room as Merrall inserted a tape in the VCR. "Maybe you should take a look at this tape. It will give some insight into the mindset of the people running the militia." She pushed the buttons.

Within a few seconds, a light flickered on the monitor followed quickly by the video of a large gathering inside an enormous auditorium with thousands of filled seats; placards and banners lined the walls. On the center stage sat a half-dozen men to either side of a podium where a speaker was engaged in a highly emotional address. Then a freeze frame of the center three men.

"This meeting took place a few weeks ago at their national convention." Merrall informed them. "The man in the center delivering the speech is Christenson. Seated to his left is Marvin Calloway and to his right is Timothy Bonner."

Several people turned their chairs to get a better view. All eyes focused on the television screen. At the podium, the six-foot-two-inch Pete Christenson, wearing dark charcoal slacks, a light blue sports jacket, and open-collared white shirt, suddenly came to life. His voice boomed out to the vast audience, mostly men, all white, a hint of fire in his eyes, "Listen to me! White European Americans will very soon become a minority in this country! The birthrate of nonwhites, racial intermarriage, added to the immense, unfair, and virulent immigration of 90 percent nonwhites will insure that our country will soon become a third world nation and send us into poverty and civil unrest." A slight pause inviting angry shouts from the crowd. "Anyone who stands up for the rights of white America is called a bigot, a racist! If a nonwhite group votes in a bloc, the press calls that 'American'! If white Americans vote in blocs, they call us 'Racists'! If they speak out for the rights of nonwhites they are called 'Americans'! If we speak out for the rights of whites, they call us 'Racists'!" His pace accelerated. His voice amplified, echoed around the auditorium, as if punctuating his message through dramatic repetition.

"Several years ago, they ran down to Jasper, Texas and couldn't print enough about the black man dragged to death by a couple of white men and yelled 'hate crime.' At the same time a little white girl was raped, murdered, and burned by three blacks and no one considered yelling, 'hate crime' at them! What the hell constitutes a 'hate crime'; only crimes against them?"

Sweat beading on his forehead and now totally in control, Pete Christenson held his airtight grip on three thousand angry minds and pushed steadily onward; his resounding reproach now blaring well above the pandemonium, his fiery words reaching out to ignite dry timber in his excited audience.

"Under the banner of freedom and democracy, they are electing their kind to key public offices and any opposition from us, the descendants of the White Europeans who fought and died to build this great country, is labeled, 'Racist'! They now use the same tactics used by the communists, label, label, and label the opposition into silence!" Another round of furious yelling filled the auditorium. Hundreds of men nodded to one another, their faces clearly reflecting the passion of their leader.

Pete Christenson continued, now spewing out like molten lava, a rapid-fire stream of hot angry words, "Nonwhites who have been convicted of crimes including use of illegal drugs, prostitution, and corruption now run many of our biggest American cities. Nonwhites have even taken control of the United States government and forced, through their powerful lobby, laws that favor them. The exploiting Jews and their cohorts seek only to continue the flow of billions of our dollars into Israel by constantly keeping their convenient, concocted Holocaust locked in our minds. The Jew parasites ignore and suppress information about the real Holocaust in Russia and those in many other countries like Rwanda and Sudan, because they don't suit their selfish purpose!"

The intensity increased as Christenson cleverly stirred the crowd like a master chef intimately preparing his favorite recipe, pausing occasionally to take in the aroma, deliberately cooking at low warmth then quickly turning up the heat. Feet pounded the floor sending a thunderous noise vibrating around the huge auditorium threatening to bring the rafters blasting down upon the gathering.

"They want to take away our weapons, our final means of protecting our white society. If we don't forcefully take back our government, if we don't aggressively protect our way of life, we will surely be doomed to become minorities in a third world nation completely governed by nonwhites."

He paused briefly to bask in the trumpeting of the crowd, mentally preparing for the final, convincing squeeze. "The America we are now quickly becoming would not be recognized nor tolerated by our founding fathers. We must act soon, or it will be too late! The time is near! Be vigilant! Prepare yourselves! The second great revolution is close at hand! The government you thought was yours now belongs to them! You must act now to defend yourself before all is lost!" His final words barely heard over the deafening shouts. "We must act now for ourselves, for our families, for our dignity, and for our freedom!" Christenson's whole body glowed with a sense of personal fulfillment, of precise execution; another ingenious creation by a master chef.

Merrall cut the sound and pushed the off button, turned in her seat, and took a drink of cold coffee. The room was quiet for a few seconds. Then she commented, "Real wacko's, huh?"

Donovan shifted in his seat, took a sip of coffee and muttered, "Yeah. These are the ones we know about. What scares me are the ones we don't know about; the ones in the shadows."

Singleton stood, stretched, and added, "There's no doubt they're serious enough to go after the president. But they want something else, something much bigger. They want—"

"To change the country," Morrison interrupted. "To burn the Constitution and create their own state, where they can perform their own 'ethnic cleansing.'"

Donovan took a deep breath before answering. "Singleton's right. They're after something big. The militia wants the country, but Fajil and the Alliance want much more." He swirled his coffee, nearly spilling it before adding, "It's gonna be fierce—and not just here in the district. Whatever's coming down, it'll be all over the country at the same time." He stood and walked to the coffee machine, commenting as he moved, "It won't be long and we'll all know what that is. But it sure would be nice if we found out sooner rather than later."

"Maybe they're not after the Capitol," Morrison commented, "They could send a missile into the White House and vaporize the president. Or, stop on Constitution Avenue and fire it straight up the yard."

Singleton suggested. "Firing a missile from any number of buildings is a no-brainer. Hell, I've been upset with the Hotel Washington being so close you could almost throw a grenade onto the roof of the White House from dozens of rooms. They could certainly hit this building with little effort. Scares the hell outta me. We should close that place."

"It would take a very high explosive device to do any damage to the White House from that hotel. Certainly not a grenade," quipped Vornas.

"What if it were a small nuclear device?" snapped Singleton. "A few years back the Russians developed a small nuclear device, a quarter kiloton or less. That technology could have moved to Iran, North Korea, and from there God knows where."

Vornas merely shrugged his shoulders in resignation. "It would be difficult, even suicidal."

Donovan spoke up. "It would take a nuclear warhead to destroy the Capitol. You'd get a lot more than just the president if you hit during the State of the Union Address. Makes perfect sense. Everything points to it. Wiping out US leadership would certainly benefit the Alliance. Fajil would become the king of assassins, and what a great way for the militia to start a nationwide revolt, a second revolution. Decapitate the government and start over from scratch. Makes good sense it's going to be a nuclear hit. Especially, if a warhead were small enough to be fired from a device mounted on a truck, or maybe fired from an apartment window. Of course, that couldn't have happened just a few years ago. However, the agency and the Pentagon tell us it's now entirely possible. Believe it or not, the age of miniature nuclear weapons is here."

Everyone wanted the subject changed. A small nuclear device would be an absolute nightmare to defend against.

"In any case," Vornas sat back, closed the file and pushed it away, fighting an overwhelming need to yawn, "we need at least one small piece of evidence that something like this is actually being planned."

"Sounded a bit far-fetched, at first," Morrison mumbled with some frustration. The extreme seriousness of their situation slammed home to them as he grimly added, "But I agree with the nuclear possibility; I mean on the Capitol, considering the people involved and the information we have."

Vornas mentioned with a weak smile, "Maybe the guys you questioned Sandra, were part of a big deceptive plan."

Donovan ignored Vornas's comment and continued with his thought, "To hit the Capitol during the State of the Union Address with a nuclear weapon would take a lot of people. Maybe even some insiders as well; people inside the Capitol, the State Department, the Pentagon. Who knows?"

Donovan stretched, and then absently raked his hair. "I think we've worked this thing to death, at least for now."

Heaving a generous, relaxing sigh, Merrall responded, "Maybe you're right. I'm saturated." She stood, put her jacket on, casually walked to the door, opened it, and turned around. "See you later, people. I'm going home and die. Maybe I'll be thinking more clearly in the morning."

"Need a ride?" asked Singleton, closing an old report detailing the assassination of Sadat.

"Sure, thanks." Sandra turned and walked out the door. They walked downstairs, out the main door and down the steps.

"How late will he work tonight?" asked Sandra as they walked across the courtyard.

"Who, James?"

"Yeah. You've been working closely for the last week or so."

"Who knows?" Singleton sensed Sandra wanted to know more. "From the little I've seen, he's mostly a creature of habit. James always arrives at work an hour early to read the news and have his coffee in peace and quiet." Singleton continued as they crossed the cement courtyard toward Pennsylvania Avenue. "He reads from a half-dozen magazines and three newspapers; *The Post*, *NY Times*, and the *Chicago Tribune*. No time to read the paper at home, too busy getting out the door. Obviously, takes no time to buff his shoes." They laughed as they turned left on Pennsylvania.

Heading up the sidewalk to the parking garage, Singleton continued "Work, sports, work, the news, and work, nothing else seems to matter to James." She hesitated, then looking over to Sandra added with a grin, "From what I've seen today, you might change some of that."

Merrall felt her skin redden.

8:45 PM

Fajil al-Said walked out onto the deck of his apartment and looked out across the Potomac River to the stream of traffic moving across the Memorial Bridge, glistening lights reflecting shimmering colors off the wet pavement.

The cool crisp air gently blowing across the balcony brought with it a virulent, deep chill. Fajil folded his arms against the cold and thought to himself, *do they know? The militia are betraying their own country, how could they be trusted?*

A jet was making its final approach into Reagan airport. Fajil's eyes moved along the gleaming skyline. *How many have followed us around as we moved about this city? Are we being lured into a snare? We are not dealing with fools. Some of the most sophisticated investigators in the world are out there.*

Fajil al-Said became worried for the first time in years and a sharp chill moved slowly down his spine, hesitating as never before, sending an unfamiliar anxiety throughout his body. Looking down to the street below, he saw a father walking hand-in-hand with his small child. Instantly, Fajil felt terribly alone, realizing he was never allowed to experience the joy of walking with his child, the pleasure of holding her close, of sharing her dreams and her life. As he looked up into the night, lights twinkling in the distance, he recalled the exact day his quest had begun, the moment the avenging angel entered his heart, even the very hour, the minute, and the second.

Fajil closed his eyes. His mind slowly whirled in a regressive spiral, back over forty hard years, locking suddenly on that dreadful day. That traumatic moment when he found his family crushed to death was forever imprisoned in the deepest recess of his memory. The cool air surrounded him as Fajil slowly opened his moist, reddened eyes to see the city lights in the distance and the Lincoln Memorial just a few miles away. His head cleared as he looked at his watch, then down again to the father and child on the street below.

Chapter Seven

Monday, January 17

With the president's speech just two days away, special security was ordered at all federal buildings in and around the district. Teams of FBI, ATF, and Federal Marshals along with agents of the Secret Service were working in various cities to determine who on the suspect list was missing or had a significant change in routine. They were searching for any clue, even the slightest indication of what was planned or from where the assault might come.

Leadership of the local militia was surreptitiously questioned and the most suspicious were detained in "unofficial buildings" and "secure homes" with addresses, which never appear on official reports. The public was kept unaware of the intense investigation and detention, verifying in the minds of the detained that the government was continuing to rule by suppression.

The Mexican agent, Antonio Vasquez, had arrived in the district and identified Roberto Santos as being the one who supervised the transfer of weapons into Arizona. Since Santos might have flown into the area with an ill-fated Texas informant, information on the Mexican was being distributed to all concerned. From Vasquez's description of the crates unloaded from the fishing ship, Apiza, handheld missiles to be used in an attack was now a very strong possibility.

3:00 PM
The Cabinet Room

Only thirty hours remaining before the address. Tension was beginning to mount. Personal composure was wearing down. For some, self-control had become nothing more than a fragile, super-heated filament waiting for the slightest thump to shatter it to pieces.

Inside the Cabinet Room, the president sat at the center of a massive rectangular table, his back to the windows through which the Rose Garden could be seen just outside. With him to his right and left were Nelson Borland, the vice president and Barry Dipaula. Directly across from him were William Russell, chief of staff, John Skinner, secretary of state, David Polchak, and James Donovan.

Polchak had requested a meeting with the president but would allow Donovan to take part in his appeal with a strong suggestion he choose his words carefully and not upset the president. Bergstrom had agreed to meet with the agents prior to his 3:15 PM meeting. Following the normal moments dedicated to transitory small talk, Bergstrom gave the floor to Polchak who turned it over to Donovan.

"Mr. President," Donovan felt Bergstrom's penetrating eyes move to the right and level on him, triggering a memory of his father waiting anxiously for an explanation. "As you know so well, sir, our task force believes that individuals from Al Qeada or some splinter group have joined with the National Militia and are planning an assassination attempt before, during, or after your speech. Most of our people believe a missile might be fired at the motorcade en route, or at the House Chamber during your address. Either scenario would call for some major changes. We request you consider them in your plans, Mr. President."

Without saying a word, and with respect for the agent's direct approach, Bergstrom looked away from Donovan's eyes to the man seated next to him. Having been given a briefing earlier by Polchak, the president was aware of the efforts being made by various agencies to protect him on his way to and from the State of the Union Address.

Looking back to Donovan, Bergstrom offered an empathetic smile and said, "Specifically, what are you asking of me, James? What do you recommend we do?"

"Mr. President, I believe, given who we are dealing with, that it might be best to submit the address in writing and have it read, perhaps, by the vice president. Another possibility would be to deliver the address yourself, but from here. That may protect not only yourself but others along the route and in the Capitol as well."

Still staring at Donovan, the president questioned the director of the Secret Service. "What do you think, David?" Then, he turned his eyes on Polchak.

"Mr. President, I consider the threat to be quite probable and support the recommendations James has submitted," Polchak responded. "I must again mention, we have no specific data to indicate an attack will occur to your motorcade or even, heaven forbid, during your address. However, this is not a casual recommendation; it's a sensible precaution. It is derived from very careful consideration by teams from not only the Secret Service but Homeland Security, the FBI, and CIA as well. Mr. President, I repeat what others have said, the international terrorists and the National Militia would benefit greatly if you were eliminated and more so with billions of people watching."

Donovan interjected, "We believe they have the capability to carry out such a plan, Mr. President. Even an attack on the Capitol is a real possibility."

"There isn't a better venue for them to make a major statement than the Capitol of the United States, nor a better event than your address," noted Polchak. "After all, sir, in actuality, this is not merely a state of the union address, it is more of an address to the entire world."

Looking now to Russell, Bergstrom continued his questioning, "What do you think, Bill?"

"Well, Mr. President, I have no doubt there is a probability that an assassination may be attempted. But assassination attempts are always a possibility. There isn't much solid evidence that a major assault is being planned during the speech. I strongly caution against appearing overly concerned, especially at this very critical time, with the deadline approaching."

"By overly concerned, I think Bill means 'frightened,'" added Dipaula. "Mr. President, as you know so well, the Alliance states would love to see you weakened. That would strengthen their resolve and perhaps even be the one thing needed to solidify their union. And, Mr. President, the National Militia might find a destabilized president would serve their purpose as well. This is time for a firm commitment at every level."

"What about a dead president?" Donovan said to Dipaula with such force he even surprised himself.

Dipaula recoiled as though he had been stabbed with a dull dentist's drill. Polchak looked sharply at his assistant.

"James, an attack upon the Capitol wouldn't make sense," Dipaula remarked. "It's too big and well fortified. But, I guess, for something to happen along the route of the motorcade, well, that does make some sense."

The president merely glanced at Donovan, as if making a quick judgment about his emotions. He then turned to Dipaula. "Any other thoughts, Barry?"

Barry Dipaula had given serious thought to the concerns expressed by the Secret Service. However, he was paid to focus on national security. "Mr. President, I consider your speech to be extremely important at this critical time. I have all respect for the perspective of our zealous colleague," he turned to Donovan, "who has quite vigorously and appropriately indicated his concern for your personal safety." He then refocused on the president, "However, while stability in Central Asia may not entirely rest on whether you deliver the speech from the podium or from that desk, another factor is extremely important. In this world, and in this situation, appearances make a critical difference."

Dipaula remained fixed on Bergstrom, everyone did. "While delivering your speech from the Oval Office may be considered a viable alternative by some, I believe you should deliver the speech in person at the podium as planned. My thoughts are based on the lack of hard evidence that an attack is actually being planned either during the motorcade or during the address. Also, I doubt that such an attack, were it to occur, could actually be successful. I would—"

"Hard evidence is a relative term, Mr. Dipaula," Donovan interrupted, his eyes growing cold. "Some would—"

"Remaining in the White House on such an occasion might send the wrong signal to individuals, international and domestic," continued Dipaula without acknowledging the agent's abruptness. "It would, without a doubt, stun everyone and doesn't seem warranted, given the actual hard data. The world is growing more unstable each day. You need to be in control and at the podium, Mr. President."

Russell nodded his agreement.

While Donovan made no verbal reply, his face shouted an angry response. Donovan's lack of fondness for politicians and political appointees was well known in the service. He considered the vast majority of them nothing more than campaign workers being paid off, or people who knew someone who was being paid off. For most, concern for the well-being of the president was nothing more than a personal concern for preserving their own positions. They reminded him of groupies, fans of a rock star who drained him of his wealth while selfishly inflating their own résumés. Many of them would gladly place the president in the line of fire if it furthered their own personal goals. To him, political people in the White House were constantly checking the balance bar, adding and removing weights, considering how far to push the president without loosing control of their cherished positions.

"What about you, John?" Bergstrom asked, needing a buffer to restrain the potential conflict between his primary defender and his primary supporter. Skinner, always a levelheaded man, had often served as Bergstrom's gearshift to decelerate to a slower, calmer pace during heated, critical deliberations. This was a good time to use him.

"Well, Mr. President," Skinner began, "my concerns are similar to Barry's. I will be meeting with Minister Malinkof a few hours following your speech and would find it very difficult to deliver the message you are considering if you were hostage in this mansion. If the evidence were more convincing, well, then any measure of protection would be explainable. But, given the amount of data available, your remaining in the White House would be a difficult decision to explicate. The proposal for some change in routine by the Secret Service and others, however, obviously needs to be given your serious consideration. Some compromise between the need to display strength and conviction and the need for prudence and guardianship of your office is definitely called for. I believe a change in the motorcade coupled with leaving a member of the cabinet in a secure place would suffice. This would be added to an already enormous defense, which your protective agencies have effectively and professionally implemented."

"Thank you, John." Looking around the room, Bergstrom focused on Donovan and asked, "Is it true the only evidence you have that an attack will take place anywhere are some vague reports from Europe, Mexico, and a few domestic reports from informants involving a federal building?"

Tense but determined, Donovan replied, "You've read the overview of our report, sir. While there are a lot of inferences, there are also some fairly convincing facts as well. To someone not involved in the daily discussion, on the surface the report would appear to be a bit flimsy, I admit. But we know the individuals we're dealing with . . ." He paused and released some frustration before continuing. "Sir, please keep in mind, it's not only the service but the FBI that is recommending changes. Again, with all due respect to Mr. Dipaula, Mr. Skinner, and Mr. Russell, as far as the Secret Service is concerned, politics doesn't enter the picture. Our responsibility is to protect you, at all costs. We believe strongly in order to do that we must request you not deliver the speech as planned."

The president sat back in his chair, looked at his watch and said to Polchak and Donovan, "Gentlemen, would you leave us to consider the dilemma you've presented us? As you can well imagine, we have many other pressing matters to deal with today. Thank you for your concern and always remember how much I admire and respect your efforts. Regardless of my decision, that will remain a certainty."

Standing and buttoning his jacket, Donovan made one last attempt to convince the president. "Mr. President—"

"James?" Polchak quietly interrupted.

"Please, David," Donovan pleaded with his boss. "Mr. President, allow me one additional thought. Since the concern is for the crisis in Central Asia and in Russia, while I'm certainly not political, wouldn't it be in the best interest of the United States to have you remain alive, with all respect, sir? I agree in part with Mr. Dipaula, the Capitol is too big and too protected for ammonium nitrate or some such high explosive device. However, one last thing we have not fully discussed is that Fajil may use a mobile missile armed with a nuclear warhead."

Dipaula's eyes began a slow, critical roll. His patience was strained.

Donovan caught the subtle criticism at the corner of his eye, almost losing his train of thought. However, he chose to ignore the looks and continued, "Perhaps, a warhead obtained from an Alliance state, maybe Iran, as the CIA believes. Also, sir, as you are aware, a few years back a former Russian spy stated quite convincingly that a group of Soviet agents were assigned to locate places within the United States to conceal small suitcase-size nuclear weapons. If that—"

"Come on, James," interrupted Dipaula with an incredulous smile on his face. "Surely you don't believe that old story!"

"It was never disproved, sir," countered Donovan.

Dipaula's mind snagged on his tone of voice and missed the message.

"Mr. President, Soviet nuclear weapons may actually have been in this country for many years." The volume of Donovan's voice had increased slightly. "If that is the case, sir, this whole scenario might pan out and a major attack on the Capitol during your speech is even more convincing. The Capitol is big, but maybe not too big for a small-yield nuclear device. Fajil may have the capability and he may have the support. I'm certain he has the motivation. The bureau believes he may actually have two nuclear weapons." Donovan let his words sink in before adding, "I hope that will contribute something to your discussion."

Hiding the sting of the nuclear jab, Bergstrom forced an uneasy smile and replied, "Thank you, James. You just made my day."

Donovan, true to his reputation, struck one final time; "Again, with all due respect, Mr. President, it's not your day I'm most concerned about, sir; it's your life—the life of the president of the United States." He knew Polchak would take him to the woodshed for that remark.

"James," Polchak quickly interrupted, "it's time to leave."

The president locked on Donovan's eyes. Everyone waited for Bergstrom to soundly put the agent in his place. Instead of taking issue, the president slowly nodded his understanding. Everyone remained quiet, even Polchak. There was unanimity in the thought, *what if Donovan is right?*

Chapter Eight

Monday, January 17, 4:15 pm

It was the day before the State of the Union Address. Fajil was in a safe house in Georgetown, together with Kamile and the entire Iwo Jima team. Weapons were rechecked and final instructions given before they turned to their individual ways of dealing with the moment. Tomorrow could well bring an end to their quest on this earth and undoubtedly mark their destiny forever.

Fajil walked out into the backyard of the house into the cool night air. Kamile followed. They sat on white metal chairs, both smoking, completely immersed in thought.

Kamile spoke first, the softness in his voice revealing a deep, unusual concern. "There is nothing more that can be done, we have covered every detail." He glanced over to his friend who was examining the blue smoke from his cigarette as it twisted and turned, and climbed higher and higher before vanishing into the cool night air.

"This smoke is like our souls." Fajil spoke deliberately, mindfully. "They may soon rise into the heavens to join our brothers." Fajil had never before spoken of death before a strike. However, this time was like no other.

Kamile said nothing. He took a deep breath and looked at the trees that lined the yard protecting them from curious eyes. As young men, they could not imagine an end to their life. Now, they measured their time in hours. Kamile's thoughts moved back over the years to a time when he and Fajil played together as children. He remembered the day

Fajil's entire family had died in an Israeli air raid at home in Port Said. His thoughts turned to his own loss. His wife, his mother, and his only child were killed while riding to market in a crowded bus. *They call us assassins*, he thought. *What, of our families? Were they worthless cattle to be slaughtered without thought or concern? They were human; creations of Allah. And what we are about to do will at last declare that fact to the whole world. We are people too!*

The two men sat for a long while, reflecting on where their destiny had finally brought them. Then, without words, as if responding to the same veiled signal, they calmly rose and went back inside.

7:10 PM, Alexandria, Virginia

It took a few minutes for Jerry Mason and William Kempner to discover they were alone in the basement of the safe house; each looking to the other for some comfort in a most uneasy situation.

"Where's everyone else?" asked a very nervous Kempner. "What's goin' on here?"

As they looked at each other, the full realization of their situation pounded down on them like a meteor from the sky. Suddenly, the door opened and three men entered the room, Samir and two gunmen. The silencers were effective and the noxious thuds came like rapid puncturing stings of deadly hornets bursting through flesh and bone. The two members of the Virginia Militia fell into pools of blood as the assassins turned, left the room. Samir closed the door behind them.

8:00 PM
The District

The storm that had been predicted for the DC area hadn't materialized. Myron Davis, weatherman for CNN, had just reported the jet stream had shifted and North Carolina and Virginia were now being pounded with heavy rainfall. In contrast, the district was rather calm in the cool evening of January 17, the night before the president's State of the Union Address.

With only twenty-four hours left, most of the military effort focused on an air attack. The FBI believed any assault on the Capitol would most likely come from the air and the military consultants agreed. Their concern was now focused on searching nearby airfields and defending the winter sky against attack planes, remote controlled small craft and helicopters. The military was not focused on the handheld missile reports, choosing to give that responsibility to the FBI, Secret Service, and ATF who would be in charge on the ground immediately around the building.

Twenty-three specialists from a number of agencies were working with the task force, another hundred in other buildings around the district. Donovan was reviewing a rough sketch for defending against an attack on the Capitol. With him were Singleton, Morrison, Merrall, and thirty-one-year-old, Chris Van Meter; all seated around a cluttered table. His voice vibrated a bit, "Does everyone have a copy of the emergency response plans for the district?" he asked, holding up a thick binder. "I mean the plan for the entire district, not just the mall area?"

"Well, I think everyone has a copy," Singleton answered. "I should verify that."

"Yeah, have someone else check. This damn thing is impossible to read, must have been designed by a group of bureaucratic lawyers. It's more political than practical."

"Can we position any additional antimissile defense on the Capitol?" asked Van Meter, a special tactics expert. "Not much up there now."

"I saw something in here. God knows what page," responded Singleton, thumbing through a thick binder.

"Anything on the Santos picture?" Donovan asked Merrall.

"Nothing yet, that I'm aware of. Oh, a few sightings, which amounted to nothing. There's still hope. Maybe, he'll turn up in the next few hours."

"Well, I hope to God we have a few hours," snapped Donovan.

"The bureau's located Chad Fletcher, the militia hit man." She sat back in her chair. "They intend to pick him up for questioning."

"He won't come easy," Donovan casually replied, glancing at the FEMA plan. "He's critical to this whole operation. Tell them to leave him alone. Follow him. Might give us more information than sounding an alarm and letting everyone know we're geared up for this thing."

Merrall reached for the phone.

Everyone worked into the night. A special team was sent to the hill to join with Capitol police in their search for an explosive device. Equipment to protect against a biological attack was moved to the rooms directly behind the House Chambers as were protective masks, suits, and other gear. All tours of the building were canceled for the next day. Only individuals with legitimate business would be allowed inside.

Switzerland
Wade Pike's Mansion

Pike stood looking out the second floor window, reflecting on his humiliation years ago. The bitter memory ignited a relentless, intense hate, which, like the end of a tormenting nightmare, instantly jarred Wade Pike back to reality. The evening colors were beginning to fill the sky as the last vestiges of the memory trickled away, leaving behind a burning commitment. He removed a speck of tobacco from his tongue, examined it, and flicked it aside saying to his aid standing patiently near the door, "Get me through to our general at the Pentagon." Then after taking a slow drag, he added, "We need to talk."

Tuesday, January 18, 2:00 PM
Day of the State of the Union Address
The District

The wind began to pick up a bit as low pressure forced cooler air into the district. Planning to avert an attack on the president was continuing in the Situation Room and in the headquarters of the Secret Service a few blocks from the White House on G Street. Most agents were able to grab a few hours of sleep during the previous night. Others were not so fortunate.

Critical meetings were taking place throughout the district. FBI counterterrorist units were preparing to locate themselves throughout the area, ready to move quickly should the need arise anywhere in the beltway. One area with quick access to the freeway system and with visual advantage to the Capitol was the Iwo Jima Memorial. A vehicle was assigned to that area; another to the Lee Mansion in Arlington Cemetery.

The Pentagon was now involved. Additional military troops were assigned to various strategic locations around the district. A call was placed from the Pentagon to a home a few miles away in Virginia. The caller had a deep, harsh, unforgiving voice.

"Fletcher, I don't want any shit! This thing has got to come down hot, heavy, and fast. We'll be sending additional troops around the city over the next few hours and you'd better get word to Pete that I don't want any slipups."

"I know, sir. We've got everything under control. Once this thing comes down, there will be no stopping it. You've done your job well and—"

"Where's Pete now?"

"Where he said he'd be."

The man in the Pentagon sat his pipe down and thought for a long stretch before ordering, "Okay, get on the phone and double check every office nationwide. Stay on that phone until you have confirmation from every region! Then report back to me on the private line."

They disconnected.

2:25 PM
The White House

President Bergstrom was sitting alone in the Oval Office reading his speech for the final time, reflecting on every pause and inflection. Tonight would be his first State of the Union Address and with the crisis in Central Asia, it had to be just right. It was only seven hours away.

A buzz at his desk.

"Yes?"

"Sorry to interrupt you, sir." It was his secretary. "You asked me to remind you about your selection of a cabinet member."

"Oh, yes, thank you." Bergstrom looked up from his desk, his mind abruptly switching subjects.

The deadline was here to select a cabinet member to remain behind in the Situation Room, protecting the line of succession. The identity of that person would be kept secret from the public until the cabinet officers entered the House Chambers for the speech. Most people, including the media, paid little notice to the one missing cabinet member but were aware of the precaution instituted decades earlier.

The discussion regarding who would stay behind had taken more time than anticipated. The vice president and the speaker were ruled out. The secretaries of defense and state, while good choices, were essential for the media in this time of crisis. Other secretaries were discussed; however, the decision was made when Bill Russell mentioned a health concern regarding the Secretary of the Interior James Kilpatrick. The secretary had been feeling poorly over the last few days and shouldn't be overly concerned about missing the event.

While Kilpatrick indicated he had the flu, Russell believed the problem to be more serious. The chief of staff recalled the incident a few weeks earlier when Kilpatrick had excused himself from a Christmas party after becoming quite ill and nearly passing out.

Bergstrom felt Kilpatrick was certainly not the best choice, given the situation. His instincts told him to leave someone with more authority and greater presence behind. However, after asking the joint task force not to panic over inferences, he could do no less. In any case, he didn't want to disappoint any member of his cabinet and this was an easy way out.

The president placed a call to Kilpatrick. Bergstrom asked about his health and then if he would mind being excused from attending the State of the Union Address. Kilpatrick, still feeling a bit under the weather, explained it was just the flu and accepted the idea of spending a quiet evening at home. To his surprise, without explaining the potential threat, Bergstrom requested he come to the White House and remain until after the address. Kilpatrick, not totally pleased, agreed to the president's request. Bergstrom scratched a note on his pad to have someone check on the state of Kilpatrick's health. Tomorrow morning would be soon enough.

Bergstrom pushed back in his chair and considered the decision he had just made. Then, placing a few sheets of paper in front of him, he began writing. In a few minutes, the president glanced up as the national security advisor entered the office, walked quietly across the room and took a seat next to his desk.

"Just one second, Barry," Bergstrom said as he continued to write.

"Yes, sir," Dipaula casually remarked as he settled into the chair.

After reading his notes, Bergstrom absently tapped the pen a few times before laying it next to the stationary. Looking over to Dipaula, he detected a more than predictable somberness in his friend. The president sat back and took a deep breath. A few quiet seconds passed before he spoke, "A great many things to worry about, Barry."

Taking a deep breath, Dipaula answered, "Yeah. Things are coming down pretty fast, Mr. President."

The president stood, walked over to a small table and poured two glasses of ice water. Handing one to Dipaula he remarked, "The address is good, Barry. As good as we can make it." After taking a drink he added, "As for the other concerns, well, we will deal with them as they arise. I'm convinced the UN will deal with the Alliance. Maybe buy us a few more weeks or months."

"I'm confident you're right, Mr. President," Dipaula answered. "But at the moment, we don't have much time. The address has to do the job or we'll face much bigger nuclear crises than Cuba." Swirling the ice in his glass, he continued, "We won't get much sleep tonight."

"The weight of the world has always rested on this very room and the men who occupy it," Bergstrom said as he returned to his desk. "Right now, that's the two of us. It's our responsibility now; comes with the job. I can't do it by myself, Barry. I need you and the others with me." Bergstrom leaned forward. "Especially tonight; especially you, Barry."

"I'm fine. Believe me, I'm fine. Just a little tired."

"Barry, we've known each other for a long time; I've never seen you when you weren't fine."

"I was told you wanted to see me," Dipaula said as he sat his glass on the table.

After reflecting a moment, the president answered, "I need a favor. I think it might be best if you remained here in the White House during the address. No doubt things will be a bit wild up on the hill tonight. It would be suffocating for you. And, as you noted, we will need some clear thinking when I return." Bergstrom sat back in his chair. "There's not much you can do up there except dodge the media."

Dipaula looked up into the president's deep blue eyes, reflected for a moment and then merely nodded his agreement, wondering what really motivated Bergstrom in asking him to remain behind.

"Good," responded the president. "That's all I wanted, for now."

Dipaula stood and as he headed for the door, remarked, "I'll be here if you need me, Mr. President."

"I'm counting on that. I'll definitely need you tonight, my friend." Then as Dipaula opened the door, Bergstrom called after him, "Oh, Barry?"

Dipaula stopped, turned, "Yes, Mr. President?"

Bergstrom looked down at the letter on his desk then back to Dipaula. "Nothing, Barry. Nothing."

A bit puzzled, Dipaula left the room.

A few minutes later, Bergstrom picked up the letter, read it, and then pushed a button on his phone. His secretary entered the room. "Yes, Mr. President?" she asked, moving toward his desk.

Placing the letter into an envelope, he said, "Mrs. Brint, if I return to the residence in a reasonable time following the address, say before midnight, please destroy this letter." As he placed it into her hand, he looked directly into her eyes and added, "If something should prevent my return this evening, anything at all, would you please see to it that Mr. Kilpatrick is given this letter?"

Unable to completely shroud her concern, Kathleen Brint answered, "Certainly, sir. I'll see that he receives it." She swallowed hard, turned, and left the room.

Throughout the region, local police together with the FBI, Secret Service, Federal Marshals, and ATF agents were rounding up anyone with a remote connection to violence against the government, especially known National Militia members. A great many people complained vociferously that their rights were being violated, self-verifying their accusations about the government. Every available law enforcement officer and special agent was working overtime.

Throughout the country, law enforcement agencies were alerted to prepare for a possible move by local militia forces over the next forty-eight hours.

Chapter Nine

January 18, 5:15 PM

In a secure room inside the Treasury Building, over a dozen people were concerned with the dangerous situation likely to slam into them in the coming hours. Donovan, Merrall, and Special Agents Van Meter, Morrison, Vornas, and Johnson were seated around a large, cluttered table. With them were members of the Department of Defense's Special Weapons Station and FBI counterterrorist experts, including Linnet Singleton. Dir. David Polchak had just arrived and was in his office down the hall.

John Stanley, from DOD Special Weapons Station, very military with short blond hair and smartly pressed brown suit, was standing behind his chair at midtable finishing his briefing related to handheld nuclear missiles. "Again, our reaction time will be in fractions of a second. We don't have the advantage of Patriot Missiles and long incoming trajectories. If it comes, it will be a short flight and faster than shit through a goose. However, we might be able to detect a laser guidance tracking beam if it was activated long enough and if we were positioned properly. We'll have a number of detection devices located around the Capitol and in the streets along both motorcade routes. Frankly, I think we're too late on this whole thing to provide any kind of effective defense. There are a great number of questions, which—"

"There are only two big questions," Charley Morrison interrupted. "Will they fire the missile from the air or from land? Will the attack be biological, high explosive, or even nuclear? All other questions are secondary."

Moore broke in, "How many additional weapons would we need, beyond what we already have up there?"

"I remind all of you, it's vital we keep the press and media out of this," Donovan responded. "A complete blackout; adding more visible hardware would only draw attention. In any case, we're using everything available." He was tired, confused, frustrated, and starting to sound like Chandler. "We only have a few hours. It's coming down too fast for last-minute suggestions."

The ring almost went unnoticed before Singleton reached for the receiver.

"This is Singleton. Right. When? What's his name? Get him over here, ASAP. Right. Thanks."

She now had everyone's attention. "I think we've got a break... maybe."

"What's that?" Donovan asked.

"A police officer thinks he ran into Santos Saturday morning. Pretty certain it was him."

Donovan looked a bit skeptical as he asked, "Why is this different from other sightings?"

"He and his partner checked the man's driver's license for a minor traffic violation. They were in a rented car. Later that day, his partner was shot to death by an unknown assailant; a teenage daughter along with him." Singleton said as she walked over to the file cabinet. "They're dropping him by for a meeting with Vasquez, the Mexican agent."

"Damn, this thing is going down," Morrison mumbled. "But exactly when? Where? How?"

"I want to see that officer when he gets here," Donovan said as he picked up a picture of Roberto Santos.

5:45 PM

With three hours remaining, word came from defense that a few additional mobile antimissile weapons were moving toward the district. In any case, reaction time would be so short the primary defense would be several small antimissile missiles already located on the Capitol with backup from circling Apache helicopters. One danger in firing the missiles would be the low angle. If they missed their mark, the missiles would hit the buildings surrounding the mall. Someone in the highest authority would have to give the order to fire the weapons. It meant the president himself.

Fighter planes from Andrews would be located just outside the downtown area, circling at three to five thousand feet, prepared to intercept incoming aircraft. The sky around the district would be closed and NORAD and Northcom fighters would be in the air over major cities.

His secretary interrupted the president as she announced that John Kindle and David Polchak were outside wishing to speak with him. Once in the room, they spent only a minute or two explaining the plans and the possibilities to him.

After a few thoughtful seconds, the president spoke, "Your plan does sound rather . . . excessive, doesn't it? The media already knows something is out of line."

Bergstrom was hoping they would agree, but knew they wouldn't. He even felt a bit sorry for them.

"Sir, we just received word that a Mexican fitting the description of a man suspected of smuggling missile launchers across the border has been spotted in the district. He may have killed a police officer a few days ago for having identified him. It's starting to look real ugly. Mr. President, it may be inconceivable for either the vice president or the speaker to be absent from the chamber," Polchak began, standing in front of the president's desk, next to his boss, John Kindle. "However, sir, that is our best advice. I believe the threat is serious enough to warrant such a decision. Specifically, sir, I recommend the vice president remain here in the residence." Polchak waited quietly, respectfully.

Bergstrom stared at the director for a few seconds, then, with slightly distorted lips caused by intense concentration and biting of the inside of his cheek, he looked again at Polchak and said, "We need another alternative. The vice president sits next to the Speaker of the House, directly behind the president. The camera will be on them the entire time. His absence would instantly send the wrong message to the world. We need another alternative, gentlemen."

"Mr. President," the director continued, "which one of your cabinet members will stay here in the Situation Room?"

The president leaned back in his chair and placed both hands flat on his desk, a nervous reaction he was working to overcome, stared at them and said, "I've decided to have Jim Kilpatrick remain here in the White House." The two men looked noticeably upset. Bergstrom continued, "I know that's not much for you to relax with, but at least you can feel comfortable that we are leaving someone here at the residence."

The president stood and walked over to a small table, poured some water as he continued, "Also, you indicated we're altering our plans for the motorcade. God knows what the press will make out of seeing your agents get out of the limo at the Capitol steps." Bergstrom chuckled at the thought. Raising the glass to his lips he said, "Damn, I'd like to see that!" He then smiled his big campaign smile.

"Mr. President," Polchak requested, "would you give Capitol security and the military orders to prepare to fire the antimissile weapons located on the top of the Capitol and the OEB, if it became necessary, even if the trajectory were low and in line with the buildings surrounding the mall?"

Bergstrom placed the empty glass back on the tray and walked to his chair as Polchak added, "I'm afraid, sir, that if we make no substantial defense, the outcome will be determined by circumstance, not by us. We're attempting to get some additional antimissile hardware in from surrounding areas and will need your approval to fire them as well."

Bergstrom leaned forward in his chair and looked intently at the two men who carried the burden of the moment. They were reasonable, logical men, responsible for his life.

"Gentlemen, this is an extraordinary request. You've already located missiles on the roof of the Capitol and, in addition to the hardware already up there, you want to bring in more? My God, you guys are taking this far too seriously for the amount of evidence you have. I'm not going to allow a major change because people have a hunch that 'something' will happen." He settled down a bit then asked, "Does the media know any details about this situation?" His face flushed.

Kindle leaned forward, a bit overwhelmed to hear the president expose the absurdity in such a frank manner. "No, sir, we have no reason to believe they do. Of course, the precautions we've taken appear to be a bit excessive to some but may not be causing the media undue concern. It won't be difficult to explain away later."

Sitting back in his seat, Bergstrom fiddled with a pencil, established a sense of calm, then continued. "Yes, I will authorize the missiles to be fired under the condition that an unquestionable attack occurs on the Capitol from, say, 8:30 PM until 10:00 PM. Not an attack on my person, gentlemen, but only if the Capitol or the White House is unquestionably under attack." Tossing the pencil on his desk he asked, "Will that be sufficient?"

Bergstrom knew these men might be correct in their assumption, yet, he could not cancel this important speech. He was definitely in a critical position and felt somewhat powerless to change events. Everyone who planned to attend the speech was already preparing to leave for the Capitol and countries around the world were ready for the live broadcast of his address. It was a show that had to go on and could not be significantly altered at this late hour.

Polchak and Kindle agreed, thanked Bergstrom, and left the president just as Barry Dipaula and speech writer Timothy Brennan entered the room.

6:00 PM
The District

Men in each of the five safe houses, some now in National Park Service uniforms, were rechecking their watches. At precisely 8:20 PM they would leave. At precisely 9:05 PM they would reassemble at three separate locations. Their weapons would be loaded at 9:08 PM and be fired at precisely 9:11 PM. Six minutes on sight, that's all—six critical minutes. Three hours to wait, three very long and lonely hours. They tried to smile. Deep in their hearts, like other men they didn't want to die far from home and family.

Fajil would be alone. He had to give the final word. At the house in Alexandria, he stood at the doorway facing the seasoned men he had trained in the hot dry hills halfway around the world. Men he had taken to the brink of death many times before. However, this time was different. This time they would move past the brink of death and cross over into the abyss of history. They would complete the greatest strike of all time. Nothing throughout history would even compare. He felt both sadness and pride in allowing them to participate. For the five militia members chosen to accompany them, he had no concern. They were, after all, traitors to their country, common criminals.

Slowly, he looked into the eyes of each of his companions, one at a time and each smiled weakly, knowing this might be the last time they would see their leader in this life.

Fajil's eyes stopped at Kamile. Kamile stepped forward and approached him. They embraced. Fajil whispered a farewell in Kamile's ear, then turned, and walked out the door.

8:00 PM
The Situation Room

In recent days, the crisis in Central Asia had dominated discussions in the Situation Room, W20. With the Chinese and Russians aiming deadly weapons and manpower at each other and the Alliance states, threatening to ignite the situation at any second, the meetings in W20 had been intense.

This evening, the Situation Room was more like a den where friends had gathered to watch the election returns or the latest bowl game. At one end of the room, five newly installed television screens were turned to the major channels, each with muted sound. The main large-screen display in the center was tuned to C-span, which showed the empty podium of the House of Representatives standing below the speaker's chair and the US flag, where in an hour President Bergstrom would appear. The stewards, in their crisp blue blazers and starched white slacks, had put out sandwiches on the fine china and coffee was served all around.

Interior Sec. Jim Kilpatrick sat in a comfortable chair, sipping a cup of coffee, staring at the television screen, the only cabinet officer in the line of succession not attending the address. He watched the cameras focused on Kindle from treasury, Giovanni from transportation, Coyle from defense; hell, even that oily son of a bitch White House Counsel Jake Venturi was there. They were keeping company with some of the most powerful public officials on earth: the Supreme Court, the combined Houses of Congress, and assorted American and foreign dignitaries.

Everybody just oozing sincerity, thought Kilpatrick bitterly, *you can't buy that much television exposure*. A former governor of Arizona, he suddenly wanted to be in the chamber, knowing his health would soon necessitate his retirement from public office. He believed the chief of staff was suspicious of his health, which may have been why the president requested he remain in the White House. He would be the only cabinet member not introduced to the world tonight, of all nights, Bergstrom's first major speech to Congress and to the world during the greatest crisis since Cuba. Everyone would be watching, but few would notice a missing interior secretary.

Kilpatrick took another sip of hot coffee, felt a strange tightness in his chest, eased down in his chair, and loosened his tie. He had avoided government doctors in recent months for fear of being forced to resign before he could establish his place in history. Only his wife and his private physician were fully aware of his condition. It had started about a year ago and came and went almost daily. However, over the last few days, it had worsened. This morning it was almost unbearable.

Federal Judge Herbert Walker, a beefy, red-faced man with white hair seated next to Kilpatrick, didn't notice the secretary slightly hunching with his right hand massaging his chest. Walker was too busy wolfing down his second sandwich. He, too, was part of the insurance policy and invited to remain in the White House during the State of the Union Address. For an emergency, he kept a battered traveler's bible in his briefcase. Having been a respected Federal judge for the district, he was soon due to retire as a specialist in the history of presidential law.

Along the polished conference table sat an assortment of midlevel staffers from legislative affairs, domestic policy, and White House operations. A handful of senior members of the National Security Council sat huddled at one end of the room. Their next briefing wasn't due until noon the next day; they had all night to work anyway. Their boss, Barry Dipaula, hadn't bothered to join them. He was in his office on the main floor, having decided to watch the address from there.

As the president's top advisor for national security affairs, Dipaula had written much of the address himself. Tomorrow, he would be called on to answer many questions and he wanted to be ready.

Chapter Ten

January 18, 8:15 PM
The State of the Union Address

The White House was bustling with activity as the president moved down the steps to basement level one. Instead of turning left to the recently decorated tunnel leading to the Treasury Building, he turned right and walked to W16. Inside the room, nine Secret Service agents staffed the Command Post.

The president poked his head in and said, "Ladies and Gentlemen, I know you're very nervous, . . . frankly, so am I. But this job is not any easier than yours and I know you'll always do your best. God willing, so will I." Recognizing the contribution he made to the tension the Secret Service was now under by refusing to change his plans, he made an unusual request, "Wait up for me. When I get back, we'll have a drink together."

"Mr. President?" Donovan approached Bergstrom.

"Yes, James," the president held out his hand.

Donovan gave him a firm grip. "Take care, Mr. President," he said as though he were saying good-bye to a friend entering critical surgery.

Donovan's words sent an unsettling, deathly chill throughout Bergstrom's body. "I will, James. Thank you for your concern."

They faced each other for a few seconds then, surrounded by a team of agents, the president turned and proceeded to the tunnel and the Treasury Building beyond, ready to face whatever nemesis awaited him.

8:25 PM

For public view, the bogus presidential motorcade departed from the White House with special agents in the president's decoy limo. It took the expected, highly visible route, proceeding down Pennsylvania Avenue toward the Capitol. People lined the streets waving to the limo. Agent Mike Forester, playing the president, felt a small tingle in his stomach. He could get to like this. Yes, he could like it very much. On several occasions, he smiled and waved to the crowds. Yes, he could get to like this, indeed.

8:30 PM

The armored limo, with the president tucked inside, pulled quietly away from the Treasury Building. Secret Service cars moved in front and back, uniformed officers led the way on motorcycles. Trailing close behind were two jet-black vehicles, an extended van, and a Suburban containing a dozen officers in military camouflage, four attack dogs sat quietly on the floor. The motorcade headed down the district side streets toward the Hart Office Building. City police unceremoniously cleared the route.

At the same moment, the vans containing the Viper Force drove through the streets to their destination. All the players were now moving, all at the same time, within a few miles of each other, all heading for the same climax, all with their specific parts to play.

At the Capitol, the news teams were at their assigned location. Barriers had been placed at a greater distance than normal. All the networks and cable stations were represented, as well as press from around the world. There were now scant reports of the seemingly extraordinary security measures imposed by the Secret Service. No hint of why.

Streets were blockaded in a four-block perimeter around the hill. A hundred eyes scanned the crowd for "lookouts" of every description.

In a private room outside the House Chamber, the vice president, speaker, and several cabinet members chatted with members of the Supreme Court.

In various places inside the Capitol, nearly all members of the House and Senate, the joint chiefs of staff, the Supreme Court and the president's cabinet awaited the arrival of the president.

The order of entry into the chambers was a matter of tradition. The members of Congress first, followed by the military leaders, then foreign ambassadors and representatives, the Supreme Court, and the president's cabinet. Finally, an appointed committee of congressmen would escort in the president.

Secret Service officers next to Vice President Nelson Borland heard the announcement from the Command Post in W16, "Boulder is in Hart."

One of the agents leaned over to Borland and whispered, "He's in Hart, sir."

The vice president immediately cut off his conversation with the speaker and said, "He's here. Let's get this show on the road."

The vice president and speaker entered the chambers, proceeded up to the podium and took their places in front of the American flag. Members of the Supreme Court proceeded along the hallway to the door at the rear of the chambers, from where they would enter following the formal introduction.

Television stations were now interrupting normal broadcasting to cover, live, the State of the Union Address. It was estimated that nearly a billion people would be watching broadcasts around the world.

8:48 PM

The assassin's vans neared their destinations; one headed toward the Iwo Jima statue, another to the Old Post Office; the third was experiencing some heavy traffic leading to Arlington Cemetery.

On both Constitution and Pennsylvania avenues, on the east and west of the Capitol were military personnel, FBI, Park Service Police, and Secret Service agents from the DC field office. Others were located at various high points in the city. Every available officer and agent was on duty. Even near the Iwo Jima Statue and Lee's Mansion.

Air traffic was holding at the local airports. In addition to Reagan National Airport, both Dulles and Baltimore were temporarily closed, resulting in backups and delays at nearly every major airport in the country. Nothing was flying over the city except the three military helicopters loaded with antimissile hardware assigned to surveillance and defense, and two fighter jets circling high above. Bergstrom was in the underground transit leading from the Hart Building to the House Chambers.

8:50 PM

The president entered the office of the speaker, just outside the entrance to the chambers. He was greeted by the secretary of the House and the key senators and congressmen designated as escorts.

Inside the chambers, the ambassadors of fourteen countries had just entered to the applause of the joint session. They were soon followed by the Supreme Court. Lining up outside the doorway were members of the president's cabinet. Soon, all would be seated and ready for Bergstrom.

8:52 PM
The Situation Room

Jim Kilpatrick sat at the table next to Judge Herbert Walker. With them in the room were a handful of staffers and two Secret Service Agents Glen Towers and Stacey Brint.

Kilpatrick was surreptitiously popping tablets to relieve the uneasiness in his stomach and hoped the heavy pressure on his chest would soon go away, as it had on other occasions. A slight bluish tinge filtered into his pale skin, tiny beads of sweat began to ooze from his body. He was determined to make it a few more weeks before acknowledging his problem. If forced to retire due to medical reasons, his service would be buried with his body; historians never treat a one-year secretary kindly. Loosening his tie, he struggled to suck air into his lungs. No, he could hold out, it would take at least two years to write a place into the books and he would buy the time. Grappling with suppressed fear, he sat upright and tried desperately to regain some control.

"Are you all right, Mr. Secretary?" asked Judge Walker.

"I'm fine; just fightin' the damn flu."

"Can I get you something, Mr. Secretary?" asked Brint.

"No thank you." An uneasy smile as Kilpatrick gently rubbed the sweat from his forehead. "Nothing; I'll be fine."

8:54 PM

The Old Post Office team left their van on Eleventh Avenue; five men walked up the steps and entered the building; three men in front, two behind. Weapons concealed under heavy winter coats. It was windy and cold and not many people were inside the building; the few that were, appeared to be occupied with concluding their shopping.

The assassins entered through the large double doorway and turned left to the main elevator leading to the tower. The elevator was located in a small room where Park Service personnel gave brief lectures to the tourists prior to their ride to the tower. As planned, they found one man on duty. He was surprised.

"What're you guys doing here? You can't—" The gun, pressed deep into his chest, ended his authoritative posture. A muffled thud and he slammed against the chair and slumped to the floor.

The second van, followed by its security car, eased up the road to the Iwo Jima statue, rounded the driveway through the trees and into the main parking area. A couple of tour buses were parked near the drop off, facing the mall. Passengers were taking pictures of the statue, most from the bus, it was cold outside.

A gray FBI Grand Marquis was parked ahead of them facing the buses; three agents inside.

The van stopped behind the last bus, its side door facing away from the statue and out to the mall. The agents focused on the van. The security car pulled in behind it. Visibility was good. Brilliant floodlights scattered light throughout the area.

Time condensed. The driver of the security car, Roberto Santos, got out and walked a few feet from the front bumper of the van, on the statue side. As Santos took a cigarette from his pocket and cupped his hand to light it, the side door of the van slowly opened.

The three men in the FBI surveillance car became nervous. "What do you think?" asked Miller, the driver.

"Wait a second," replied Becker, the agent in back.

Ahead of them, two men in black coats exited the sliding door of the van. They moved slowly up the side of the buses, out of view of the Marquis. One of them was Kamile.

Agent Becker instinctively whispered, "That guy in front looks familiar; the big one. Isn't that the Mexican everyone's looking for? Call it in. I'm gonna check the other side." He got out of the car and began walking toward the van, making a crunching sound as he stepped gently on the frozen grass. The parking area was curved. He could see part of the bus in front. Becker walked further along the grass. The tour bus now shielded the van.

8:56 PM

The speaker in W16 came to life, "We have a man matching the description of a Roberto Santos. He just arrived at our station and it appears something is in the works. We'll investigate and get back to you."

Donovan could hardly breathe. He turned to Merrall. "If that really is Santos, it's about to happen."

8:57 PM

Near the Iwo Jima statue, the agent on the passenger side got out of the Marquis and began walking toward Santos. Two members of the Iwo Jima team, Radwan and Zaki began preparing the missile launcher.

Kamile walked the length of the first bus before he saw agent Becker directly in front of him. Immediately, he raised his machine gun and fired. Becker hit the ground in a swarm of bullets. Santos dropped his cigarette and blasted the agent coming toward him.

Agent Miller reached for a machine gun as he pushed the panic button on the dash, sending an immediate distress signal to the FBI. He threw open the front door and ran alongside the tourist buses. Miller sent three rounds into Roberto Santos. Within seconds, the agent bolted into the air, hit by a furry of bullets. Kamile and Samir lay prone on the frozen grass ahead of him, smoke rising from their weapons.

At the same time, the third van sped up a narrow winding road in Arlington Cemetery. It was headed for a spot near Lee's mansion.

Security guards, alerted by an electronic alarm, were moving to their vehicles. Military personnel on duty near the main entrance were now in pursuit of the van. Interception would be difficult. The hill was crisscrossed with many winding roads.

The distress signal from the Iwo Jima statue rang through the command center at the FBI's Hoover Building. The Secret Service Command Post inside the White House was immediately notified. From there, the alert was transmitted to agents on the hill.

9:00 PM

The door of the House Chambers opened and all present came to their feet as the secretary of the House appeared and solemnly announced in a very loud, deliberate voice, "Ladies and Gentlemen, the president of the United States."

Chapter Eleven

January 18, 9:01 PM
The Capitol Building

Having been announced by the secretary of the House and escorted by a congressional committee, President Bergstrom had just completed his triumphant walk from the rear of the chambers and turned left to greet his cabinet members. After a few words and smiles with Secretary of State John Skinner, he turned to his right and walked to the center podium, just below the speaker and vice president, both applauding with enthusiasm.

Special Agent James Howard turned pale. He opened the door of the House Chambers.

The speaker presented Bergstrom, once again, to the Congress and the traditional second applause was roaring through the room.

9:02 PM

A large number of Capitol Police, National Park Police, and a dozen FBI and Secret Service personnel surrounded the Capitol.

Capt. Bill Rogers, one of many military officers stationed just outside the House Chambers, held a special scope to his eye and scanned the area toward the mall, looking for signs of a laser beam. Lowering the instrument, he relaxed his eyes and lit a cigarette, inhaling it deeply.

He took a second drag, dropped his cigarette to the ground, placed his shoe on it, and smashed it out. The burning ashes flew in the wind a few feet from him, swirling up behind an overhang. His eyes followed the tiny cinders gently floating into the air and suddenly locked on a tiny reflection of light in the tower of the Old Post Office. He stepped over to clear himself from the branches and raised his scope to examine the image. There it was, a strong laser beam moving from the tower directly to the House Chambers. Just as suddenly as it had been activated, it was extinguished. Rogers wondered, did he actually see a laser? Did he imagine it? No, he did see it; and it was aimed at the Capitol. The captain almost shouted into his shoulder microphone.

In W16, Gregg Lawrence, a thirty-seven-year-old communications expert, and Linnet Singleton were sitting with other agents assigned to the Command Post. Donovan and Merrall were standing next to the communications desk. The call came in at 9:05 PM.

"We have it! I repeat, we have it! A targeting laser has been set on the House Chambers coming from the Old Post Office. Three sightings! What do you advise? Repeat, what do we do with this thing?" It was an agent from the DC field office located outside the Capitol.

Donovan shouted, "Tell them to fire a missile at it, immediately! Destroy it, do you hear!" Turning to the others in the room he added, "That was Santos! It is happening!"

Lawrence returned the shout, "Wait a minute. Fire a missile at the Old Post Office? Maybe it's not a laser!"

"We don't have time to over think this now, Brian!" Donovan shouted. "Tell them to destroy the damn thing, now! Fire a missile, damn it! There's no doubt this thing is going down!"

Charley Morrison, the shift supervisor, said to himself, "Heaven help us." He immediately transmitted to the Capitol. "Destroy the damn thing, and do it now! Do you hear me? Now! Fire a missile at the Old Post Office tower! Now!" He thought to himself, *Damnit! If Donovan is overreacting, we're gonna be in deep shit!*

The chambers became very quiet as the president began his address. Instantly, the words "Capture Boulder" rang in the ears of every Secret Service agent in the room. David Polchak had issued the command to secure the president; to capture Boulder! He was now putting his ass on the line as well.

Agents close to the president looked to their immediate supervisor, James Howard. Howard froze for a moment, and then he shook his head, saying, "No!" He stepped outside the chambers, and shouted into the microphone, "What's going on Command? Why capture? The man is speaking and a billion people are watching!"

Lawrence answered quickly, "A laser beam has been set on the outside of the chambers. I repeat, you have been marked by a targeting laser! Director's orders! Capture Boulder! Now! Capture Boulder!"

"The president is speaking, for God's sake!" Howard was almost shouting.

Lawrence quickly answered, "It's the director's orders! It's not your call, Howard . . . damnit . . . it's not your call!"

9:07 PM

Antimissile crews at the White House and the Capitol were alerted; an attack was imminent. Military personnel near the Air and Space Museum scanned the monitors. They attempted to align their missiles on the post office. Police and military personnel, as well as FBI agents, were on their way to the Iwo Jima Statue, Arlington Cemetery, and to the Old Post Office shopping complex.

In the Secret Service Command Room, W16, orders were shouted to agents in the Capitol and on the streets.

Gregg Lawrence looked at Donovan and Merrall. The three of them knew they were no longer in control. It was now up to the FBI counterterrorist units, the military, and, of course, the assassins themselves. The only hope now was to get the president out of the House Chambers and into the underground passage as quickly as possible. That was the responsibility of the Secret Service agents in the capitol.

TV sets in the Command Room were broadcasting the president's opening remarks. Viewers in the room could see the president pause, then, look slightly to his right and down. He was looking at Howard and Kindle, two men who were about to take the biggest step of their lives and stop the president of the United States during a major State of the Union Address.

With his eyes fixed on the television screen, Donovan's pulse soared as his mind churned up a fury of vital questions, *Are Howard and Kindle going to act? Can they do it? They have to! There's no doubt now. Now, Howard! Now!*

9:09 PM

The laser guidance system from the Old Post Office was once again tested for a single and final second. The launcher from the Iwo Jima Memorial was sighted along the laser path.

At the cemetery, the second launch team pulled to a stop near a clearing having a line of sight to the Capitol. Not the designated area, but they were being pursued, unable to get to the mansion in time. They exited the van and started to remove the missile launcher. Police vehicles came at them fast from front and rear.

Assassins stood at both ends of the van, firing into the night. Two police vehicles swerved off the roadway, windshields shattered. While one vehicle knocked down a row of marble gravestones, the other slammed into a tree.

Additional police and military vehicles joined the storm of bullets. Within a minute, all the assassins were occupied, returning fire. The launcher remained in the van with its deadly ashen steel growing colder by the second—the unarmed nuclear payload firmly attached.

Helicopters moved in over the van. Their searchlights flooded the area. Another helicopter was heading for the Iwo Jima Statue, responding to the FBI alarm.

9:10 PM

Both Howard and Kindle approached the lower podium to the right of the president. The vice president and the speaker looked down. They were confused.

The president cleared his throat; stared directly into Kindle's eyes. In that moment of silence, his eyes asked the obvious question, *is there an impending danger? Is it for real?*

The answer came in Kindle's face, *Yes, Mr. President; we now believe it is for real. It's going to happen.*

The president looked at the audience and calmly said, "Ladies and Gentlemen, will you excuse me for a moment." He turned to his right and began walking slowly down the steps. Agents moved to the top podium and reached for the vice president and the speaker.

At first, there was absolute silence in the chamber. Then, whispers, as people looked at one another. Viewers across the United States and around the world sat in stunned silence, wondering.

Barry Dipaula, alone in his office at the White House, stared hard into his TV set as if he could somehow penetrate the borders and look deep into the House Chambers. His mind was now filled with a thousand fears.

Agent James Howard moved to the microphone and calmly announced, "I'm James Howard of the Secret Service. Cut the cameras. Will you all please immediately exit the chambers and the Capitol itself. It appears we have a serious bomb threat. Please move in an orderly fashion through the rear doors and exit the building as quickly as possible."

In the Command Room, W16, everyone was frozen to the TV screens. Reality hit. A major disaster was about to happen.

James Donovan looked over to Gregg Lawrence and said, "My God, it is going to happen. Better place tighter protection around the mansion. Reinforce the man in the Situation Room. Son of a bitch! It's really going to happen!"

Without hesitation, Donovan turned and ran down the hallway.

9:11 PM

Fajil stood among trees high on a hill near the National Cathedral. He looked at his watch. "*It is 9:11 PM*, he thought. *America will now have another 9/11, far greater than the first.* Then, he whispered to himself, "Send forth the angel of death, Allah's mighty arm of justice!" Looking high into the night sky, as if heaven were listening, he said aloud, "For you my wife and my child." He pressed a button on his transmitter.

Simultaneously, the laser beam from the Old Post Office hit the precise spot on the outside of the House Chambers. The missile from the Iwo Jima Memorial sprang from its launcher and flew like the angel of death through the still dark night, two hundred feet above the ground, passing to the left of the Lincoln Memorial, to the left of the Washington Monument and on toward the Capitol.

Marine guards reacted quickly. The antimissile rockets located on the capitol burst into the frigid night sky, flames pushing them increasingly faster and faster over the frozen lawn and out over the mall. Both soared high on a miscalculated maneuver to meet the rapidly incoming missile whose tremendous speed had taken it well past the intercept point. One missile flew over the Lincoln Memorial while the other headed for Arlington Cemetery and the heat of the security helicopter hovering near Lee's Mansion.

A fraction of a second later, the deadly missile from the Iwo Jima Memorial made a direct hit on the spot marked by the laser beam.

The earth shook. Buildings shattered. The House side of the Capitol disappeared in a soaring flash of fire, dust, and smoke. The ground moved buildings for miles and brought instant destruction to everything five hundred yards up the mall.

The White House moved with the shock wave and its reinforced windows thundered. Room W16 went silent. Millions of viewers watched empty screens, while television directors and technicians sat in complete shock.

In Moscow, in an office near the Kremlin, Russian officials and agents looked at one another in silence. It was 5:12 AM, and they had risen just to hear this speech live. They were confused and looked to each other for an answer to the president's strange move from the podium, followed by a blank screen. The same scene was repeated in China and more than two hundred other countries around the globe. No one outside of Washington knew what had happened.

9:12 PM, the Situation Room

The lights suddenly flickered. The screens went blank, then a harsh static filled the room with a ghastly white light. Abruptly, the violent shock wave hit them, shuddering the broad table, glasses clattering aimlessly across its polished surface. A bucket full of ice, already sitting precariously near the edge of the table, leaped off, its contents scattering like jewels on the wine-colored carpet. Everyone looked down at it. One of the NSC staffers rose from his seat, moving toward the television controls. "What the shit's going on?" he stammered.

After a few seconds, Barry Dipaula rushed into the room. His stomach churned. He looked at Donovan. "Do you believe the House Chamber was hit? Could it have been another building?"

"I don't know." Donovan paused then started to respond, "Why didn't you—," but quickly caught himself. Personal expressions were of no use now. The two men looked intently into each other's eyes; Dipaula expressing his guilt, Donovan suppressing his anger.

Kilpatrick looked up at Dipaula and quietly asked, "What does that mean, Barry?"

A bit dazed, Dipaula responded, "It could mean that everyone in the House Chambers, including the president and his cabinet, may be seriously injured or . . ."

"Or what . . . ?" His body trembling uncontrollably, Kilpatrick knew what Dipaula meant. The thought terrified him. He never considered the possibility such a catastrophe would actually happen. He wasn't capable of assuming the presidency. They had to be alive! Just one of them had to survive.

"I . . . I don't know, Mr. Secretary. However, if that explosion is what we suspect, it could mean that you, . . . sir, . . . there is a possibility, just a possibility, that you may soon become the president of the United States."

That thought sent a chill up Dipaula's spine. Immediately, he cursed himself for not insisting the vice president remain in the White House or that Bergstrom deliver the speech from the Oval Office. Now, with Kilpatrick the possible successor to Bergstrom, and with the cabinet and Congress in all probability seriously injured, the future became an appalling nightmare.

Dipaula looked around the room and realized, for the first time, everyone was focusing on him. Their eyes reflected the emptiness he felt. As far as he knew, the leadership of the American government could, as of a few seconds ago, have been nearly eliminated.

"I don't have to tell any of you what may have just happened," he said, almost in a whisper. "Before we move too quickly; Donovan, find out as fast as you can the extent of this situation. Was that explosion actually on the hill? If so, what is the extent of damage? If not, where was it? Remember, people, there was a report of a possible attack somewhere in the district. We may have just experienced an explosion in an unoccupied building. Keep that in mind until we learn more."

"We're on it now." Turning to Secretary Kilpatrick, Donovan continued, "Mr. Kilpatrick, we'll have to take you to a more secure area, sir. Will you please accompany these men to the shelter down below?"

"Yes, of course," responded an unnerved secretary of the interior, trying to ignore the irregular pounding of his heart, the tightness in his chest.

The agents immediately escorted Kilpatrick to the door and moved quickly to the emergency elevator. As they proceeded through the doorway, Kilpatrick began to struggle with his breathing. Clutching his chest, sweat pouring from his pallid face, eyes opened wide, he stumbled and fell to his knees, pulling at his collar. The elevator doors closed forcefully against his legs then opened again.

Towers and Brint reached for the secretary and attempted to raise him to his feet. Kilpatrick's body went limp, breathing stopped, panic filled his eyes.

"Code Red; Kilpatrick's down!" shouted Brint; his words cracking into the ears of everyone nearby.

Donovan raced down the hallway toward the activity; reality growing with each fleeting step, the unconscious man on the floor in front of him might at that moment be the president of the United States.

After dragging Kilpatrick back into the hallway, Towers felt for a pulse. Finding none, they moved him to the Situation Room, laid him on the floor and prepared for CPR.

"We have cardiac arrest!" yelled Towers as he cleared the airway. "Take the air; I'll take compressions!" he shouted to Brint.

"Get the staff doctor down here fast," Donovan shouted into his mic. The president's physician was on Capitol Hill and most likely lost in the explosion.

"Bring the AED," Towers shouted. The defibrillator was kept in the medical room on the first floor. He exposed the chest, rechecked for a pulse, no breathing. The two agents set to work in a desperate attempt to revive Kilpatrick who was unresponsive, pale, cool, and clammy.

As Brint forced precious air into the secretary, Towers compressed his chest. Donovan stood by, feeling helpless, quickly realizing what Kilpatrick's death would mean to them all.

Suddenly, Brint jerked back hard, head swiping to the side, face covered with vomit. The agent, determined not to loose the man lying cold below him, quickly wiped himself, cleared Kilpatrick's mouth and resumed the breathing, a slight stench went unnoticed in the air.

The AED was rushed into the room by two agents and several members of the staff.

Donovan opened the kit and began immediately to shave the secretary's chest. He then removed the bag valve and mask, installed them, hardly missing a breath.

"Anything?" asked Donovan as he squeezed the bag.

Towers leaned hard against the chest.

"Nothing!" answered Brint.

Donovan checked the terminal connections, pushed the "on" switch and waited for the engaged system of self-checks to complete its cycle. "Back away!" he yelled. "Back away!"

Everyone stopped. Brint leaned backward. Towers sat back on his heels.

"Analyzing! Checking movement!" shouted Donovan, clearly in charge of the AED.

Then, a recorded voice screamed, "Stand clear! Stand clear!" the machine shouted. "Stand clear!"

Donovan placed his finger on the shock button and yelled, "Shocking! Shocking! Shocking!" He pressed down. Kilpatrick's body arched as the electrical impulse shot through him.

A few seconds passed before the machine voiced, "No shock advised! Check pulse!"

Brint and Towers moved simultaneously to CPR. Donovan waited one long minute and again shouted, "Stand Clear! Stand Clear! Shocking! Shocking!" Kilpatrick's body bowed up again.

"No shock advised!" screamed the machine.

Dr. Terry Maddock sped into the room and without hesitation shouted, "What's his down time?"

Brint responded, "Six, no, seven minutes!"

"Medical history?"

"Unknown," yelled Brint. Then he looked up and asked, "Anyone know?"

No answer.

"Let's insert the endotrachial tube," Maddock said as he calmly knelt down and removed the tube from its holder. "Hand me the bag," he ordered Towers. Inserting the bag to the ET he said, "Get an IV going. Epinephrine. Sodium Bicarbonate. How much down time now?"

"Nine minutes!" It was Brint.

"Hit him again!" Maddock said.

Donovan immediately yelled, "Stand Clear! Stand Clear!" Kilpatrick arched once again.

A few minutes later, Maddock asked, "Down time?"

"Twelve minutes!"

"Who's in charge here?"

"Right now, it's Barry Dipaula," Donovan answered.

"Ask him what he wants to do."

"I'm right here, Doctor," Dipaula said, as he moved next to Maddock.

"He's been down a long time. What do you want me to do?"

"Continue," there was no hesitation in his voice. "We need him alive."

Another five minutes; more air, compressions, shocks.

"He's down seventeen minutes," Maddock announced. "Medically, he's gone."

Donovan leaned over and said, "Keep working doctor." Sweat pouring from his face.

"He's gone! It's been seventeen minutes," answered Maddock.

Dipaula looked down into nothing, realizing the impact of the doctor's words.

"Open him up, Doctor!" shouted Donovan.

"What?"

"Open him up! Massage his heart; now!"

"That's ludicrous!"

"Now, Doctor! Now!"

"He's gone!"

Without warning, Donovan pulled his pistol and pointed the gun at Maddock's head and shouted, "Open him up, damn it! Now!"

Maddock, in complete shock, unable to comprehend what was happening, yelled, "He's brain dead, you idiot!"

Everyone was stunned by Donovan's reaction. No one moved a muscle.

"Now!" shouted Donovan. "You have to save him. He may be the president!"

The president? Maddock, dazed, looked down at the lifeless body of James Kilpatrick. *The president?* Taking a deep breath, he looked up at Dipaula and said, "I can cut him open, but do you want a president with irreversible cellular damage—a vegetable?"

"Open him now, Doctor!" Donovan's eyes made no allowance for further discussion, the pistol pressed solid against the doctor's temple.

Dipaula placed his hand on Donovan's shoulder and said, "He's right, James. It's been almost twenty minutes. It's over."

The gun didn't flinch.

"It's over when I say it's over!" Donovan's voice didn't weaken. "You stay the hell out of this, Dipaula! We're now in my area of responsibility!"

Sandra Merrall moved through the stunned agents, knelt down and said to Donovan, in a near whisper, "The doctor's right. It's been too long, James. He'd be a vegetable. No good to anyone. Let it go, James. Put your weapon away."

Donovan held steady for a few seconds. No one moved. His hands trembled. He looked up at Dipaula. Tears welled in his eyes as he lowered the weapon and sat back on his heels. It was over.

The secretary was pronounced dead—likely a massive heart attack, but assassination was also a strong possibility. Everything he ate and drank during the day, and especially in the evening, would be carefully analyzed.

"Good God," whispered Judge Walker to no one in particular. "Is he really dead? What the hell's goin' on here?"

"You didn't know about his condition, Doctor?" Dipaula asked Maddock.

"No," the distraught physician replied. "Did you?"

Dipaula didn't respond, simply looked toward the blank television screens. *What have I done? Russell suspected Kilpatrick's health. Why didn't I listen? I didn't listen to any of them.* He turned to the people in the room and said softly, "For the time being, no one must know what has happened in this room. Everything that has taken place in this room must, I repeat, everything must remain highly classified. No one, even elsewhere in the residence, must know of Secretary Kilpatrick's death. Everyone here will remain in the compound and out of communications until further notice, until we have more information on the attack on Capitol Hill. No one must enter or leave this room without my instructions."

Turning to Donovan, who appeared to have regained his self-control, he asked, "James, are you okay?"

Donovan slowly nodded and answered, "I'm fine. I'll be okay."

"Good. That's good. Assign agents to seal the door. Allow no one in and no one out without my permission. As you put it so well, this is now a matter of national security; my area of responsibility."

Without the words, each of them knew what Dipaula was saying. If the Capitol had just been destroyed, no one must know the one person left behind in the White House to protect the line of succession, was now dead.

Dipaula appeared to be the obvious authority in the White House. The people in the Situation Room were looking at him, glad to have someone in charge. An intense feeling of aloneness suddenly engulfed him. His head began a slow swirl, like a ghostly merry-go-round, alternating stabs of guilt rising and falling in his mind. Sweat began to bead on his forehead. He turned and headed down the hallway to the men's room. An uncontrollable shake quivered throughout his body. His mind fought to deny what he knew had just happened. He absently turned on the cold water and splashed his face, attempting to wash away the nightmare. With hands on both sides of the wash basin and his warm tears mixing with the cold water, he felt a tremor start way down in the pit of his stomach. The tremor turned to convulsions, followed by a terrible chill, then a strange liquid filled his mouth and his bowls threatened to release their contents. Suddenly, a hand tightened on his shoulder and seemed to hold back a terrible evacuation. Dipaula looked up into the mirror. It was a woman next to him. It was Sandra Merrall.

"Are you alright, Barry?" Merrall asked, her voice fluttering.

Her words echoed in his mind as he fought to regain control.

"Ye . . . yes, I'm fine," he stammered. "I'll be fine; just such a shock."

Merrall rubbed her hand across his back and the warmth returned. He pulled a towel from the dispenser and wiped his face. When he turned around, Merrall was gone. Within a minute, Dipaula was back in the hallway and standing next to Donovan.

The two men paused just long enough to acknowledge each man's sudden loss of control and feeling of vulnerability before they turned and walked quickly down the hall to the Command Post in W16; both hoping to learn the Capitol had been spared. As they entered the room, field agents were receiving critical information from throughout the city. All reports were the same: an explosion, perhaps a low-yield nuclear explosion, had hit the Capitol. The assassins had succeeded. Everyone now realized this was the beginning of an excruciating nightmare that would soon engulf the entire world.

Chapter Twelve

9:40 PM
The White House

The White House switchboards were overloaded. One call from FEMA was of particular importance. The green and white presidential evacuation helicopter, Bronco, had been dispatched to the White House. Bronco was prepared to transport the president or his successor to either Andrews Air Force Base or the underground White House a few miles north of Camp David.

While in the Command Room, Dipaula was given the message about Bronco. He knew the evacuation procedure. Twice since taking office, the Bergstrom administration participated in trial runs of a massive evacuation involving thousands of high-level and critical government employees, including the president and his closest staff.

Dipaula knew the chopper was rapidly approaching and the crew would expect to be met on the south lawn by the acting president. *Not this time*, thought Dipaula. The chopper would be ordered to remain on ready status near the South Portico. It would give him time to think of a logical reason for Kilpatrick to remain in the White House. With the crisis in Central Asia poised to explode at any moment, news of Kilpatrick's death would have to be withheld until some order was established and any survivors in the line of succession were identified.

The US Military immediately went to threat level ConDelta and Charlie Alert. In a hundred places outside the district, automatic defense systems were being activated. Military satellites had begun their search of the skies for booster flame while land-based radar stations were looking for incoming aircraft and missiles. There was no doubt a warhead had been delivered, but how? And from where? And by whom?

Alaska

Staff Sgt. Clinton McDaniels, glad to be inside on such a bitter cold and windy night, was on duty at the Star 18 early warning station on the Alaskan North Slope when the "Red-Alert" light and audible signal came on. The shrill whine of the computer tone jolted him out of his seat like a noisy dentist's drill. Leaping up, he spilled coffee over his fatigues, reached for the phone and immediately connected with the Watch Duty Officer Lt. Neil Travis.

"Yeah? This better be good, McDaniels."

"Sir, . . . the alert signal is on. Repeat, on." Taking a deep breath he continued, "Doesn't look like a drill, sir."

Travis put down his stale ham and cheese sandwich and said, "Chill out, McDaniels, I hear it. Alert, Maj. Campbell, reset the alarm, and get Strategic Command on the line for confirm."

"Yes, sir!" responded McDaniels, reaching out to reset switches. Other operators had a similar alert status, and were staring at McDaniels. The same situation was occurring along the entire line of defense.

9:40 PM

Initial assessments arriving at the Secret Service Command Room inside the White House indicated the House side of the Capitol building was completely destroyed. With its thick-riveted shell of brittle cast iron, the dome had partially collapsed. The Statue of Freedom could no longer be seen towering over the massive building. Miraculously, the Senate side of the building, while seriously damaged, appeared to be substantially intact. To the south, directly across Independence Avenue, windows in the Rayburn, Longworth, and Cannon House office buildings were blasted to dust.

To the east and across First Street, the ornate Jefferson Building of the Library of Congress was severely damaged from blast and debris. Up the street from the Jefferson Building, the Supreme Court Building was still standing, its white marble facade densely pocked from flying shreds of metal, concrete and wood.

West, toward the mall, and just below Capitol Hill, the Botanical Garden Conservatory with its broad face of latticed glass panels lay flattened and smoldering like the wreckage of an exploded dirigible. Further west, buildings of the Smithsonian Institute were severely damaged.

Close in, the huge reinforced windows of the Air and Space Museum were shattered, exposing the nation's aeronautical treasures to violent forces. The airplanes and space vehicles were smashed and thrown like toys into odd arrangements.

A fraction of a second after the blast, a low intensity heat wave had pulsed away from the chambers, traveling almost a mile from the hill, leaving a path of broken trees, scrubs and overturned vehicles. Hundreds of small fires had sprung up throughout the area. Immediately outside the south wing of the Capitol, lay scorched walls and disintegrated human flesh. Unfortunate survivors who had been a short distance from the building, now lay about, sight and hearing gone, reason lost forever, life oozing from their hammered bodies; men, women and children, reporters, onlookers, law enforcement, and military personnel.

The massive granite obelisk and centerpiece of the district, the Washington Monument, appeared to have sustained only minor damage. Directly in the pathway, in the very center of the mall, it had remained as defiant as its namesake and stood firm against the crushing force of the blast.

Further west, to the end of the mall, beyond its reflecting pool, the Lincoln Memorial stood unharmed. Inside, the dispirited figure of Abraham Lincoln seemed to gaze up at the wreckage of the Capitol as if he were required once again to witness his country in a major upheaval and take upon his shoulders the heavy burden of a nation in disarray.

The low blast of the quarter kiloton bomb spared the mall from major destruction. As reports continued to come in from agents around the city, those in the Command Room at the White House were anxious to hear a word of the president. Had he left the House Chambers in time? No one was more concerned than Barry Dipaula.

At 9:41 PM the urgent call from the State Department came through for the cabinet secretary in charge at the White House. The Under Secretary of State for Political Affairs, Marty Castellano, was working late in his office at state when the news was received. His senior watch officer had entered the room within seconds of receiving the alarm. Moments before, the undersecretary knew something was seriously wrong when his screen went blank and the shock wave jarred the massive building on C Street.

June Cooper, Castellano's personal assistant, was with him in the room watching the president's speech. Her eyes filled with tears as the watch officer explained the reported cause of the sudden loss of picture. Anticipating numerous calls from embassies around the district and from American embassies around the world, Castellano wanted instructions. After being informed Kilpatrick was not available, he insisted the call be transferred directly to Dipaula. Without hesitation, Dipaula took the call.

"Barry, what the hell's going on?" Castellano's voice was shaking as he rubbed his hand over his moist, bare scalp and stared at the static on his television screen. Shock had equally blindsided everyone in the district and, like everyone else; Castellano was searching for clues, hoping to gain some insight into what had just happened.

Dipaula stood near a small desk in the Situation Room, receiver in hand. His friend's shaken voice amplified the thousands of actions and reactions he knew were happening worldwide. He paused to collect himself and then spoke softly into the receiver, "Marty, we're not exactly sure what just happened. We believe the Capitol, or . . . at least the House Chambers," Dipaula felt the tremor coming once again. He felt faint, took a deep breath, leaned lightly against the wall and continued, "The chambers was hit by a bomb."

Silence. Both men were trying to find words. Letting his eyes drop to the desk in front of him, Castellano whispered desperately, "Oh my God." Tears welled involuntarily in his eyes.

"Marty, until we have more information on the extent of the situation I recommend you just stall everyone and anyone. Do you understand, Marty?"

"Barry, do you think they got the president or the secretary? Damn! The Congress? The Supreme Court? Jesus Christ Almighty, do you realize how many ambassadors were in that room?"

"Marty, I don't know how secure this line is. We won't—"

"Barry, is the cabinet member there? Is he—"

"Don't panic, Marty. Don't let hysteria cause people over there to do or say anything dangerous. Stall, Marty. Just stall."

Dipaula sensed the desperate need for absolute secrecy in an immensely complicated crisis. "Listen to me clearly, Marty. Just listen! I don't want to repeat this again. It's critical you stall. Give your people instructions to delay. Tell them to wait for specifics. Is the deputy secretary there with you?"

"No, he's in Europe; a hell of a time to be out of the country."

Dipaula took a deep breath and continued, "Then you have to assume you are in charge. Do you understand, Marty? You are in charge!"

Unconsciously tapping his fingers on the desk, Castellano continued, "We're going to be inundated with calls very quickly. The ambassadors from a dozen countries were in that room. What do I say?"

Dipaula realized the undersecretary needed some direction. His concern for the president and the line of succession had caused him to completely forget the foreign ambassadors. "We think the explosion was isolated to the Capitol itself. Write a general release and get over here as soon as you can. Leave someone with brains there to handle the situation."

Castellano glanced over at Cooper sitting in the green leather armchair, noticing her attempt to follow the conversation. Remembering the evacuation procedure, he asked, "Are you people staying in the White House?"

"Yes, for now."

"Let me know what to say, Barry. For Christ's sake, don't hold back." Castellano took deep breath and continued, "I know this isn't a good time to ask . . ., but do you think our families are okay?"

"I don't know, Marty. I . . . I think so. We believe the explosion was isolated to Capitol Hill. We really don't know. I've really got to go; a lot to deal with here. Check back in ten or fifteen minutes. Let me know as soon as you're able to contact the deputy secretary. He's to return immediately." Dipaula paused again, and then continued, his voice choked with tension. "Remember, Marty, delay. Don't let anyone over there panic. We don't want hysteria. Do you understand? The release should say something like 'It's too early, and more time is needed to assess the situation,' or something to that affect. Deal with things yourself, Marty, at least until you feel comfortable enough that someone else can handle it. Then get the hell over here as soon as you can."

Castellano leaned forward in his chair, rubbed his forehead with his left hand and said, "I'll get back to you in a few minutes. Shit, I can't . . . this couldn't have happened at a worse time . . . with the Alliance, the Russians, the Chinese, the Israelis and the whole damn Middle East, and Central Asia flaring up again. Sorry, I'll get back to you, Barry." Taking a deep breath he closed, "Good luck over there. This is the shits."

Dipaula placed the receiver into its cradle. *The shits?* he thought. *What an understatement. Damn, I don't want this. It's too much for me. David, wherever you are, hang on. You've got to be alive! I can't handle this! It's not my damn job! I give advice; I don't make critical decisions! Be alive, damn you!* The tremor began to rise in his body.

5:25 AM, Moscow

Moscow was eight hours ahead of the district. At 5:25 AM, the large hairy hand of the president's aide on foreign affairs, the barrel-chested, thick-browed

Anatoli Karzinski, picked up the phone in the president's office. "Da," came a deep, irritated grunt.

"This is Kalingkov. We have just received word from Washington a serious explosion of an unknown cause has occurred in the area of the Capitol." The deputy chairman of the Russian Committee for State Security was noticeably strained. "We do not yet know the extent of damage." He waited for a gentle rolling thunder in response. It came.

"Kalingkov, tell Chernosvitov to come here immediately!" Karzinski's thunder was somewhat louder and sharper than Kalingkov expected.

Kalingkov hung up the phone and turned to his boss, "Karzinski wants you over there immediately."

Chernosvitov rose from his chair, faced the others, and said, "I want a direct line to the Washington embassy when I arrive in the president's office, do you understand? I want either Tarasavitch or Igmanov on the line." Walking to the door, he continued, without looking back, "I prefer Igmanov. Yuri, come with me!"

After Chernosvitov and Kalingkov had crossed the courtyard and arrived in the president's office, they were taken immediately to the Strategy Room deep inside the massive cream yellow buildings of the Kremlin.

In the large, high-ceilinged room were six of Russia's most powerful men. A deep chill made each breathe clearly visible. In the center of an oversized rectangular table, sat brown bottles of fruit juice, mineral water, a bottle opener, and a number of drinking glasses resting on a paper-thin glass tray. Next to them were several platters of hard biscuits and cookies. An ornate, tarnished silver samovar and matching silver glass holders sat on a table against one wall. Steam from the samovar filled the room. The atmosphere was quiet, almost scholarly.

"The embassy is on the line for you, Chernosvitov," bellowed Karzinski from the far end of the table, his grossly large, unshaven eyebrows slightly furrowed. "It's Igmanov." His face tightened. "I'm surprised he's home," he scoffed.

Karzinski hated the grip Chernosvitov had on the Washington embassy through Yuri Igmanov. He knew Igmanov was enjoying his assignment and attended every social function possible in his expensive Italian suits and Mercedes sedan, circulating throughout Washington like a wealthy western playboy.

Chernosvitov left the room for a few minutes to take the call in a private office and then returned just before President Masarov entered.

Masarov had been awakened one hour earlier to watch Bergstrom's speech in his office at the Kremlin. Even with the time difference, he insisted on hearing it live. The Central Asian problem was escalating rapidly and the Chinese were threatening his borders. Perhaps a world war was inevitable. Bergstrom's words would be critical.

Aware that something serious must have occurred in Washington, Masarov took his place in a simple hardwood chair at the center of the table and quietly asked, "What has happened?"

Chernosvitov spoke first, "A few minutes ago there was an explosion in the area of the Capitol while Bergstrom was delivering his speech," He paused.

Masarov's eyes twitched slightly, as if he had been pricked by an unseen needle. *So that's why communications was lost?* he thought.

No one spoke. Chernosvitov broke the momentary silence, "We do not yet know if the Capitol itself was the target. If it was, the situation is grave. In the room with the president were Vice President Borland and his complete cabinet, with one possible exception. We are reviewing the tapes to find out who that member is. Also, most likely every member of the leadership of the United States government was present. The embassy believes, from their view of the situation, all may be dead." He hesitated before giving them the final blow. His voice slowed, "The explosion may have been a small nuclear device."

Chernosvitov looked casually across the table at a very staid General Obidiov and studied his normally impenetrable face, slowly discovering the reflection of his own thoughts. *Could it have come from our own arsenal?*

Maxim Obidiov, military advisor and first deputy minister of defense, was also chief, general staff, Russian Armed Forces; the most powerful military officer in the country and one of the most dangerous men in the world. While he appeared to serve Russia, Obidiov was loyal only to himself; a continuous, tormenting migraine for Masarov.

At the mention of a nuclear device, all eyes widened, focusing sharply on Chernosvitov, who sat back grimly and waited for questions. After receiving none, he looked again at the president and said, "The embassy is still on the line if you wish to speak with them."

Evgenii Malikov, director of the Crisis Management Team, looked across the table to Obidiov. Instantly their eyes locked; their glance spoke volumes. At least four men in the room knew the type of weapon that could have been used. Chernosvitov noted the private exchange.

Masarov looked at each man, unable to believe what he was hearing. He lingered for a few seconds on Asgini Chernosoki, advisor to the president on general staff work, a loyal friend, before focusing on Igor Malinkov, minister of foreign affairs, also his trusted supporter. Both men were slightly pale and merely stared back at him.

Now in his late sixties, Masarov, a graying, portly, but still a handsome man, remained in good shape. His wife, Elena, had died during the summer and he now threw every moment into his job. Her loss was the greatest pain of his life. At least she had lived to see the fall of communist authority and his rise to power. His three children had moved away from Moscow; choosing to let their father handle his grief by total immersion into running the country.

With the most influential leadership in the world possibly gone, Masarov realized his decisions in the coming hours could be pivotal for his nation and for the world. Turning to General Obidiov, he now realized the greatest danger could come from within his own country.

Chapter Thirteen

9:40 pm, Capitol Hill

Only scattered rescue operations had begun on Capitol Hill. The DC Fire Department and FEMA had not yet fully responded with their recovery teams. Radiation counts would be taken before a full-scale rescue would take place. The night sky around the Capitol was set ablaze with the red-orange glow of a thousand scattered fires. The Capitol itself had an eerie incandescent glow coming from within where small isolated fires burned unabated.

Few survivors in the area ventured up the hill. Most were attempting to move away from the Capitol.

Taxi drivers, chauffeurs, and press people, brave enough to hazard moving close to the smoldering buildings, joined with military, security, police, and emergency response personnel in a series of sporadic heroic attempts to locate survivors near the entrances. However, not many were brave enough to enter the south building, for fear the roofing would further collapse or that falling debris and building fragments would create additional jeopardy to themselves, or anyone who might be trapped alive. On the north side of the Capitol, a few individuals bravely and impulsively ventured inside, responding to desperate cries for help, unable to stand and listen. Their fervent compassion would soon be harshly rewarded with generous symptoms of deadly radiation.

The subways beneath the House Chamber leading to the Rayburn and the Cannon buildings were severely damaged. The Senate Chamber to the north was substantially intact, but the halls leading to the rotunda were blocked and darkened.

Spectral figures walked around in a daze; sightless, deafened, isolated. Electrical cables and exposed wires dangled from sheared walls and huge pieces of concrete lay scattered about. Narrow flames shot up everywhere like a thousand dying fingers pointing accusingly toward the heavens. In other places, the evening cold was quietly entering through the debris in countless cracks and holes finding its way deep inside the crushed concrete structure, as if the old building was loosing the warmth of life and had slowly begun to die.

9:44 PM, the Situation Room

Dipaula had just ended a call from the Pentagon similar to the one with Marty Castellano at the State Department. However, the Pentagon seemed to be a little more authoritative. While they were unclear about who was actually in charge in the official chain of command, they were confident in their ability to insure that proper steps were taken to defend the United States. While this gave some comfort to Dipaula, it also triggered a peculiar sense of concern. Again, he was careful to not reveal that Kilpatrick was dead.

"I will be in the communications center if you need me," Dipaula said to those in the Situation Room as he turned to the door. "Remember, this room is sealed and . . . I mean sealed. Come with me, Craig." He had established some control.

They went down one level to the White House communications center. With state-of-the-art equipment, the center operated on its own source of power and was still functioning. Conversations stopped as Dipaula and Craig Thomas, the forty-four year old senior deputy assistant for National Security Affairs, entered the room.

"Get me Skywatch One, now!" Dipaula shouted. "Craig, jump in anytime with suggestions. I need some help here."

Skywatch One was the 747 command plane of the former Strategic Air Command. The Strategic Air Command had been downgraded in 1992 but still maintained a squadron of communications and strategic aircraft in the air twenty-four hours of every day. Its commander was responsible for national security during emergencies and had the capability of responding to a crisis if the United States was under attack and the president and his successors, as well as the Pentagon, were out of contact. At present, this appeared to be such a crisis. The power of the commander of Skywatch One was impressive. Under very stringent circumstances, he even had the capability of ordering a nuclear retaliation.

"Skywatch One is on, sir," a young female Air Force sergeant shouted.

Dipaula picked up the receiver, breathed deeply, and said, "This is Barry Dipaula, who am I speaking with?"

"This is Gen. Mark Bradley, sir," a slight static in the line. "I understand we have a very serious crisis."

"Yes, General; it appears your orders under G5B are operative. However, we believe this is a nonaggressive situation and does not require retaliation. I repeat, this appears to be a nonaggressive situation. Do you understand?"

"Affirmative, Dipaula. You consider this to be a nonaggressive situation. Do you have your circumspect code?"

"That code is not yet available to us but will be shortly, General." Dipaula sat next to the console and slowly rubbed his head. "The executive case was in the explosion, but we are in the process of retrieving the codes from the receptacle here in the White House. I believe you can access your initial orders without the executive code. Is that correct?"

"Yes. However, I'll need your part of the code at some point. I will advise you of my orders under G5B in a few minutes. We're receiving some heavy communications traffic. I'll get back to you. It appears the Pentagon is somewhat confused, as are Omaha and Andrews. Get me that code, Dipaula!"

"Yes, General. Please get back as soon as possible. I must repeat, this is most likely a limited terrorist attack and not an act of aggression. We will have the executive code within the next few minutes."

Dipaula stood, turned to Thomas and said, "Get as many of the NSC people together as possible, as fast as possible, along with the directors of the Homeland Security, FBI, CIA, and NSA. Have them meet us in the Situation Room. Deputy Secretary of State Castellano, will be here soon. Have the Crisis Management Team report here immediately and get the lead Secret Service agent in here fast."

Thomas turned to leave, but Dipaula continued, "Find out who in the residence can be of value and get them down here on the double. See if there're any cabinet rank people here. I hope to shit there is." If any cabinet rank members were in the executive mansion, they would have authority; they could take control of the situation. He wanted desperately to hand his responsibility to someone, anyone. If that wasn't possible, he needed all the advice he could get, and now.

Dipaula turned to the communications staff sitting at the table, and by their blank stares, knew he was the designated hitter, the one who had no choice but to call the shots, at least for the moment. "Get me the ranking civilian and military officers at the Pentagon, and the director of FEMA." He was determined to find the one person who was now in charge of the government, determined to give up the spotlight and be rid of the enormous weight now placed on his shoulders.

9:48 PM, North of the District

A Park Service van moved along Highway 66 west toward the Beltway. Kamile and his five men from the Iwo Jima team were quiet, reflective as they weaved in and out of traffic. Law enforcement radios were broadcasting emergency instructions and patrol cars had taken positions throughout the area. Occasionally, a police cruiser would speed past them going in the opposite direction, heading toward the city; lights flashing, sirens blaring. Fajil was in a dark blue Regal traveling north on Highway 66 west, about three miles ahead of Kamile and his team.

9:58 PM, Room W16

The Command Post received word that, most likely, the weapon had been fired from the Iwo Jima Memorial over the mall to the Capitol. Witnesses near the statue and the Old Post Office reported brown government vans being involved in both areas. The Command Post notified police authorities to be alert for National Park Service vehicles and approach them with caution.

Forty-six minutes had passed since the explosion, yet it still remained an illusion to James Donovan. He was in the Command Room relaying information to Lucas Chandler at the service's headquarters a few blocks away on G Street. He was doing the same with the Washington field office on Connecticut Avenue, in the Washington Square Building. No scenarios during his training prepared him for this situation. The worst disaster to ever face the United States would now necessitate the greatest manhunt in American history.

White House Security Coordinator, Dep. Asst. Dir. Raymond Holmes, rushed over from the Secret Service office in the Treasury Building to take charge of security within the residence. Director Polchak was on his way to the White House from his office on G Street to speak with Holmes and Dipaula.

In the Command Post, agents were listening carefully to every incoming call. It was becoming more apparent the president was, in fact, dead. Even if by some chance he was not killed on the hill, he would most certainly be dead from radiation within a few days.

Abruptly, a call came in from district police on New York Avenue near Florida.

"We have a National Park Service van in traffic on New York proceeding toward John Hanson. I repeat, we have a Park Service van in line. Approaching and will investigate. Stand by."

The microphone remained open as officers left the vehicle. Immediately, shots could be heard over the radio, like popcorn slowly beginning to explode against a metal lid, followed suddenly by rapid bursts.

"Officers down! We need help! We need help! Officers down!" The radio continued for a few seconds to broadcast gunshots and then went silent.

"Can we get a chopper over there?" shouted agent Marshall.

"One's on the way," Van Meter replied.

Two officers lay wounded on New York Avenue. Another was dead. The few police officers available responded to the desperate call for help.

The van sped along New York weaving in and out of traffic, a single police car in pursuit. It turned left onto Bladensburg Road cutting across the center line and bouncing off the curb hitting the left rear fender of a 98 Chevy and, with little hesitation, raced toward South Dakota Avenue.

In a few minutes, the two lanes ahead were blocked by a long line of slow moving vehicles attempting to leave the area. The van swerved to pass a delivery truck and crossed over to the oncoming lanes. As it cleared the truck, it cut sharp, returning to the right lanes to avoid a head-on with an approaching pickup, then slid on the icy roadway, impacted the back of a passenger car, and came to a stop as the delivery truck smashed into its back bumper.

The driver attempted unsuccessfully to restart the van. The passengers threw open the side door and ran with weapons in hand through traffic toward the National Arboretum. Police cars were pulling up to the rear of the delivery truck as the driver of the van jumped down from the open door and sprayed one of the cruisers with a deadly burst. He then turned and ran between cars, heading for the Arboretum.

Six police officers and two civilians died before the five assassins who had set the laser from the Old Post Office were shot to death amid the trees and frozen fountains of the nation's showplace garden.

Moscow, 6:20 AM

The morning sunlight had not yet pierced through the clouds suspended over the gold domed Kremlin Cathedral and early morning traffic was still very light. Most of the people moving about the city knew nothing of the drama unfolding in the capitol of the United States, and now in the Kremlin.

In the Strategy Room, President Masarov and the others were joined by fifteen people; members of The Congress of People's Deputies, the president's council, the Ministry of Defense, foreign affairs, intelligence analysts from the Ministry of State Security, and members of the Crisis Management Team headed by Yevgeni Malikhov.

Malikhov and his team had conducted joint exercises with the United States crisis team on a number of occasions in the late '90s, and early in the new century. Members of both teams had become working colleagues over the past few years.

General Obidiov was thoughtfully responding to a question from the cautious Malikhov. "Yes, there has been evidence of communications between the White House and the Skywatch aircraft. It appears that Gen. Mark Bradley is in charge of the aircraft. He has, or someone has, issued orders for a military alert; however, only within the borders of the United States. At present, there does not seem to be an immediate threat to our forces or to anyone. But that could happen at a moment's notice."

Obidiov was a hard-liner. He strongly disagreed with the new policy of exchanging military information and didn't trust the United States, especially its military leaders. He was hardened by the Chinese theft of nuclear secrets from the United States, the world's greatest arsenal. He was determined that would not happen in Russia.

It was Obidiov who had worked with the powerful, secret organization, Soyuz, which operated in the late eighties. He was prepared to take necessary measures when power was finally transferred to more reasonable people. It was already many years overdue.

Soyuz had been formed years earlier in response to the liberal measures initiated by the Gorbachev administration and was composed of influential people in government, military, and the so-called private establishment. While some minor members were known, and a few killed during the '91 coup attempt, the most powerful still remained in the shadows.

Yevgenii Malikhov offered a suggestion to Masarov. "Perhaps, since the secretary of state has most likely been killed, you should call the White House and ask to speak with the person in charge, that should be . . .," he said, looking down at his papers, "Secretary Kilpatrick, if our information is correct. It appears a junior officer, Castellano, may be in charge at the Department of State. I believe in this state of emergency we should bypass them and go directly to the White House."

The room was quiet. Masarov spoke, "Yes, this is a good idea." Then, looking down the long table to one of his advisors, he continued, "Place the call, Chernosoki."

Karzinski took a long drag on his cigar and said with a deep growl, "Why would they have such heavy communications between the White House and the Skywatch aircraft and why would the aircraft be issuing so many orders?" The room fell silent again as everyone thought about the ominous question.

Karzinski continued, "If someone were in charge on the ground, would the aircraft be so active?"

A somewhat nervous Malinkov looked at Chernosvitov and spoke, "Karzinski raises an important question. What do the official reports from the State Department say about this man Kilpatrick?"

Chernosvitov looked directly at Karzinski and said, "Of course we have his background. Copies of career and profile are being made as we speak. From what I have seen, he is of moderate competency, of ordinary intelligence. When the copies arrive, I will discuss specifics of his personality. Of this particular incident, we have seen only one release from the Department of State and you have read it. They also have said this man, Kilpatrick, is in charge at the White House." Chernosvitov looked down at the report in front of him, "The American Ambassador Stewart, is here in Moscow and will keep his line open to us."

Masarov gestured slightly to Chernosvitov, "Have Igmanov check on this man Kilpatrick and continue to monitor carefully communications between the aircraft and anyone else," he ordered. "I want your office to bring all the important literature on Kilpatrick to me immediately, including your analysis of his capabilities and weaknesses." He then turned to the head of the crisis management team. "Yevgenii, who would be in charge if this Kilpatrick were not in the White House? Who is second in command?"

"Considering the loss in the Capitol and our review of the tapes, that would most likely be either Russell, the chief of staff, Linda Martin, the trade representative, or Barry Dipaula. These three were not seen in the television recording and may not have been in the building. They may be in the White House. All three, I believe, have the ability to make sound decisions. We know little of the capability of Martin, although we must assume she has Bergstrom's respect. Chernosvitov should also provide information on her as well."

"Why do you mention this woman, Martin?" asked Masarov.

Malikhov shrugged his shoulders and said, "I'm not certain of her authority in this crisis. Her position is stated to be of the cabinet rank. While she may have little practical authority, it is unclear what her official authority might be under their law."

"Can you speak with any of them?"

"If I can use the emergency telephone, it should be possible."

"Then do it; and I suggest you try now!" With the military conservatives and possibly even the hard-liners in his Ministry of Security looking for an opportunity to seize power, Masarov wanted to know, which American he must deal with in this moment of great crisis. "Get me Lee Pong."

The foreign minister stood and walked to the phone.

Chapter Fourteen

Interstate 270

The brown van, now heading north away from the district, was in the I-270 Technology Corridor a few miles north of the Democracy Boulevard overpass. Freezing rain kept them from moving any faster than thirty-five miles an hour. The strained defroster and noisy windshield wipers barely kept their vision clear enough to move over the frozen highway.

The silence in the van was suffocating, almost lethal. Only the steady clicking of the wipers and the low roar of the defroster disturbed the private thoughts of the six assassins. Kamile sat in the front passenger seat, his eyes riveted on the road ahead. He turned a switch on the receiver. The reports blaring over the radio were good news, but incomplete. They were professionals and knew that neither victory nor defeat had yet been determined. Had they killed everyone?

Looking through the noisy wipers to the icy road ahead, each concluded in his mind that it no longer seemed to matter. They had done their best; what they were trained and prepared to do.

10:18 PM, the Situation Room

Twelve members of the National Security Council and Joe Sullivan, deputy director of FEMA, were in the Situation Room with Dipaula. They were awaiting the arrival of other council members and members of the Crisis Management Team. Deputy Chief of Staff Sean Kennedy and Assistant Staff

Secretary John Newman, were taking care of business on the main floor, as was Deputy Assistant to the President Mary Metzger.

"Ladies and Gentlemen," Dipaula opened the meeting. "As you know, we must make a number of important decisions very soon. The press, media, and state houses need information. He leaned forward in his chair and continued, "They have no idea Kilpatrick is dead. I believe, for the time being, it must stay that way." He wiped away a faint hint of sweat from his upper lip.

Dipaula then expressed their responsibility as clear as he could. "This is a hell of a mess. Since we are the only ones who know the full extent of the problem, like it or not, it will be up to us to make the primary and crucial decisions. We didn't ask for this responsibility. I see no volunteers in this room. But we're here. It's in our laps. We'll do what we need to do."

As Dipaula listened to himself, he was beginning to understand the significance of political role playing. How often he had smugly criticized his friend, David Bergstrom, and those men and women around him who pretended their position, who daily played a role in accordance with the great titles they had accepted. After years of relative comfort in being a detached advisor, able in most cases to speak and to behave as he wished, circumstance had now brutally compelled Dipaula to become an impersonator, an actor. He now had to play an overpowering role and he knew the fate of the nation, and maybe even that of the world, depended on how well he played his critical part.

"As far as we know, succession stops with Kilpatrick," Tom Stratton said. "Is there any policy for this situation? Surely, someone's already thought of this possibility. It is incon—"

"We have the FEMA plans, as weak as they are," Dipaula interrupted. "However, we're checking to see if we have anything in the contingency files for loss of the complete line of succession. As far as I know, we have nothing. There—"

"Previous administrations had contingencies," Craig Thomas noted. "They named individuals to something like a secondary line of succession, senators and congressmen, and others. Probably wasn't constitutional."

"There's some logic for cabinet rank members," Stratton said. "Maybe even the director of the Office of Management and Budget, the trade representative or the chief of staff. They may have some authority."

"Unfortunately they're not here," said Phillip Page. "Most likely wouldn't have much authority anyway."

Terry Kovach entered the room. He looked in the direction of the covered body lying on a small table near the wall. His look of surprise stopped the conversation.

Kovach, chief of the White House Command, Control, Communications, and Intelligence Office, was also a member of the Crisis Management Team. The team was composed of a half-dozen key American officials such as the secretary of defense and the chairman of the Joint Chiefs of Staff. The Russians had a counterpart team with members of equal rank.

"Terry," Dipaula said, maintaining a steady voice, "That's Kilpatrick. A heart attack. Either couldn't handle the heavy burden, or the victim of an assassination. We don't know which. Frankly, at this moment, it doesn't really matter."

Kovach sat down. He looked around the table, and then muttered, "This is a hell of a mess. Shit, Barry, what the hell have you been releasing to the press?" His tone changed as reality swiftly hit home. "What's going on here? The Goddamn Capitol has been blown apart. They're all probably dead up there. Now, Kilpatrick!" He looked around the room, mouth slightly open. "You people have been lying your asses off, haven't you? Son of a bitch!" No one said anything.

"Have we had any contact with the Russians or the Chinese?" George Guyette asked, wanting to change the subject and give Kovach a chance to cool down and catch up.

"Yes," Dipaula said, a bit relieved. He looked at Kovach and said, "I'll brief you in a minute, Terry." Turning back to Guyette, he continued, "Tarasavitch called for 'whoever is in charge.' We stalled him, but I'm sure we'll get a call from Moscow very shortly. He wouldn't settle for the formal release issued by state; insisted on calling here directly. So has Ambassador Wu. They believe the Alliance is responsible. They may expect us to immediately retaliate against the Alliance states."

Dipaula looked at his notes and continued, "The British, French, Germans, Israelis, Canadians, and twenty or so others have called state as well. Many lost their ambassadors. Some have insisted on calling here directly. We've been successful in convincing them we're too busy to respond. They've been referred back to official information being released by state. They've been told Kilpatrick can't take their calls. The British are requesting an emergency meeting of the UN Security Council, maybe within the next few hours. Everyone suspects the damn Alliance or Middle East extremists. The secretary general also called and wants some answers. He—"

"He isn't particularly a problem right now," interrupted Thomas. "His staff appears to be giving us some room. Castellano seems to be keeping it together, so far. He's a good man."

"Thank God we've got him at state," Stratton remarked.

"Stalling may work for a while," Thomas speculated, "but soon they'll insist on specifics."

"Yeah, I know." Dipaula took a deep breath and slumped a little in his chair. Looking at Kovach he said, "Terry, we're gonna need your help on this one, especially on reading the Iranian, Chinese, and Russian reactions. We'll need to know who is responsible, at some point. But, for now, we have a much more significant crisis to face. Can we hold this world together for the next few hours?"

10:20 PM, Room W16

The Command Room resembled a hospital waiting room as agents stood around, anxious to hear a word from the field. Every one of them filled with intense guilt.

Donovan stood with Agent Linnet Singleton at a small table near one wall, looking down at a detailed map of the city. Singleton knew the district as well as anyone, having lived here for many years, long before joining the FBI. She had earned a justified reputation with the Secret Service for endurance while serving with them on protective duty for Sen. Maxwell Hodge during his difficult presidential campaign against Bergstrom. She was a tough and highly intelligent agent and knew she had a long night ahead. Her reputation would be tested beyond her own imagination.

On the map were highlighted locations of Park Service vans already stopped or investigated. Vans were the only lead available and had to be worked as thoroughly as possible.

Interstate 270

Inside the Beltway, traffic was beginning to increase. A great many people were attempting to leave the area, even amid reports the radiation had quickly subsided and was only a threat immediately in and around the collapsed House Chamber.

Further from the district, the traffic was light by comparison. A state patrol car was parked among the trees on the Maryland side of the Potomac River dividing Virginia and Maryland, slightly ahead of the large blue sign reading, "Maryland Welcomes You." However, the visitors now crossing over the bridge were not the kind of people for which the sign was intended.

As the van slowly drove past the partially hidden patrol car, Corp. Manny Pitusia, seated on the passenger side, casually remarked, "Interesting, wonder where he's going."

Officer Steve Connely, sitting behind the wheel, remembered the alert, "Yeah, better call it in."

Capitol Hill

The wailing sound of sirens pierced the cold night air. Emergency lights bathed the mall in a flashing sea of bright blue and red. The scene from the rescue helicopters hovering over the Capitol was surreal. In one of the heavy Chinook lift and transport helicopters hastily brought in to raise the massive chunks of concrete and marble, Navy Chief Brad Sabo just shook his head in disbelief. The destruction was beyond anything he had imagined. He had been told it was bad, but not this bad.

Emergency broadcast crews raced through the city side streets to both Capitol Hill and the White House. The media and press were now demanding particulars about who was truly in charge at the White House. They needed to be dealt with.

The White House

The Command Room was the nerve center for the Secret Service. Communications constantly flowed in and out. There were so many reports, they had become desensitized to minor tragedies. One incoming call, however, instantly captured everyone's attention.

"This is the Maryland State Patrol. We've sighted a brown National Park Service van heading northwest toward Gaithersburg on Highway 270 near Rockville. Do you want pursuit?"

The call hit the crowded room like a hammer through a thick pane of glass. Agent Marshal, sitting at the control panel, unable to conceal his excitement, quickly answered, "No! Keep under surveillance! Do not attempt to apprehend! We will respond in a minute. We need some time, Maryland Patrol."

"Roger," came the reply, almost incidentally. "Don't worry. We don't intend to lose him."

Marshal turned to the others and said, "What do you think?"

10:28 PM, Atlanta, Georgia

In a busy Atlanta studio, CNN was analyzing the situation with the usual speculation from hastily assembled experts. Similar discussions were taking place on every major network both in the country and around the world. Broadcasts were nonstop.

Karl VanKeller was moderating. His guests were John Baldrige, former White House correspondent, and Margaret Livingston, former deputy director of FEMA. VanKeller was speaking. "Who precisely makes up the president's cabinet and the line of succession beyond the Speaker of the House?"

Livingston, a slim forty-six-year-old with brown shoulder length hair, read from a list held in her somewhat shaky hands. "The cabinet comes next, which includes the heads of fifteen executive departments; the secretaries of agriculture, commerce, defense, education, energy, health and human services, Homeland Security, housing and urban development, interior, labor, state, transportation, treasury, and veterans affairs, and the attorney general. Under President Bergstrom, cabinet-level rank also has been accorded to the administrator, Environmental Protection Agency; director, Office of Management and Budget; the director, National Drug Control Policy; and the US Trade representative. We believe they were all lost, with the exception of Secretary Kilpatrick, who remained behind. He may be in the White House, Camp David, or another secret location."

"Yeah, Kilpatrick. Earlier, we were discussing the military, in light of the extreme tension around the world, who is responsible for our military?" VanKeller asked, his eyes darting to the numerous staff behind the cameras.

"It's FEMA's responsibility to locate and authenticate the successors to both the president and for military matters," Livingston added, "the successor to the secretary of defense."

VanKeller appeared to listen intently but was looking slightly over Livingston's head for cues from the station staff. They were waiting for a live broadcast from the District. He was a poised, sophisticated journalist in his midforties with just the right red and gray tie and dark blue pinstriped suit. This was the greatest moment of his career. What a story! Millions would be watching him at this very moment. Slightly nervous, the moderator adjusted his stylish glasses and asked, "Have they authenticated that Kilpatrick is the presidential successor?"

"Yes, most likely they have," Livingston answered.

Livingston had been out of her position at FEMA for four years but still felt confident she had accurate data. She was one of the hundreds of former government employees, and now university professors, lecturers, and authors, being called to studios around the country for just such a discussion.

The moderator then asked the question millions of viewers wanted answered. "Mrs. Livingston, in your opinion, who, in light of the crisis in Europe, Asia, and the Middle East, is presently in charge of the military if Kilpatrick has not yet taken the oath of office?"

Livingston smiled weakly. "Karl, this is a question which can only be answered by those people manning FEMA's Central Locator System. I really can't answer that question."

Suddenly, she realized where she was and what impact her obvious uncertainty must be having on the millions of Americans sitting anxiously at home as well as many millions more in other countries. She quickly added, "But you can be sure the proper person is in charge and the country is operating as we have planned and practiced and drilled for many years. The best minds available are unquestionably in control, I'm very confident of that based on my years of experience working with highly qualified and professional people."

VanKeller thought as he turned to face the camera, *Confident, hell! You're scared shitless like the rest of us.* Responding to signals from behind the camera, he turned and spoke directly into the lens, "We will now go live to the district." Seeing a frantic director waving a cue card, VanKeller pressed hard on his loose earpiece and quickly continued, "No! I'm sorry; we will now reexamine the video of the House Chambers prior to the explosion."

The video appeared on the screens of millions of viewers around the world. "As close examination appears to indicate," voiced VanKeller, "Secretary of Defense Martin Coyle, and the Chairman of the Joint Chiefs of Staff General Thomas Orr, are in the chambers. However, we believe the deputy secretary of defense is also in the room." The video froze and a circle appeared around a man in the upper gallery.

VanKeller's voice continued, "It is our understanding the next three people in order of the line of succession to the secretary of defense would be the Secretary of the Army Frank Penata, the Secretary of the Navy Andrew Morgan, and the Secretary of the Air Force Jack Crawford. We cannot ascertain from the footage if any or all of them are in the room."

The screens returned to the studio as VanKeller turned back to Livingston and Baldrige. He continued, "It is my understanding the person in charge of the military, through ten or fifteen levels of succession at least, is in every case a civilian, is that correct?"

"Yes," Livingston answered, "it goes all the way down to such people as the many assistant secretaries of each branch of the military and in order of their length of service. All, I might add, to be determined by FEMA and its locator system." She looked down and thought to herself, *as long as they can be located and authenticated in time to prevent the military itself from taking control.*

"It must be pointed out, Karl," interrupted Baldrige, "that the secretary of the interior, James Kilpatrick, is most likely the legitimate successor to the presidency and therefore exercises full control over the military, regardless of who the successor to Mr. Coyle might be."

"This raises an important question," VanKeller said. "If Kilpatrick is not yet sworn in, and the White House is still unclear on this matter, does that mean he cannot exercise control over the military?"

Livingston and Baldrige looked at one another. They weren't sure what the answer was, but they knew that if the military controlled the defense establishment, a power-hungry general could assume extraordinary authority.

VanKeller focused sharply on the voice in his ear and then hastily reported, "We have just received some unconfirmed reports of explosions in various cities around the country. In Minneap . . . no, in Indianapolis, Billings, Santa Fe, Decatur, and Rockford, Illinois. We will give you further details when they become available. There has been conjecture over recent weeks that the National Militia has been planning to strike against the federal government at some point. That now appears to be happening."

A distressing silence filled the studio as technicians and guests looked at each other, grim expressions all around.

Chapter Fifteen

10:30 pm, the White House

At the White House, the media and others were kept at a distance by police and two companies of army troops from the Twenty-second Military Police Battalion from Fort Meyer, which now surrounded the residence. The press had set up cameras in Lafayette Park across the street. Armored personnel carriers, heavily armed soldiers, and military police formed a complete circle outside the black metal fence surrounding the White House, the Old Executive Office Building, and the Treasury Building. Heavily clothed, thick-gloved uniformed officers of the Secret Service were scattered inside the White House fence throughout the extensive yards and gardens, some in dress uniform others in black combat fatigues, guard dogs chained nearby. It was a cold night, and the reporters could see each man's breathe in white plumes against their camera lights. Sirens blared in the distance and the eerie silence surrounding the White House reflected the grave situation. A ghostly haze shrouded the mansion.

10:31 pm

Unmarked vehicles were traveling a safe distance both behind and in front of the Park Service van as it moved slowly along Highway 80. In addition, the Maryland Sate Patrol had deliberately positioned vehicles at major exits and at vantage points located along the interstate. A few police vehicles made brief observations while traveling in the opposite direction, on the far side of the grassy median.

"Central One, this is Maryland Command, are you there?"

"Yes, Maryland Command, this is Central One, go ahead." Terry Forester was handling the communications in W16.

"Sir, we're wondering if you plan for us to apprehend the vehicle. The longer we delay, the greater the risk."

"Maryland Command, do you have any airfields near the area?"

"We'll check."

"Thank you."

A few minutes passed, then. "This is Maryland Command; do you read me, Central?"

"Yes, we're here," Forester answered. "Go ahead."

"We do have a small local airport in Frederick, just north of where the van is now located. It's heading in that direction. We estimate about five minutes to the exit leading to that airfield."

"Thank you, Maryland, could you cover the field just in case, at least until the van passes the exit?"

"I think so, Central. Let me off and I'll give it our best shot. We'll have to use local law enforcement."

"We can't afford to lose that van or its occupants." Forester's voice hardened. "Do you understand? This is the highest priority and a matter of national security. Is that clear, Maryland Command?"

"Roger, security, I understand. We have so many vehicles on this I'm more concerned that one will actually collide with the van than I am about losing sight of it."

Forester turned to the other agents in the room. Donovan, Lawrence, Singleton, Van Meter, and Charlie Morrison were there, along with Sandra Merrall.

Donovan spoke first, "The helicopter can take us to that airfield?"

"I think you'll need Dipaula's approval for that, James," Morrison answered.

Donovan was convinced he could do nothing from here. He had to get to the van. "I wanna be there when they stop that van." His jaw tightened.

The radio came back to life, "Security, this is Maryland Command."

"Go ahead, Maryland."

"The van has turned off the Pike onto Highway 70 and it is heading in the general direction of the Frederick Municipal Airport. Please advise."

"Stand by, Maryland Command."

Donovan's heart began to race, he spoke in a whisper, "They're heading for that airport?"

Morrison took the microphone and said, "Does that airport have tower control?"

"One second, security. Local police believe there is no tower located at that airfield. I repeat; no tower. It's a small one."

Morrison turned to Donovan and said, "If there's no tower, we are not able to close that field. They would have known that. If they plan to fly out, this could be the one."

Donovan almost shouted to Morrison as he turned toward the door. "Alert NORAD to send a fighter to Frederick. And have the police cover that field, out of sight. They are not to move unless absolutely necessary."

Moscow, 6:40 am

It was morning. The reddish-brown overused and underrepaired sanding trucks clattered loudly in protest as they rambled down the wide, frozen streets. There was little traffic, but near the train station, the queues for food and gasoline had already begun to form. A pale hint of sunlight appeared low in the dark Moscow sky. The call from the Russian Embassy in Washington interrupted intense discussions in the Strategy Room. It was from Igmanov, for Chernosvitov.

Chernosvitov grabbed the receiver and almost raised his voice, something he seldom did, "Yes, Igmanov, what do you have?"

"Our people have returned from the White House. There are military guards closing traffic for blocks around the House. On the roof of the house, the Executive Building and other buildings, we can see armed guards, some behind machine guns and grenade launchers. Policemen are on the side streets leading to the White House. The house is indeed heavily fortified. Only a few people have been allowed to enter. But when the people who have entered are identified, we will notify you. Some may have entered through underground passages. After we are through with this conversation, we will transfer the information we have to you."

Chernosvitov was anxious. He knew that radical forces would soon pressure Masarov, a pressure he might not be able to resist.

"Hold a moment, Chernosvitov, we have the White House on line," said Igmanov.

After a few minutes Igmanov came back on the phone. "We have just spoken to Craig Thomas. He indicates that the military are on alert here in the United States and tells me that many special response units are also on alert worldwide. They may place their entire military on full alert within the hour."

"How do they sound?"

"They are very direct and slightly hostile but is understandable," Igmanov responded.

"Igmanov, tell the Americans that President Masarov wishes to speak with the person in charge and will be using the direct line in ten minutes. Do you believe they will be prepared to discuss the situation with him?"

"I don't know who is in charge. But they could hardly refuse a call from Masarov."

"Then speak with them immediately . . . and keep this line open." Chernosvitov handed the receiver to his aide, breathed deeply and entered the Strategy Room.

There was a new odor in the room, a rich aromatic smell. Chernosvitov realized what it was. Someone had brought in a carton of American Camel cigarettes.

10:50 PM, the White House Situation Room

Nearly two hours had passed since the attack. The White House was now in a state of controlled response. Every line was being used to communicate with FEMA, the Pentagon, special emergency teams, various police districts, state offices, and news centers from around the world. Extra staff was being located to assist. The atmosphere was extremely tense.

Kilpatrick's body had been taken to a secure room down the hall from the Situation Room. Secret Service agents stood guard. Knowledge of his death would be on a strict-need-to-know basis. Nearly all who worked frantically in the upper floors of the White House were completely unaware of the secrets being discussed in the floor below.

The Situation Room had a large gathering of support staff from various White House Offices. Lt. Gen. George Glazer, military assistant to the president and director of the White House Military Office, was needed. He left Fort Bragg and was on his way to the district.

Marty Castellano had arrived and Dipaula insisted he remain in the mansion to communicate directly with state and through them to embassies around the world.

The people in the Situation Room were not dissimilar from the many ordinary men and women throughout history who, for a few decisive moments, were charged with making instantaneous critical decisions in defense of their nation. For some time, they had been discussing the likely person, or persons, to legally exercise leadership in this crisis. The US Constitution seemed to be of little help. The lone member of the situation support staff assigned to emergency planning, Joseph Adamson, could shed no appreciable light. According to the National Command Authority, someone in the defense succession was legally in control of the military. Soon that would be clarified. But the haunting question remained, who was legitimately in control of the government?

FEMA's locator system was damaged by either the electromagnetic pulse emitted by the nuclear explosion or by overloaded power lines, or any number of problems with numerous microprocessors and semiconductors. They couldn't locate nor authenticate anyone. Many internal inspectors predicted this vulnerability over the years, but their warnings only agitated impudent, disinterested ears. Nothing resulted from their complaints. The main office at the Federal Center Plaza was now working to correct the problem.

The Deputy Director of FEMA, Joe Sullivan, was in the Situation Room and was forbidden to leave. He had earlier been persuaded, after a great deal of thought, to report to his director that Mr. Kilpatrick had chosen to remain in the White House. The unparalleled deception was now widespread.

Jerry Gannon, slim, forty-two years old, and fourteen years with the National Security Council staff, was highly respected by his peers. In most emergencies, Gannon, a magna cum laude from Princeton, waited to evaluate the discussion before sharing his thoughts. The time had now arrived.

He shifted his gaunt frame, cleared his throat and said, "Barry, one thing we could be missing is that it may not be just one person who should be making decisions. Let's not forget the power of the governors. Perhaps, they, working together, really constitute the leadership of the country when succession ends. If the entire line of succession and the Congress is eliminated, it's clear that no one has the authority to govern the country or to elect or appoint a president."

Carol Cassatt, a slightly corpulent forty-six-year-old with eleven years on the situation support staff, toyed with the collar of her blouse. "We can't really forget the NCA," she said. "Does the military have any official political power in a situation like this? I know they have some retaliatory powers. But do they have power to declare military or martial law?"

"Carol has a point," Gannon remarked. "If there is no identified head of government, one of our military generals might impose martial law. That's not unheard of. Actually, it may be the right thing to do."

Dipaula looked at Cassett, took a deep breath and then nodded a reluctant agreement. "Interesting you should say that, Carol, General McCloud at the Pentagon has informed us if he doesn't hear from Kilpatrick to the contrary, he'll shortly place our international forces on full alert. It appears he's presently ranking general in the Pentagon and seems to be in control of the military, legitimately or not. He's concerned about the situation in the Middle East and Central Asia, and well he should be."

"What about General Sanchez?" asked Sullivan.

"We can't locate Sanchez." Dipaula cleared his throat and added, "Being the deputy chairman of the Joint Chiefs of Staff directly under General Orr, he's likely the highest ranking military officer left. As far as the civilian chain of command, someone named William Styka, an assistant deputy secretary of, I believe the army, just might be the ranking civilian over there."

"Jesus, can you believe that?" Cassatt sat back in her seat. "How far down do we have to go?"

Two Secret Service agents and three marine guards secured the door to the Situation Room and blocked Donovan from entering. One of the agents knocked on the door. Phillip Page opened it part way and looked out.

An agent outside the door announced, "Sir, Agent Donovan would like to speak with Mr. Dipaula. He says it's urgent."

"Who did you say?"

"Agent Donovan, sir; he says it's urgent."

"Donovan, come in." Page noticed other agents moving and quickly added, "Just Donovan, no one else."

The tension was electrifying. It charged everyone in the room, much like the tingling moments before a lightning strike. Conversation stopped as Donovan entered.

Dipaula walked around the table and approached Donovan. "What do you need?"

"Barry, the persons we believe responsible for the assassination are approaching a small airfield in Maryland. We need to get up there fast. We need Marine One. It's on the south lawn?"

Dipaula nodded his agreement. He looked deep into Donovan's eyes. His jaw locked. "If we don't bring them in soon, the National Militia will continue to spark revolutionary fires all over this country. They're raising hell right now, James, but things could get worse in a few hours. Take whatever you need. And, if possible, take the sons of bitches alive. I don't want 'em to hang. I want to rip their insides out myself."

"You need to call the security desk and authorize it?"

"I will. Good luck and keep us informed."

Donovan turned toward the door and stopped. Turning back to Dipaula, he said, "I know what you're carrying."

"I know you do, James. You carried it for a long time yourself, thanks to me."

"Yeah. Sandra's going up there with me."

Dipaula felt a delicate sting. "Tell her, good luck and take care. That goes for you too, James."

After Donovan left the room, Dipaula, sat back in his chair and arced his spine. The stress was affecting the muscles of his back. They burned and ached, adding to the relentless tension. He once again felt a surge in his stomach. A terrible feeling of aloneness, of insufficiency, moved through him. Closing his eyes, he attempted to regain control, knowing he could not withdraw from the enormous decisions that had to be made.

The room was silent, as if everyone distinctively sensed Dipaula's internal struggle and related to it. Before the silence became unbearable, Agent Van Meter opened the door.

"Mr. Dipaula, sir."

"Yes," Dipaula opened his eyes and sat up straight. "What do you need?"

"Sir, the president's secretary, Mrs. Brint, has something for Secretary Kilpatrick. She said it was urgent, sir. Something left for him by the president."

Dipaula looked around the room. They were now aware of how effective their story had been. Even Mrs. Brint had been deceived.

"I'll be right there." Dipaula stood and went to the door.

Outside the room, no words were exchanged as he embraced Kathleen Brint. After a few seconds, the secretary said, "Mr. Dipaula, the president gave me a letter for Secretary Kilpatrick. He said it was to be given to him if he did not return to the White House in a reasonable time. I think he meant . . ." Tears flowed from her eyes.

"Mrs. Brint," Dipaula said softly. "I'll give the letter to the secretary. You go back to your office and rest. I'll let you know the minute we hear anything from Capitol Hill."

Dipaula took the letter. After Mrs. Brint had left the hallway, he entered a side office and sat down at a small desk. For a few seconds he merely looked at the envelope. Then he opened it and removed the letter, which read,

Secretary James Kilpatrick:

If you are reading this letter, I will assume the worst scenario may have occurred and the entire cabinet, with you as an exception, has been lost. You may now be the president of the United States. I would not have selected you to remain behind if I did not have confidence in your ability to serve in this high position. You will find a number of personal notations in the lower right drawer of my desk in a small metal box. The notes are my personal recommendations should I fall victim to an assassination. For now, however, I have chosen to leave you with my most respected friend and advisor, Barry Dipaula. Trust him in all things. He is above reproach and a man of highest integrity. Do not fail to keep him close to you as you struggle with the decisions of your time. You need him, the country needs him. Also, I rec . . .

Dipaula didn't finish the letter. He folded it, placed it back into the envelope, slid it into his pants pocket and returned to the Situation Room.

After taking his seat, Dipaula spoke up without hesitation, "I'm sorry for the delay. A few things needed to be taken care of." Then, with a new sense of confidence, he began as though no time had passed nor any interruption had occurred. "By the way, General McCloud is having a hard time believing Styka has any authority. I suggest—"

"Hates civilians telling him what to do," interrupted Cassatt.

"Anyway," Dipaula continued, "at least for the time being, we should continue to keep Kilpatrick's death quiet, even from the military, including McCloud and the people over at the Pentagon. At least until we locate Sanchez. Overreaction by the military could trigger serious consequences in Central Asia and in Russia."

"McCloud's a redneck asshole," lampooned Cassatt.

"Yeah, anybody but McCloud," added Gannon. "He wouldn't hesitate to take over. He once said the military's the fourth branch of government. He's dangerous."

Dipaula took another deep breath, leaned forward and continued again, "The president expressed some concern regarding his speeches. Seems he's become hardened as he nears retirement. He might have some political aspirations. None of that matters now. We've contacted FEMA to find out who has authority over McCloud. With the top brass killed in the chambers and with the locator still out, it will be a while before we know precisely who's in charge of the military. As I said earlier, we're inferring it's the Secretary of the Army Frank Penata, wherever he is."

"He may have been on the hill as well," Craig Thomas added.

"Yeah," Dipaula continued. "As the list in front of you indicates, after the secretary of the army, it's Andrew Morgan, secretary of the navy, then Jack Crawford of the air force, and so on." A few people seated around the table picked up the individual reports and shuffled through them, trying to locate the list. "The Secret Service is checking the video tape to see if they can identify everyone."

Carol Cassatt seemed to share Dipaula's concern, as did most around the table. As an intelligence analyst, she had major responsibilities on the White House Situation Support Staff. Her specialty was military matters and her reports were always extremely accurate, objective, and specific.

Cassatt slowly rotated the coffee cup between her palms, watching the black liquid gently swirl back and forth. Suddenly, she pushed the cup a few inches away and said, "Considering the Central Asian problem and the hard-liners in Moscow, our automatic response systems give me some concern. They could set off an uncontrollable reaction in other countries; could cause some major catastrophe beyond anyone's control. Since our own military has been of some concern here, I believe it's essential we maintain, and even maybe enhance, the appearance of Kilpatrick's presence and control here in the White House."

She hesitated a second to check reactions, and then continued, "I only hope extreme elements in Iran, Russia and China don't overreact and Masarov keeps a cool head and tight reins."

A few people around the table shifted uncomfortably in their chairs while several others nodded an uneasy agreement.

George Dansie, a dedicated NSC staffer, looked extremely frustrated. "Come on now. Cut the shit! Who really believes our own military would be anything but sensible in this situation? You're getting carried away with military bashing! Hell, they're all patriotic Americans. They defended this country with their lives. More than most of you in this room have done. Surely, you aren't comparing them to power-crazy Muslim extremists or even the damn Russian hard-liners. I see nothing wrong with telling them what's going on. As a matter of fact, I think we have to! Hell, that might be what's necessary to keep a lid on overreaction. This hoax is wrong! Keeping a crisis of this magnitude from our own military authorities is ludicrous not to mention extremely dangerous. Glazer will damn sure agree when he arrives."

Gen. George Glazer was military assistant to the president and director of the White House Military Office. He had retired six years earlier after distinguishing himself both in the Gulf and the Iraq war and was in the air and on his way to Andrews from Fort Bragg.

Jerry Gannon looked slowly around the room, now containing eighteen very anxious people, then directly toward Dansie. "You may be right, George, but why take the chance that McCloud, or others, might be so damn patriotic as to actually believe they should play a major role by rationalizing it's their duty and obligation."

"That's a pile of crap!" shouted Dansie. "And you know it!"

Without taking his eyes off his enraged colleague, Gannon continued, "Have you forgotten Haig, George?" more than a little fire in his eye. Then looking back at Dipaula, "All we need now is a general with an 'I'm in charge' attitude."

Chapter Sixteen

10:53 pm
The Situation Room

The half-dozen telephones in the room rang simultaneously. Bill Macintee lifted the receiver closest to him and listened for a few seconds. Placing his hand over the mouthpiece, he said, "It's the Russians, their embassy. It's none other than 'Igmanov the Great.' He wants to speak to whoever is in charge of the country. Sound familiar? Or to you, Barry."

Dipaula picked up the receiver in front of him. "This is Barry Dipaula."

"Mr. Dipaula," a mature female voice, "can you speak with Mr. Igmanov from the Russian Embassy? He said it's urgent."

"What isn't urgent tonight?" he mumbled, more than a little irritated. "Okay, put him through."

"One moment, Mr. Dipaula, I'll connect Mr. Igmanov," replied the operator. "Go ahead, sir."

Dipaula spoke first, "Misha, I'm sorry we're extremely busy here. Nothing has changed since Thomas spoke to you last."

"Yes, well, I'm certain you are very busy, my friend. I am merely, well, calling to tell you that our President Masarov will be placing a call on the direct line within the next hour. Will the person in charge speak with him? Of course, he is a bit concerned about the intensified military activity and questions who is in charge of your military. He is also concerned about a number of matters."

Dipaula was getting cottonmouth and could feel the moisture forming under his shirt. Igmanov was searching.

"Misha, we really are trying to understand this situation ourselves. I would suggest you inform Moscow not to irritate things by taking any unnecessary military action. We may be a bit uncertain about what has happened here in Washington, but we are not in the least bit uncertain about what must be done to protect this country and its interests around the world, including the Middle East and Central Asia."

"Yes, well, I do understand, Barry. Please do not misinterpret my call or the president's call. We are obviously concerned over this tragic situation, which places not only your own country but also ours in a very dangerous situation. Without your president's influence, Iran and the Alliance states may take a military offensive, one that could quickly involve our country."

"I know that, Misha. Please, I have to go now." Dipaula wanted to get off the line for fear he would say too much to the head of the elite corps of Russian spies. He could feel Igmanov analyzing his every breath and inflection.

"Well, yes, of course. The president will be calling soon. I feel it is important to tell you, Barry, even in this difficult time for you that our government cannot tolerate the slightest threat to our borders. I am certain our military would respond forcefully if retaliation were to occur within our region, even under your present crisis; that is why President Masarov must speak with whoever is in charge of your government and soon. Do you understand, my friend? He does not wish to believe your military is completely in charge, or that perhaps your internal militia is involved in a major revolutionary move—a move connected with individuals in other countries."

"Misha, there is no—"

"Excuse me, Barry, but there are major acts of hostility occurring across your country at this very moment. It appears your government is not in absolute control. How can—"

"They're unrelated, Misha! Everything is under control here. Just—"

"Unrelated? I am not implying that you, personally, are involved in a conspiracy. But our president would consider unauthorized leadership of the United States government a very dangerous situation."

"Is that all, Misha? We have matters to deal with."

"I know you do. Keep in mind, Barry, your country is unlike any other. If an angry population has decided to revolt, well, you control an enormous power, which could be released by the slightest push on a button."

"Good-bye, Misha. I hope you're as concerned about who is in charge of your military as you appear to be about ours and I hope you are as confused about this situation as I am."

Dipaula sat his receiver down as he considered, *Do the Russians actually believe that a coup is in progress? That the damn militia is that strong? Good God, I never thought of that. Damn, how could anyone think such a thing would be possible in the United States. But, in their culture and especially their history . . . it just might make sense. Hell, coups are almost an annual occurrence in many countries. With reports of scattered violence in different parts of the country, it does appear the National Militia has declared war. Maybe they actually have.*

Dipaula, deep in thought, lowered the phone into its cradle. With a quick blink he turned back to the others and said, "Masarov will be on the direct line within the hour. Who should speak with him and what should they say? Any thoughts?"

Terry Kovach, senior negotiator with the Russians, spoke first. "I have a major concern. If the right person does not answer that phone, the Russians will suspect Kilpatrick is not in control. Anyone short of Kilpatrick won't work."

"As a matter of fact," added Thomas, "if the media does not see Kilpatrick soon, they'll begin to speculate themselves. Shit, everyone will."

"We can only sell this thing for just so long," Kovach warned. "We either find a solution fast or we produce Kilpatrick. We have no other option."

"Dammit, Terry, you know that's impossible," Guyette said with no attempt to repress his irritation.

"Is it impossible?" replied Phillip Page. Page, thirty-six, from Stanford, worked on Bergstrom's campaign as a freelance strategist. With Page, you got unconstrained creativity with a little traditional thinking.

The room was silent for a few moments, then Page continued. "If we could sit the secretary up in a chair and take a photo for the press corps, it might pass." He then added, matter-of-factly, "It doesn't appear his face was damaged."

The room was silent. A few frail smiles appeared. Sounded like Page. However, over the years they all had seen enough of his wild ideas actually succeed that he wasn't completely ignored.

"Shit, you're not serious," said George Guyette. "My God, that's crazy. Who the hell are you kidding? Who'll put color back into his face?"

"And then, what happens when it's discovered he's been dead all this time?" asked Terry Kovach. "Hell, they might think we killed him. Shit, that's crazy, even for you, Phil."

"Masarov will be on the phone before long," Dipaula said. "Who should speak to him?"

"You see now what this stupid deception has led to?" Dansie said as he rose to his feet. "What right do you have, Barry, or any of us for that matter, to lie to the country and the whole damn world?"

"Calm down, George!" Gannon snapped.

"Hell no, I won't! It's time to end this crap! Who the hell are you people? What right do you have to keep this critical information from anyone? Who the hell do you think you are? I'm goin'—"

"Sit down, George!" Dipaula shouted. He wasn't making a request. "We need to discuss this right now! We need everyone's input, including yours. We don't need to criticize each other's motives and we don't need emotional outbursts. Sit the hell down."

"Screw you, Dipaula! You're an advisor. No authority in this situation! You've been pretending you don't like the spotlight, you don't like the leadership, the power!" His face solidified. "Well, I think you're liking it now; a bit too much, if you ask me!"

"No one's asking you, Dansie," yelled Gannon. "In any case, who else is there?"

Dipaula was surprised by Gannon's endorsement.

"Well, in case you people forget, there's the American people and the generals you're so damn afraid of," Dansie snapped, his fists tightened. "It appears you only have faith in yourself! That's your style, Dipaula. You only have faith in yourself." He walked toward the door, "What's that you said about an 'in charge attitude,' Gannon? What about you people? You're so damn arrogant you can't see that attitude in yourselves!"

"That's enough, Dansie!" Cassett yelled. She started to get up. Not a man in the room wanted to mess with her.

"Oh you're a good one, Carol." Dansie wasn't intimidated in the slightest. "You've been after my ass for a long time. Well, you got yourself into a pile of shit and you're trying to drag the whole damn country in with you."

"After your ass, George? Your ass?" she said with an agitated sneer. "If I were a man, or, even if you were a man, I'd be tempted to kick your ass around this room!"

"The hell with you guys." Dansie moved to the door. "I'm not taking part in this irrational and dangerous charade. Responsible people need to know what's going on in this room." He was immediately blocked by one of the Secret Service agents.

"Get the hell out of my way!"

The agent didn't move.

Turning back, he asked, "Am I a prisoner of war, Dipaula?"

Dipaula wanted to kick Dansie's ass himself. "George, no one is leaving this room. And you're not a prisoner of war." He stood and walked over to Dansie. "Believe this or not, George, your opposition gives us a good balance. I know Terry isn't a hundred percent with us as well. The two of you are really needed here. Please sit down, George, and help us work through this thing. Please."

Thinking for a few prolonged seconds, Dansie took a deep breath and said, "Do I really have a choice here, Dipaula? Really, a choice?"

"Not really, George."

After shaking his head in resignation, Dansie walked over to his seat, sat down, steaming as if he had just completed the Boston Marathon in record time. The room was crammed with a tense silence, broken only by the rustling of a chair and a nervous cough.

Gannon's earlier remarks and his vote of confidence had produced a peculiar feeling in Dipaula. He felt a strange surge of energy come over him, a birth of confidence, as if he were being transformed into the role he had merely been playing over the last few hours. Dipaula became a bit troubled that Gannon might actually have jolted loose a latent ambitious side of his personality, one he had fought to suppress over the years.

10:55 pm, the South Lawn

Donovan quickly stepped up the ladder and entered Bronco as the engine came to life. Smoke came rushing into the cold air as drooping blades slowly began to spin and gradually level with the increased speed. The calm night air at the South Portico of the White House was shattered by noise from the presidential helicopter as Gregg Lawrence, Charlie Morrison, Linnet Singleton, and Sandra Merrall followed Donovan up the ladder and through the doorway. Seven members of the Secret Service assault team in black combat uniforms filed in before the door slammed shut. Uniformed officers of the Secret Service watched as the olive green and white chopper, Marine One, lifted off the frozen lawn.

The Situation Room

Dipaula turned back to business. "We must decide now; do we continue the charade or start to level with, at least, some people? It's looking more like some sort of insurrection is taking place across the country. Igmanov made that quite clear. If we don't reveal everything or . . . and I hate to say this . . . become more aggressive in the charade, I agree with Carol, we're going to loose it. I'm not sure what would happen if the country and the world knew the United States was without legitimate leadership."

Craig Thomas shifted in his seat and broke in, "Pentagon and state are convinced the men responsible for the destruction of the capitol are agents of the Alliance. People, that's an act of aggression against the United States, on a par with the bombing of Pearl Harbor. If they are responsible, we could be facing a major world catastrophe. In reality, we may have as much control here as a blind pilot in a hurricane."

Dipaula nodded slightly then continued, "It's quite clear most of the world believes the Alliance is responsible for our situation. If the facts here in the White House were revealed, Iran might move against Iraq and Israel. If they did, the Alliance would be forced to react, which would bring all of NATO, including the Russians, into the crisis. If the Russians get involved, China would most certainly respond. And who knows how North Korea would react. Certainly, any move on their part would ignite all of Asia. We cannot, no matter what the pressure, break the secrecy we've established. Kilpatrick must remain alive. Otherwise, world war three could be just hours away."

"I agree. We, somehow, have to control the situation or it'll control us," Page replied. "We have no choice but to take some action now. If we—"

"It's my opinion we don't tell the Russians, Chinese, Israelis, or anyone else anything," interrupted Gannon. "Why the shit should we? By the way, people, I for one, haven't forgotten Haig. Why he—"

"Hold it a minute," Dipaula interrupted. "I think Gannon was onto something a while back. Maybe the governors of the individual states have more power than we're aware of." His eyes turned to the tall, quiet man at the end of the table as he asked, "Judge Walker do you have any insight into the power the governors might have in a situation like this?"

Judge Herbert Walker had been in the Situation Room since 8:00 PM and had sat through the heart attack of Secretary Kilpatrick and all the discussions, which followed. Neither his years as a judge nor his years as a congressman had prepared him for this.

Everyone in the room now focused on Walker. He moved his six-foot-two-inch frame a little in his seat, swallowed gently, and allowed his eyes to circle the room slightly below the ceiling, hoping to read some wisdom in the light green trim.

"Well," Walker began, trying to calm his nerves, "it does appear the highest easily identifiable elected officers of the country are presently the governors of the individual states. If one were to imagine what the framers of the Constitution might consider to be the highest authority in such a situation, one likely possibility would be they would select the governors, especially if the governors were to act in concert."

"Are you saying, Judge Walker," Tom Stratton asked, "that if the governors elected a president, it would be permissible under the spirit, if not the letter, of the Constitution?" Like the others, he was anxious to find an answer, any answer.

"No, no, no," Walker continued, hands raised, palms out, a slight protest to Stratton's statement. "I'm only speculating here. The union is, after all, just a union of individual states. If the highest elected representatives of the people are now the governors, then it should hold true that, in an emergency such as this, they would hold the highest power. As we know, they can even appoint senators and representatives, should the need arise. Why couldn't they have the power to take whatever action is in the best interests of the people of their individual states; and by so doing, act in the best interests of the entire country?"

Walker had everyone's attention. They were hoping he would provide the answer, any answer. After a few seconds he continued, "It appears you haven't forgotten Haig. Certainly, as well, none of you have forgotten Jerry Ford. The people didn't elect him either for the office of vice president nor for the office of president. If governors can appoint congressmen and congressmen can, in turn, elect a president . . . why couldn't the governors in a national emergency simply elect a president, at the least an interim president?"

Cassatt sat back in her chair and acknowledged, "It's not possible to have a general election fast enough to protect the interests of the United States; especially after hearing comments regarding the tense situation in the Middle East and Russia."

"I agree," added Thomas. "However, there is another thing to consider. According to the National Command Authority, a successor to the secretary of defense has authority for military action if there's no established successor to the president."

Walker chimed in, "And by the way, this is very important; it was never intended by our founding fathers that the military, on its own, would have extreme authority in any domestic situation. Keep this firmly in mind, ladies and gentlemen; martial law should never be called by a military person."

Gannon quickly added, "Also, people must accept not only the decision of who will serve as president but also the method by which that person was selected. I agree with Judge Walker, they would most likely accept a decision of the governors. I know I would."

Cassett leaned forward, "I agree with Jerry. I think that would be true of world leaders, as well. They're going to be very concerned about how we determine who is in charge." Sitting back she added, "With everyone apparently lost on Capitol Hill and with Kilpatrick dead, I think the governors could well be our answer."

The room was completely quiet as if a curtain of intense thought were suddenly pulled across their collective minds.

Dipaula stood, somewhat confident a massive weight was about to be lifted from his shoulders. "I can't imagine going more than a few hours without a president, even in the best of times. The last time we had a few hours without a president was immediately after Kennedy's assassination. But even then, we had a complete line of succession to keep the continuity. That's obviously not the case now. The governors need to make the choice. As Jerry indicated, successors to the secretary of defense might well control the military, but we need a political leader everyone will accept. The governors will have to make that call."

Kovach stood and walked behind his seat. The others were quiet. Most were looking down at their hands or at the piles of scattered papers on the table. While realizing they had no real constitutional power, each knew they were the only ones available to set the course for the country. The fate of the nation and the stability of the world depended on them.

Kovach put his hands on the back of his chair and leaned forward. "Ladies and Gentlemen, I believe this extraordinary situation calls for extraordinary action. First, I think we must continue to convince everyone outside this room that Kilpatrick is alive and in charge. The United States in panic, equals a world in panic. Next, it is my opinion as well, that we should gather every governor possible for an election. I also agree with Barry, that it must be done at the earliest possible moment, maybe even before daybreak in the district, certainly before noon tomorrow."

The room was silent. Then, Macintee, playing with his pencil, said, "You can't be serious, Terry. The sun will be up in eight hours. Specifically, how do we do that? Even conceding that it would be possible, what happens when governors arrive in the district? People will immediately know we have a serious leadership problem here."

"Why do they have to meet here?" asked George Dansie. "Why not somewhere else; maybe Andrews or Camp David?"

Everyone was quiet. Dansie? A constructive idea from Dansie? Everyone choose to resist making an issue of his unexpected input; pleased there was some growing unity around the table. Even Cassett gave a subtle smile but made no comment.

Guyette got more involved, "If that's what you think should be done, then George is right, why does it have to be here? Shit knows, this city is in a state of chaos. You couldn't conceal that much high-level traffic. We still don't know the radiation threat outside this building. Anyway, it would take a lot more time to bring everyone here. Maybe somewhere in the center of the country."

"In any case," added Thomas, "the media is getting mean as hell. Have any of you watched the latest rundown on the networks? They're yelling for information from us, or Kilpatrick, heaven help him."

"Yeah," speculated Gannon. "If a Middle East or Alliance country was involved in the assassination, where will they strike next, and how soon? If they can hit Washington, they can hit Moscow, Beijing, Tokyo, London, Paris, anywhere."

"Hell," said Mcintee, "we don't have time to get a bunch of politicians together; and dammit, you're talking fifty of 'em, in one meeting, trying to make a decision like this. Damn." He sat back and let the red drain slowly from his face, triggered more by fear than by anger.

The room was respectfully silent. After gaining some control, Guyette took a deep breath and quietly continued, "You may be right, Bill. The first priority is to keep this world from blowing up because the military acted where we should have. Hell, maybe you're even right about the governors." He lowered his head and took a deep breath.

Dipaula moved once again to bring order, determined not to let this opportunity escape. These were people who, under normal conditions, were very logical and creative. He spoke noticeably louder and faster than usual. "Ladies and Gentlemen, unfortunately, we do not have the wisdom and guidance of the Constitution. As far as we know, it has no provisions for the loss of the complete line of succession and the loss of the complete Congress. We have only our best judgment to depend on. By giving this problem to the governors, the highest elected officials of this country, we could relieve ourselves of this responsibility. For me, the sooner the better. Now, I suggest we spend time discussing ways of stalling President Masarov, and others, and ways of getting the governors to one central cloistered place, in secrecy, as quickly as possible and pray to God they can elect a new president in time. Anyone have a problem with this plan?"

Kovach shifted in his chair and, with a slight body tilt, spoke, "Not about what you propose, Barry. I'm sorry, but I would like us to reconsider letting at least the British, Israelis, and the Russians know a little about what's going on. I don't think they would want us to panic anymore than we would want them to panic."

"Terry, do you mean we should tell the Russians, maybe even the British, everything?" Dipaula asked. "That Kilpatrick is dead and that we intend to bring the governors together to elect an interim president?"

"That's right," answered Kovach. Chuckles rippled around the table. "Wait a minute. It's just a thought. Where Russia is concerned, I'm certainly only referring to Masarov and the friendlies, not Obidiov and his gang. I agree it could be an absolute disaster if they found out; Masarov wouldn't last the day."

Looking around the room, Dipaula asked, "What do you think, ladies and gentlemen? No abstaining. No one has the luxury of remaining quiet at this table. We're going to face this crisis together. A good friend reminded me earlier that we are the people. The country belongs to each of us. I remind you, in this room, there will no longer be any abstentions."

Surprisingly, many of them thought it might be better to trust Masarov. This would be a major decision, which could be either a big step forward out of this nightmare or trigger a major disaster.

Dipaula had the attention of everyone, but his confidence was threatening to fade once again. He had to get rid of the problem before he made any more mistakes.

Chapter Seventeen

11:25 pm, Frederick Municipal Airport

The small private airfield was dormant, frozen, and shrouded in darkness except for a few automatic lights in empty offices. A gentle icy breeze blew through a few anchored garbage cans, around the deserted metal hangers and moved out over the frozen fields surrounding the area. The evening fog had now formed a thin layer of ice on everything including trees, buildings, and the runway itself. The airport was deserted on the late January night, and was as silent as a long abandoned mining town.

Aviation Way ran east and west parallel to the main runway. The airport buildings were lined primarily between the Avemco building to the far west with its five flagpoles standing watch on the front lawn and the Frederick Community College buildings to the east, its beige sign held green letters reading, "Aviation Technology Program." A series of metal hangars ran the distance between the two.

In the center of the hangars was the empty fire station with large red letters mounted on the roof, spelling the word "PIPER"; and across a small parking area from the fire station stood the well-known Airway Cafe. The small white building with blue trim had been a local landmark for many years, since the 1950s, not changing much over time. The second floor of the cafe housed the airport authorities, when they were here. During the summer, hundreds of small aircraft lined the field, and the parking areas scattered about were always full. Not tonight. Not on this cold, quiet January night.

An Exxon station was located immediately inside the fence separating the field from the buildings, near the runway, about a hundred feet from the cafe. During warm months, it pumped thousands of gallons of fuel per day for men and women who would impatiently fly away seeking relief from the worries of everyday life. The station now sat cold and silent on the dark frigid landscape.

Bailes Lane and Hughes Ford Road were the branches leading to the airport, both connected with Patrick Street, the main arterial, forming a rough triangle. On cold winter nights, they were seldom traveled by anyone but local farmers. Tonight, however, they had already carried more than a dozen cars from local and state police toward Aviation way and the small municipal airport.

Undercover vehicles from the county sheriff's office arrived first, followed by Frederick city police and the state patrol. Along both approaches, restless farmers, alerted by the peculiar traffic, looked out their windows, inquisitive, confused, and a bit upset.

The vehicles pulled onto Airport Way and scattered, some going west into parking areas behind the gray Avemco building, others taking positions between and behind buildings both to the east and west of the Airway Cafe.

Two squad cars pulled onto the taxiway and immediately disappeared across the runway toward a white cone-shaped building in the distance, hidden in darkness on the opposite side of the field.

Unnoticed by the police cars and concealed from view by the darkness, a small six seat aircraft sat quietly on frozen dirt near the end of a cross runway. Inside sat a lone man at the controls. He observed the cars driving onto the airfield and watched silently as they disappeared into the shadows, taking positions behind buildings.

Inside the plane, Fajil slowly picked up the transmitter and flipped the "on" switch. The radio clicked.

"Hello, hello." Fajil, huddling low in the small aircraft, spoke a little above a whisper.

The Park Service van had turned off Interstate 70 onto Monocacy Boulevard and was moving down Patrick Street, headed for Bailes Lane, now less than four minutes from the airport gate. A man in the front passenger seat of the van picked up his radio and acknowledged the call. "Yes."

The voice from the plane spoke, "They are here. I will be ready for you." He hesitated and then continued. "We will need cover. Do you understand?"

The van replied, "It will be done." Kamile set the receiver down and closed his eyes.

In exactly two minutes, Fajil set the switch of the special designed twin rotary engines to "on," pressed several buttons and the propellers began to move, with each explosion they slowly filled with life. The engine noise was low at first. Soon, the engines came to life. Several dozen pairs of eyes began to frantically scan the darkened airport for the source of the faint rumbling noise.

In the police cruisers, no one spoke, windows were lowered. Like frightened deer in a forest, men raised their heads slightly as their eyes scanned the runway. Echoes bouncing freely from the metal buildings made it difficult to determine the exact direction of the sound.

The van proceeded down Bailes Lane and approached the airfield from the east; police vehicles tailing in the distance. Suddenly, before reaching the center of the field and the Airway Cafe, it turned right and entered the area between the Community College building and a series of long parallel hangars. A hundred feet beyond, the van turned left onto the runway and suddenly increased speed.

Halfway down the runway, directly in front of the cafe, the driver spotted small lights in the distance; a plane. The plane sat at the far end of the cross runway to his right. The driver pressed the break pedal. The van slid a dozen feet on the ice. In front of the Exxon station, two members of the Iwo Jima team leaped out of the van, guns at the ready. The van slipped on the ice, then accelerated directly toward the plane.

The tailing police cars entered the gate and headed toward the van, no longer keeping their presence a secret. Radios in the hidden squad cars began to vibrate with shouts of, "Where is that plane? Stop the plane! Stop that damn plane!"

Fajil eased the aircraft onto the runway. He pressed tightly on the brakes and revved the engines to full force. He could feel the added power; the militia had done its job well. The plane began to vibrate violently. Fajil's hands and feet fought to hold back the intense forward thrust.

The van reached the plane about the same time the first police car tailing them was riddled with machine gun fire from the two assassins on the field. It swerved and went crashing into another car to its right. Metal and glass flew in all directions.

Officers began returning fire as Kamile and the remaining assassins sprung from the brown van and ran toward the small plane. Kamile, Zaki, and Samir jumped through the doorway.

Lights began to flash from all directions. Police cars suddenly appeared from between the hangars both east and west of the cafe and from behind the Avemco building. Fajil tightened his grip and pushed forward on the throttles. The last assassin to enter lost his grip on the doorway and almost fell to the tarmac as the plane moved forward. He leaped into the opening, banging his knee on the metal floor.

The assassins on the ground locked sights on a police car passing the fueling station and riddled it with machine-gun fire. The car swerved crashing into a second unit approaching parallel from its left. At the same time, a fuel truck parked nearby erupted in a volcano of flame, burst open by the explosion of a thrown satchel charge. The conflagration lighted the runway like an exploding volcano. The police returned fire toward the two men standing like spectral giants in an incomprehensible setting, back-lighted by a fiery, frozen landscape. Others directed their bullets at the plane, now loaded with five of the most sought-after assassins of all time.

A fiery barrage filled the air. The aircraft roared down the runway toward the oncoming police cars. Gunfire from the vehicles was no match for the two machine guns blasting twenty rounds a second, smashing windshields and exploding side glass into the pursuing cars. Grenades were thrown in the pathway of oncoming vehicles, shattering the night with powerful concussions and puncturing the darkness with blinding flashes. A grenade was thrown into the Exxon station; the explosion ripped it apart and set it ablaze.

The plane lifted up just as it passed behind the two condemned men who were now laying a protective cover of bullets, shrapnel and flame. The plane nearly hit a runaway police car with its dying driver slumping over the wheel and its wounded passenger desperately reaching for the door.

Instantly, exploding out of the night, the incoming helicopter, Marine One, containing Secret Service agents suddenly blasted into view as it flew over the hangars from the west between the cafe and the blazing Exxon station, its powerful engines muffling the gunshots and bright spotlights illuminating the deadly scene below.

Without looking behind, the assassins on the ground, now firing their last bullets in a protective shield, raised their left arms with clenched fists to their leaders who lifted into the sky over them. It was a farewell salute to their brothers who gave them the ultimate opportunity to die as martyrs, a tribute to their lives; assurance of a better life to come.

Fajil immediately banked the plane to the left to escape fire from the police below. Suddenly, from his right, without warning he saw the blinding lights from the approaching helicopter.

The chopper swerved to the left to avoid a collision. It then banked right to pursue the plane. The passengers inside Bronco were moved violently about as the chopper maneuvered over the field.

Police on the ground fired a few shots at the helicopter before they realized what was happening. The shock in their eyes at seeing the presidential seal and the markings of Marine One was just another of the barrage of surprises they had already experienced. Their attention quickly returned to the two assassins on the ground and, in a few seconds, hammered them into the pavement.

A half-dozen determined police officers died to assure these assassins would never raise their hands in salute again. A dozen more lay seriously wounded on the concrete amid the flaming wreckage scattered about the Frederick Airport.

The fleeing plane gained altitude and speed as it attempted to escape the pursuing helicopter.

Inside the chopper, Donovan's eyes were glued to the aircraft ahead. He shouted above the roar of the engine, "Don't let them escape. Get Andrews on the radio. Find out where the hell's that fighter we asked for!"

Donovan adjusted his infrared binoculars aimed at the rapidly disappearing aircraft, listening to the pilot feed their exact location to White House Command and to Andrews.

Both aircraft were now gaining altitude and heading north into the dark winter sky.

7:25 AM, Moscow

In the Strategy Room, much was being discussed about the call to the White House. What would they do if Kilpatrick refused to speak with them? Should they aggravate a dangerous situation by actually placing their military on alert? They had already stopped all traffic through Russian air space and had reinforced the Kremlin and Parliament security. Whoever attacked Washington might also be ready to attack Moscow.

Yuri Kalingkov entered the room and stood by the president.

"Yes, Kalingkov, what is it?" Masarov asked crisply.

"We just received word from the embassy that the White House requests you not place your call as planned but wait for Kilpatrick to gather enough information to be of use in the conversation. We do not know what the reason might be, but we were asked to hold your call until we hear from them."

"I believe they are in a very difficult position." Chernosoki was the first to respond. "This Kilpatrick may be going to ask for our assistance for something. We should be careful of forcing them into anything. We do not know the American who is now burdened with this great crisis. I believe we should delay your call. To force their position would be dangerous."

"General Obidiov, what do you think this is about?" questioned Masarov.

Obidiov withheld his true opinion, determined not to say the wrong thing. Much depended on keeping his thoughts to himself, for his concerns went well beyond this crisis in the United States.

Obidiov had risen to his present high position through political pressure. He replaced Gen. Igor Dmitrievich Lizchev whose deliberate political approach to crisis made him a threat to conservatives. Lizchev was one of a select few military leaders to plan the pullout of Afghanistan and one of even fewer to mastermind the withdrawal from Eastern Europe, but he was too liberal and too old to continue in power. The men who met in Kremlin shadows discussed covert methods for returning to the old way, to be rid of Lizchev. Obidiov was one of their most influential leaders. Masarov was pressured for over a year to give this post to him. The president now considered it one of his worst appointments.

"Perhaps, they do not wish too many ears to hear what they must tell you," Obidiov replied. "I believe that everyone in leadership may have been killed. Perhaps this man Kilpatrick may not be in the White House. He might be moved to a more secure place or . . . maybe he too has been eliminated." Obidiov began to feel very proud inside for even suggesting such things. He used fear, as always, to bend others to his will. "Dead men cannot speak. He may be dead."

Masarov thought for a moment and then said, "We will wait. You may not be so wrong, general." Looking down, he repeated to himself, *you may not be so wrong, you bastard.* Masarov poured some mineral water. Everyone relaxed for a few moments; all except Anatoli Karzinski. Like Obidiov, he thought this was the time to act decisively and not wait. The American military themselves just might be responsible.

11:30 PM, the Situation Room

Phillip Page shifted in his seat, severely troubled by what they were attempting to do. He listened to the debate regarding the role of the governors, how the Russians would respond, what the media was doing and what was happening in the city. He cleared his dry throat with a short rasp cough. Clearing his throat again, slightly louder this time, he blared out, "Barry, can I say something?"

Dipaula glanced at him, "Of course."

By this time, there were eight members of the National Security Council Staff in the Situation Room. Being the only official member of the National Security Council itself, Dipaula had been declared the highest-ranking official in the White House.

Page, only one year on staff, raised his voice slightly, still looking down at his clasped hands, which were resting uneasily on the table, "Can we get the special agent in charge of the Secret Service in here, I have a question, which might help?"

"Okay, Phil. Mind telling us why?" asked Dipaula.

"I have an idea, Barry. I just want to follow it up, if you don't mind. It won't take more than a minute." Page sat upright, feeling a bit more confident.

"Okay, if you think it'll help." Dipaula was trying to keep some order to the situation. A clear idea openly expressed might lead to a solution. Even a temporary relief from the intense stress would be welcomed. Fatigue was obviously setting in. Dipaula quickly added, "Look, Phil, let's not take much time. As you know we need to work on the governors' meeting." He had respect for the staff member but could not relinquish authority to Page or anyone else in the room.

"I'll be right back. I have a few calls to make," Dipaula said as he moved to the door. "Craig, take over."

11:37 pm, The Situation Room

Van Meter entered the room. Thomas turned and said, "This is Agent Chris Van Meter. Phil what did you have in mind?"

"Chris, is there anyone available to either the Secret Service or the FBI with the ability to duplicate the voice of another person, a human synthesizer of sorts?" asked Page.

Van Meter looked at Thomas, unaware of Page's train of thought.

"Yes, sir, I believe there are such people. We don't have anyone here in the mansion; but I'm certain the CIA, NSA, and the FBI have access to such people."

Van Meter was curious about such an odd question. However, his discipline wouldn't allow a sign of concern. Trying not to let his eyes wonder from Page, he continued, "I don't know how people like that function. However, I believe they would need the person's actual voice to work from and, as I understand it, they could in turn pronounce, or duplicate, the words very closely."

"Chris, can such a duplication be detected easily?"

"Sir, I don't know much about it. There's a way to analyze a voice to determine its authenticity, but it would take some time to do. You really need the advice of an expert. I'm sorry, that's not me."

"Thank you, Chris." Thomas wasn't sure where this was leading. "You may leave now, but would you stay close by; we may need you for something very quickly. By the way, how did the press conference go upstairs with the deputy press secretary?"

"Not very good, sir; they're waiting to speak to Kilpatrick. Everyone was very understanding but rather impatient, to put it mildly, sir."

"Thank you, and please stay close by," Thomas requested as he escorted the agent to the door.

"Certainly," replied Van Meter as he moved between the special agents stationed just outside the room.

Thomas turned to Page, "Well, Phil, you've got our attention. Do something with it." He returned to his seat.

"I believe we might be able to keep the Kilpatrick story alive, so to speak, if we release a recording. We might have a way to deal with Masarov, as well."

A negative attitude filled the room like an unwanted visitor. No one smiled; it was too serious for that.

"Why do that?" asked Thomas.

"It's 11:50 PM. We believe the nation needs an elected president before morning. The governors need time and complete secrecy to make that decision. If that means deceiving everyone, so be it. The payoff is well worth the deception. You didn't seem to like my photograph idea. A counterfeit voice may help. I think it should at least be considered, if only as a last resort."

A few minutes later, Dipaula entered the room, now convinced Kilpatrick must remain "alive" until the transfer of power is complete. Surprising warmth flowed through his body as he walked to his place.

He leaned forward, hands flat on the table, and spoke with an even, calm voice, "I have, on my own responsibility as the highest-ranking official present and with your firm consensus, ordered that the governors be contacted immediately. They are to be informed of our present situation and requested to proceed immediately to . . .," glancing down to his papers, "McConnell Air Force Base, Kansas for a meeting absolutely vital to the national security of the United States. The meeting will begin at 7:00 AM Kansas time, approximately nine hours from now. Purpose of the meeting will be to elect a temporary president and vice president of the United States before noon Washington time. The meeting time and location will remain highly classified. Absence from the meeting will be the responsibility of each governor, answerable to the people of their state, the people of the United States, and their individual conscience. Only the governor is acceptable, no other state official will be admitted to the meeting. I have already taken the liberty of informing Gov. Gary Dupree of New York of the situation. He is the chairman of the National Governor's Conference and will also assist in contacting the governors regarding the meeting. Without his support, too many very difficult questions could jeopardize this meeting. Governor Dupree has agreed to the Kansas site and to contacting the governors."

Dipaula's words brought a sudden relief throughout the room like a cool breeze on a hot Louisiana day and lifted some of the burden they had carried for the past few hours. Responsibility for solving the crisis would soon be shifted to those who had the elected authority to deal with it.

While a great deal of personal relief could be felt, Dipaula knew the danger that lay ahead in the hours before the governors could act. Iran might unilaterally strike against Israel, which would bring all the Alliance countries into a state of war. He also knew, if China and Russia decided to engage the Alliance states, the world would soon plunge into a nuclear war.

Dipaula felt the heavy responsibility and the need to keep things together. "We will authorize any federal military support required. Secret Service and FBI agents in each state capital will immediately locate and visit the governor to personally discuss our specific problem. Edward Clarke and David Polchak have agreed to coordinate the effort. In the meantime, both Governor Dupree and I will personally contact the individual governors who are officers of the National Governor's Conference to serve as the Executive Committee for the proceedings." Dipaula stopped and waited for comment.

A knock interrupted the discussion. Page opened the door. It was agent Van Meter. "Mr. Page I have a possible alternative to your request, sir."

Van Meter entered the room.

"What's going on Phil?" Dipaula asked. He felt a bit offended he was not informed, not a part of every discussion, every decision. It was a strange feeling and he quickly dismissed it.

"We might have some helpful input here, Barry," Page said. "Let's hear what Van Meter has to say. Go ahead, what have you got?"

"Well, sir, I attended a nightclub act in Georgetown a few nights ago," he said to Page. "They featured a comedian who could give excellent voice impressions of everyone from Presidents Bergstrom and Clinton to Jimmy Stewart and John Wayne. He took requests from the floor and did remarkably well. He is very impromptu. I'm certain, sir, with a little practice, he could impersonate anyone you might be thinking about. If that's what you're after."

"Can you locate him in all the confusion?" Page asked. "Within the hour, I mean?"

"I don't know. I could give it a try. We will also continue to locate specialists at the FBI and CIA. However, if I might add, I believe the comedian would be more convincing and spontaneous. He's really good, sir."

Dipaula thought for a few seconds, realizing where this plan might lead, then decided to trust his instincts. "I think I see what you're after Phil. Agent Van Meter, do whatever is necessary to bring this man to us within the hour and do it in strictest secrecy. No one, not even the individual involved; no one but you must know why. Limit the number of agents who know it's happening. Do you understand our problem?"

"Yes, sir. We'll do our best." The agent gave a slight reassuring smile and left the room.

Chapter Eighteen

12:05 AM
Washington DC

Van Meter and five agents were moving through one of the tunnels between the White House and the Treasury building, heading to the Washington District Hotel just up Pennsylvania Avenue toward Georgetown. The Georgetown cabaret manager had informed them comedian Bob Caridene was staying at the District. The cabaret, along with other businesses, was closed following the explosion.

In the communications center of the White House, Dipaula was speaking in turn with the principal governors who would make up the Executive Committee at McConnell Air Force Base. He was careful not to mention Kilpatrick's death and knew Secret Service agents would give the exact details in private meetings.

The agents in charge of the Secret Service offices in each state capital were being informed of the situation by code through the special communications office in New York.

In state houses, hotels, and private homes, thirty-six governors were being informed of the situation in Washington, DC. They were asked to take the most expedient method possible to arrive at McConnell Air Force Base before 7:00 AM, Kansas time.

Four state governors were out of the country and unable to be reached with any security. The governors of the Virgin Islands and Puerto Rico were not informed, again for security reasons.

12:14 AM

The Secret Service command room beneath the White House had alerted all airfields in the flight path of the assassin's aircraft to track them on radar. Having received instructions, the Harrisburg, Pennsylvania tower had immediately focused attention toward the south. The aircraft was now on the screen.

The streets around the White House were jammed with rescue vehicles, members of the press and media. A few curious people walked the streets. However, Pennsylvania Avenue was nearly empty along the blocks immediately west of the White House toward the Washington District Hotel. A curfew had been placed on the city.

Agent Van Meter and his band approached the intersection of Pennsylvania and I Street. A red awning hung over the sidewalk in front of the Washington District Hotel. They quickly entered the doorway and walked through a very small lobby, up four steps, turned left into a smaller room containing the registration desk.

The two men behind the registration counter watching a thirteen-inch portable TV were shocked as five very imposing men in dark overcoats approached them.

"Can I help you gentlemen?" asked the clerk. The bellman remained quiet, just staring, considering a dash for the emergency exit.

Van Meter held up his identification and said in a very serious, authoritative voice, "We need Bob Caridene's room number."

"Just a moment, sir," said the clerk as he placed his hands on the keyboard. He typed several mistakes and then said, "He's in room 3728, sir; third floor up."

"Where's the elevator?" asked Van Meter.

"Around the corner to your left."

Van Meter turned to Agent Micheles and said, "Bill, stay here and ask these gentlemen to keep our visit confidential."

Turning to the clerk he said, "It's imperative Mr. Caridene does not know we are here. Please call and tell him you have received an urgent fax for him and the bellman is bringing it up now. If he says to keep it here or to read it to him, tell him he's already on his way up."

"Yes, sir." The clerk was too nervous to refuse any request from agents of the Secret Service. Especially when they looked this determined and appeared to be in the process of arresting someone in his hotel. The remaining agents followed Van Meter to the elevator. The clerk called after them, "Room 3728 will be to your right, sir. But you should be careful using the elevator. If the electricity goes out again you could get stuck."

Another agent remained outside the elevator facing the lobby. Unable to leave the city, most hotel guests were in their rooms watching the reports about the tragedy unfolding only a few miles from their hotel. Part of the city immediately adjacent to the hill had been evacuated due to the threat of radiation. However, the evacuation area was limited to avoid panic and additional congestion. Fortunately, the Washington District Hotel was not on the evacuation order.

The hotel was built in the 1930s and remodeled several times. However, the elevator still required an operator. The agents had to wait for the bellman to enter behind them. He closed the door, pushed the metal gate closed and moved the lever to the up position. The elevator began to rise.

Lying back against several pillows, his short hefty body swooping down in the cheap mattress, Caridene guzzled his third beer from the modest, scantly stocked minibar. Electricity had been restored to this area an hour before and he was now in his underwear watching the television news reports. Just like his career, things appeared to be going up in smoke all around him. Over the past few years, booze had been a fickle companion. While the first few drinks refreshed his mind with confidence the big time was just a phone call away, later drinks brought a miserable reminder that he wasn't getting any younger and time was running out on his career.

The comedian was a good-looking, divorced thirty-eight-year-old who wished he were anywhere but in the district on this night. Tonight was different, different for everyone. Bob Caridene was not in the mood for comedy tonight. He was thinking of the coincidence of being here in the nation's capital while such a tragic and historic event was taking place. Everyone knew where they were and what they were doing when Kennedy was shot and when they heard of nine eleven, this would be the same. People would forever talk about what they were doing when the Capitol exploded. He would have nothing exciting to tell them; just having a few expensive beers in a cheap hotel.

The phone rang. Caridene picked it up.

"Hello."

"Mr. Caridene, this is the front desk."

"Yes."

"Mr. Caridene, I hate to bother you, sir, but we just received an important fax for you. The bellman is bringing it up." The clerk was too nervous to deliver the message. The speaker was Agent Micheles.

"Who's it from?" asked Caridene, a bit confused, caused in part by the booze.

"Not sure, sir. The bellman will be there with the fax momentarily."

"Okay," replied Caridene with a growing sense of concern. *Shit, who would be sending me a fax tonight?* he thought, reaching for his pants.

In a few seconds, the knock came as expected. Caridene walked to the door and asked, "Yeah, who is it?"

"Mr. Caridene, this is the bellman. I have a fax for you, sir."

Caridene removed the chain lock and opened the door. Agent Van Meter placed his foot in the doorway as Caridene's eyes widened in shock. Obviously, this was not the bellman.

Van Meter held his identification to the startled man and said, "Mr. Caridene, don't be alarmed. I'm Agent Van Meter of the United States Secret Service."

Caridene was instantly paralyzed, holding tightly to the door.

Van Meter continued, "We are here on a matter of great importance and would like to speak with you."

Looking down at the identification, then further down to the foot in the doorway and then back to the agents behind Van Meter, Caridene began to recover some control, "Do I have any choice?"

"I'm afraid not," replied Van Meter with a steady authoritative voice.

"What if I say, I'll call the cops?"

"Mr. Caridene, we are the cops," countered Van Meter.

Moscow, 8:20 AM

The city awakened to the horrifying news. Russians focused intently on interruptions to normal broadcasts, urgent reports were being carried on every radio and television across the country; many now wondering what effect such a tragedy would have on their future. Without the powerful support of the United States government, would their country be thrust into a political tailspin? Would civil war or martial law drag them back in time to the dark days of communism?

12:25 AM EST

In Command Room, W16, a contingent of Secret Service officers was dealing with reports from the Capitol regarding rescue operations. Also being monitored was the chase now taking place in the skies over southern Pennsylvania.

The president's helicopter was not equipped to follow the small aircraft into the night sky. Donovan, Lawrence, Morrison, and Singleton, together with Sandra Merrall were forced to land at the closed Baltimore International Airport. Marine One would head back to the White House. The agents would need a small plane to continue the chase.

Airports along their route, including Harrisburg tower in central Pennsylvania were tracking the plane containing Fajil, Kamile, and three other assassins. In addition, an Air Force A-10 fighter from Andrews had locked on.

The A-10 was flying close by, remaining in both radar and visual contact with the small aircraft. This was not a difficult maneuver for the fighter. It had excellent maneuverability at low speeds and low altitude. Well suited for darkness, the Thunderbolt II was operating its Night Vision Imaging System; and the pilot was equipped with night vision goggles. Its bubble canopy gave Maj. Kevin Braun good visibility. His 30-mm Gatling gun could fire nearly four hundred rounds per minute if necessary. If he needed more, he could use his Sidewinder missiles. Major Braun watched the small plane as it flashed over the snow-covered fields three hundred feet below and six hundred feet ahead.

A hundred miles to the south, five Secret Service agents and one very overwhelmed comedian raced through the tunnel from the Treasury building to the White House. Caridene was nearly exhausted as he entered the basement of the residence. He was taken immediately to room W14 before being allowed to catch his breath.

Effects of the three beers were now returning as the initial shock of the last few minutes had began to wear off. He had no idea why he was now in the White House. He could have been transported by space ship to an alien planet and not have been more dumbfounded. The comedian sat in a padded green chair in a small meeting room. In front of him was an oblong table made of beautiful cherry wood. If it were made of gold, Caridene would not have noticed. Secret Service agents stood both inside and outside the door.

In a few minutes, Dipaula and Van Meter entered the room. Dipaula introduced himself; an unnecessary formality as Caridene recognized him immediately.

Dipaula explained the entire situation to the comedian who sat in an obvious stupor. "And so, Mr. Caridene, we're asking you to do something extremely important for your country."

Caridene looked up at Van Meter, then to the agent with his back to the door and finally to Dipaula. "Mr. Dipaula, you want me to try and fool the president of Russia into believing I'm Secretary Kilpatrick?"

"No," responded Dipaula. "I don't want you to try. I'm asking you to succeed in fooling him. Just to, try, as you put it, would be a dangerous misunderstanding. I'm also asking you to speak to the American press, by radio, and convince everyone around the world you are Kilpatrick."

Bob Caridene, felt a sudden dizziness come over him. He had an eerie sense of being in a bizarre dream. Taking a deep breath, unconsciously brushing his thinning hair with his left hand, he said, "Mr. Dipaula, if this is half as serious as you say, . . . damn! How much time do I have to prepare?"

"Mr. Caridene, thank you. Well, to be honest with you, we would like you to release something to the press in about an hour, at 2:00 AM. I've written some things for you to say. We'll have a dry run in forty-five minutes. If we agree it's passable, you're on. If you aren't ready at that time, we can delay a short while."

Caridene took another deep breath and let it out slowly. He forced a frail smile, raised his eyebrows in reluctant submission and said, "Where are the tapes? I'll let you know after I hear his voice. Two days wouldn't be enough, but forty-five minutes, hell, I'll try . . . well, you know what I mean."

1:27 AM, Pennsylvania

The plane containing the assassins was flying low over the fields near Lancaster, Pennsylvania, being tracked by the Harrisburg tower several hundred miles away and by the A-10 somewhere above and behind in the dark sky.

"We must land," Fajil said, his eyes focused on the ground below. "We are quickly losing fuel. The tanks have been damaged."

"Can we reach our airfield?" asked Kamile.

"If we land at any airfield now that we have been discovered, we assuredly will be met by the police."

Kamile merely nodded. Looking down in the darkness to the ground below, he asked, "Can you safely land this plane in one of those fields?"

"We will land on a road. The military aircraft will not be able to follow us." Fajil was seldom nervous. However, this was the second time in the last twenty-four hours.

The moon peered through the scattered clouds; shafts of light fell on the frozen earth several hundred feet below. Fajil looked up and back to his left. The fighter was there. The mysterious helicopter was gone, not having been seen for some time.

They flew over the Amish farms near the city of Lancaster, Pennsylvania. Fajil spotted a narrow country road, lined through the icy fields dotted by an occasional farmhouse. He circled; noticing the jet would be unable to land and no city lights were near the area. They would have time to seize a vehicle and escape before police could arrive.

Maj. Kevin Braun, in the A-10, watched the plane go into a tight circle. He spoke into his radio, "Target is circling and appears to be preparing for a landing on a small road. Our location is . . ."

The plane with James Donovan and Sandra Merrall aboard was about sixty miles behind and closing but couldn't hear the transmission. The message was relayed to the FAA plane as the wheels of Fajil's aircraft hit the pavement of the small country road, precariously bouncing from side to side. At the same time, contact was made with Pennsylvania law enforcement offices and the FBI.

The plane taxied down the narrow road, blowing a very thin layer of powdered snow in twin rooster tails making it easy for the fighter pilot to observe. Fajil eased the plane to a driveway in front of a farmhouse. The assassins jumped from the plane and raced toward the house. Time was critical. They needed to transfer to a vehicle without delay.

The jet continued to circle the area at low altitude making it impossible for anyone to sleep. For miles around, homes were filled with stirring family members, confused by the loud noise of a jet aircraft overhead. Some even suspected a storm until the same thundering noise continued to repeat itself.

Harrisburg tower was able to track the small plane down to an altitude of four hundred feet before losing it. The controller also reported the exact location of the downed aircraft to FAA and to state police.

The assassins ran up the steps of the farmhouse and burst through the unlocked door. They were confounded by the sight in front of them. Standing in the candle-lit hallway, bedroom doors on both sides, were two bearded men, three women, and two small children, all in their night clothes.

"We need a vehicle," demanded Kamile. "Where is your car?"

The oldest male replied, "We have no car." He was shaken but in control.

"Give us the keys to your car old man!" Kamile shouted as he moved forward.

Fajil grabbed his arm and said, "These people are Amish. They do not own vehicles. Is that right old man?"

"That is correct."

It was 1:37 AM; and like a strike of lightning from the heavens, the worst of the new century suddenly invaded this quiet Amish community and the assassins had picked the worst of places to set down.

Chapter Nineteen

1:44 am, EST

During the first few hours, while electricity was lost, most people in the district were unaware of the extent of the problem. When power was restored, reports of the low radiation threat and local damage estimates kept most people from panic.

Across the United States, newscasters were speaking on camera to experts who freely offered suggestions on what should be Kilpatrick's responsibilities and how order could be quickly restored. Tapes of the devastation were available to stations outside the district, produced by news teams sent in by local Virginia and Maryland stations.

Nearly every governor was now aware of the situation and it came as no surprise to them why the White House was not releasing more information. However, a few were suspicious after hearing only preliminary information regarding a secret meeting being called at McConnell Air Force Base. One such governor was Canton B. Haynes of West Virginia.

Governor Haynes was visiting relatives in Big Run, thirty miles east of Charlestown. A special agent was on his way but had not yet arrived in Big Run. Agent Ramon Vines was in his office in Charleston and on the phone with Governor Haynes.

"Mr. Vines, I realize you're calling at the request of Mr. Kilpatrick; but if you can't offer a plausible reason for such a meeting, I can assure you I'll not be present."

"Governor Haynes, the agent in charge of our Charlestown office will be with you shortly, sir. He will discuss the purpose of the meeting with you directly."

"Yes, I understand and I'll wait his explanation. However, since I can't speak directly to Kilpatrick, it'd better be a compelling reason or I'll be damned if I leave West Virginia in this time of crisis. Do you understand?"

"Yes, sir, I do."

Governor Haynes hung up the receiver and turned to his long-time and very trusted friend, Martin Husak.

"Marty, somethin's seriously wrong. It just may be possible this whole goddamn thing is a ploy ta get the governors wiped out. Shit, it may be those goddamn Arab Muslim bastards playin' us for suckers. Maybe it's the stinkin' militia. How do we know that Dipaula or even Kilpatrick himself isn't somehow involved with this conspiracy? Shit, there's no reason on God's earth to put the governors of all fifty states under one roof after what just happened over in DC."

"I don't know, Canton; maybe there's more to the explosion than we've seen on the news. Kilpatrick may have some important reason to speak to all the governors. God knows he's gonna need a lot of support. If Congress is completely wiped out, he needs the governors to get involved, and fast."

"Any case, I'm asking for additional security people to be here when the agents arrive. I don't trust anybody right now."

Haynes picked up his phone and called West Virginia National Guard Cdr. Gen. Milton Cory, and arranged a military aircraft to be ready in Charleston for a flight to an unknown location. He requested a helicopter and additional security people be sent immediately to Big Run for his transfer to Charleston. Additional state troopers were ordered to his cousin's home. After all, it was the White House that had made the request and it was Secret Service agents that were fighting the winding West Virginia hills on a cold winter night to reach him.

A similar scene was occurring in many states around the country. A number of governors were just now being reached while others had been notified an hour before. Planes now began lifting into the air and state executives from across the country were racing to attend a secret meeting on an air force base in Kansas.

9:45 PM
Sitka, Alaska

The governor of Alaska had flown often but never in a fighter like the one rushed down from the Twelfth Fighter Squadron at Elmendorf Air Force Base in Anchorage. It was essential he use the Air Force F-15 Strike Eagle. It was the only available fighter jet with two seats capable of reaching Kansas. The jet had twin Pratt Whitney engines, each capable of generating thirty thousand pounds of thrust. Since the normal weight of the jet was forty-five thousand pounds, the pilot could accelerate from idle power to maximum afterburner in only four seconds.

The F-15 eased its way out onto the Juneau Airport runway, frozen snow banks on both sides, the deep blue Mendenhall glacier off its left wing. Gov. James Warren began to pray. He was genuinely scared to death and had debated not going; telling himself it wasn't necessary for all the governors to be present and he probably wouldn't arrive in time anyway. However, his patriotism compelled him to board the aircraft, shaking to his toes, locked tightly in his flight suit. To do otherwise would have shown him a coward in the face of a national emergency, and he knew the feeling would be unbearable.

The pilot turned onto the runway and sat for a moment looking down its long path, then up into the dark sky overhead. Knowing the takeoff would be unusual for a civilian, he explained to the governor the Juneau airport was not an easy place for an F-15 to take off. The governor's lips tightened, his eyes dilated, and his knuckles turned white.

Col. Chuck Hanson continued his explanation, describing how the plane would be heading over the city of Juneau, which was surrounded on three sides by mountains. The pilot would have to take off, turn a sharp right, and immediately cut engines to prevent slamming sideways into the mountains. The plane would slowly drop for a few seconds. Then, Colonel Hanson would point the nose to the sky and kick the F-15 Strike Eagle with all she had.

The governor listened quietly to the vivid takeoff description, pleased to know what to expect, while horrified at the thought. He began to feel his stomach tighten, blood leave his head, and a slight nausea taking control.

"Are you ready, Governor?"

The governor's eyes began to widen, his body began to shake, and he realized the plane had better leave immediately before he threw up in his mask.

"Colonel, if you don't get us off the ground now, I'm getting out!" He shouted.

The pilot smiled as he eased the throttle forward, releasing the brakes. The governor's head pressed back against the head rest and his eyes glassed over as the fighter blasted down the runway, twin flames shooting out behind as it rapidly gained speed, and in one instant, shot straight up into the night air. Colonel Hanson wasn't certain of the exact words coming through his earphones, but he thought it sounded like "Soonnnnoffffaabittcchhhhhh! Hoollly shhiitttt!"

2:05 AM, Washington, DC

The microphone bank was prepared in the Communications Room. Caridene entered, escorted by Chris Van Meter. In the room with the technicians were four Secret Service agents along with Barry Dipaula, Craig Thomas, and Jerry Gannon, a friend of Secretary Kilpatrick.

Dipaula smiled empathetically toward the comedian, who was about to give the performance of his life. Caridene smiled back. Dipaula escorted him to the chair behind the desk covered with the pictures of Kilpatrick, as requested by the comedian.

"I hope these will do, Mr. Caridene," said Dipaula calmly, trying to relax the performer.

Bob Caridene was now in as much control as possible under the circumstances. "Mr. Dipaula, do you mind? I need to read the speech one more time."

"Mr. Caridene, you just let us know when you're ready. The dry run was good enough. Do the same now and we'll be fine," answered Dipaula, taking a chair opposite the comedian.

After rereading the script, Caridene sat up straight, closed his eyes for about thirty seconds, cleared his throat and then looked at Dipaula. "This would be easier if you hadn't been so wordy." He took another deep breath and nodded, "I'm as ready as I'll ever be. Let's go."

Dipaula returned the nod and waited. A technician adjusted his earphones then spoke quietly into his attached microphone, "Let's do it." A few seconds, after the stations had been interrupted and they were live from the White House, the technician pointed to Dipaula, saying in a nervous whisper, "Go!"

Dipaula then nodded reassuringly to the comedian.

Caridene took a deep breath and began, "My fellow Americans, I am Secretary of the Interior James Kilpatrick. This is truly a moment of deep tragedy for us all. Reports indicate that President Bergstrom and members of his cabinet may have fallen at the hands of assassins. I now may be the sole remaining member of the president's cabinet. The Constitution places responsibility for the high office of president upon me through the line of succession. The oath of office is not at present required for me to act in this capacity. I, therefore, will not take the oath of office until it has been determined, beyond reasonable doubt, that President Bergstrom, Vice President Borland, the Speaker of the House, and my fellow members of the cabinet are, in fact, lost. I have now legitimately directed all necessary action to protect the security of the United States and to maintain order. Our military is prepared, standing ready, and vigilant. With the assistance of local officials and law enforcement, order is being rapidly restored to the District of Columbia and throughout the area."

Caridene was doing an excellent job. His voice was a bit shaky at times, but this was acceptable; Kilpatrick would be under great stress. He continued, "I have also requested counsel and support from the governors of the states to assist me in this time of crisis."

"There does not appear to be a threat to the security of the United States nor does there appear to be a greater conspiracy. I ask you, my fellow Americans, to pray for me and for our country. Our hearts go out to the families of those who perished this evening while in service of not only the United States but many foreign governments as well. Let all of us face the hours ahead with the same strength and determination with which Americans have always faced disaster, . . . with courage, conviction, and faith in God. I appeal to your good judgment and request your calm, controlled, and prayerful support. Good night, and may God bless us in this time of grave affliction and bitter test."

Caridene pulled back from the mic, sweat beading on his forehead.

Dipaula leaned forward and took over. "This is National Security Advisor Barry Dipaula. Secretary Kilpatrick has done an exemplary job in bringing order not only to our domestic circumstance, but he has given great assurance to leaders in other countries." It was the first time he placed himself directly in the spotlight. "We have been in direct contact with President Masarov of Russia, Premier Lee Pong of China, President Valasione of France, the secretary general of the United Nations, Prime Minister Thomas King of Great Britain, and with many heads of state throughout the world. All agree, the world is not in an immediate state of crisis as a result of what has happened here in Washington. We are not in immediate danger of war nor do I believe we are in immediate danger of further assassinations. It is our belief this act was singular in nature and isolated, directed only at the Capitol. As you may know, there have been a number of terrorist incidents reported in various parts of the country. We suspect that local extremist groups have taken advantage of the tragedy here in the Capitol to attempt to cause hysteria among us. But they will not prevail. Local officials have done an excellent job in handling the incidents and limiting their effects. While the situation is in control here in Washington, we all acknowledge that we have many difficult hours and days ahead. I will speak with you again in a few hours when we should have further information to share. It is our hope to be able to call a press conference later this morning. Once again, our country is in no immediate danger and we have already begun the painful recovery process on Capitol Hill. We should know more in a few hours. Thank you."

The technician waited for ten seconds to insure the White House deputy press secretary was speaking and then looked at Dipaula and nodded, "We're off. But please, gentlemen, walk out of the room before talking, just in case."

Dipaula stood, closed his eyes briefly, and took a deep breath. Craig Thomas walked over to Caridene. Thomas stood patiently, then Caridene looked up at him, fear in his eyes. As they walked through the door into the hallway, Caridene, asked, "How was it?"

Thomas looked at Gannon, and asked, "What do you think, Jerry?"

Gannon smiled, placed his hand on Caridene's shoulder and replied, "You did just fine. I think even I would have been convinced. Anyway, it was good enough to satisfy people for a few necessary hours."

Alex Bernard sat in his car parked in front of the damaged Air and Space Museum. Bernard was a reporter for the Washington Post and had been so for more than a dozen difficult years. He knew everyone in town and had the dirt on most of them. He was trying to visualize what his ears had just heard, but Kilpatrick's face was not materializing. *What the shit?* he thought. *What's wrong with that broadcast? Kilpatrick's voice? Reminds me of someone else; but who?*

The White House

Caridene, Gannon, and Dipaula reentered the communications room and walked over to the familiar table. No one spoke. Caridene sat in front of the red phone, a technician next to him on his right, Dipaula to his left.

Dipaula turned his chair slightly toward the comedian and after a few seconds said, "Now, Bob, this call will be short. You've read the general script. Look it over again and let me know when you're ready. There are two things to keep in mind. One, don't let him engage you in small talk. And two, don't stay on for more than one minute. No more than sixty seconds. Do you understand?"

Caridene nodded and wiped the sweat beads from under his nose. He closed his eyes for a second and thought, *Where the hell am I? Shit, an hour ago I was in a small hotel room minding my own business, having a beer, scratching my ass, a miserable two bit comedian, looking for a chance at the big time. Now I'm sitting in the White House, the damn White House for Christ's sake, impersonating the president of the United States and getting ready to talk to the president of Russia. This isn't for real. Holy shit! One hour from watching a disaster on television to being in the center of it. Damn, when people ask me what I was doing the night of the big explosion, will I have a story for them. Hell, it won't matter. They'll probably kill me for what I'm doing.*

Dipaula continued, "Once you feel comfortable that you understand the script, please give it to me. You must appear completely spontaneous. Being nervous is not a problem. However, you must flow with the conversation."

Caridene looked around the room containing a dozen people. He leaned over to Dipaula and whispered, "I've had three beers and two cups of horrible coffee tonight and my brain is swimming in piss again. Any chance I can go to the rest room?"

Dipaula smiled and told Agent Van Meter to escort Caridene to the men's room.

After returning, Bob Caridene, a third-rate American comedian, began the final preparations for what would be his greatest performance.

After a few minutes of silence, Caridene uttered, "Okay, let's do it."

Dipaula nodded toward the technician who immediately placed the direct line to Moscow.

Chapter Twenty

Moscow, 10:20 am
Near the Strategy Room

General Anatoli Karzinski, aid to President Masarov, picked up the receiver, "This is General Karzinski."

"General, this is Barry Dipaula. Mr. Kilpatrick would like to speak with President Masarov, if possible."

"Yes, Mr. Dipaula, he is here. One moment please."

President Masarov was called to the small room. He sat at the desk and took the phone from Karzinski.

"This is President Masarov."

"Mr. Masarov, this is Barry Dipaula, sir. I have Mr. Kilpatrick here for you. According to our Constitution he now has authority of the president of the United States."

"Thank you, Mr. Dipaula. I understand."

Dipaula handed the phone to Bob Caridene who had photographs of Secretary Kilpatrick in front of him next to photos of Masarov.

As he took the phone from Dipaula, Caridene sat up straight and spoke clearly, with some authority, "Mr. Masarov, this is Sec. Jim Kilpatrick. This is our first opportunity to speak. I apologize for not being able to have a word with you earlier."

"Mr. Kilpatrick, I have deep sorrow for the great tragedy which has taken place in your country. It is my hope that you will know the Russian government considers this to be a global tragedy."

"Thank you, Mr. Masarov. We have not been able to clearly determine responsibility, but we shall do so as quickly as possible."

"Yes."

Twenty seconds had passed. Only forty remained. No small talk.

"Mr. Masarov, I'm certain you understand there is extremely pressing business here, which must be dealt with immediately. If you will allow me, I will call you in the morning to brief you in detail. We may have significant matters to discuss at that time."

"Yes, I do understand, Mr. Kilpatrick. Do you have any unilateral concerns aimed at our region of the world in response to this crisis?"

Forty seconds, and only twenty to go.

"Mr. Masarov, I really must go. Other United Nations Security Council members are awaiting our calls. In the morning we will have a better picture of what has taken place. I hope you will also allow me to get back to pressing matters and wait a few hours for us to gather data."

Dipaula held up the notes for the comedian to see, pointing to one note in particular.

Caridene nodded and then continued, "Be assured, Mr. Masarov, we are in control of both the military and the government. There is no question of leadership here either by the military or the government and the transfer of essential power and authority has already taken place. I ask that you do whatever you can to influence Iran and keep them in restraint."

"Yes, Mr. Kilpatrick, I understand. I will do my best. However, we are somewhat concerned of the status of your military. During this time of confusion, this enormous crisis, will anything be done without your orders? This is of great concern."

One minute and ten seconds. The technician was getting nervous. Too much time and Caridene might slip or the Russians would have more than enough tape for a routine security clerk to analyze the voice pattern for everything from sincerity to anxiety level to authenticity. It might take time for them to retrieve original voice prints; but in this crisis, everything would move faster than normal.

"I assure you, Mr. Masarov, I have authority and control here." Caridene's heart was racing, fully aware he was taking too much time. "The military is acting on my orders. You can be assured that no one here will act without my explicit instructions. While a full transfer of authority has not officially taken place, our military will not act without my instructions. I'm sorry, Mr. Masarov, but I must leave you now. I will call you in the morning."

One minute and thirty seconds had passed. The technician was starting to move in his seat. He was not willing to risk telling Caridene to get off the line. If Dipaula was leaving the comedian alone, so was he.

"Yes, Mr. Kilpatrick," Masarov wanted to learn as much as possible. "I—"

"Mr. Masarov, I am sorry, but I truly must go. Good-bye, sir, and I will speak with you in a few hours."

"Yes, of course, Mr. Kilpatrick. I hope that your country will take the sound course in this moment of tragedy and, I must add, global crisis."

"Thank you, Mr. Masarov, and good-bye." The impersonator handed the receiver to Dipaula who listened for a moment and heard the final, "Good-bye, Mr. Kilpatrick."

It was done.

After Dipaula placed the receiver in its cradle, the room remained absolutely silent. Technicians stared at Bob Caridene who sat frozen, face in his hands, elbows on the table.

Dipaula put his right hand on Caridene's shoulder, "Some day, Bob, you will know how important that call really was. You may have just earned your place in the secret files of history. For now, you have only our thanks and admiration. You did an incredible job. I'm sorry to ask; but we would like you to stay here, at least until sometime tomorrow."

Caridene looked over at Dipaula and merely said, "Right now, I need that rest room again." Everyone laughed. It was the most comforting laugh he had ever received from the most appreciative audience he ever had.

2:35 AM

In the Situation Room, Dipaula reported the newscast and phone call appeared to be successful and that forty-three governors were now informed and should be on their way to McConnell Air Force Base, Kansas.

"I believe, ladies and gentlemen," Dipaula poured himself another cup of coffee, "that soon this thing will be out of our hands, thank God. I have alerted General Bradley that the governors are on their way to McConnell Air Force Base where they will be voluntarily sequestered."

"You know, Barry," interrupted Jerry Gannon, "this sounds like an American version of the College of Cardinals." A weak smile as he added, "All we need is white smoke when the president's elected."

"You're not far-off," acknowledged Dipaula. "We expect all the governors to be present between 6:00 AM and 7:00 AM Kansas time. Not bad if it works. What we need to do now is—"

A loud buzz on the intercom from the White House Staff.

Dipaula pushed the button.

It was Special Agent Mary Simons. Her voice was obviously shaken, as she said, "Mr. Dipaula, you asked for an update. We've just received reports of additional violence; this time at federal buildings in Boise, Cheyenne, and Jackson, Mississippi, sir. In addition, an Amtrak rail has been destroyed outside Reno, Nevada. A power station was hit near Raleigh, North Carolina. FBI and local law enforcement have taken militia groups into custody in a dozen other places." She paused, then, "Oh, yes, there's a shootout now taking place outside Montgomery, Alabama. We're not sure how serious that is."

"Damn!" Dipaula said as he gritted his teeth.

"Look's like a war has started," Dansie said to no one in particular.

"Shit," whispered Cassett as she sat back in her seat. "The ignorant bastards."

People in the room looked at each other in a strange mix of confusion and depression. Things were rapidly falling apart.

Dipaula thanked Simons, clicked off and turned back to the people seated around the table, "Right now, that's no concern of ours. Shake it off. We can't focus on outside issues. Law enforcement will deal with the militia. We have our hands full here."

They were exhausted, but none more than Bob Caridene. He was taken to a small office next to the Situation Room for rest and security. He might be needed to perform again before the crisis was over.

2:40 AM
Near Lancaster, Pennsylvania

As the fighter blasted overhead once again, animals stirred and moved about in a dozen barns scattered along the countryside. It could take four or five miles for the fighter to make a low pass. While they could see and hear the jet, it was difficult for the local police to identify the exact area where the assassins had landed. The fighter relayed the exact location, but most of the police cruisers lacked the technology to make use of his coordinates.

Major Braun was making one of his last flyovers, when the first patrol car arrived. The cruiser stopped several hundred yards from the small plane, now icing over in the frigid wind, forty feet from the farmhouse. The A-10 buzzed the house then flew off into the darkness.

2:42 AM

From the newsrooms of the major networks and cable stations, Kilpatrick's statements were being broadcast worldwide. A photograph of the rather unknown secretary was being displayed on millions of TV screens while the voice transmission of his brief speech was on the air in over a hundred languages. The man who had worried about not having his place in history, was suddenly given a bright spotlight on a worldwide stage.

Following the address, US experts were called in to analyze his statement. They were repeating once again words from the Constitution related to the line of succession. Interviews were being broadcast with law professors, former congressional and cabinet members, military generals, law enforcement officers, disaster relief and rescue specialists, representatives of foreign governments, terrorist specialists, and any other specialist available.

Not many people in the United States had gone to sleep before President Bergstrom had started his address. Only a relative few had remained unaware of the amazing, historic events which were now taking place. In a few hours, they would encounter an ironic twist of fate; they would awake to a nightmare far more frightening than any experienced while they slept.

Moscow, 10:50 AM

The question being discussed around the table in the Strategy Room at the Kremlin related to a possible rebellion taking place within the United States.

Gen. Maxim Obidiov was speaking, "I know a little of this General Bradley. His records indicate he was assigned to the White House advisory staff for two years. During that time, he could have masterminded a coup and prepared himself for duty aboard the aircraft, Skywatch, for this very moment. Also, he is a friend with Gen. Jake McCloud, who we believe is presently the ranking military officer at the Pentagon. McCloud is a most ambitious man. I believe him capable of any action, which would offer him greater power."

Alexai Chernosvitov entered the room and took his seat. Obidiov glanced intently at him and continued with his scenario. "McCloud is a complex, threatening, and troublesome man. He would be difficult to deal with. But it was Bradley who placed the military on alert immediately after the explosion. I believe he could be involved. Perhaps even Kilpatrick, now the most powerful man in the United States, could be involved as well."

Chernosvitov reset his earpiece and stood up suddenly, his voice steady and firm, shocking the room, "President Masarov, may we speak in private?"

Masarov looked deep into Chernosvitov's eyes. Pushing his chair away from the table, the president stood without saying a word and followed his trusted friend out of the room to a nearby office.

"What is it, Alexai?" asked Masarov.

"You have spoken with Kilpatrick. While his words are of little importance, the sound of his words has proven to be significant. We have reason to believe the man you spoke with may not be Kilpatrick."

"What?"

"We have analyzed his voice patterns and compared them to recordings of Kilpatrick's voice. Our preliminary analysis indicates there is no match."

The Russian president could feel the emotional pain deep in his chest. Masarov thought to himself, *What is Chernosvitov saying? Was Obidiov right? Is there really a military coup taking place inside the United States? Has the military or National Militia actually taken charge?*

"Chernosvitov does the voice impression of Dipaula match the real Dipaula? He would most likely be an essential part of any revolt and appears to be the spokesman. Recheck the voice, then contact me immediately."

Chernosvitov said nothing, waiting for Masarov to continue.

After a few seconds, Masarov asked, "Could the White House be taken over by the military?"

The minister of security answered, "Yes, reports from the embassy indicate the building is like an armed fortress. It appears the military may have taken over. However, one cannot be sure. We have already checked and all indications are that Dipaula is for real."

"Let us keep this disturbing news to ourselves. It would be a very dangerous weapon at this critical time," the president warned.

All eyes were on Masarov as he entered the room and took his seat at the head of the table. He looked down at the papers in front of him and, after a few seconds, raised his head and said, slowly and calmly, "Chernosvitov, get the embassy on the phone and tell them to meet immediately with Dipaula. If he refuses, then get Kilpatrick on the phone. I will speak with him once again; directly with him."

Obidiov, suspecting something was seriously wrong and now feeling more confident he was correct, looked at Masarov and asked, "What if they both refuse?"

Masarov moved his head slowly to his military advisor and replied, "Should they both refuse, General, I will instruct you to immediately place our military on full alert and be prepared to aim your weapons toward the Alliance states, and . . ." he hesitated, . . . "toward your targets in China. But," he quickly added so all could hear, "you will not do so until I, personally, give you the order!"

Complete awareness penetrated each man in the room. This could well be the most dangerous moment in history, the beginning of the end. No one could imagine this scenario, not since the eighties. If a country as powerful as the United States were in the hands of a renegade military force, perhaps influenced by the militia movement, then anything would be possible, even total destruction of the planet. They would control the greatest nuclear arsenal and military might in the world and pose a serious threat to the entire planet.

Masarov lowered his head again and thought to himself, *why now? Why now?*

Chapter Twenty-One

3:11 AM, White House Communications Room

Barry Dipaula was speaking with Governor Hollis of Texas, who was about to depart for McConnell.

Sgt. Kerri Daniels, White House special operator, interrupted Dipaula. "Mr. Dipaula, the Russian embassy is on the line. They say it's critical they speak with you, sir."

"Governor, I have to run. Please contact me if I can be of any assistance. We have an open line to Kansas. They're making all necessary arrangements and security will be very tight. We need a president before noon our time, Governor. Do whatever you can to meet that deadline."

"Thank you, Mr. Dipaula, we will." The governor hung up the receiver.

The national security advisor turned to the special operator and said, "Connect them."

"Hello, this is Barry Dipaula."

"Barry, this is Mikhail Igmanov here."

"Yes, Misha, why are you calling? They said it was critical."

"Yes, well, Barry, it is. You see it has become quite necessary for us to have a meeting as soon as possible."

"Misha, I told you we are extremely busy here. We have no time for meetings with anyone outside the White House. Besides, Masarov has spoken to Kilpatrick and they agreed to remain in control, not to overreact, have additional discussions in the morning; just a few hours from now."

"Yes, well, Barry, it does appear that Mr. Kilpatrick said just such a thing. Well, we are, uh, long time friends. Surely, you will understand when I tell you, well, it is not a request. My government has listened quite intently to every word and inflection spoken by Mr. Kilpatrick. It is now insisting that you and I meet immediately."

"Misha, I—"

"Or, I will be forced to ask you, well, rather difficult questions about Mr. Kilpatrick over this telephone, one, which we both suspect has many ears."

Dipaula thought to himself, *the conversation between Masarov and the impersonator had taken place only an hour ago. Now the Kremlin is insisting on a face-to-face meeting. They've analyzed the voice and must know that Kilpatrick was not on the phone. They must have checked the voice patterns. Shit! Why do they have to be so goddamn efficient? Their plumbing doesn't work, their telephones don't work, for Christ's sake their people don't even work. But their goddamn voice analyzer does. Shit!*

"Okay, Misha. We can meet, if you insist." Thinking for a few seconds, he continued, "Can you recall the morning we met by accident while you were with the ambassador and I was with Congressman Emerson? The day I was jogging and you made the remark about my fitness?"

"Yes, of course. You were finding it difficult to breathe, if I recall. I hope that is not the case now, my friend." He was tempted to comment on Kilpatrick's ability to breathe as well but thought that would be too injudicious.

"I will meet you there thirty minutes from now. And Misha, we cannot speak freely if you are a walking transmitter. Please do not compromise our discussion."

Dipaula knew Igmanov would remember the location of that meeting. He never forgot anything. That's why he was head of the elite corps of the Ministry of Security and why he was trusted at the Kremlin, even beyond the Russian ambassador himself. While they only met on rare occasions, they knew everything about the other. When you study a person as much as they had each other, a special bonding takes place.

If they knew Kilpatrick was not on the phone with Masarov, they would assume he was dead. That would surely panic the Russians. Shit, the hardliners might overthrow Masarov and move against Central Asia. He had to calm them until the governors elect a new president. But that wouldn't be for another eight to ten hours, at best. Anything could happen in that long span of time, and probably would.

3:20 AM, Washington, DC

Reporter Alex Bernard had taken brilliant notes of the rescue operations at the Capitol and was heading toward the White House using a myriad of side streets to avoid roadblocks. As he proceeded down E Street toward St. Dominic's between Sixth and Seventh, he was listening to a repeat broadcast of Kilpatrick's address to the nation. When it was completed, Bernard felt a sick feeling in his stomach.

He drove down Maine Street past the waterfront restaurants. That voice. He had heard Kilpatrick on a number of occasions and it sounded like him, but—something was strange.

His car was going under the Fourteenth Street tunnel when, like an unexpected jolt, it hit him. He almost lost control of his car. His head jerked involuntarily. His eyes widened. It was Kilpatrick's voice which had confused him. It was curiously familiar. Damn, it sounded like that comedian. What was his name? The one Bernard had seen two nights before in Georgetown. What the hell was his name? "Caridene ... Bob Caridene," he said aloud, alarming himself. "That funny shit. No ... no, there's no way. Why? Why does it sound like Caridene?" *Why?* he thought. Again, he said out loud, "You dumb shit! That's ludicrous. The stress must be getting to me."

He continued down side streets, his mind trying to confront what he had voiced aloud. A dumb thought. But just in case, he turned his car west and headed toward the Lincoln Memorial and the Kennedy Center on his way to Georgetown.

Barry Dipaula and three Secret Service agents moved through one of the tunnels leading to the Treasury building. They entered the building and went up two flights of stairs to the south entrance.

There, four other men who would act as cover joined them. The door opened and the eight men walked out onto the concrete entryway used earlier by Agent Van Meter and the comedian impersonator, Bob Caridene.

Once outside the entryway, they proceeded across Van Buren Drive to the small park on the opposite side. It was cold and dark. Only a few rescue vehicles and police cars were moving about. The military was now in the city protecting the capitol area and the White House. The hour of the day didn't lend itself to a full scale martial law such as the one following the assassination of Dr. Martin Luther King. It would come at daybreak.

Military guards were posted around the area, some in the park. They knew the men exiting the Treasury Building were government agents.

The eight men walked to the center of the park and then split, two in one direction, three in another, and three in yet another. Dipaula and his two Secret Service escorts went across Fifteenth Street toward the mall.

It was 3:45 AM and time to meet with Igmanov. They walked quickly down Fifteenth and crossed Constitution where four men were waiting near the Old River Gate building. The small stone building was used as a watch gate in the early nineteenth century. It was here that Igmanov and Ambassador Tarasavitch had seen Dipaula jogging.

The Russians were waiting when Dipaula and his protection arrived. The Americans walked up to the Russians. Dipaula extended his hand to Igmanov. The two shook and immediately turned to walk along Constitution. The mix of American and Russian agents followed them; Americans behind Dipaula and Russians behind Igmanov.

The moon was breaking through thin clouds and a cold wind had begun to blow softly across the mall. The sight entranced each of the men now walking slowly up Constitution.

The Capitol, lit by portable floodlights, glowed like an apparition in the night, a broken white memorial over the crushed bodies lying deep inside. Half-dozen helicopters hovered over the scene, searchlights illuminating the rubble below, emergency lights flashed like strobes on broken walls. Hundreds of rescue workers were scattered among huge pieces of white granite, like ants over a broken cube of sugar. Police, emergency aid, and military vehicles packed the streets in all directions, lights flashing, speakers blaring. The building looked like something on a Hollywood set, an illusion, a figment of the imagination. However, what was happening both on the hill and down the mall near the Washington Monument was very real indeed.

Igmanov was first to speak, "Barry, thank you for coming. Well, uh, I believe you know why Masarov insisted on this meeting."

"No, I don't know, Mikhail, why?" They continued walking but didn't look at each other. Both were staring down the mall toward the Capitol.

Suddenly, Igmanov stopped and turned to Dipaula. The escorts closed a short distance behind. The two men faced each other. The mood suddenly turned serious.

"Barry, we know that Mr. Kilpatrick is not in charge at the White House."

Igmanov was bluffing. He knew the voice was not Kilpatrick's, but he didn't know who was in charge at the White House. As always, he was searching.

Dipaula wasn't about to bring anything to the conversation until it was clear what Igmanov knew and what he merely suspected.

"Mikhail, perhaps you should get to the point. What does the Kremlin want? Surely, it's not to have you and me walk around in the cold night and play cat and mouse. We're friends now; it's not like the old days."

"Yes, well, you are very correct. Barry, President Masarov takes your masquerade as more than a personal insult; he considers it an insult to our country. Masarov believes the deception is part of a larger conspiracy. The situation poses a substantial threat to our country and to world peace and he is prepared to commit the military might of Russia and its allies if you do not immediately and satisfactorily explain the true situation at the White House. The question is, my friend, who is in charge of both your military and your government?" Igmanov didn't mix words. He was ordered to be firm and direct, and he was.

While not knowing how much the Russians actually knew, Dipaula realized he could not lie; Igmanov would know. Taking a deep breath, he decided to tell him the truth about Kilpatrick and in so doing risked destroying the hard-won stability between the two nations.

McConnell Air Force Base, Kansas

It was 2:30 AM central time, 3:30 AM in the east; six hours since the tragedy on Capitol Hill. The military base was teeming with activity. The meeting room chosen for the governors was in the middle of the base, just below the Officer's Club. This allowed for sufficient meeting rooms, refreshments, and the necessary security.

A command post had been set up to track the governors' arrival and to coordinate their transportation to the Officer's Club. None of the governors had yet arrived, although several were expected before 3:00 AM.

The base was closed to civilians and state police were guarding the roadways to the airport. No traffic was allowed in the area unless it was related to the incoming visitors. Due to the hour, most locals had no idea what was taking place in their small community, nor its relationship to the catastrophe in DC.

While the enlisted personnel had no real knowledge of who was responsible for this high level of security, nor why all of this was happening; most assumed it was in some way related to the situation in Washington. Some of the troops even speculated that Kilpatrick himself was being brought here for protection.

Only the top brass knew the real reason for the drama unfolding in this relatively unknown base in Kansas.

Security of the nation and, perhaps even the world, was about to be determined by the people arriving in the dark of night.

3:56 AM, Washington, DC

Igmanov walked next to Dipaula and listened to the series of events covering the last twenty-four hours being slowly and carefully described to him. Even after Dipaula finished, they continued to walk in silence. Soon both men stopped simultaneously, as if by signal, and turned to face each other.

"Barry, are you telling me that no one in the leadership of your government has survived?"

Barry Dipaula knew he had gone beyond the point of no return, believing President Bergstrom would have done the same. Now, this one Russian knew the nation's critical secret. What would he do with it?

"Yes, Misha, they're all gone. However, as you know, it's often the appointed staff that runs the everyday business of government. We both know that's a curse as well as a blessing. When you have a truly democratic bureaucracy, you will understand more clearly."

They turned and began to walk back down Constitution toward Stone Gate. Dipaula, with his hands joined behind his back, and Igmanov, with his hands in his coat pockets.

"What will your government do now, Misha?" asked Dipaula.

"I don't know, my friend. How long do you think the governors will need to elect a new president?"

"Hard to say; but we don't have a lot of time. If Iran and North Korea follow through on their threats, we may not have enough time. The governors were told we needed to have someone elected before noon our time. That won't be easy. We're not certain yet if this is even going to be legal under our constitution. We don't even know how it will be done. But I think it will work, get us through the next few months."

"Yes, well, again, are you certain all your leaders have been killed in the explosion?"

"Indications are that no one is alive up there. We must assume that to be true. The new president will be a president pro-temp for a short time with, we believe, necessary power given any president. He won't take the oath of office until we are certain of the extent of the loss, but he will be in charge."

Igmanov stopped once again and turned to Dipaula. He knew how much this man had revealed to him, how vulnerable he now was, how vulnerable they both were.

"Barry, do you think your military will take control?" Igmanov continued. "President Masarov is very concerned about this possibility."

"Misha, most of our military leadership is unaware of the extent of our situation. They are following the orders of their commanders and the person they believe to be Secretary Kilpatrick. They will be told the moment a new president is selected by the governors. We have asked the most senior generals of all branches of our military to stand by and await further instructions. I am convinced they will follow the wishes of the governors."

Igmanov looked Barry Dipaula directly in the eye and said with more than a slight touch of ridicule, "You are convinced? You are convinced, my friend?"

Igmanov did not take his eyes from their mark. "What you and I believe your generals will do is of little consequence. What they will in fact do, is of great consequence. And what our generals believe and do may be of even greater consequence. There are great forces at work in my country, as you know; people who want to return to the old ways. The contested areas are many, my friend, and the dangers are very real. Some diseases are often contagious and spread rapidly. Our concern is that whatever has afflicted you will emerge within our own country very soon."

Dipaula nodded his head in agreement and merely said, "Obidiov?"

"Yes. You have McCloud, we have Obidiov, and others. Barry, the situation in my country is far worse than perhaps even you know. May I bare my soul as you say? We are allowed to have a soul now, you know."

"Of course." A slight smile.

Igmanov took a deep breath and taking Dipaula by the arm, turned and began walking, "You have revealed much to me. I will do the same. You certainly are aware of most of what I will say, I know that. Following the breakup of the Soviet Union and withdrawal of our army from parts of Europe, we had . . . well . . . nearly five million men in our military, most within the borders of Russia. We had no way to accommodate or feed them. Many of the officers who had lived the good life in Berlin, Prague, and elsewhere were now forced to live in tents or with their families. We had five million men with basically no place to live. In the early nineties, there was a very strong move to form an alliance of military officers; a union of sorts. However, during the end of the last century, our country found new wealth in our oil and gas fields. Life became good for most of our citizens. The military union went into a sort of hibernation. When Yeltsin was gone, the hard-liners saw a new opportunity. They began to move more openly during Putin's time and had some influence on him as you know. This influence grew when the price of oil and gas began to drop and as our standard of living dropped with it. When Masarov came to power, things changed. He decided to develop new oil and gas fields in the difficult regions in the arctic. Masarov set them back once again with his reforms. They became committed to getting rid of him. Well, last year that military alliance was fueled by the old men who once lived the good life at home, including some of my former colleagues from the KGB. With the anti-American, antidemocratic movement growing stronger every day, some of our generals have convinced others in high places that now is the time to return to the old order. Their comrades from the Ukraine and other republics of the old soviet empire are moving with them. Masarov's acceptance of the financial support from your country was too much for these desperate men."

The two men, followed by their security escorts, walked solemnly down the sidewalk toward the Lincoln Memorial. The lighted Capitol, with rescue helicopters and crews of disaster relief specialists, glowed in the distance behind them.

Igmanov continued, "A few months ago, there was a meeting held near the Black Sea. This group of men decided the mistakes of the nineties would not be repeated. The plan they had worked on for years was updated and their patience was growing rather thin. The crisis in Central Asia, caused by the Alliance of terrorist states, presented an opportunity to make Masarov look weak. The Chinese attacking us at our border in response to our, shall I say, delaying, our energy shipments to them was perhaps the final straw. The plan is very well structured my friend. President Bergstrom's decision, and I assume you participated, to give us a large loan, set back their plan. However, things have changed in the last few hours. And the situation you have described to me at this moment is just the situation they have waited for. If they realize that you have no leadership, they will assume no one will move against them nor come to the aid of Masarov. I am certain they will execute their plan. I have no doubt that if they learn of the situation tonight, tomorrow they will move against our government. This time, unlike the last time against Yeltsin, the army, and perhaps many of the people, will be fully behind the takeover. Within hours, our world could be moved back more than twenty years."

The wind began to blow. Both men buttoned their heavy black coats.

"Most Americans do not fully understand my country, Barry." The Russian continued. "You realize how situations can quickly reverse. The inability of democracy to fully work in my country has led to many problems with the people. These men can succeed. I do not doubt that, my friend; and you should not either."

Both men stopped. Igmanov took a handkerchief from his pocket and blew his reddened nose. His eyes betrayed his distress. "The generals of the world are the dangerous ones," he said. "Bureaucrats often play their senseless mind games, but generals . . . generals are trained to kill, to act quickly, and decisively."

Dipaula understood immediately what Igmanov was saying. He looked back at the agents escorting them, determined they had heard none of the conversation.

Dipaula looked again at the one man who headed the most powerful unit of Russian security in the United States, a man with a voice to the president of Russia. Igmanov was also looking casually at the escorts.

The national security advisor said in a quiet whisper, "I understand your situation. Of course, there is nothing I can do to help. You now hold the important information that is known only by a few people. Hopefully, Masarov and Chernosvitov will not reveal the truth about Kilpatrick to a wider circle. Both of our countries face serious consequence if the information is misused. With Bergstrom gone, Masarov must stay in control until we elect a new president. Do you know our saying, Misha, 'the ball is in your court'?"

Igmanov smiled weakly and nodded. He took a deep breath, turned, then looked back to Dipaula and said, "I believe you have another saying, my friend, 'Up the creek without a paddle.'" They both smiled an anxious, deeply concerned smile. His escorts followed, as Igmanov turned and walked away.

4:05 AM, Washington, DC

While the meeting between Barry Dipaula and Mikhail Igmanov was concluding, reporter Alex Bernard was heading to the nightclub in Georgetown. His mind whirled with questions; *was the voice of Kilpatrick really the voice of Bob Caridene? Shit, if this was true. Good God!*

He stopped his car in front of the Georgetown Cabaret Club. As suspected, it was closed. Every place in town was closed. The electricity was still off in some of the district, but not in Georgetown. However, it was late and most people were either out of town or at home watching the television news reports. The area was deserted.

Bernard picked up his car phone and called his office. After a few attempts, he connected asking that someone locate the name and telephone number of the owner of the club. He lit a cigarette and drove slowly around the area waiting for the reply.

Chapter Twenty-Two

3:42 AM, The Amish Countryside

The Amish family looked out the window of their farmhouse as the police officers walked out into the dark night. On the narrow road in front of their house were seven police cars with red and blue lights swirling, four from the sheriff's office and three from the Pennsylvania Highway Patrol. Many more were on the way—many more.

The area was being surrounded in an attempt to keep the fugitives confined and away from any city where escape would be more probable. After pushing the small aircraft out of the way, police vehicles moved from the narrow roadway. All eyes then looked to the sky.

Within minutes, two tiny pinpoints of light appeared above the distant horizon to the east and steadily enlarged into bright powerful beacons. As the roar of the engines intensified, the oncoming plane dropped out of the sky on a direct course for the flares lining the roadway. It descended rapidly before impacting hard on the pavement, jarring violently, swerving, its brakes squealing, nearly hitting a police cruiser before coming to a stop near a small ditch running alongside the road.

The door of the FAA plane opened and James Donovan, Sandra Merrall, Linnet Singleton, Gregg Lawrence, and Charlie Morrison stepped out. They walked directly to the police officers assembled near the farmhouse. Two law enforcement officers were waiting for them.

"Donovan?" asked the lieutenant, reaching out his hand.

"Right."

"I'm Jeff Myhre; sheriff's department. That pilot made a hell of a landing, sir."

"He'll never do it again with me on board," replied Donovan with a nervous grin.

"I'm Sergeant Fowler, state patrol. Must be some pretty important characters to take that risk."

"They are."

After brief introductions, Donovan asked, "Have you set up roadblocks around the area?"

"Yes, sir, we have." replied the lieutenant. "We're blocking roads within a five mile radius. Not completed yet, but shouldn't take long."

"These are Amish farms, as you know," the sergeant said. "The Amish are peaceful people. They can't defend themselves, or won't. They have no guns. The only weapons they have are farm tools. They haven't seen real violence since the school shooting a few years back."

It was cold and the moonlight wasn't strong enough to offer much visibility. Donovan briefly recalled the school shooting, then scanned the countryside, saying, "The best we can do for now is seal off the area and wait until morning. We need some helicopters in here fast and a lot more men people; maybe the National Guard."

2:50 AM, McConnell AFB

Col. Tom McCannon, commanding officer of McConnell Air Force Base, stood next to his dark blue limo. He was watching the approach of a twin-engine jet inbound from Lincoln, Nebraska, carrying Gov. Jack Waynright, the second governor to arrive. Gov. Janice Olbright of Missouri landed a few minutes before. The plane touched down, taxied the length of the runway, and circled back to the small terminal where Colonel McCannon was waiting.

As the Nebraska National Guard jet approached the terminal, the lights of an Air Force T-38 Talon could be seen in the distant sky as it headed down for its final approach. Aboard the trainer was Gov. Ralph Buchanan of Oklahoma.

Another aircraft, a few miles away in the sky, was approaching; behind it, about five miles, was yet another plane. Both planes held governors headed down out of the night sky for an urgent meeting in a room beneath the Officer's Club. Within a few hours, most state executives would have arrived. It was now a dark 3:05 AM in Kansas and cloudy at 12:05 PM in Moscow.

The Kremlin, 12:05 PM

Chernosvitov raised the receiver from its cradle. He sat silent for a full minute. Slowly he looked at the door to the Strategy Room. What was he to tell them?

Igmanov was reporting that his meeting with Dipaula had been completed and he was convinced the situation was stable, for the moment. While he knew more than he was able to reveal, he could say no more. When Chernosvitov insisted, Igmanov merely answered, "I am convinced that it would be extremely hazardous for me to elaborate further using this system of communication."

Chernosvitov became inflamed, "You are convinced? You are the ultimate judge on what is important and what is not?"

Igmanov held his ground, "Alexai Mikhailovich Chernosvitov, I am telling you that I cannot elaborate at this time. You must understand, the situation here is stable and poses no threat to our country. However, if certain elements in Moscow speculate incorrectly, then the situation might change. You must understand. It cannot—"

"Listen Igmanov," the temperature rose quickly, "it is you who must understand! Now, listen carefully. Do not misunderstand any of my words. Mikhail Nikolavich Igmanov, you will report everything, everything the American told you, every detail, by diplomatic channel directly from you to me and you will do it within ten minutes. Now do you understand?"

Diplomatic channel referred to the highly classified transmission, which transferred data through a complex series of harmonics combined with an intricate internal code, a code within a code, within a code. It was changed by the hour, and if need be, even by the second. If required, it could even adjust to the voice track of both the person sending and the person receiving. As such, it could be personalized to specific individuals as Chernosvitov was ordering; only they could send and receive.

There was a brief moment of silence. Igmanov took a deep breath and said, "I understand, Alexai. Please put President Masarov on the line."

Chernosvitov was infuriated by the impertinence of his subordinate. He nearly crushed the phone in his powerful hands before he calmed down slightly and said, deliberately, "Within ten minutes, Igmanov. This is the end of our conversation."

With that, Alexai Chernosvitov hung up and disconnected the direct line with the embassy in Washington. He speculated about what was going on that Igmanov would want to bypass his boss? What was wrong in Washington? Igmanov was out of character and that warranted great concern.

Outside the office door, having overheard the raised voice of Chernosvitov, Vadim Polozko curled his eyelid in deep thought. He turned and walked away.

4:10 AM, Washington, DC

The Hoover Building was filled with a frenzy of activity on all floors. Calls were coming in from two dozen fronts scattered across the country. Three calls had been received claiming responsibility for the attack on the Capitol. Not entirely unusual but not expected. Hundreds of others were now tying up the switchboard as agents moved quickly with state and local law enforcement to contain and prevent the violence and terrorism, which had begun several hours before.

Something big was going down. If allowed to rage out of control, to expand beyond the present flashes, the militia revolt could sweep the country like a relentless wildfire and cause widespread death and destruction before being extinguished by force or burning itself out. No one thought seriously that a revolution would take hold, but none doubted it could wreak havoc upon the wounded nation if it remained unchecked.

Reporter Alex Bernard was driving north on Marianne Street, a few miles from the Hoover Building, when the call came in from his office.

"Bernard, here!"

"Kevin, I've got that name and number for ya."

"Great, let's have it." Bernard pulled his car to the curb and snuffed out his cigarette in the ashtray, sparks falling to the floor mat. He picked up his pencil and notepad from the passenger's seat and began to write.

After hanging up, he dialed the home number of the owner of the Georgetown Cabaret Club. The phone rang four times and then a deep raspy voice came on the line.

"Yeah."

"Hello, Mr. James Schulen?"

"Yes, who the hell are you?"

"Mr. Schulen, this is Bob Caridene's cousin. I must speak with Bob immediately. It's an emergency, sir," said Bernard.

"Who'd you say you were?" answered Schulen, obviously disturbed by the call.

"Bob Caridene's cousin. It's an emergency. I've got to speak with him immediately. Can you tell me where he's staying, Mr. Schulen?"

"How'd you get my number?" asked Schulen.

"Bob gave it to me," said the confident reporter.

"Then why didn't he tell you where he was staying?" asked the club owner.

"It's a long story, Mr. Schulen. This is an emergency, sir. Please tell me where I can reach Bob. I'm sure he will explain everything to you in the morning." His voice urgent, Bernard continued, "Please, I don't have much time. One of his close relatives is believed lost in the tragedy on Capitol Hill, his father."

Schulen thought for a second and said, "What the hell's going on? First the police call and now you." The stress was just too great for him. "He's at the Washington District Hotel on Pennsylvania, or maybe "I" street, ah, one or the other; they connect somewhere near Pennsylvania."

"Thank you, Mr. Schulen. Thank you so much," Bernard disconnected.

The police! Holy shit!

Bernard pulled out onto Marianne, made a quick U-turn and headed for Pennsylvania Avenue and the red awning of the Washington District Hotel. It was on "I" where it joined Pennsylvania.

Bernard parked his car in front of the awning and walked quickly to the front entrance. It was locked. He knocked several times until the night clerk cautiously approached the door.

The clerk would normally expect to see one of the many street people who often came over from the park across the street. However, tonight he was expecting anything. Sirens were still constant, but general traffic was thinning out after having been steady a few hours earlier. He was relieved to see a man in a sports jacket and open collar. Behind the man was an expensive-looking sports car. He was certain the Secret Service didn't drive such high-priced vehicles, at least he hoped not on his taxes.

The clerk yelled through the door, "Whadda ya want?"

"Sir, I'm Mr. Bob Caridene's manager, Bill Striker. I must speak with Mr. Caridene immediately. He's a guest in your hotel. His father was critically injured at the Capitol and he has to know immediately," answered Bernard.

"You're too late," replied the clerk.

"What do you mean?" asked the reporter.

"I mean he's not here."

"Where is he? This is an emergency."

"I'm sorry," said the clerk. "Mr. Caridene's not here. Come back in a few hours. He may be back by then. If you like, you can leave a message."

"Where is he? I have to speak with him now. A few hours will be too late," shouted Bernard.

"That's too bad. He's not here. I don't know what else to tell you, buddy." replied the irritated night clerk.

Bernard realized he was getting nowhere fast. He reached into his pocket and pulled out a one hundred dollar bill, held it up to the window and asked, "Will this refresh your memory? Do you know where he is?"

The night clerk looked behind him and back at the bill, obviously battling with his conscience. It was a quick battle; the bill won hands down, no contest. After all, he was only temporary and no one would know. No big deal. If the government was lying about the radiation threat, he just might be dead before long and who would care?

After taking the bill through the crack in the double doors, he said, "The police came and got him."

Bernard's heart began to pound. "What police?" he asked.

"The feds," came the reply as the bill was quickly shoved into a pants pocket.

"What feds? The FBI?" asked Bernard.

"No." The night clerk knew there was one more battle to win and the enemy was weak.

Bernard pulled out his wallet; only a fifty, two twenties left and a few ones. He handed them to the clerk, showing him the empty wallet.

"The Secret Service," said the clerk with a smile as he pulled the money through the crack.

Bernard's heart stopped. His breathing began to accelerate. He was stunned.

"When?" asked the reporter.

"Couple hours ago," responded the clerk.

His thoughts began to spin wildly as he turned toward his car. *I'm sitting on the biggest scoop of my life. I've got to get to the office. I can't risk the phone.*

As he turned the ignition key, another thought hit him. *What the hell's going on? If Caridene is impersonating Kilpatrick, we have no president. Holy crap!*

The consideration of a scoop seemed insignificant in comparison to the probability that the nation was without a leader. His mind began to spit out thoughts like a rotating fireworks display. *Is this a conspiracy? Is it the National Militia? Who's in charge at the White House? What the hell's going on?*

He drove away from the Washington District Hotel, turned left through the campus of George Washington University and down Twenty-third Street, made a slight adjustment to avoid the crowd at GWU Hospital, and headed toward the Lincoln Memorial. The traffic was light near the Memorial Bridge when he thought to call his contact at the Pentagon, Gen. Clayton Hendsley. He owed Hendsley a big favor from the summer when the general told Bernard about a large sum of money being piped to Israel for insurgency action in Libya. Now he would owe him another one. Hendsley would know how to check out the situation at the White House. The reporter realized this was big shit national security stuff. But a scoop didn't mean diddly squat if there was no free country to read it.

It seems the White House is lying to everyone, he thought. *Is it possible that a conspiracy could exist here in the United States? Of course, it has to be an internal conspiracy if the White House is involved. It's the damn militia; it has to be. If so, General Hendsley would know what to do. Good God!*

In eight minutes he had Hendsley on the phone. The general was at the Pentagon with a number of other officers. Most officials in government were glued to their television sets or their command stations. They arranged to meet at the Pentagon within thirty minutes.

4:20 AM, The Pentagon

General Hendsley, sitting back in his padded swivel chair, took a long drag on his cigarette as he listened to the remarkable story and speculation being offered by Alex Bernard. As the reporter continued, Hendsley found it becoming more and more credible. After all, Bernard was no fool. He had written Pentagon and Defense Department stories just as Hendsley had secretly reported to him over the years. Accuracy was Bernard's trademark. Hendsley hated the private sector and all civilian sons of bitches who ripped off the government. Every chance he could, he would give Bernard a scoop to uncover the bastards.

General Hendsley waited until the reporter was finished and then said, "Alex, if what you're saying is true, General McCloud has to be told immediately. He's in charge here."

They both sat in silence, thinking of how the story would sound to General McCloud. After a few seconds, Hendsley said, "Let's do it. I think you're on to something, Bernard."

"Will he get pissed?"

Hendsley, with a knowing smile, responded, "No. He won't get pissed. I think he'll be pleased you stopped by."

Pleased? thought Bernard. *That's a funny choice of words.*

They walked down the hallway to the office of three-star Gen. Jake McCloud, now in charge of the army. McCloud was not in the room. However, it appeared that everyone else was.

General Hendsley walked in and asked for McCloud. A major responded, "Sir, General McCloud is down in the secure area, room E1214. Can I help you?"

"Yes, Major. You can get General McCloud on the line for me," replied Hendsley.

"Yes, General; I'll try. But General McCloud is quite busy, sir."

"I know he is . . . but try, Major," Hendsley said with the assured voice of authority.

Fifteen minutes later, in room E1214, Jake McCloud was listening to the same incredible story Hendsley had heard a few minutes earlier. The initial reaction was the same, disbelief.

Gen. Jake McCloud felt much taller than his six feet two inches. His close cropped hair was a direct throwback to his youth and the time spent as a tobacco sharecropper's son. Fifty years earlier, his father successfully milled into him that good men don't drink heavy, don't sleep late and they always, always fear God and have neatly cropped hair. Every Wednesday night, Sunday morning, and Sunday night, his lead-thin father and mother would sit next to him and his three brothers in the back row of a small Baptist church in rural southeast Kentucky. Little Jake listened intently when the preacher raised his worn bible and shouted about the righteousness of the Lord. At nearly all services, his mother sang in the choir and his father was asked to say the opening or closing prayer. Jake remembered, like it was only yesterday, his father rambling on in open petition with nearly every other word being "Lord." He still listened to it daily in his mind, *Lord, thank you, Lord. We thank you, Lord, for our pastor, Brother John, Lord. Lord, keep our families on the righteous path. Lord, make our children, Lord, grow in your kind and merciful love, Lord, and maketh not a den of iniquity of our country Lord. And, Lord, drive away all stain of sin from this land.* In the last fifty years, Jake McCloud never left that back pew, he merely brought the world into it with him and his father was as ever present in his mind as his brightly polished stars.

After Bernard finished, McCloud looked at Hendsley and said in a slow even tone, "Hendsley, if this reporter friend of yours is an idiot, tell me now and save yourself a really big enema. We're faced with a national disaster and none of us has the time to listen to fantasy bullshit." Looking to Bernard and then back to General Hendsley he continued, "Do you believe what Bernard's saying?"

Hendsley knew that McCloud was hoping for confirmation. "Jake, I believe it's entirely possible," he said, and not a word more.

"The big question is, is Kilpatrick for real?" Bernard offered a suggestion. "General McCloud, call the White House and ask to speak to Secretary Kilpatrick. Ask him a simple question, one that an impersonator wouldn't know. If he's right, no problem. If he can't answer you, well . . . big problem."

McCloud's face brightened a bit, "Now why would I do that?" he asked.

Hendsley quickly responded, "General, can you afford to risk the defense of this country by not asking? What if that's not Kilpatrick? What if there is a real conspiracy going on at the White House? Dipaula has been telling everyone that Kilpatrick is in charge. Can we honestly say that he is telling the truth?" Then he settled back in his chair and added thoughtfully, "Don't forget the National Militia, Jake."

McCloud's head raised slightly.

Hendsley continued, "What if Dipaula, or others in the White House, are actually running things and Kilpatrick is really dead." Adding again, "Can't forget the militia now, can we Jake?"

"Militia?" McCloud repeated the words. *The National Militia*, he thought. *No, we can't forget the National Militia.* Turning to Bernard, he asked, "If I did speak with Kilpatrick, what would I ask him?"

The reporter spoke slowly, "About ten years ago, Kilpatrick was a congressman from the state of Wyoming. He was on the committee that formed a new national park, it was called 'Rocky Butte National Park.' The park is very small and was formed to protect a few Indian battle sites. Ask him to tell you the name of that park. Not a difficult question for Kilpatrick."

Taking a deep breath, McCloud looked at Hendsley, their eyes locked. Then turning back to Bernard, he asked, "What did you call that damn park? Rocky Butte?"

Bernard said calmly, "Yes, General, Rocky Butte National Park."

Five minutes later, McCloud was connected to the White House on a priority line. They were getting Barry Dipaula.

In a few minutes, Dipaula came on the line, "General McCloud, we're very busy here. What can I do for you?"

"Mr. Dipaula, I must speak with Secretary Kilpatrick immediately."

"I'm sorry, general. Mr. Kilpatrick is very busy and can't come to the phone just now. Can I help you?" replied Dipaula.

"Mr. Dipaula, we have a real serious situation here and I can only relay it to Mr. Kilpatrick," said an adamant General McCloud. He had a passionate dislike for bureaucrats, like many in the Pentagon.

"General McCloud, I can't interrupt Mr. Kilpatrick just now. I'll have him call you as soon as possible," replied an irritated Dipaula.

"Mr. Dipaula, you may have an even greater crisis if you do not have the secretary call me within the half hour," responded an equally irritated General McCloud. His numerous medals and his bright stars gave him the confidence needed to parry this chicken-shit appointed civilian.

Dipaula was extremely tired. This had been a very long night. His patience was also wearing thin. "Are you trying to tell me something, General? Do you actually believe the national security advisor cannot hear what you have to say?"

"Mr. Dipaula, I must speak to the secretary and I mean soon. If you don't understand the importance of keeping this department informed and in direct contact with the man who may be the commander and chief, you had better consult with your textbook or someone who does." The general was not impressed with the civilians who shielded the president from the military. It really pissed him off.

Chapter Twenty-Three

2:00 AM, PST, Spokane, Washington

The dark blue van moved east on Trent at exactly fifty miles an hour, not wanting to attract attention. It turned north onto Argonne and within ten minutes turned left onto the Mount Spokane Highway. Ahead, two miles to the northwest, along a hillside was the massive Avista Utilities main power station, which serviced the Spokane area and much of Eastern Washington and Northern Idaho. The van eased off the highway and onto a dirt road, lights out, now heading between two frozen wheat fields and directly toward the station. As he slowed, the driver could just see the outline of a car parked in the darkness a hundred feet ahead.

The van came to a stop about ten yards from a fifteen-foot-high wire fence topped with spiraling razor wire. Parked ten feet ahead of the van, a green Spokane county sheriff's cruiser sat quietly in the dark. Two men jumped out of the van as the uniformed driver of the cruiser opened his door and walked back.

Within five minutes, a gaping hole eight feet square had been cut from the fence. The van moved through the hole and across the secured area surrounding the power station. The driver slowed to a stop a hundred yards from the building containing the main transfer couplings. He quickly stepped out of the van, set a switch, pushed down on a small lever and ran back to the fence as the van accelerated toward the station. The driver cleared the hole as the enormous explosion rocked the ground and sent a huge fireball high into the air, lighting the hillside for miles around.

The cruiser sped away on Mount Spokane Highway as nearly all electrical power in the region was suddenly turned off.

5:06 AM

The telephone rang in room E1214 of the Pentagon where McCloud and Hendsely waited. Against a mild protest, Bernard had been taken to another room for a quick breakfast and had not returned as yet. General Hendsley picked up the receiver. "General Hendsley."

"General, is General McCloud there? This is the White House," said the communication's officer sitting next to impersonator Bob Caridene.

Hendsley turned to McCloud and handed him the receiver, "It's the man."

McCloud grabbed the receiver. "This is General McCloud."

"Hold one moment for Secretary Kilpatrick, sir."

Caridene looked at Barry Dipaula standing next to him. Dipaula smiled encouragingly at him. Caridene was not comfortable. The effect of the beer he had drank in his hotel room, coupled with only an hour of sleep, was causing him to feel extremely fatigued. The strong coffee seemed to cause him to become even more disoriented. He took a deep breath and remembered what Dipaula had said, "Don't talk for more than a minute." *Tell a comedian he can only talk for a minute, now that's a real joke,* he thought while clearing his throat.

"General McCloud, this is Secretary Kilpatrick. What's this about?"

"Mr. Secretary, we have people here who are being asked to carry out some strong acts of faith, sir. It's imperative we put their concerns to rest soon, Mr. Kilpatrick."

"What concerns, General?"

"They suggest I ask you a question, Mr. Kilpatrick. Sir, can you tell me the name of the national park in Wyoming you helped to establish? The one you sponsored while in Congress."

There was silence on the other end. Caridene looked at Dipaula who was listening to the conversation on another line. Dipaula's eyes were glazed in thought. *What is the name of that park?*

Caridene's eyes reflected some of the panic he was experiencing. He quickly sensed that Dipaula couldn't help and he said into the receiver, "General McCloud, do you realize the seriousness of the situation here in the district? Surely you're not calling, in the midst of this crisis, to question my identity. You idiot! Do you have any idea what's happening in this city?"

The general hesitated, then continued, fully committed, "Sir, please answer the question. If you do, I can assure you I will offer you my complete support or my resignation immediately, whichever you choose."

"And if I refuse to play your silly ass game, General?" replied Caridene.

"I don't know, sir," responded McCloud.

Caridene looked pleading to Dipaula and the others in the room. Dipaula indicated with a gesture for Caridene to hang up, mad.

"General McCloud, I want to see you in my office immediately. Do you understand me? Here in the White House, Damn it!" Caridene hung up.

Caridene looked at Dipaula. The smile was gone.

McCloud set the receiver down.

"Well?" Hendsley asked.

McCloud said nothing, he was deep in thought. He retrieved the receiver and punched in a number. The two men sat quietly, waiting for an answer. The general seemed preoccupied. Then he said into the receiver, "This is McCloud. No. No. I know about that asshole Fletcher. He was the wrong man for the job. Not careful enough. Screw Fletcher! Now shut up and listen! Get into the district as soon as you can. It appears we have a situation at the White House which needs immediate attention."

Silence.

"Yes, I know how busy you are!" his voice raised. "This is more important than anything you're dealing with right now. It's absolutely critical! I think you'll find it of great interest. Move us ahead on our calendar by months if not years. Call me when you get in." He disconnected.

"Was that who I think it was?" asked Hendsley.

"Yes," answered McCloud. "Things have been accelerated a bit, Clayton; quite a bit. Get our special unit ready. We're gonna need 'em."

Moscow, 1:30 PM

Inside the Kremlin, Anatoli Karzinski turned the corner and continued down the long dimly lit corridor, his hard leather shoes echoing ahead of him in the deserted hallway. Within a few seconds, he slowed his pace and cautiously looked about. Satisfied he was alone; he opened the door and entered a small room. After walking a few feet, he entered another, much larger office. Seated at a table in front of him were Gen. Maximum Obidiov and Vadim Polozko. They were obviously waiting his arrival.

"What kept you, Anatoli?" the hard voice of Obidiov.

"You're too impatient, General," Karzinski said as he walked toward the table.

"We don't have time for the usual bullshit, either of you," admonished Polozko, "There is no time."

"Patience is not your virtue either, Vadim," Karzinski replied as he took a seat. He added without hesitation, "From what you have overheard, Polozko, I am certain our friends are now in charge in the United States."

"That is the case," added Obidiov. "Masarov is too weak to realize the terrorist has taken out their entire leadership. Chernosvitov must surely realize the seriousness of the problem. Word has come that—"

"You have received word from them?" asked Karzinski, slightly raised eyebrows, as much excitement as he ever displayed.

"No, not from them. But it is a matter of time. In any case, our responsibility is not to wait for events in the United States to develop. It is time for us to move; to regain our own country. The world is now in chaos. There will be little opposition from anyone, especially the United States. Others have their own concerns to scrutinize."

"You always make it sound so simple, General," Karzinski mumbled.

"It is simple, Advisor Karzinski." Obidiov shifted in his seat. "You need only to take care of your responsibility and the rest will fall into place. I have made certain our military will be placed on high alert; weapons will soon be fixed to designated points. At the precise moment, when I alone give the word, the weapons will lock onto their true targets. Less than eight hours from now, Lebanon and Israel will occupy everyone's attention while we move to regain our country." He sat back in his seat. "Masarov will see our alert as a response to the crisis in the United States and in Lebanon, nothing more. When the final word is given, our forces here will insure that Masarov and his comrades are quickly eliminated in one move. Within an hour of our emergence, the country will be ours. All the design—"

"As always, Maxim, you have great respect for your plan and little for Chernosvitov's intelligence," interrupted Karzinski. "As I have continually advised, he is cunning. A man not easily—"

"I agree with Anatoli," added Polozko. "Chernosvitov is no fool. He must be taken out first, and soon. He may already be—"

"Nothing can stop us. Not Chernosvitov! No one," insisted Obidiov, with a wave of his hand. "We will move as planned; every step as planned. You have more faith in the minister than in yourself. If you are not convinced of our superiority, then . . ."

"I am as committed to this responsibility as you are, General," snapped Karzinski. "We all are!"

"Hold it!" Polozko almost shouted. "I agree, we are all committed to this event. It is only that our nerves are straining, nothing more." Turning to Obidiov he continued, "General, you are still the one to give the initial order. The military is yours. After you have secured the military, we will do our part. But Chernosvitov must go first!"

Some last minute details were discussed before the meeting was concluded and the three men turned to their personal responsibilities, fully united in their effort.

5:30 AM, Amish Countryside, Pennsylvania

A sliver of light appeared along the eastern horizon as Secret Service agent Charlie Morrison worked with Linnet Singleton and the FBI to coordinate the security net placed around the countryside. Helicopters were being brought in along with military and police aircraft. A portable communications center was being transported from the state's Disaster Relief Agency and the Pennsylvania National Guard was sending troops to the area. Every available law enforcement officer was being activated.

James Donovan, Gregg Lawrence, and Sandra Merrall were working with Lancaster County Sheriff Marlin Reid, and Highway Patrol Lieutenant Dave Hanson. A detailed search of every farmhouse in the area was necessary and would begin as soon as possible after sunrise, now only minutes away.

When things had quieted down a bit, Donovan and Merrall walked quietly away, down the hard dirt path next to the Amish farmhouse. It was cold and they wore heavy blue highway patrol parkas. They were exhausted.

The light from the morning sun was appearing over the horizon to the southeast. A gentle breeze was blowing across the fields. They stopped to view the peaceful country scene and saturated themselves with the moment of peace in the midst of destruction and chaos. They blocked out the distant noise of the police radios and the movement of vehicles. Only the breeze was allowed to enter their world.

The sky was now filling with morning colors.

Sandra spoke first, "It's been almost twelve hours since this nightmare began. It seems like light-years away." She smiled briefly. The smile disappeared as she continued, "A few hours later, we're standing in the middle of an Amish farm, the nation without a leader, and madmen terrifying this gentle countryside." She wanted the nightmare to go away, to never have happened.

"Sandra, I remember talking with you a few days ago about the simple life some people live. The Amish, for example, no cars, no telephones, no televisions, no traffic jams, no guns, no running for planes, no concerns for stock market crashes, no . . ." James was releasing tension. Neither of them had slept for over thirty hours and had no idea of when they would be able to sleep again.

"Sandra, since we can't do anything for an hour or so, why don't you lay down in one of the cars and get some rest?" James was feeling the strain himself and he knew Sandra was on the edge of exhaustion.

If they hadn't walked into this peaceful field, the adrenaline would have continued to flow. But this moment of silence had relaxed their bodies. The adrenaline had decreased and was no longer keeping them fully awake.

"I don't want to leave this field. I want to stay here."

Sandra knew the harsh reality of their situation was only a few yards away. What was happening beyond this field was painful and meant adjustment and uncertainty. It meant facing up to the fact that the nightmare was for real.

Donovan knew what she was feeling. He felt the same. He took her into his arms and held her tight. This field was like an oasis in a horrible nightmare of death and destruction. They began to relax and feel the warmth of each other.

"I'm concerned about Barry," Sandra whispered. "He's stuck in the middle of this catastrophe. He doesn't have a field like this to run away to."

Donovan looked to the horizon and said, "Men like Barry place themselves in difficult situations. They get some, some kick out of making the difficult decisions. Barry wouldn't admit that, I'm sure. I don't know. I believe he'll make the right decisions to get us out of this mess. He has to—"

With explosive force, the loud roar of an HH-60 Pave Hawk helicopter broke the silence as it suddenly hammered the ground bringing them back to reality, to the world beyond the field. It would be some time before they would know a peaceful moment again.

The chopper slowly descended onto the roadway as James and Sandra hurried back toward the dozen police cars parked next to the fences.

Capt. Earl Hillman of the Pennsylvania Highway Patrol and Gen. Richard Whitsett of the National Guard jumped from the doorway, followed by half a dozen armed soldiers, as the giant blades slowly wound down. Gregg Lawrence quickly escorted them to the makeshift operations area where a large group had assembled.

Lawrence stepped forward and said, "Gentlemen, this is James Donovan, assistant director of the Secret Service and special agent in charge here. Carl

Miller head of the FBI unit has not arrived yet. We expect him soon. This is Sandra Merrall of the bureau's counterterrorist unit."

"Thank you for your support, gentlemen," Donovan said as he shook hands. "As you know, these men are wanted by the Federal government and we ask that the fugitives be placed under FBI custody."

"Not a problem, Mr. Donovan," responded General Whitsett. "If these bastards are who I think they are, they would be safer under your custody than mine."

"That's right," Captain Hillman concurred. "How many federal agents are here, Mr. Donovan?"

"We have twenty-six here and another two dozen on the way both from the district and from around the state. About forty men from the special antiterrorist unit from Quantico will be arriving shortly as well. As you seem to know, we believe these men were involved with the mass assassination at the Capitol."

Captain Hillman took a deep breath. The other police officers standing nearby now fully realized as true what they had merely suspected.

"Exactly who are these men, Donovan?" asked Hillman.

"We're not certain; but we suspect international terrorists, perhaps the National Militia. That's only a guess. We really don't know. From the shootout in Maryland, they're definitely involved with the attack on the Capitol. In any case; these men are extremely dangerous. Expect a lot of civilian casualties. No doubt they'll use hostages if it comes to that."

"Perhaps we should get a negotiator here in a hurry," Hillman commented.

Donovan looked at him politely and said, "Well, Captain, if we were dealing with individuals trying to make a political statement, I would agree. But these men are international assassins and not the least bit interested in statements. They've already made their statement. They'll either escape or they'll die. You'll find it difficult to negotiate with them. I don't believe it's possible. But I suppose it's best to have a negotiator present, just in case."

The discussion went on for another ten minutes. Sheriff Marlin Reid explained the roadblocks and patrols covering the fields and farmhouses. They had expanded the net to include enough territory that even riding on horseback at full speed, they could not escape the secure area.

Distant gunfire stilled the conversation and all eyes scanned the horizon in the direction of the shots. Car radios came alive with desperate shouts as helicopters sped across the skyline. At least one of the assassins had been located.

A few miles away, two against twelve was not good odds; at least not for the Lancaster County sheriff's deputies. While they had the assassins, Radwan and Zaki, pinned down under a wood bridge, they had wisely accepted the warnings from the FBI and had the good sense to wait for reinforcements.

Beneath the bridge, huddled against the rocky bank just out of sight, Radwan turned to his companion and said, "I believe Allah has marked this place for us, my brother."

Zaki, also sensing his last moments were upon him, answered, "If it be the will of Allah, then let us take many with us."

They removed the explosive devices from their jackets and placed them on the icy ground. Without words, their eyes expressed agreement about what must now be done. Soon, more police would arrive and there would be no chance for surprise. They had to act now, while the police on the ground above them were still unprepared.

The helicopters appeared in the sky at the moment they sprung from beneath the bridge and ran forward, throwing explosives and firing their weapons. The local police were completely surprised by the attack and hesitated a few critical seconds before returning fire.

Bullets filled the air as shouts of pain followed a steady blast of deadly gunfire. Hurled explosives sent men and weapons flying into the air. Radwan and Zaki had changed the odds dramatically before the helicopter landed and reinforcements set foot on the ground.

Turning to rush the helicopter, a barrage of gunfire riddled the two assassins. They fell in unison upon the frozen weeds and rocks, their bodies wasted, their souls rising to Allah.

Chapter Twenty-Four

3:02 AM, Los Angeles, California

The brown *Conklin Industries* truck turned the corner from Valley View onto the narrow two-lane Vista Drive and headed north. A 1996 gray Crown Victoria followed close behind. A few minutes later, the two vehicles eased up to the massive Conklin Microwave Relay Terminals high atop Adrianna Point. Two thousand feet below and eighteen miles to the southeast, the city of Los Angeles sparkled in the distance. In the dark of night, streams of flowing lights, silvery white and red, marked the vast freeway systems, which linked the enormous city. While millions slept, thousands moved through the area going about their nightly routines.

The Crown Victoria came to a stop two hundred feet from the outer fence, just outside the ring of floodlights. The driver of the truck moved forward into the bright lights of the main gate, which locked the fifteen-foot-high outer fence.

There were three security fences, one inside the other, and twenty-five feet apart. Their gates were offset by eight feet, making it nearly impossible for any vehicle to ram straight through to the inner area. The two inner fences were somewhat smaller; all with barbed concertina wire rotating around the top.

In the center of the silent compound were several small utility buildings and four three-hundred-foot towers soaring high into the sky, loaded with microwave dishes. The towers transferred vital communications signals from Rose Peak, seventy-five miles to the northeast, into and out of the greater Los Angeles area, a critical communications link with the outside.

A small security station was located next to the main gate. As the truck slowed to a stop in front of the gate, a confused armed guard stepped through a small door. Approaching the driver, he asked, "Heh, Mike; what you doin' here this time a night?" A cautious tone in his voice.

"Got those new generators we've been waitin' for," the driver answered with an easy smile.

"Didn't expect 'em till later in the week. What's the deal?" The guard remained a few feet from the driver, his hand resting casually on the handle of his weapon.

"Mr. Lawford said to have 'em here before sunup. Mornin' crew's gonna install 'em."

The guard's eyes searched along the side and under the truck as he said, "It's not on my papers. When'd you find out?"

"Bout seven last night," the driver answered calmly. "Told me to get 'em up here early."

"It's three o'clock for Christ's sake." The guard was now looking toward the empty passenger's seat. "Damn early."

"That's what I was told, early," Mike said with a stifled yawn.

"We've got a security alert, Mike," the guards eyes now focused thoughtfully on the driver. "Can't let you in without some verification."

"Shit, Henry, it's me for God's sakes." The smile less sincere.

"Sit tight, Mike. I need to get some clearance here." An unsympathetic voice. "Shouldn't take long."

The guard started to turn as the driver spotted three men in black combat uniforms slip through the small door and into the metal building. To regain the guard's attention, he quickly asked, "What's goin' on, Henry?"

The guard turned back; he was unaware of the intrusion. "Something about the bomb that hit the Capitol tonight. Got everyone jumpy. Special alert. National Militia thing."

"Yeah, heard about it. Damn, it's the shits. Not good for the country. Killed the president an all. We got some hard times head of us."

"Yeah, just—"

Two sharp thuds and the guard hit the ground. Immediately, several more thuds sent two inside guards following Henry to the eternal reward. A silent alarm was pressed before the remaining two security guards and three men on night shift were brought down.

Exactly five minutes from the truck's arrival at the relay station, the four towers were blasted to pieces by massive explosions. At nearly the exact moment, in other remote areas around the city, two additional relay stations were destroyed.

The lights of the city still sparkled and the cars continued on their way, but communications with the outside world was almost completely cut off.

At 3:12 AM PST, the Crown Victoria with six men inside passed two law enforcement vehicles that were speeding toward the burning relay station.

6:15 AM EST, the White House

Barry Dipaula was having orange juice and sweet roll in a private room with Howard Imhoff, deputy director of the CIA, and Elliot Doering, director of the FBI. They had been reviewing reports from McConnell. So far, eighteen governors were safely on the ground. It was 5:15 AM in Kansas. The remaining governors, who would be able to join their colleagues in the opening session, would arrive within the next two hours.

Governor Imanoia of Hawaii, aboard a yacht twenty miles off the Hawaiian coast near the island of Oahu, had been contacted late. He was now being transferred to an Air Force jet on Oahu for a flight to the mainland and on to McConnell. He would be the last to arrive and would be absent for the majority of the discussion. Nevertheless, he was determined that Hawaii would not be excluded from decisions in time of great national crisis; Bergstrom had been a close personal friend.

Dipaula continued his discussion, "And it appears that Igmanov reported the situation to Masarov directly and hopefully," he lowered his voice, "he will contain the information . . . as well as his generals."

Imhoff took another drink of coffee and said with a slight twinkle in his eye, "I wonder what General McCloud will say when he finds out about Kilpatrick. That old son of a bitch will hit the roof. Dipaula, you'll be in the hot seat for a while. He doesn't like to take orders from civilians to start with, but to take orders from a nonelected civilian would really piss him off. Anyway, that bastard would love to have control of this government. Why Bergstrom kept him as general of the army is beyond me. Maybe, you ought to have that comedian call him up and fire his ass."

They all laughed for the first time since the two had joined Dipaula in the White House a few hours earlier.

"Shit, now is the time to get rid of a whole bunch of bastards. Why stop with McCloud?" added Doering.

"We haven't heard from McCloud since he was ordered to come to the White House," Dipaula noted. "Could be a problem; he's not a predictable man. Elliot, have your field offices been able to send personnel with the governors?"

"Yes. The governors have been surprisingly cooperative. That's a bit strange to me. I know West Virginia raised some hell, but most of them have been pretty controlled. It scares the hell out of me, as well, to think they're all in one place, especially after last night." Doering stopped for a moment, leaned forward and continued. "Barry, some questions have been asked."

"No doubt; I've been asking a lot of questions myself."

"About you, I mean." Doering paused.

Dipaula looked up, obviously alarmed. "What questions?"

"Don't get excited, Barry," Doering said. "But questions have been asked about why you've been making all the critical decisions in this crisis."

Dipaula's eyes narrowed, his face reddened. "What does that mean, Elliot?" The anger issued from every pore on his face. Dipaula set his cup down hard on the saucer, the loud clap magnified the tension now rapidly building.

"You've been using everyone from the Secret Service, the FBI, the military, even the governors." Doering attempted to keep a calm voice. "People are asking, why you? Why are—"

"Why the hell me, Elliot? Why me, for Christ's sake; why not me!"

"You were involved in picking the location of the meeting." Imhoff said.

"Hell yes, I was! So were a number of other people."

"Now, don't get excited, Barry," Doering's hands went up.

"Exactly who is asking these questions, gentlemen?" Dipaula's anger had reached a boiling point.

No one spoke. The two officials looked at each other then back to Dipaula.

"What people, gentlemen? Who specifically?" Dipaula persisted. "The two of you? Someone else?"

Silence.

"You weren't around during the process," Dipaula said. "No one with any White House authority was here, but me. The whole nation was focused on this house. No! The whole damn world was focused on this house. They expected some assurances the country was secure. Kilpatrick was dead! The entire weight was on me. I've done nothing to hurt the country."

"We're not saying you have, Barry," Doering said, with an undeviating tone.

"I selected the site after considering suggestions from Governor Dupree, the National Security staff and General Bradley aboard Skywatch," Dipaula continued, the apparent insult was more than he could bear. "He's been informed of our situation from the very beginning. It was our joint decision to withhold information about Kilpatrick from anyone until the governors were notified and on their way to McConnell. I'm not part of any damn conspiracy and have no intention of overthrowing this government—what the hell's left of it!" Looking directly at Doering, he added, "It would take an imbecile to even suggest such a thing!"

Dipaula had worked without sleep and under extreme stress for almost twenty-four hours, was tired and extremely irritated, absolutely incensed by the accusation. He knew his decisions would someday be criticized, but not this soon and not by these men.

Imhoff was a bit shaken by the intensity of Dipaula's words. He took a deep breath and spoke, "Barry, don't get upset. You know we have to be certain there's nothing more than meets the eye. What happened last night was no accident. We want to be certain that what happens this morning in Kansas is exactly what you've told us and what we believe will happen."

Dipaula stared at Imhoff. He squinted slightly as his lips pursed. "Howard, are you insinuating that I am in anyway connected with a conspiracy?" His eyes were now blazing. "Damn it, Imhoff! You went along with this whole damn scheme!"

Dipaula looked at Doering. "You too, Doering, you went along with this whole plan. Surely, you men aren't positioning yourself to avoid a potential firing squad?"

"Careful, Barry," interrupted Imhoff. "We have to ask these questions. The press will! The governors already have. And sooner or later, the new Congress will. Barry, we believe you did the right thing. But, in all honesty, we will check everyone involved in the decision to select McConnell Air Force Base before that meeting starts. After what happened last night we're not taking chances with the lives of the highest-ranking elected officials in the nation. It's too damn important to worry about anyone's ego, Barry—yours included!" It was now Imhoff who stiffened.

Dipaula settled down a bit. Anything was possible after what had already occurred. He realized suddenly that new sensations were somehow transforming him, causing him to enjoy the power, to consider himself above reproach. He thought to himself, *Donovan was right; I really was just an advisor. But now, I've become more, much more; and as bad as it sounds, it feels good. Hell, I've been making all the big decisions. Of course they're concerned.* He knew they were right; he could be part of a larger plan.

"Barry," Imhoff said in near monotone. "Governor Dupree called, requesting you fly out to Kansas. He indicated most of the governors have no real sense of the international situation at this point and don't understand the importance of the noon deadline. They need to hear directly from you why it's so critical to have a president in place this quickly. They're not fully aware of the situation between Lebanon and Israel and how they could bring other countries into a nuclear conflict. Dupree thinks they will delay the decision unless convinced otherwise. You appear to be the only person who can do that." After a slight pause, he added, "What should I tell him?"

Dipaula slowly looked around the room as if searching for the answer in some shadowed recess of the walls. Funny he had never really looked up at the walls before, never noticed the unusual design of the border. How many hours he had spent here in this room and never really noticed much of the detail. Looking down, he realized that somehow he would have to be in two places at the same time, the White House and in a meeting room in Kansas. The governors would need to hear details of the crisis and its global significance, the reason the nation needed a leader now.

A strange feeling came over Dipaula. For most of his life, he appeared to stand outside the spotlight, preferring to play the game from behind the scenes, a coach not a player. Now, believing himself to be more qualified than any of the surviving players, he felt a burning compulsion to run onto the field and control the rapidly changing events. He now wondered if this crisis had caused a bizarre transformation in his personality, or, perhaps, in actuality was he sensing an emergence of a long suppressed drive to take charge, to stand center of the spotlight.

"OK, I'll go out there. But the situation here is critical as well, so I can't stay in Kansas for more than an hour at most. I'll do my best to give them the full story and calm some of their concerns. Without their decisions this situation will most likely explode beyond anything you or I can imagine."

6:30 AM, Outside of the White House

Gen. Jake McCloud, outside the metal fencing on Pennsylvania Avenue, leaned casually against his sedan, an icy wind moving about him. He had ordered a large military police unit to position itself along the fence. Maj. Brian Holster stood next to him. Both men were staring directly at the front entrance to the mansion; steam coming from their mouths.

"What do you think General?" asked Holster as he buttoned his overcoat. "Could it be possi—," his words were cut sharply by a loud rumble moving toward them on Pennsylvania Avenue.

McCloud looked to his right and caught sight of a caravan of military vehicles containing heavy weapons nearing the Old Executive Office Building. He said absently, "It's time to bust up their little party, Major," as he moved toward the trucks.

Within ten minutes a small arsenal of weapons stood ready outside the black metal gates. The sight of weapons pointing directly at the mansion, stunned district police, Secret Service officers, and the marine guards above the White House and the OEB. The military officers wanted to protest but didn't challenge the man who could be the highest-ranking officer of the entire army; especially, not General McCloud. Not in this crisis; it would be like challenging a superior officer in time of battle.

Major Holster remained next to the general as he eyed the placements. Satisfied all was well, McCloud then reached inside his jacket and removed a pipe.

Holster immediately retrieved his lighter and held it up, "May I give you a light, sir?"

"Yes, thanks, Major," the general replied, tipping his head.

"That's an unusual pipe, sir."

"Huh?"

"Your pipe, sir; the lion head, I mean. It's an interesting design."

"African," replied the general as he sucked in. "It's an angry lion," he added, his teeth clamping tightly to the stem. "Just like me." Turning back to the mansion he repeated, "Angry, just like me."

Both men stood quiet for a few minutes, eyeing the surroundings. McCloud was planning his next move. Then he said, "Get me a phone, Major."

"Yes, sir."

Within minutes, McCloud was punching in the numbers.

Several rings.

"Hello," came the answer.

"Pete?"

"Who's this?"

"McCloud."

"Don't know any McCloud."

A pause; then, "Your friend, Joshua."

"Where you at?"

"In front of the house."

"What house?"

"The house, damnit." McCloud's patience with the cat and mouse was gone. "The White House. Get your ass over here!"

"You're on a cell phone, Mc—," almost a slip. "Are you inside, or outside?"

"I'm outside, for the moment. As soon as you get here, I'm goin' in."

"We'll be there in an hour or less. Don't do anything until I get there."

"I'll be here. Things have moved into overdrive, Pete. This new development is just what we needed. Get over here fast."

McCloud disconnected. He turned to the Holster and grunted, "Get Hendsley on the line."

Gen. Jake McCloud knew he would soon become the mighty right arm of the lord. His father would be proud. All along they had planned to disrupt the country after the explosion and move quickly to form an all-white state and it was even believed they would be able to replace many of the departed congressmen with their own people. But none of them had any idea they would now be facing a complete, total rebellion involving the takeover of the White House itself. McCloud was stretched tight with enthusiasm. *They said it couldn't be done in this country*, he thought. *Well, we're about to do it.*

The Kremlin, 2:30 PM

Chernosvitov sat in the room with Masarov as the president listened to the computerized message from Igmanov. It came over Diplomatic Channel and was coded for Masarov's voice alone. After listening to the message, Masarov removed his headphones and wrote on a piece of paper, "Kilpatrick is dead." He handed it to Chernosvitov, obviously concerned that the room contained a listening device.

"I understand now why Igmanov wanted to conceal this information and why he directed it to you," acknowledged Chernosvitov.

"He was concerned that such information would be dangerous in the hands of certain individuals," replied Masarov. "Is it possible for others to have listened to this message?"

"No, it's not possible without this device. I will shred this paper immediately."

"Yes," replied a thoughtful Masarov. "It is time to take some action of our own, my friend." He rubbed his eyes, considered what this meant, then stood and walked back to the Strategy Room where his chief advisors and leaders of the military, including Obidiov, waited. Obidiov was the one man capable of misusing the information now possessed by only two people in

Russia, information that could convince him that a military coup was taking place in the United States.

Masarov walked to his seat at the middle of the table. All eyes focused on him. Everyone knew he had received a message from Igmanov about the meeting with Dipaula, but no one dared ask what the message contained. They waited for the president to inform them.

Masarov cleared his throat and merely said, "Will you all please leave, except for you Obidiov. You stay."

At first the men looked at one another, as if to find support for a mass protest. Seeing that no one was willing to be the first to challenge Masarov, they left, with little attempt at concealing their indignation. Secrets were being withheld from them and soon Masarov and Chernosvitov would pay heavily for this humiliation.

After they had left, Masarov asked Obidiov to sit next to him. Obidiov now suspected that he was correct; a coup had occurred in Washington. While he fully understood the role played by his associate, Wade Pike, he now felt that someone in the United States had taken it a step further. Now he would be able to obtain even more power and influence. Masarov had been a fool to take the soft approach with the United States. They were imperialists and only wished to make Russia soft so they could continue to take whatever they pleased in the world, as they had been doing since the traitor Gorbechev. Obidiov had gained some control over Yeltsin, and even more over Putin, now Masarov would be brought to his knees. Obidiov would emerge as a new force in Russia, and perhaps someday, even the world.

Masarov looked into the eyes of the commander of the military and said softly, "You were wrong, General. It appears the situation in the United States is stable."

Obidiov had always pretended to be friendly with Masarov and Masarov had reciprocated with the same charade. Now, the pretense was over. Masarov continued, "General Obidiov, you are relieved of command of the military until further notice." Obidiov was shocked. "This can be a private matter between you and me until I reinstate your authority, or you can be foolish enough to make it a public matter. If it becomes public, it will become permanent! Do you understand?"

Regaining some control, the general said defiantly, "Why are you doing this? What did the message tell you, Masarov?"

Masarov continued to stare into Obidiov's eyes, and then said quietly, "Chernosvitov?"

Obidiov looked around the room. Chernosvitov had appeared behind him. "Why is he here?" he asked in a tense voice.

Masarov continued in an even tone, "You are now under the protection of the Ministry of Security and will be confined to your office here in the Kremlin. It will be a pleasant time if you allow it to be. It will be most uncomfortable if you do not."

Obidiov's look of defiance turned to puzzlement, "What does that mean? What are you saying?"

Masarov nodded to Chernosvitov. The head of the State Security placed his hands on the shoulder of the general and said, "General Mikhail Tevernoich Obidiov, you are now under the protection of the Ministry of Security by order of the president of Russia."

Four well-armed agents entered the room. Obidiov looked at Masarov, fire in his eyes. Masarov looked away, back to the papers in front of him. He could no longer allow Obidiov the opportunity to move against him.

Chapter Twenty-Five

6:30 AM, McConnell AFB, Kansas

The base was closed. Every military officer and enlisted man was armed. Personnel carriers with mounted machine guns surrounded the base. Special antiterrorists units were flown in from Fort Bragg to assist. Military aircraft were in the air and fully armed. The base was completely secure. The dark night had helped conceal the activity from the local population, but noise from the unusual air traffic was noticed. Thirty-six governors were present in the ballroom inside the Collocated Club. Five governors were still on their way.

Members of the Executive Committee of the National Governor's Conference were meeting in committee in the formal dining room, adjoining the ballroom. Present were Governors Daniel Hiller of Michigan, Gary Dupree of New York, Edgar Myrick of California, Leslie Nealley of South Carolina, and Michael Cary of New Hampshire. Gov. Anthony Bennet of Oregon was ill and could not participate.

Gov. James Hollis of Texas was asked to sit with the Executive Committee, around a brown rectangular table. Gary Dupree was chairman of the National Governor's Conference and would serve as the chairman of this committee.

Dupree offered a suggestion, "Since we have no precedence for such a meeting, and indeed for such a decision, I suggest we discuss first the reason we are here and second, what we believe our real authority in this situation might be."

Edgar Myrick spoke first, "I'm certain we've each thought over the situation many times during the last few hours. It would be extremely difficult and dangerous for the nation if it had to wait several months to elect a president, vice president, and staff for the White House. The country would not, could not, function. Who else can offer the necessary leadership if not the state governors? If the Congress were present, obviously they would be the proper electors, under the Constitution. Unfortunately, we believe the assassins were thorough. I assume one might build a case for the electoral college. However, this would be a rather lengthy process involving too much time and stress for the nation and the world."

"I agree with Barry Dipaula," Michael Cary of New Hampshire added. "I think we're the only ones to restore order. He was absolutely correct in calling this meeting and I also believe we should act quickly to elect a president pro-temporary to serve until a proper election by the people can take place. It's my understanding Dipaula will arrive here within two hours. The man is under exceptional stress. The American people have no idea what he has given to this country over the last several hours. If someday we give an award for secret valor, he'll be the first in my book to receive it, I'm certain followed by many others."

They seemed to agree. No one could think of how the country would run without a president and Congress. But they needed to hear from Dipaula exactly what was going on at the White House and around the world and how quickly a president would need to be in place.

No observers were allowed in the club. The governors were sequestered and the meeting did somewhat resemble a conclave of the College of Cardinals, just as Jerry Gannon had joked about in the Situation Room a few hours earlier.

Noise in the main assembly room began to swell as the governors were having a number of separate discussions, awaiting directions from the committee now meeting in the adjoining room. In one such discussion, Gov. Joan Everett of North Dakota was questioning the proceedings.

"I believe we need to know a great deal more about what is going on in Washington before we take any drastic measures. Good, God, we hardly know anything about the condition of the poor souls on Capitol Hill."

"I couldn't agree more, Joan," responded Adkins of Missouri. "We have no Constitutional authority to elect a president. This meeting is totally out of line, not to mention somewhat dangerous. Could even be extremely harmful."

"Well, you may be right," chimed in Woodruff from Idaho. "However, I understand the situation in the Middle East and in Central Asia is demanding immediate attention. If that is the case, I believe we may need to act quickly to protect the security interests of the United States."

"I'm not certain that any crisis is more significant than the crisis here in our own country," countered Everett. "We should proceed with caution and only after we know more about the situation. It's been less than twelve hours since the explosion and we still have little information to go on. We're toying with the Constitution. Hell, shouldn't this be the job of an electoral college? Isn't that what the system calls for?"

The debate continued.

8:10 AM, Pennsylvania

The morning sun had finally risen above the frozen Amish countryside casting a strange pale greenish yellow color into the dawn sky. A slight breeze kept the temperatures down to below thirty degrees. The house-to-house search would soon begin. There had been no sign of movement anywhere following the gunfire, which left three police officers dead, seven wounded, and two assassins blown apart in the middle of a rock-filled ditch three miles from "point central," the name given to the spot where the assassins landed.

In a wooden farmhouse several miles away, an Amish family faced a nightmare of horror as two desperate men peered through a slit in the curtains at the helicopters flying low overhead. It was impossible to leave without being seen.

Kamile released the worn curtains and turned to face his companion, Samir. "We will be forced to take these people with us when we leave." Wiping sleep from his eyes, Kamile continued, "We may never see our homeland again. But, if we must die, we will die knowing we have completed our work."

Samir, merely nodded his agreement. Thick stubble covered his cheeks and fatigue lines etched his skin.

If only we could get one of the helicopters to land or, perhaps, get to a vehicle, we would have a chance. But how? Kamile thought. Their situation appeared hopeless.

He looked at the Amish family, seated in a circle on the floor, backs to the center. *What a different and selfish people,* he thought to himself. *They are content to hide from the real world. They don't care about the evils of this planet, only their own selfish needs. People starve to death each day and suffer great injustice yet it means nothing to them.*

The family didn't look directly at their captors but continued to face the wall in silence. Even the three young children sat quietly in the circle, alarmed but yet obeying their elders.

Looking out the window at the farmhouses in the distance, Kamile wondered, *Where are you my brother? Were the gunshots for you?* In the distance across the rolling fields, he could see police vehicles moving slowly up the road toward the farmhouse. A military helicopter hovered over a field about a mile away. Another was in the air several hundred feet above the approaching police vehicles as they came to a halt in the roadway about a half mile from the house, engines idling. The sweep had begun. Soon they would search house by house; the net would begin to tighten, threatening them with death.

Samir was not worried. He had known this moment would arrive and was rather surprised they had been able to escape capture this long. A mission such as this into the very heart of the United States would mean his death. He knew that it would happen, but he also knew that his family would never know hunger again.

7:15 AM, McConnell AFB

In the Executive Committee meeting, Leslie Nealley, the silver-haired governor of South Carolina, shifted in his seat, adjusted his glasses and after some thought, said, "Why don't we break into Republicans and Democrats and each party nominate candidates for president and vice president. Then, turn the names over to the main body for election?"

"Not a bad idea, Leslie, since you Democrats are in the majority," quipped Hollis of Texas, a down-home boy with some of the Bush pomposity.

"Governor Hiller, any suggestions?" asked Dupree, hoping to involve every member of the committee.

"Well, gentlemen," replied the Michigan governor. "I believe the will of the people is precisely what we're here to serve." He leaned forward. "It's often argued they do not elect a person, but a system, a philosophy if you will. If the people elected a Republican president, then, perhaps we should consider the president pro-tem should be a Republican."

"Oh, of course," Neally bantered. "That would make sense from your perspective."

Myrick cleared his throat, accepting his turn, "Let's go back to the purpose of our being here, to recommend a method by which the body of governors will elect a president," he said. "Should that be their will, and I'm not certain it will be, it is not our purpose or concern to decide whether the president should be a Republican or a Democrat." Adjusting his glasses he continued, "Since this crisis is nonpartisan, I believe the election should be nonpartisan as well and the system we propose to the main body should allow for that to happen."

"Then you don't think we should ask each party to nominate its own candidates?" asked Dupree.

"Correct," replied Myrick. "Well, that's my thoughts." A hint of uncertainty.

Ignoring Myrick, Hiller, from Michigan, interjected, "Should we go back to the last election and select Governor Powell of North Carolina? He came closer to winning than any losing candidate in recent elections, with the exception of Gore. Millions of people supported him."

"Thank you, Dan." Dupree said, feeling the need to maintain control. "Gentlemen, I agree with Governor Myrick; I believe it's our responsibility to select a method not a candidate."

"Is everyone certain that the Constitution does not have a provision to cover this situation?" asked Hollis.

"The founding fathers never anticipated this situation," answered Dupree. "No one did,"

"Someone did," grumbled Nealley.

Their eyes turned toward the governor from South Carolina.

"The assassins and their sponsors thought about it," Nealley whispered sadly.

The discussion continued for another half hour before it was interrupted by a knock at the door. Gov. Michael Dolin of Nebraska stuck his head through the doorway. "Pardon me, gentlemen, all the expected governors, with the exception of the governor of Hawaii, have arrived. We're ready to begin. I hope you fellows can bring some order to this meeting."

So did they.

"Before we go into the room," Dupree said, "there are two people I've asked to join us. One is Edith Castle, my personal secretary, and the other is Prof. John Baumann from New York University, a specialist on the US Constitution. Both will be of great help in recording and answering technical questions. Are there any objections to my proposing them to the governors?"

There were no objections. Someone needed to make official recordings and they would most likely have need for a Constitution specialist.

"Thank you, they will be the only two nongovernors allowed into the meeting."

Several large television monitors located in the primary meeting room were broadcasting live from DC. The now familiar scenes showing the Capitol partially destroyed, and the heavily damaged buildings, which surrounded it, flashed before them. The pictures made everyone in the room shiver with a deep chill of concern about the future of the country. Depression hung over them like a fog, reminding them of the horrendous loss of so many friends and colleagues. It also made them realize the enormity of their responsibility.

The Executive Committee entered the room solemnly and without a word. Governor Dupree moved to the small podium set up in the front of the room, and the committee took their place at the long table to his right. The other governors took their seats at nine circular tables in the room.

Dupree began, "Ladies and Gentlemen, we are confronted by a historic moment. Never, since the very beginning of our great nation, have a small band of its humble citizens been faced with the monumental task of dramatically shaping its destiny. Like our founding fathers, we do not have the Constitution to guide us. Our own hearts and minds must suffice. My friends, we may proudly represent our individual states, but for now, I ask you to stand and join with me in the Pledge of Allegiance to the one flag, which stands above all others, the flag we have this day been called to defend with all the wisdom the Almighty will give us. Following our salute, please remain standing for a moment of silence, each reflecting on the need for wisdom and our dear friends and colleagues who have been lost to us."

The entire assembly stood, offered the pledge, many giving strong emphasis to the words "one nation under God" and remained standing for over a minute in silence. Many eyes were filled with tears, and hearts ached at the decisions that had to be made in the agonizing hours ahead.

Dupree then continued, "Thank you. Please be seated. Now, ladies and gentlemen, with God's help let us begin the task of restoring order to our country. Everything depends on us, and rests only with us. I would like to introduce the temporary Executive Committee. Of course you know them well, but we must adhere to formality, for history's sake, which will be the case throughout these proceedings."

8:40 AM, Washington, DC

In room W16, the Secret Service Command Post, information was being reported by the minute regarding the tense and dangerous search going on among the Amish farms of Pennsylvania.

It was not known if any of the assassins were still in the district. However, the Secret Service and the FBI were conducting an intense investigation, including dusting for fingerprints in the lobby of the Old Post Office Building, and vehicles in Arlington Cemetery, at the Iwo Jima Memorial, at the National Arboretum and in the small plane outside the Amish farmhouse.

They were especially interested in examining the bodies of the assassins killed in the DC area and the bodies flown in from the small airport in Maryland. Undoubtedly, more bodies would soon be arriving from the fields of Pennsylvania.

Radiation levels near the Capitol were still too high to allow access without protective clothing. However, the counts were low enough to permit free movement over seven hundred yards from ground zero. Anyone still alive who had been within a mile of the Capitol at anytime during or after the explosion was encouraged to proceed immediately to one of the area hospitals. Rescue operations had been intensified over the last three hours.

In the Situation Room, members of Homeland Security, the NSC staff, the NSA, CIA, and FBI were making hundreds of decisions. Dipaula was on his way to Kansas and it was up to them to continue managing the situation at the White House.

General McCloud had been invited inside the mansion but refused to enter. He remained outside with his troops, their weapons still pointing at the White House. This created a very difficult situation for those inside. The media was attempting to make sense of this developing story. Fortunately, McCloud refused to be interviewed by the media and kept them away from his lines. He was now preventing anyone from entering or leaving the residence and demanding that Secretary Kilpatrick come outside.

Craig Thomas was utterly furious. He had attempted to speak with the general but to no avail. It was a standoff but wouldn't last long.

Chapter Twenty-Six

Moscow, 4:45 pm

Masarov was alone. Chernosvitov entered the room. The president was seated with his elbows resting on the hardwood table and his fingertips touching, pointing skyward like thin pillars in prayer. The head of security walked over and stood by the president and waited, not wanting to interrupt his thoughts.

"What is it, Chernosvitov, my companion in crisis?"

"We have just received word that the White House is surrounded by the military."

Slowly looking up, Masarov calmly asked, "What are you saying?"

"A change has occurred. The military are pointing their weapons toward the White House." He paused to wait for the president to take the blow.

With a look of disbelief, Masarov asked, "What do you think is happening?"

"I don't know. I hope Obidiov is not correct."

"Does he know of this development?"

"I don't believe he does. He has been isolated."

"Keep him that way until we have more information," said Masarov, as he looked back at the papers in front of him. *What would Dipaula do now that the military appeared to be aware of the situation in the White House?* Masarov thought to himself. *What if the generals do attempt to take over the United States? What should we do?*

"Place a call to Dipaula. I must speak to him myself." The president spoke the words but didn't hear them. His thoughts were miles away.

Chernosvitov left Masarov alone for the moment but returned ten minutes later. He entered the room and stood before the president. "The news gets worse, I'm afraid."

Chernosvitov handed Masarov a message, which said, "Obidiov has notified the military to stand on full alert and our missiles were ordered to specific targets, many in Central Asia. It was signed by Gen. Igor Bumanish, head of the Russian Army forces."

Masarov turned crimson and instinctively ripped the paper. He was furious. "How could this have happened, Chernosvitov?"

"Obidiov was given information by an aide who relayed orders back to military command." He stood in silence for a few seconds then quietly asked, "Shall we cancel the alert?"

Masarov, still red, turned to Chernosvitov and said, "If you don't . . . I will cancel Obidiov." After a brief pause for self-control, he muttered grimly, "This could well end everything; if anyone ignites even the tiniest spark."

8:50 AM, Pennsylvania

Farm by farm, the search continued. For Kamile and Samir the moment of truth was coming inexorably closer. The two vehicles, which had arrived earlier, remained parked a few hundred yards from the house. Another had now driven around to the back of the farm. They could see men and cars surrounding the buildings up the road. In the distance, fully armed and manned attack helicopters were suspended over an open field. Swirling clouds of steam rose from their jade metallic bodies prepared for instant and deadly fire.

Kamile turned away from the window, dropped his machine gun to his side, leaned back against the green papered wall and wiped moisture from his face. Why was it taking so long? What was the delay? The area was filled with enough military and police forces to control the situation. Why did they take so long?

A few minutes later, Kamile watched as Assault Team One quickly moved up the frozen dirt road toward him and began surrounding the farmhouse. His thoughts wondered to another time, of the days before the attack on the Capitol, sitting with his friends in the safe house in Alexandria. Most of them were probably now dead. Perhaps, soon he would join them. Kamile looked from behind the curtains at the silent, frozen landscape and knew that soon, death would be moving out there, coming for him.

9:00 AM
The White House

The men and women in the Situation Room were anxious as a call was placed to Barry Dipaula who was aboard an Air Force Nighthawk now over Kansas. The jet began its descent toward the runway at McConnell as the call was connected.

In the Situation Room, Craig Thomas's voice had a slight tremor, "Barry, you better get on the line with Masarov and speak with him, and now!"

From across the table from Thomas, Stratton almost shouted, "You've got to do better than that. Masarov won't believe you've got control with McCloud standing outside aiming cannons at the mansion. That Goddamn idiot!"

"Barry, what if we bring the Russian ambassador and Igmanov here to the White House?" Macintee suggested. "And let them call Masarov from here."

Dipaula, his voice echoing through the conference phone, asked, "Why, Macintee? What will that solve?"

"That may not be as stupid as it sounds," said Phillip Page. "Maybe, Tarasavitch and Igmanov will be able to convince Masarov everything's under control."

"There's no way Tarasavitch will come to the White House under these circumstances," Dipaula said as the Nighthawk began its final approach. "But give it a try. Craig, go out again. Tell McCloud he can enter the mansion with his personal weapons and a small security team. He can even leave word if he doesn't return in an hour they can blow the place to hell. General Sanchez is scheduled to arrive here in Kansas within the hour. Hopefully, he'll kick McCloud's ass back to the Pentagon and out of our hair."

Sanchez as deputy commander of the Joint Chiefs of Staff was now identified as the highest-ranking military officer in the United States.

"Phil, go to the Communication's Room," Dipaula instructed over the conference phone. "Get Igmanov on the line for me. Then patch it up here. No, change that. We're almost on the ground. Call the Kansas meeting and get a number where you can reach me. Oh, any word, . . . what's going on with the militia?"

"They've destroyed a number of buildings and power stations, but so far there's only been fourteen fatalities; most on their side. FBI reports the shootout in Alabama is over. No new reports of outbreaks in the last few hours. Hopefully, it's fizzling out."

"Okay. I'll get back to you. We're on our way down." Dipaula switched off.

8:25 AM, Kansas

The governors were called to order as Barry Dipaula was escorted to the podium. Governor Dupree began the introductions, "Ladies and Gentlemen, you all know Barry Dipaula, the national security advisor. Barry and his team at the White House have done a brilliant job of keeping things together. Some of you may question his decisions, but none of us can question his motivation. He has some important information to share with us, which might shed light on our purpose for being here. Barry."

Dipaula stepped to the podium, not comfortable with the spotlight even under the best of situations. Clearing the tension from his throat he began.

"Ladies and Gentlemen, it's with a great deal of sorrow I must inform you directly what you already know, that we have overwhelming evidence to indicate the president of the United States and his cabinet have been assassinated. The Secretary of the Interior James Kilpatrick died upon hearing the tragic news. We have no one in the Constitution's line of succession.

"Adding to this unspeakable tragedy, the crisis in the Middle East is worsening by the hour. As some of you know, Israel has given Lebanon an ultimatum. They are to turn over the individuals suspected in the attempted assassination of their prime minister last month and agree to verifiably destroy the nuclear warheads owned by the Alliance states and now believed stored in Lebanon. The deadline will come at eleven here in Kansas, at noon in the district. It is conceivable that Lebanon may at that time make a defensive first strike against Israel. The Israelis have alerted their forces and it appears they are preparing to defend themselves even if it means having to defend against the nearby Alliance states of Syria and Iran. Only the leadership of the United States and Russia can deter them. If we do not have a president elected by that time, the country and the world will be placed in high risk."

Dipaula took a drink to clear his throat, and his mind, then continued, "The Russians have placed their military on high alert and are faced with a coup d'etat. If the hard-liners in Russia succeed in overthrowing Masarov, they will also undoubtedly enter the picture. The Chinese have already moved at least five battalions of troops and heavy artillery into the border region near Russia. Obviously, they are very concerned about a sudden change of leadership in Russia. I'm certain you are aware of the recent border clashes between these two superpowers. As you can see, the wrong move by any single country of nearly two dozen can start a deadly chain reaction.

"Due to the explosion on Capitol Hill, there are celebrations in Iran, Libya, The Sudan, and Lebanon, and other countries sympathetic to these

Alliance states, such as North Korea. You may not be fully aware, but these countries jointly have control of at least one hundred high kiloton nuclear weapons. They could in fact have more.

"Within the hour, the United Nations Security Council will meet to discuss this crisis as it relates to the United States and the world. I had our deputy ambassador to the UN spend a few hours with us in the White House. She has agreed to attend the security council meeting and to withhold information related to Kilpatrick's death. However, I would hope you could give us some direction in this area.

"I know you are disturbed about what you are being asked to do here. There is no clear-cut direction given by the Constitution. One thing I have kept in mind, the writers of our Constitution were ordinary citizens, people who loved their country. They were merely human like each of us. While they covered most areas of concern, they could not foresee the situation we now face. In their time, it was inconceivable that the elected national leadership of our nation could be wiped out in one blow.

"In any case, it is probably true you are now the highest elected authorities in the United States. Acting in concert, your decisions would most likely be accepted by the people of our country, especially in this time of emergency. And other countries, including those of the United Nation's Security Council, would most likely accept your decisions as well.

"Of course, you could choose to take more time than I have suggested. However, with all due respect, I mention that while you deliberate and ponder this question, the nation and the world moves closer to chaos and annihilation. You can wait until tomorrow to gather more data, or you can act now. It is my considered position to wait would serve neither you as individuals nor our nation.

"Those of us in the White House are not elected officials. We have no direct authority to make the critical decisions. If you do not act, . . . no one will, with the possible exception of our military. They will continue to take whatever action necessary to defend the best interests of the United States. However, they have no power to negotiate, or install civilian authority. You are the obvious body to do so and in my estimation, the only body able to do so. I have been assured by our ranking military officers that whomever you elect to serve as the president of the United States would be respected as such by the highest-ranking military officers of this country.

"Of course, I can answer a few questions but must go back to the district as soon as possible. My taxi is being refueled as we speak. I have every confidence that you will do what is required in this crisis. You will save the day not because you are superhuman but precisely because you are merely human. Not because you are governors, but because each one of you is as patriotic as those men assembled in Philadelphia over two hundred years ago. Our nation is in its greatest hour of need. Only you can save her."

Then, he added, "On a personal note, I will be ready to support the decisions you make here, as will all the men and women in the White House, in the State Department and in the military. We acknowledge that you have full authority."

He then paused briefly before continuing, "Ladies and Gentlemen, your goal is clear to me. Elect a president and vice president of the United States, and do it as quickly as prudence will allow. May God bless you in your effort."

The room was silent for several onerous seconds. The national security advisor answered a dozen questions before concluding his presentation. Thirty minutes after he arrived, Dipaula turned, shook the hand of Governor Dupree and left the room.

The Nighhawk was refueled and shot into the sky headed back to Andrews at mock two.

Chapter Twenty-Seven

10:05 am, Amish Countryside

Kamile moved away from the window and let the curtain drop casually back in place. The search of the adjoining farm was now complete. The police and military vehicles stood in a frozen circle facing the farmhouse. Other vehicles were also starting to move down the road toward them. One of the military helicopters now slowly turned on its axis and faced the house.

Kamile looked at Samir and said in a low, despondent voice, "They are coming. Let us prepare the others."

The two men walked into the room where the Amish family was quietly sitting. None of them had moved from their assigned position.

Pointing to the eldest man, Kamile said, "You, you will be first. Come here!" The man stood up and walked through the doorway behind the assassin.

Kamile took the old man into the kitchen and forced him to look out the window. He could see police and military vehicles lining the front of the house, heavily armed men behind the vehicles, others lying prone, weapons aimed at the building.

Suddenly, a voice on the loudspeaker ripped through the silence, "All of you in the house, listen carefully, this is the police. Remain in your home. I repeat, remain in your home until we call you out. Stay away from the windows and doors!"

The old man exposed no sign of fear. Men of the modern world had invaded his peaceful farmland once again with their violence as they had years ago in a small one-room schoolhouse.

"Those men are here to kill," Kamile whispered. "That is all they know."

"You have entered my home without invitation," the old man said as he peered through the curtains. "You have threatened the lives of my family. We are a peaceful people." Turning to face Kamile, he continued, "Whatever quarrel you have with them, it does not involve my family."

Kamile had seen this defiant look before; the courage of simple men. It never impressed him; it enraged him. "Old man, you have spent your life looking the other way while millions starve to death and are beaten and imprisoned. You live a life of plenty while the world starves in filth and suffering. I have no pity, no mercy on you or your family. The children, for them death may be more just than living their life in a cave of ignorance, self-indulgence, and indifference to the sufferings of others." Taking the man down a hallway and into a bedroom, he ordered, "Sit on the floor and do not move or you will all die."

The man looked up at Kamile and said, with unmasked defiance, "It is the Lord God who determines who will live and who will die. The reward for disobeying God's law is death itself and it will be given swiftly to those who defy his law."

The man's arrogance shot through the assassin, filling his body with sudden rage. "What do you know of God, old man?" Kamile shouted in anger. "You, who hide behind the walls of this place and pretend to serve God." His emotions exploded in unchecked frenzy as he pointed the weapon at the man's head, nearly pulling the trigger, "You are the worst of hypocrites; hiding behind the ways of other times and other hypocrites. You turn your eyes from the world outside because you are not men enough to live in the world your God has created." Moving forward, his fingers tightened on the trigger, tension mounting within him fueled by stress and fatigue of the past hours. "I should kill you right now," his hands shaking, his face snarled, "so you could see the hate in your God's eyes." Moving closer, "You hide in the shadows of the past and cloak yourself with a robe of religious arrogance." The gun was now pressed firmly against the old man's forehead, into the skin, forcing his head back. "You know nothing of Allah, only your own needs," Kamile continued to shout, "The people in this country are devils and you may be the worst among them."

Kamile, breathing intensely, pulled the weapon back, leaving a deep imprint on the man's head. Catching his breath, he turned and walked away. Within a minute, he returned with a young man. "This is your father?"

"Yes," replied the young man.

"Then you will go and tell those outside they have found what they are searching for. Tell them we demand a car to take us to an airplane capable of flying for over a thousand miles. If they do not comply with our demands, your father will be the first to die. Do you understand?"

The young man looked down at his father and replied, "Yes, I understand."

The men outside waited for Team One to declare the adjacent farmhouse to be secure. The leap-frog pattern wasn't flawless, but it was effective.

A dark blue police car was parked directly in front of the house. Donovan and Merrall peered over the hood of the car and into the window.

"James?" Merrall whispered, her eyes not leaving the farmhouse. "James, look there!" Sandra almost shouted.

The curtain was moving slightly.

"There's something wrong here," Sandra whispered. "Something's really wrong."

Donovan took a deep breath and replied, "Yeah, I feel it too."

A movement at the front door. An Amish man with his hands behind his head, moved slowly from the open doorway. Fingers moved to triggers as the loudspeaker blared, "Stop, don't move any further. Hold your fire! Hold your fire!"

The young man stopped on the porch, shaking with fright.

"Possible trouble with Team Two! I repeat, possible trouble, Team Two!" Donovan voiced into the microphone.

"Roger, Two! What is it?" Linnet Singleton replied.

"Not sure," answered James. "What's your situation?"

"We're in the process of removing the family. It appears we're stable here. Should we stop the evacuation?" Singleton asked.

"No. Just speed things up if you can. Let me know when you're finished and then stand by, we may need you over here," answered Donovan.

Singleton moved quickly to evacuate the house. In front of her, a man holding an infant came through the doorway.

Lawrence shouted to him, "Hurry! Out here to the van! Fast!"

The man with the baby walked quickly to the other family members and waited with them for the last man to come out.

"Is that all?" the sheriff shouted to the family standing in a tight huddle behind the security van.

"Yes," replied the man with the baby.

The Amish family was loaded into the van and taken to the schoolhouse. Linnet Singleton immediately pressed the transmitter and said, "Team Two? This is One."

"Linnet, this is Donovan," came the reply. "What's your situation?"

"We have the family out and are securing the home."

"Linnet, stand by. We have a hostage situation. Have Martin get over here fast."

"Martin's on his way. We'll stand by here." Singleton could sense the tension in James's voice. The moment they had waited for had finally arrived.

Donovan turned to Captain Hillman of the Pennsylvania State Patrol and said, "They're secure for now, no one can leave! Let's not aggravate the situation." His words faded beneath the roar of the HH-60 Chopper now circling the house. Donovan shouted, "Order that helicopter to get the hell out of here and completely out of sight!"

A few seconds later, Hillman watched the helicopter move away. He took a deep swallow, gathered his thoughts and shouted to the man on the steps, "Move forward, down the steps and walk slowly toward the car," he said.

The young man did as he was told and stopped a few feet away on the frozen ground. He was still in his nightclothes; shivering in the thirty-two degrees and four-mile-an-hour wind, which gently moved around the house and through the vehicles surrounding it.

"Now walk slowly behind the cars," shouted Hillman.

The young man walked between the vehicles and stopped. Donovan gave him a quick search and pulled him behind a van then asked, "Who are you?"

"My family is in there with two men who have weapons."

"What's your name?"

"My name is Ezra. They said if you do not give them a car and take them to an airplane, they will kill my family. They are madmen! They will do what they say. I know it! My little sister was killed by such a man."

"Calm down," James whispered. "We'll do whatever possible to help you and your family. You've got to tell us what the situation is inside the house; every detail."

9:15 AM, Kansas

Dupree left the Republican Caucus and walked up the secured stairway to the room above where Gen. James Sanchez had arrived a half hour before.

The sixty-two year old, six-foot-three-inch Sanchez, was brought to McConnell Air Force Base to make a statement of support and loyalty for the new commander in chief following the swearing in, which everyone hoped would be soon. He was now fully aware of the situation. Each of the highest-ranking generals and admirals of the military forces was on standby for a priority phone call from General Sanchez. With one exception, Gen. Jake McCloud, he wasn't taking any calls.

Military officers, military police, FBI, state security officers, and Secret Service agents waited on the main floor of the Officer's Club. They continued their casual conversations while focusing sharply on the convention chairman as he entered the room. No one spoke to the governor as he walked across the floor to Sanchez.

"General," said Dupree.

"Governor," replied Sanchez. "How are things progressing?"

"Okay, I guess. Do you know who the lead Secret Service agent is?"

"Yes, I believe it's a Mr. Johnson. That's him over there," Sanchez answered, pointing to Terry Johnson who had arrived from Washington DC an hour earlier.

"Thank you, General," replied Dupree. "What's the military situation?"

The general looked around. "Can we go to a more secure area, sir?" asked Sanchez.

"Yeah. There must be another meeting room up here."

After finding a small room down the hall, General Sanchez ordered security guards to be stationed outside the room. The ranking Secret Service agent, Terry Johnson, was asked to join the governor and the general.

"Johnson, how are things at the White House?" asked Dupree.

"Governor, it isn't real stable right now. Networks have been going nonstop since the explosion. Everyone's becoming more aware of the real situation. They're demanding Secretary Kilpatrick give a live press conference. The tension's unbearable. It's—"

"What about the military?" interrupted Dupree, turning to the general. "How are they holding together?"

"Well, Governor, to be honest, we're having some difficulty," responded Sanchez. "The troops here in the states are on full alert. The Russians and Israelis have just placed their military on full alert as well. The major Alliance countries have directed their weapons in all directions. The damn Chinese have moved several divisions into the area near Russia. I have unconfirmed reports of weapons fire at Dushanbe, near the Afghan border and also at Lahore, near the border between Pakistan and India. Israel is becoming paranoid of every move around their borders and may strike Lebanon at any time. If they do, this whole damn thing will go up in smoke. The US Military can't sit by and watch things happen. At some point, someone needs to call the shots, so to speak."

"Mr. Johnson," Dupree, stroked his hair, "can you put me in touch with Barry Dipaula; on a secure line?"

"Yes, sir. I believe so," replied Johnson.

In seconds, Dupree was on the line with Dipaula who had just arrived at the White House from his whirlwind visit to Kansas.

"Gary, I hope things are moving along quickly over there," said Dipaula. "We've used up about all the time we can here. It's approaching critical mass."

"I know, Barry. We're moving as quickly as possible. No one is stalling. Not an easy call, pal. Appreciate your coming out. Believe me, it helped," replied Dupree.

"Yeah, I understand. We'll do whatever's necessary, Governor. But let me know immediately when it happens."

"Barry, believe me. You'll be the first one outside this room who'll know," answered Dupree. "By the way, your man is convincing. I heard him earlier. Can he continue to calm matters?" asked Dupree, referring to a second and somewhat less successful broadcast given by Bob Caridene.

"I really don't believe so, Governor. I don't think it'll work anymore. That avenue has been used up. The press, politicians, and diplomats from every corner are now demanding the man be physically present for some kind of press conference. The pressure's great here. Please don't delay any more than necessary." Dipaula's voice lowered and he said slowly, "I believe you must act quickly or it won't matter to any of us. We won't just be a country without a president. We may not even be a country."

"We have most of the details worked out," replied Dupree. "The battles have been fought. Only the voting remains. It should be fairly cut and dried, I believe, I hope. If we can—"

"Hold it Governor," Dipaula snapped. "What is it Page?"

Dupree could hear the conversation and he listened intently.

"We've got a big problem," Page said, nearly out of breath. "That brainless asshole McCloud is attacking the mansion."

"What! Shit!" Dipaula's face flushed. "That ignorant bastard!"

"What's happening, Dipaula?" questioned Dupree. "What the hell's happening out there?"

"I don't know, Governor. But I've just been told McCloud is attacking the mansion. Is General Sanchez there?"

"Yes."

"Put him on! I need him to cut an ugly wart off my ass before it sends the White House up in flames."

Dupree quickly handed the phone to Sanchez.

10:40 AM
The White House

Outside the mansion, McCloud's troops had leveled the main guardhouse, driven a gaping hole through the fence, and moved over the remains. His troops were now facing a wall of uniformed and plain-clothes agents, many lying prone on the icy lawn, weapons in hand. The marine guards atop the mansion and the Old Executive Office Building were stunned, not knowing who to fire upon. McCloud's own troops were feeling an intense uneasiness, moving only on the reactions imbedded into them over years of military training. The commanding general was issuing orders; they had no choice but to obey. But the White House for God's sakes? The White House!

Pete Christenson stood across the street watching the unbelievable scene before him. A battlefield completely surrounded the Treasury, White House, and Old Executive Office buildings. *Now is the time*, he thought to himself. *In the next few minutes, I'll finally be in the Oval Office.*

A few feet inside the fence, McCloud raised his bullhorn toward the rooftop and shouted, "The White House and surrounding buildings are now under martial law. You men on the roof, this is Gen. Jake McCloud, ranking officer of the entire US Military. There has been an attempted coup here in the district by the National Militia and their sympathizers. The complete line of presidential succession has been eliminated. The man inside this building pretending to be the acting president is an imposter. We are moving in to secure the building. You are now being given a direct order to lower your weapons." Lowering the horn, he continued, "To you men in front of me, any resistance will be met with full force. Now, drop your weapons or you will be fired upon."

Inside, in the Situation Room, Dipaula was on the line with General Sanchez. "McCloud is immediately outside and forcing his way into the building. We've told him where you are and why you're there, General. He won't listen to any of us."

"Barry, he's giving us an ultimatum," Page shouted. "Ten minutes or he's coming in!"

"Gotta go, General," Dipaula said, his hands shaking in anger. "We're about to have a full-blown siege here. You have to move fast and stop this runaway asshole or he'll destroy this building and maybe the country along with it!"

"I'll try, Dipaula. I'll do what I can from here!"

"Do something, now, General! Anything! Now!"

"Where's General Glazer?"

"He should be on his way here. We don't have much time."

"We'll get you some help, and soon," the general almost shouted. "Hang in there as best you can."

"Barry, you'd better hurry," shouted Page. "A lot of people are gonna die up there!"

Chapter Twenty-Eight

11:00 AM, Pennsylvania

Steam rose from the nostrils of men lying on the ground, nervous fingers resting on anxious triggers.

The voice shouted through the doorway, defiant, assured, "You know who we are and what we are capable of doing. Therefore, you will bring an airplane to take us away from here. If we do not leave this house for the airfield in five minutes, I will kill one of these people."

Donovan knew he wasn't about to change anything. "It will take some time to get a plane to the airport. A plane with the capability to fly that distance will have to be brought in. This little community obviously does not have such a plane," answered Donovan, not sure if what he was saying was correct. In any case, it sounded good and could buy some valuable time.

"Then, we will wait at the airport in the van. Once the plane is loaded, we will release some of the hostages. When we reach our destination, unharmed, we will release the rest. No one will die unless you choose so. You will keep the radio in the van, do you understand? Do not damage the radio in the van."

"I understand," replied Donovan.

"Do not mistake my demands for mere requests."

Donovan's eyes were red with the loss of sleep, yet he had to act soon and he had to think with a clear head. He rubbed the fatigue from his eyes and said, "Captain, get me some specifications on the nearest airport large enough to handle a plane with that range, and where we could manage the situation."

Donovan moved next to Sandra Merrall. "Any ideas? I could sure use some help here."

"James, I think we may have to go through the motions, at least to the airport," Sandra replied. "I don't think they'll kill the family if you do what they ask. It's not their style. Either way, if you rush them, it's over. We both know they'll never be brought to trial or see the inside of a prison. There's been too much killing, James, too much. Not these people. We'll never take them alive, but we might be able to save an innocent family. I say let 'em go."

Donovan walked over to the microphone and said, "This is James Donovan. We're going to have an airplane brought in. It would be best if you waited here for an hour or so before transferring to the airfield. It may take some time for a plane that size to be located. You will be more comfortable in that house. We understand the airfield is not very large. It could be a difficult landing and takeoff for a plane with the range you're requesting—maybe, impossible."

No answer from inside.

A car was approaching from their right. It was a vehicle with FBI Special Agents Martin, Singleton, and Steward along with Secret Service agent Gregg Lawrence. Like someone from home, they were a comfort to Donovan in this volatile situation.

Time was running out. Suddenly the voice from the house shouted, "Donovan, do you hear me?"

"Yes, I hear you."

"You have five minutes from now to move the van to the house steps. Only the driver is to be inside. Otherwise, the van must be empty. The side doors must be open and facing the steps. You have only five minutes. If you do not move quickly, someone will die."

"Will you let the women and children go if we do as you ask?" questioned James.

"I will decide such things, not you. But, if you do as we say, someone will be released before we depart for the airport. Remember, no one in the van except the driver. Don't try anything foolish. The plane must arrive at the airport in one hour from now or we will be forced to do something for which you will be responsible. We have been told there is an airport near Lancaster, a city close by here. No more delays. You now have only four minutes."

Donovan looked at the lieutenant and asked, "Do we have an option?"

"I don't see one."

"Captain?" asked Donovan.

The captain shook his head and said, "He'll most likely kill someone if we don't bring the van up."

"Okay. Mays, Nelson," Donovan said, "have your sharpshooters ready. Get someone to drive the van and let's get it up to the house before he starts shooting."

A member of the FBI assault team climbed into the van and sat behind the wheel. Police and National Guard vehicles pulled away from the front of the house, making room for the van.

The van backed up onto the yard as Lawrence and Singleton approached Donovan and Merrall.

"Looks bad," said Lawrence.

"Brian, Linnet, it's good to see you guys." Donovan meant it.

"Another flight from the district is landing at the airport as we speak," Linnet said. "Seven people from the service and twelve more from the FBI. I'm not sure who's in the group, but I'm glad they're here. Also, it appears the Lancaster Airport is the closest manageable airport."

James slowly nodded his head in agreement, his eyes locked on the van, now coming to a stop in front of the steps. Its side doors were open and facing the front door of the house, just ten feet away.

Captain Hillman laid the microphone in the front seat of the patrol car and walked over to Donovan. He pulled the top of his padded dark blue jacket tighter, feeling the morning chill.

"What did you find out?" Donovan asked the Captain.

"Mr. Donovan, the Lancaster Airport has a runway of about five thousand feet. They tell me it primarily serves single and twin-engine aircraft. 737 or MD-80 normally require about seven or eight thousand feet. In the cold, they can land on a shorter field. However, they think, in this weather, they will need a minimum of sixty-five hundred feet."

"Someone else will have to make the call on which plane," Donovan said, his eyes still glued to the scene in front of him.

Everyone waited. The house was quiet. The agent sat uneasy behind the wheel, looking at the front door of the house, one hand on the door handle, the other on the wheel.

"We still have one person missing," Gregg Lawrence noted. "He could be anywhere. Should we freeze things as they are, or continue the search?"

Donovan was certain Fajil was not in this house. He was a loner. "Once this van has cleared the area, continue the search. The people at central can be of help. They're in better shape to deal with the situation than some of us who're running on fumes."

At the schoolhouse, which was built following the school shooting in 2006, police officers waited for the van with the Amish family just released by

Team One, to arrive. Twenty minutes had now passed since it left the house. It was a little late, but nothing to be alarmed about, not yet.

Police vehicles were scattered around the countryside keeping watch over roads and fields, trying to cover an area ten miles in radius from point central, the distance believed necessary to contain the fugitives.

A police vehicle was parked at the side of a meandering, tree-lined country road near a small wooden bridge. Two state patrol officers were standing on the bridge looking up and down the icy stream. One held a cigarette in his gloved hand. The other had both hands in his jacket pockets. A sheriff's department van approached from around a curve.

One of the officers removed his hands from his jacket and signaled the van to stop. Seeing it was a sheriff's van with two uniformed officers in the front, the men on the bridge weren't too alarmed. The vehicle came to a slow stop. A trooper casually tossed his cigarette over the bridge and asked the driver, "Where are you headed?" His eyes peered into the van at the Amish family sitting quietly in the back.

The driver, obviously stressed, replied, "Listen to me very carefully. Don't overreact. There is someone in this van with a grenade and a handgun. He'll pull the pin if you don't do exactly as he says."

The officers were stunned. "What?"

The deputy in the front passenger's seat looked grim. "He wants you to throw your guns into the river. Now!" the driver said, his voice cracking a bit.

They hesitated. The driver repeated, "Now! Please!"

The state troopers reluctantly threw their side arms over the rail and into the stream.

A loud voice from inside the van ordered, "Both of you move to the side of the bridge in front of the van and lay down with your faces to the ground."

The officers did as they were instructed.

The side door opened, out came a young woman and a sturdily built man with a baby in his arms.

11:10 AM, The White House

The scene in front of the White House had turned ugly. McCloud and his troops filled the barricaded stretch of Pennsylvania Avenue and the streets surrounding the compound. The general looked at his watch and then shouted through the bullhorn, "Two minutes. You have two minutes to drop your weapons. If you do, no one will get hurt."

"General," Major Holster interrupted. "Pete Christenson is here, sir."
"Christenson? Where?"
"He's over there, sir; across the street."

McCloud could see the president of the National Militia standing in the midst of several dozen onlookers. To his right was Vice Pres. Marvin Calloway.

"Good," murmured the general. "The time has finally arrived."

Capt. Bernie Waltrip standing next to Holster asked, "Who's he Major?"

McCloud softly replied, "Your new president, son."

Waltrip looked closely at the man in the park. "Who did—"

"General McCloud, this is Special Agent Van Meter," the agent shouted loud enough for all to hear, as he stepped from behind the armed uniformed officers outside the entrance. "I repeat, you are in a secure area protected by the United States Secret Service. Move your troops away from the building. You are committing a federal felony and will face serious consequences. You have no authority here, General."

"Cut the shit, Van Meter! Drop your weapons, now!" responded an enraged McCloud. "Your coup is finished. This is the United States of America. You people destroyed the Capitol, but you won't take over the White House."

Uncomfortable thoughts raced through the men standing around the general. *Is the general right? This is the White House! Why are we attacking the White House? This is insane! That's the Secret Service for God's sake!*

"General. There's been enough bloodshed," shouted Van Meter. "We've asked you to come in. Back your men away and come inside. See for yourself what's happening here. We don't have—" Suddenly, a loud pounding from above broke his sentence.

Everyone looked to the sky. Half a dozen military helicopters swarmed in over them. Four came to a stationary position two hundred feet in the air, forming a rough circle around the confrontation taking place on the front lawn. The roar was deafening. Two others flew over the mansion and lowered onto the south lawn, not far from Marine One, which had returned from Maryland.

The heavily armed choppers sent a tornado of violent turbulence blasting down on the scene, sending an ear-splitting, pounding thunder echoing off the frosted walls of the mansion. Men on the ground shielded their faces from the freezing chill descending rapidly on them from above.

"Screw you!" yelled McCloud over the noise. "I know what's goin' on. Do you deny that the man speaking for Kilpatrick is an imposter?" Looking up in anger, he shouted, "Who the shit ordered those choppers?" His voice lost in the noise.

"General," Van Meter's voice wasn't going anywhere, not penetrating the vibrating, bone-jolting noise. He dropped his weapon and with hands extended in front of him, palms up, he moved forward and stopped a few feet in front of McCloud. "General!" he yelled. "Come inside and see for yourself!" he pleaded, eyes squinting from the fierce wind.

Face red with anger, the general shouted back, "You bet your ass I will, and one minute from now. Tell the choppers to move away or I'll blast the building right now!" Moving the bullhorn across the lawn in front of him, McCloud clamored, "Drop your weapons and move out of the way!" Turning back to Van Meter, he screamed, "Is he an imposter? Answer me, Van Meter! Is the real Kilpatrick alive inside, or is he dead along with the rest?" Then, staring directly into VanMeter's eyes, he stated as softly as a preacher at a funeral, "You now have thirty seconds."

Van Meter couldn't hear, but he could read the general's lips as he backed toward the front entrance.

The choppers hovered directly over the scene. Determined eyes of pilots aimed the cannons at the soldiers standing behind McCloud. Then, as suddenly as they had descended, the choppers backed away and circled high into the sky. The men on the lawn watched as they climbed up and away; three, four, five hundred feet before coming to rest in the sky above.

11:18 AM, Pennsylvania

The dark blue and white police car pulled up to the roadblock near State Route 41 and Valley Road. Five officers were standing near their vehicles.

"Where are you guys goin'?" asked the officer on the road. He looked into the car and saw two police officers in the front seat and two Amish women and a small child in the back.

"The little boy needs a doctor. The women won't let him travel by himself. I don't mind, it gets me out of this situation for a while."

"Yeah, don't want to get your tail shot off, huh."

"Or froze to death like you guys." The driver smiled and pulled away.

The Amish family was now reported missing from the schoolhouse. A search began for the missing van.

Chapter Twenty-Nine

11:20 am, The White House

McCloud looked up from his watch and shouted, "Time's up, Van Meter!"

"Stay back, General!" the agent yelled.

"Take it, men!" McCloud said as he stepped forward.

"Don't do this, General!" shouted Van Meter.

"You did it, Van Meter! You and that conspirator traitor, Dipaula," he screamed as he moved forward. "You killed the president and now the mighty right arm of God is gonna take you out!"

McCloud and his men were now twenty feet from the thick line of Secret Service agents and thirty feet from the main entry doors.

"Stop, McCloud! Stop now! This doesn't hav—"

"Move your men back, General!" Dipaula shouted, standing alone in the open doorway behind Van Meter and his men. "Now, before it's too late!"

Catching sight of Dipaula, a sadistic grin came over McCloud's face. "Dipaula! So, you're still here; thought you might have run along with the other political cowards." The grin widened.

McCloud turned slightly to his left and shouted to his men, "That man in the doorway, Barry Dipaula, has been giving orders from inside this house. He has been deceiving all of us, the entire world, into believing that Secretary Kilpatrick is alive and well. All the time, Kilpatrick has been dead; killed at Dipaula's orders!"

Dipaula said nothing.

"He's dead, isn't that right, Dipaula?" McCloud shouted.

The heavily armed soldiers behind McCloud had their weapons leveled on the men in front of them, but their eyes focused on the man standing in the open doorway. The scene was frozen as everyone waited for the national security advisor to answer.

Dipaula walked through the line of agents and stood a few feet from McCloud. After staring into the General's eyes for a few seconds he turned to the men around him and said, "The only conspiracy taking place here is the one led by General McCloud, and you will become part of it if you continue this assault. This man is part of the National Militia. They are out to take the country by force. Drop your weapons. This is still a democratic country, governed by laws; laws that even the military must observe."

"It's too late for your canned speeches, Dipaula," McCloud shouted. "This country is finished with talk from people like you, Bergstrom and the rest. You've trampled on the words, 'In God we trust.' You've blasphemed the sacred words, 'One nation under God.' You've used the Constitution for your own selfish gains and it's time to be done with you and start over again."

"With you and Pete Christenson, General? You two are the great revolution; the new beginning?"

"That's right, Dipaula, and tens of millions with us. You're history. Today you're nothing but history—a bad dream. President Christenson will give us a new beginning. We will again become one nation under God."

The nervous soldiers around McCloud looked to each other, now more uncertain than ever.

"What's your new position going to be, General," Dipaula asked. "I can't see you playing second fiddle to Christenson. What's your new role; commander and chief?"

"I'm merely God's servant, Dipaula; something you can't understand. God will place me where I can do his work. He always has. He has a place for me."

"He certainly does, General. God has a special place for men like you. You think you can take this country simply by taking this house? The country is more than a building. It's free people and their constitution—a constitution, which allows for change by votes not by bullets."

"You're wrong, Dipaula. The Constitution says it's not only the right but the duty, the obligation, of the people when ruled by tyranny to take their country back by force, if necessary."

"Tyranny? Ruled by tyranny?" Dipaula looked around to the troops and said, "Do you believe, really believe what the general is saying?"

"Damn right they do, Dipaula!" McCloud yelled. "Now step aside."

"You'll have to go through me, General," Dipaula declared, his fists clenched.

"You want to be the martyr, eh, Dipaula?" He raised his pistol. "Self-righteous to the end."

"I don't want to be a martyr, General. Do you?" Then turning his eyes to the troops, he shouted, "Over the last few hours, this man's militia has been blowing up power stations, federal buildings, and killing innocent people." Then, looking at a young African American staff sergeant he added, "They want to form an all-white state. Is that what you want to support? Do any of you want to die in the uniform of this country while supporting a madman? Look up there!" he yelled, pointing to the sky.

As the fully armed choppers fanned out six hundred feet above the scene, a dozen men walked out of the White House; seven in military uniform, one with a megaphone in hand. They stepped through the agents holding position at the foot of the steps and moved next to Dipaula. Three of the twelve had stars on their shoulders. In the center was Lt. Gen. George Glazer, in charge of the White House Military Office. Chris Van Meter moved forward with the men and stood next to Dipaula.

McCloud looked at the imposing strength, silver stars mixed with silver eagles. He was definitely outflanked.

Glazer stepped forward, holding a remote microphone that transmitted to the speakers located throughout the compound. "I am Lt. Gen. George Glazer, military assistant to the president and director of the White House Military Office. I am in charge of all military personnel on White House grounds. Four star General Sanchez is in command of all US Military forces worldwide and has authorized our mission here. With me are Maj. Gen. Samuel Reisenauer from Andrews and Brig. Gen. Anthony Scarfo commander of the US Army Post at Fort Bragg, North Carolina. General McCloud is here in a renegade capacity and not acting under authorization of the United States Military." Looking directly at the distraught man in front of him, Glazer continued. "General McCloud, by authority of military statues, we hereby relieve you of all command." Looking about, he added, "Troops previously commanded by General McCloud are immediately placed under the command of General Reisenauer. You men are to stand down and immediately remove yourselves from the compound."

"Don't move an inch!" shouted McCloud. "This is part of the conspiracy! Prepare to fire!"

No one moved.

"General McCloud, you will immediately hand over your weapon!" demanded Glazer. "Now, General!"

"You're full of rat shit if you think I'm gonna give in to your insurrection." He raised his pistol toward Dipaula and squeezed the trigger.

Instinctively, Van Meter dropped in front of Dipaula taking the bullet in his chest, as the loud report exploded into the air. Everyone froze. Dipaula reacted instantly and vaulted over the falling agent, reached out and deflected the weapon as it fired its second shot into the frozen dirt. He then rolled over the general, knocking him to the ground.

McCloud swung his elbow around, catching Dipaula on the forehead, smashing him back. Like a field of surprised crickets, dozens of loud clicks filled the lawn as weapons suddenly cocked, barrels pointed directly at the defeated general's head.

Major Holster started to turn away. Captain Waltrip eased his rifle into the major's ribs, "Not a good idea, Major."

Not willing to give up, McCloud shouted, "You men are protecting an imposter! Don't you see, you're taking part in an attempt to overthrow your own government?" His eyes widened and glassed over, "Listen to me, your freedom depends on it! You don't want be part of this immoral, bloody coup! You fools! You idiots!"

Silence. He lowered his weapon and laid back on the icy grass, completely drained. "Lord, I'm sorry, Lord. It almost worked, Lord" he muttered. "Lord, it almost worked, Lord."

Across the street, in Lafayette Park, Christenson and Calloway backed away from the scene, a half-dozen men following. Turning, they began to walk briskly up the street.

As the members of the National Militia approached an intersection, a dozen men moved in front of them and leveled automatic weapons on them.

"Hold it! This is the FBI. You men are under arrest," shouted the lead agent.

Christenson turned to see a dozen more directly behind. He stepped forward and said, "What's going on, here? What do you mean, under arrest?"

11:23 AM
Pennsylvania

The midday sun had warmed up the area slightly, but the men outside the home were feeling the chill of the morning breeze.

"James, we've just received a report from FBI Deputy Director Clarke," reported an FBI officer. "That van carrying the Amish family from the last house hasn't arrived at the school yet,"

"That's not good," said Singleton. "We've been here a long time and they left before we did. I saw the van pull away myself."

"Damn!" exclaimed Lawrence. "What the hell went wrong?"

Lieutenant Nelson noticed a movement at the window. "There's activity!" he shouted.

As everyone stared at the house, an Amish woman appeared in the doorway wearing a white robe, her hands tied behind her back. She was followed quickly by another woman.

Soon all the family members, one man, two women, and three children, were standing on the porch near the door in a semicircle, tied together at their hands and waists. Two men with pillow cases over their heads, slits cut for their eyes, moved into the middle of the group. They both held a grenade in one hand and a machine gun in the other.

"Hold your fire!" ordered Captain Hillman. The assault team froze in a ready position. Dogs stood poised, ready to leap the twenty yards onto the white porch.

"Listen to him!" yelled Kamile. "These people will die if you do not listen! We have pulled the pins from the grenades. We are leaving. The airplane must be waiting for us or one of these people will die. Do you understand me, Donovan?"

Donovan raised his head above the car and shouted, "We can't promise the plane will be there when you arrive. It has to be located first. We need more time."

"Listen to me, Donovan. I will not repeat myself. If the plane is not at the airport when we arrive, one of these people will die. We are not so foolish as to be led around like children as you delay for time. If we do not reach the airport in the time I think is reasonable, we will kill one of these people. You must also understand, I know much about aircraft. In this cold temperature, such a plane could land on a very small runway. Perhaps a DC-9 or 737 would be sufficient. Perhaps even a corporation jet. Do not play silly games with me. I am no fool."

Donovan knew he could not respond. This man was indeed no fool. They had to let them go or risk the lives of innocent people. Sandra was right; enough people had been killed this past fifteen hours.

The circle closed behind the assassins and they moved toward the wooden steps leading down to the van.

Donovan shouted, "You said you would release some of these people before you left this house. Show us your word is good."

"We will release one if you do not attempt to stop us," answered Kamile.

The assassins entered the van, shielded by the Amish.

"He speaks good English," said Linnet Singleton.

Sandra answered, "Yes, he is either Fajil or Kamile."

"What do you remember about Kamile?" asked Donovan.

"He's intensely dedicated to Fajil," she responded. "Evidently, they were kids together. He was a dedicated family man. He had a family. Maybe he likes kids, I don't know."

The assassins immediately dropped to the floor of the van and pushed out an eleven-year-old girl before the door slid shut.

"Take us immediately to the airport," Kamile shouted to the driver. "Do you understand this?" He held up the grenade. The pin was definitely pulled; it was alive.

The girl didn't move from outside the van. She banged her fists on the door and shouted, "Let them go! Let them go! Momma, I love you. Poppa, don't let them do this."

She continued to pound on the door. Her father, Ezra, broke from behind the protection of the squad car and ran to his daughter. She was still hitting the door with her fists as he grabbed her. The van slowly moved away.

Two police vehicles led the van down the narrow country road in the direction of the Lancaster Airport. Behind the van were a dozen vehicles, blue and red lights flashing.

The road ahead was cleared. Four helicopters were ordered back into the air. An aging Aerospatiale Puma from Lancaster Airport with six men on board and a converted Agusta A109 Mk II Plus used by the Pennsylvania State Patrol eased up and off to either side of the van, maintaining two hundred feet. The Air Force Pave Hawk moved behind the caravan loaded with a dozen men.

A new EH101 helicopter from Baltimore with fifteen heavily armed men on board flew low over the trees to take a position in front of the motorcade. As it approached a small bridge, the pilot saw a sheriff's van hidden in the trees near the end of the bridge.

"Kim, down there!" he shouted to his copilot.

"Better call Central. Looks like the missing van."

The Kremlin, 7:40 PM

Masarov was in his office with a half-dozen men. "A few minutes ago, our military was ordered to stand away from full readiness," Masarov spoke with as much confidence as he could collect under pressure. "I am convinced neither the Americans nor the renegade Alliance pose a direct threat to our country and the new President Kilpatrick of the United States has taken sufficient control of their military."

Masarov had spoken both with Tarasavitch and Igmanov, now in the Russian embassy, and decided to trust Dipaula and the American civilians in the basement of the White House. In doing so, he knew he risked the security of Russia and perhaps that of the entire world. He was the one man in Russia holding the world together on a gamble, determined the generals would not lead the world into nuclear disaster. He had hoped the threat would have ended with the treaties of the early nineties. That did not happen.

"Masarov," asked Chernosoki. "You have been given the responsibility to defend the people of Russia, but are you so sure of Igmanov, or of this man, Dipaula? Are you so sure that what is happening in the United States is being, this minute, controlled by one man, this unknown man, Kilpatrick? What if the rebel militia forces control their nuclear arsenal?"

Neither Masarov nor Chernosvitov had told anyone in the room that Kilpatrick was dead. They had to avoid a careless mistake that could launch World War III. Anything that hinted of a provocation was to be avoided.

"Chernosoki's concern is well spoken," Yuri Starastinov calmly remarked, a hint of rebuke in his voice.

Chernosoki looked at the vice president with some surprise, as did the rest.

Starastinov continued, "Perhaps, this man, Kilpatrick, is a prisoner, or perhaps Obidiov is correct, he is dead. No one has seen him since this event began, so it's conceivable he is dead. If that is the case, then we may be dealing with a very dangerous situation indeed. If the world's greatest nuclear arsenal is in the hands of terrorists, we may have little time remaining to defend ourselves. We must move now to counter any provocation from the Americans."

Masarov didn't like what he heard. He looked directly at the vice president and said, "I believe that Igmanov is telling us the truth. I myself have spoken to Kilpatrick. Are you questioning me as well, Starastinov?" *There, I've done it! The president of Russia is now a part of the charade,* he thought.

Starastinov was nervous as he looked around the room to determine Masarov's support. Was it time to take control of the government?

"I do not say you are lying, Masarov, nor do I say you are a fool," responded Starastinov, "I am merely saying that the Americans are very good at deception. There has been some questioning, even in the United States, as to this man, Kilpatrick. No one has seen him. The television is filled with questions about this man. If what Obidiov and Chernosoki say is true, if this man is not in control of the military, then would you have us sit by and allow our country to be placed in a vulnerable position?"

Masarov remained silent while Chernosvitov spoke, "I believe Igmanov, and I believe that Masarov is still the president of Russia. I have a suggestion. If we do not see convincing evidence that a president, a civilian, is in charge of the government and the military forces of the United States within an agreed-upon time, then the military will again be placed on high alert and we will make preparations for war."

The men in the room were quiet, reflecting on the compromise. Then, as if on cue, they looked to Masarov. He sat with his arms on his desk, fingers entwined, looking at each man and then back to Chernosvitov.

"What time are you suggesting, Alexai?" asked Masarov.

"I think six hours would be sufficient."

"That's too long!" insisted Chernosoki.

Masarov was pleased that Chernosoki was even agreeing to the plan.

"Okay." said Masarov. "If we have not received sufficient proof that the United States is controlled by a civilian who is in charge of its military and there is no military threat against our region within, well . . . four hours, we will place our military again on full alert. We will then take the necessary steps to insure the defense of our country and prepare an offensive against the Alliance countries or anyone who threatens us. Until that time, no one is to leave this building or make any contact with the military unless I instruct it. You, Chernosoki, will remain in this room with me."

Chernosoki did not like the compromise entirely but felt he had a chance to get his way. In any case, he remembered the fate of his friend, General Obidiov. In four hours, they would be prepared to order the forces of Russia and the Ukraine on full alert and move to overtake Masarov. They would then move against the southern states.

Yes, thought Chernosoki, *in four hours, we shall see who is in control not only of the United States, but perhaps we shall also learn who is in control of Russia. You have four hours to live old man. You have sealed your own fate.*

Chapter Thirty

11:45 AM, Pennsylvania

Donovan, Merrall, and Lawrence were in the back seat of the moving patrol car. Captain Hillman was driving and Linnet Singleton was sitting in the front passenger's seat. They were traveling directly behind the van carrying the Amish family and the two assassins, Kamile and Samir.

The chatter on the car radio was suddenly interrupted by an alert. "This is Point Central to Unit One."

Captain Hillman picked up the microphone and said, "This is Unit One, Hillman here."

"This is Morrison, sir. I'm patching a patrolman through to you."

"Captain," the patrolman came on, "We have located the missing van and it appears the last man is out. He escaped from the last house; dressed as an Amish, holding a child with a grenade under the blanket. We didn't look close enough after getting your urgent call and the family didn't alert us for obvious reasons. Team One didn't find his weapon in the house. He had it blocked up inside the chimney."

"What's the situation now?"

"He took a patrol car and four hostages, two women, a child, and a sheriff's deputy. We have an All Points out for the patrol car. They passed through a roadblock at Valley Road where it crosses Route 41."

"Roger, we copy. Let us know the progress." Turning to Donovan, Hillman said, "Well, we now have two hostage situations."

Donovan shook his head and said, "The other guy may be the worst. We suspect he masterminded the assassination in DC."

"The guy in the patrol car must know of our situation here," Lawrence said. "I'm certain he's listening to our radio transmissions."

"James, do you think he'll head for the airport?" Linnet asked.

"That's a strong possibility. Captain, slow the car; I need the car in back of us."

"You got it."

The captain rolled down his window and with his left hand motioned for the car behind to move alongside. The car pulled out of line and came up next to Hillman. The officer lowered his window.

"We're going to transfer two passengers to your car," the captain yelled. "Don't use your radio. I repeat, don't use your radio."

The officer in the other car nodded his head. The cars slowed to a near stop. The two men quickly transferred cars and at the next intersection, turned left away from the motorcade.

The caravan moved through the frozen countryside, occasionally passing a police blockade; patrolmen, weapons in hand, stared at the van as it moved by. The Amish countryside was now experiencing the violent tornado of modern civilization roaring through its quiet community.

10:50 AM, Kansas

The knock from the Republican caucus came first. Edith Castle opened the door and was informed the Republicans had selected their candidates and would wait to be summoned. She went to the caucus chairman, Governor Kerry Donaldson from Kentucky, and told him the Republicans were waiting.

In a few minutes, acceptance by both Democratic candidates was announced to the caucus, followed immediately by a thundering applause from the main assembly room signaling the Democrats had reached a decision. It took another ten minutes for the governors to gather once again in the main assembly room. Now, the final decision would be made.

12:01 PM, Pennsylvania

It had been fifteen hours since the explosion on Capitol Hill. The convoy of National Guard and police units was now moving south on 501 toward the awaiting Lancaster Airport, keeping the assassins and their hostages heavily confined.

The control tower, located on a frozen grassy field to the north, stood alone like a faithful sentry. Its brown-windowed control room sat on a white sixty-foot-high pedestal. The entire structure looked more like a huge trophy than an air traffic control tower. Framing its base on three sides was the small parking area, which now contained employee, police, FAA, and FBI vehicles. South of the control tower, on the opposite side of the runway, the terminal and hangar area could be clearly seen.

Police vehicles lined the road, having been in place for almost a half hour. Proceeding down Airport Road, the motorcade again turned left, entering the terminal area. Driving a few hundred feet into the terminal compound, it arrived at the east corner of the Lancaster Airport Authority Building where it turned left once again onto a narrow paved road giving access to the aviation buildings now straight ahead. Immediately past the building, the lead vehicles stopped and waited for a sliding metal gate on the right to squeak open, providing access to a rough, unpaved road leading directly to the runway.

An hour had passed since civilian personnel had been cleared from the airport. Local reporters were also restricted from the area. Tension hung like a thick, dense fog.

Slowly, as if leading a funeral procession, the two lead patrol cars turned right, drove through the open gate, and moved across the bumpy access road, then turned right again onto the taxiway and headed toward the terminal.

Following closely behind the lead cars, the van turned right onto the open taxi area inside the fence. Behind the van came the caravan of cars and trucks containing federal agents, policemen, National Guard, and various assault units.

The motorcade pulled onto the tarmac, the hostage van securely tucked between a dozen vehicles. Inside the van, the two assassins appeared less confident and arrogant.

Sitting on the floor of the van, Kamile realized this would be a long perilous journey home. For a brief moment, his mind yielded to the exhaustion of the last thirty-two hours as it slipped into a semiconscious world where fantasy blends with reality, consciousness releases its grasp, and the overwhelming desire for escape blocks all external stimulus. For a few brief seconds he floated off, escaping to a world far away where friends laughed and danced in the cool desert night. Suddenly, Kamile snapped back into reality. He was breathing heavily as his eyes caught Samir's, and he realized his companion was aware of his momentary escape from the terrible danger they faced.

Kamile knew it would be easier to just die here, in this strange land, among these even stranger people. Shaking his head slightly, his unshaven face tensed as he smiled and looked at Samir. Samir nodded his awareness, forcing a weak smile in return. Both knew they were nearing the end of their lives.

A new and affectionate union immediately formed between them. They had shared much over the few years of their relationship, but now, they were bonded by their imminent deaths, a bond shared by men dying in battle, away from all things familiar. Their eyes moistened and the salty, stinging sensation caused them to again, focus on the situation at hand. This could be their last moment together in life, and they chilled at its passing, and of the unknown to come.

The lead car came to a stop on the icy tarmac. The other vehicles slowed, preparing to take up positions near the van. However, Kamile ordered the driver to leave the convoy and move further out onto the runway. It was allowed to continue unabated, stopping a hundred feet from the army of vehicles now assembled, its warm exhaust floating up into the cold Pennsylvania sky. The escort helicopters touched down at various places around the field.

The MD-80 was not in sight. It had entered the air at the Harrisburg Airport as the motorcade crossed Millport Road and was beginning to circle about fifty miles to the north, staying out of visual range. The plane would come in for a landing only when ordered to do so by Edward Clarke.

Canadian authorities had been alerted. They had agreed to allow the MD-80 to enter Canadian airspace and to allow American chase planes to follow, should such an option be required. Canadian authorities had been in constant contact with the FBI for the past hour and had placed antiterrorist units on alert, in the event they would be needed. However, the Americans had no intention of allowing the departure of the plane unless it was absolutely necessary.

On the opposite side of the field from the van, two dark green AH-64 A/D Apache attack helicopters were stationed on the frozen ground between the runway and the control tower, blades whirling, cannons now leveled at the van. A third chopper, an unarmed OH58N observation aircraft, came in loud and low from the east and made a slow, deliberately intimidating pass, hovering for a brief moment directly over the van.

As he steadied the chopper, Chief Warrant Officer Robert Li found it difficult to believe his eyes. On the icy ground below him, police, military, and federal vehicles sat motionless, facing the isolated van. The only movement was the spinning lights from atop the patrol cars. On the grass to his right sat the Apaches, and near them, three small armored vehicles. After moving over the scene, he slid the rear of his chopper around and made another low, deliberate pass over the van before positioning himself about a hundred feet off the ground at the west end of the runway, facing the bizarre scene. His two crew members sat fixed in their positions, now content to watch the drama unfolding on the extensive spectral stage which lay below, patiently waiting for others to determine the role they would play.

"Now, Donovan, you will order the plane to land," instructed Kamile from within the van.

"This is Special Agent Edward Clarke. Donovan is not here. I am presently in charge," responded Clarke, who was standing behind a state patrol car about a hundred feet from the van.

"You are a fool, Clarke. I am the one in charge here! Order the plane to land. If it is not on the ground in fifteen minutes, one of these people will die. Every fifteen minutes after, we will kill another. If you choose, we will sit here for an hour and a half. Only you can save the lives of this family."

After a few seconds, Clarke said, "Let me have that mic. Dale Hayden, this is Ed Clarke, are you there?"

"This is Hayden."

"Dale, did you hear his latest demands? Can we get the plane here in fifteen minutes?"

"I heard, but we can't comply, sir. You should be ready for at least a half hour." Hayden was stalling for time, knowing the channel was open to the assassins inside the van.

Clarke realized his situation. He turned to Sandra Merrall and asked, "Sandra, any suggestions?"

"Ed," Sandra said in a weary voice. "They'll kill anyone who stands between them and freedom. If you can't neutralize them, then let them go or people will die. Things are rather simple with these guys; take 'em at their word."

Clarke nodded, picked up the mic, "This is Edward Clarke of the FBI. Are you listening in the van?"

"We are here," came the reply.

Ed Clarke was well trained, but this was his first crisis leadership position, his first real test. He too had been awake for almost thirty-three hours; too long.

Kamile's raspy voice came on the radio, "You now have twelve minutes," he said.

"It will take at least a half hour to get that plane in here," Clerke responded. "You must wait. Surely, you realize we're doing all we can. We have complied with all your demands. For the sake of those innocent people, be reasonable about our situation. We want you out of here as much as you do. But we can only do so much in such a short period of time. If we—"

"You want to give the aircraft more time. I agree. But thirty minutes from now, the airplane must be on the ground here or all these people will die. All of them! There will be no more discussion, Clarke."

The radio went silent. The wait had now begun.

Across the field, atop the tower and its supporting white pedestal, half-dozen high-powered rifles held by expert marksmen were aimed at the now-covered windows in the van. Below them, on the ground, army personnel carriers of the Pennsylvania National Guard and two armed helicopters waited. Behind the personnel carriers were several military trucks containing equipment, including weapons and explosives. The combined firepower from the various police agencies, FBI Special Forces units, Secret Service, and National Guard troops surrounding the van would be enough to instantly disintegrate it. Lancaster Airport had become a heavily armed battleground.

The relentless wind had intensified the cold, causing a brutal stinging sensation on the face of National Guardsman David Boyd as he stood beneath the tower. He held his thick gloves over his mouth and nose, shielding them from the freezing air. He turned slightly to his right to observe the approach of a sheriff's cruiser, a lone deputy behind the wheel.

The car passed next to the door where Boyd stood, rifle over his shoulder, hands to his face. The cruiser moved forward, coming to a stop behind a five-ton military truck. Immediately in front of the truck sat one of the armored vehicles.

Private Boyd stared at the deputy as he stepped out of the car, turned, and walked directly toward him. *What strange eyes*, he thought. It had been a long cold day for Boyd. Now he would find relief and rest, forever.

Not far away, Clarke reached for the telephone, which was connected to the command center at the FBI building in Washington. He recommended to his superior, Elliot Doering, that the plane be allowed to land at Lancaster. The alternative would lead to the death of at least one hostage, maybe all of them. Since the attorney general had been killed on Capitol Hill, Doering had to make the call.

12:20 PM, the Hoover Building

The Task Force Command Center on the sixteenth floor of the FBI building was filled with agents from administration, criminal, and counterterrorist units. Several were speaking with officials in Canada, Lancaster, and the

White House. Others were making contact with FBI units along the route of a possible hostage flight and with Andrews Air Force Base.

Dir. Elliot Doering was in the command room observing his team and making suggestions when the call from Clarke came through.

After disconnecting with Clarke, Doering turned to his assistant and ordered, "Get me the pilot." The line was immediately connected.

"This is Elliot Doering, director of the FBI; can you hear me, Captain?"

The distant voice came through with minor static, "Yes, sir. I can hear you well. This is Capt. Kevin Holbrook, Mideast Airlines; a former colonel in the Air Force Special Services."

"Captain, you understand the situation, so I'll be brief," responded Doering. "The principal officials on the ground in Lancaster are FBI Deputy Director Edward Clarke and Secret Service Assistant Director James Donovan." Doering hesitated and then continued. "Edward Clarke is the person in charge at the site. You are now instructed to land your aircraft. Following your landing, you will verify all orders and instructions with Clarke prior to taking any action. I will now turn you over to FAA Dir. Mel Collins."

"I understand, sir. I'll do whatever you suggest. Are you aware, sir that I've been given specific orders to carry out should we lose contact? You're aware of my cargo?"

"Yes, on both points, Captain," replied Doering.

"Captain, this is Mel Collins, of the FAA. If you are ordered to take off from Lancaster by Director Clarke, you will be instructed by the FAA to alter your course after flying over Niagara Falls. Two Canadian fighters will enter US air space to escort you to an airfield near the Canadian border. The American fighters will remain behind you and out of visual sight. Canadian air control will direct you to land and you are ordered to follow their instructions."

"The runway at Lancaster is 3,600 feet," the captain came back. "We'll need all that, maybe more. Give us some clearance in case we overshoot."

"We'll do."

"We'll need all the distance on takeoff as well."

"Hopefully, Captain, you won't have to leave the Lancaster Airport."

"Yes, sir; I copy that."

Chapter Thirty-One

12:50 PM, The Lancaster Airport

The assault team stood their ground, waiting for orders. Within a few minutes, the Mideast MD-80 was seen above the horizon cutting through broken gray clouds, heading down from the west toward the runway, landing lights on. Flaps fully extended, the aircraft gradually moved in from the west toward the airport.

At 12:53 PM the plane cleared the police cars on 501 between Thomas Farms and the Business Park. It hit the front edge of the runway and sped past the waiting van with reverse engines blasting against the winter air, brakes fully applied. Smoke rose from the tires as the friction threatened to rip the wheels from their mountings.

The Mideast jet rolled fifteen feet over the concrete edge and came to a stop on the frozen ground. It turned slowly and moved over the rough field back onto the pavement, and headed toward the army surrounding the van.

The loud shrill of the two tail-mounted engines covered all noise on the field. It seemed to crack the delicate icy atmosphere, almost piercing the eardrums of the special forces units lying on the pavement. The plane taxied to a stop near the hostage van.

Suddenly, speakers in dozens of cars blasted to life. "Are you there, Clarke? This is our demand."

"This is Clarke. What's going on?"

"In a few minutes, we will move this vehicle to the back of the plane. Lower the rear stairway of the aircraft, now!"

"I don't believe there is a rear stairway on that plane," answered Clarke.

"Lower the rear emergency stairway, now or one of these people will die." Kamile was no longer willing to negotiate. He would live or die, but he would be in control.

Clarke ordered the stairway to be dropped. In a few minutes it was lowered to the concrete runway. Ten years ago, Clarke had given up cigarettes. Oh, how he needed one now!

"You will order all to leave the plane. I mean all; including the flight crew and those hiding inside. Now!" shouted Kamile.

Jim Lane, the special negotiator, tried again to speak with Kamile. He was beginning to realize how ineffective his techniques and training were in this unique situation. These were the most effective assassins in the world and he was no match for them. Their demands were nonnegotiable.

In a few minutes, Captain Holbrook and his copilot, walked down the rear stairs and stood a few feet out onto the concrete.

"Now, have the military forces leave the aircraft!" shouted Kamile.

"There is no one else aboard," answered Clarke.

There was no response from the van for nearly a minute. "You are lying. But it will be of no importance to us. If they do not leave in one minute, someone will die."

"What do we do, Mr. Clarke?" questioned Mays. "He's not kidding."

Clarke appeared to be frozen in thought. No sign of action.

A long minute passed.

The van eased toward the rear of the aircraft, circled, and stopped within feet of the stairs. An alarm came from the spotter high on the control tower, "This is Position One. The side door on the van is opening."

"Hold your fire," shouted Ed Clarke. "Hold your fire. Position One, what's happening?"

"They're leaving the van," came the reply.

Clarke leaped from the trailer and headed toward the armored vehicle located fifty feet from the rear of the MD-80. He looked to his left as he ran, a dozen agents moving next to him. He could see a huddle of bodies at the rear stairway. Clarke swung around the armored vehicle and yelled for a microphone from the driver of a cruiser parked alongside. "Can anyone identify the targets?" he shouted.

"Sir, this is Position Two. Our position is not good."

"This is position One. We have three men, two holding children, and two women walking toward the aircraft."

"Can you mark the targets, Position One?" Clarke shouted again.

"Don't know."

"Hold your fire," Clarke yelled into the mic, his mind whirling.

Then, sensitive receivers heard the tired, raspy words, "Up the stairs."

At that moment one of the men with a young boy on his shoulders, began to back up the stairway holding the railing with his left hand and the weapon in his right. The others hesitated. One of the women began to climb.

In a few seconds, three people were on the stairway. Two men remained at the foot of the stairs with a woman and child.

"Hold your fire," warned a strained Ed Clarke. "Hold your fire. Any thoughts, Position One; anything at all? Can you get a clean shot?"

Samir stooped to enter the aircraft, keeping the child's head below the frame. He moved quickly to inspect the toilets, the seats, and the cockpit. *Where are they?* he thought. Returning to the stairway, he spoke in a low voice, "The main area is clear. What of the cargo bay?"

From beneath, the raspy voice said, "Do not be concerned. If they are in the cargo area, they can do no harm inside the passenger area. You, the pilot! You will join us. Now! The copilot will move away."

Holbrook stepped forward and stopped a few feet from the two men.

"Now, move to the stairs and back up," the man with the raspy voice demanded.

One by one, the remaining members of the group backed up the stairs following the pilot. A man with a child was the last to enter the aircraft.

In less than two minutes, all of the occupants of the hostage van were on board the MD-80. Everyone suspected the last man to enter was Kamile but could not chance a shot.

Suddenly, to everyone's dread, the rear stairway began to rise. In fifteen seconds, it was completely retracted, and locked into place. Over two hundred heavily armed men watched in silence.

"Will you shoot the tires?" Lane asked.

Clarke turned around and looked directly at Lane. "No," he responded. "We will allow the—" At that instant a rapid series of deep pounding blasts stopped him in midsentence.

Following earth-shaking concussions, several large balls of fire shot up from the area near the control tower. The five-ton truck was blown apart and the entire top of the control tower exploded sending shrapnel hundreds of feet in all directions. The two gunships immediately lifted into the air, moving away from the explosion. One was struck by flying metal. It spun wildly, moved sideways, and drilled into the concrete, sending a fireball of burning fuel across the runway.

"Fajil!" shouted Sandra Merrall standing outside the cruiser, a few feet from Clarke.

"What?" yelled Clarke. "Who?"

"Fajil!" shouted Merrall.

Another explosion and one of the personnel carriers burst apart and flew up into the sky. At two hundred feet in the air, the remaining Apache swung around facing the fire and smoke below. The observation helicopter at the west end leaped into the air and darted for the control tower area. The black smoke rose high into the sky as the chopper swung its tail around, searching for those responsible.

The engines of the MD-80 sent an ear-piercing, high-pitched shrill across the area. It began to move forward heading to the west end of the field.

Fire trucks, emergency vehicles, and armored carriers headed across the runway toward the tower area, barely escaping the engine blast from the MD-80. A fire truck nearly hit the forward section of the aircraft, which was now moving quickly to the west.

The small chopper dropped down over the entry road leading to the tower parking area. James Donovan jumped to the ground, pistol in hand. Fajil was here and Donovan felt a personal obligation to either capture him or blow him to hell. Blazing debris and shreds of metal lay strewn about. Men in various uniforms rushed around the area, weapons and emergency equipment in hand.

Where are you, Fajil? Donovan thought. He had forgotten the aircraft, which was now turning east at the far end of the runway. Donovan hesitated for a moment, *Where would he be?* Looking around, he continued to question himself, *is he in the tower? In one of the vehicles? Where? Where?* He ran to the front of the building. The burning truck and personnel carrier were sending flames high into the air.

He looked directly into the face of each man he passed. "What do you look like now, Fajil, you bastard?" Donovan muttered to himself as he stopped amid the chaos and desperately looked from man to man. *I'll know your eyes.*

Inside the cockpit of the MD-80, Kamile held his pistol to the back of Holbrook's head. The explosions outside had jarred the plane and the fireball had lit up the cabin like a spotlight. Kamile knew it had to be Fajil. He moved back into the cabin and stared out the window toward the control tower.

The military had completely surrounded the area and it was obvious that Fajil would be unable to reach the plane. Thoughts quickly raced through Kamile's mind. Should he wait? Should he stop the plane and insist that Fajil be allowed to join him? In the fire and confusion he realized that if he delayed, all would be lost, even Fajil. Kamile moved back into the passenger compartment.

Running back into the parking area amid the chaos, fire, and explosions, Donovan looked at the heavily damaged control tower. The door was open, men rushed into the building with fire extinguishers and weapons. He focused on the door for a few seconds, then moved toward it as two men came out carrying a stretcher. He looked directly into the eyes of the first man, then into the second. Neither was Fajil. He moved forward toward the door as the stretcher passed. The man's face was covered with ash and dust, his eyes were closed, body covered by a gray blanket. Donovan turned and watched as the stretcher was placed into the ambulance a few feet away. He began to move toward the ambulance and was struck in the back by a National Guardsman who was rushing from the doorway.

Regaining his balance, Donovan approached the ambulance as the doors slammed shut and the stretcher-bearers headed for the front of the vehicle.

"Hold it!" Donovan shouted to the driver. Holding his wallet with Secret Service badge into the air, he yelled, "Get away from the ambulance! Now!"

The driver shouted to his partner, "Move away from the truck. Something's wrong."

As the two men backed away from the vehicle, Donovan grabbed a guardsman standing nearby and ordered him to prepare to fire as he opened the rear doors. The guardsman lifted his rifle and pointed it at the back of the vehicle.

Donovan stood to the left side of the ambulance, gun in his right hand and slowly opened the door with his left. As the door swung fully open, he heard a shout, "James!" It was Sandra Merrall running toward him.

"Stay back, Sandra," yelled Donovan. "Stay, back!"

Merrall froze in her tracks.

Donovan climbed into the ambulance, pistol in hand. He moved forward and rotated the pistol around the head, the cheek and the mouth of the man on the stretcher. After forcing the man's eyes open he examined them, and then pulled back the blanket. A gaping hole containing severed tissue and dried blood caused him to realize this was definitely not Fajil.

The guardsman at the rear of the ambulance looked toward Merrall and back at Donovan, who was now aiming his weapon at the head of the injured man on the stretcher. The guardsman focused his dark narrow eyes on Donovan. He deliberately looked back toward Merrall.

Donovan relaxed a second then examined the victim's features. He was not an Egyptian. He may be Latin, but this man was not from the desert. Donovan turned to face the open doors. The guardsman was gone, and so was Sandra.

Suddenly, like a bolt of lightning it came crashing into his consciousness. *It was Fajil. The guardsman! It's Fajil!*

He jumped from the rear door and looked around but couldn't locate either of the two. He started to panic. He ran toward the field and saw the MD-80 moving down the runway toward the east. He gave it no attention. Despite the chaotic noise, he heard the faint sound of a helicopter engine revving, louder and louder. He spun around. The small chopper lifted from the ground. Sandra was in the front passenger's seat next to the pilot. The guardsman was seated directly behind the pilot. Donovan realized it was Fajil. And he had Sandra!

The helicopter lifted off and began to turn, facing away from the field. Looking up, through the windows of the chopper, James Donovan looked into the eyes of Fajil al-Said. Each recognized the other, knew he was facing a formidable and determined adversary.

Fajil looked to Merrall and back to Donovan. A twisted smile; he had the ultimate hostage. A momentary glance out across the field and he identified the MD-80 now moving along the runway.

Maj. George Montgomery, the helicopter pilot, had spoken with Donovan for over a half hour as they waited at the airport. He instantly recalled Donovan's words; *He is death itself, the man responsible for the disaster in Washington. He won't get away.* Montgomery looked down into Donovan's eyes, then out to the blazing inferno before him. It was his decision whether this man would escape to kill again or be brought to justice.

Fajil yelled, "Move the helicopter out of here now, or the woman will die!"

Montgomery looked to his right. Merrall wasn't frightened. Her eyes seemed to tell him, *It's your call. Do whatever you think best.*

Sandra Merrall then moved her right hand slowly down and across her waist toward the weapon strapped to her belt. Fajil raised the rifle barrel and jabbed it to the back of her left ear. "Take it by the handle and drop it to the floor." Merrall did as she was told.

Montgomery looked down to Donovan as the chopper began to lower. Fajil, for the first time in his life, felt a strike of panic. Had it come to this? Would an insignificant helicopter pilot be his demise?

As the chopper lowered, Fajil looked about the ground. Only one man stood in wait. *How foolish*, thought the assassin. *He should have called for help.*

The chopper was now within a few feet of the ground and Sandra Merrall leaped out the door. Immediately, the pilot shut the engines and jumped to the ground only to have his hip and back splattered by lead from Fajil's weapon.

The helicopter pounded into the ground as Donovan took aim and fired into the cockpit, the bullet glancing off the windshield. Fajil raced from the doorway as the chopper bounced again, leaned sideways, and balanced upright.

Donovan fired into Fajil's arm, hoping to just wound the man; he wanted him alive.

Fajil hit the ground and rolled to the side; firing at Donovan, hitting him in the arm with two rapid thuds, spinning him to the ground.

Merrall fired from behind the chopper, but Fajil had already lined his weapon and sent bullets flying into her right arm and her head. She was blasted to the ground. Rolling to one side, she took aim and squeezed off three rounds at the fleeing assassin as he ran for the base of the tower. She slumped to the ground.

Donovan fired toward Fajil, hitting the corner of the building splintering concrete, then moved forward in pursuit. As he neared the corner, he slowed, crouched down, eased around to face an open area. Guardsmen and police were running toward the airfield. Fajil wasn't there. He stood with his back to the wall, catching his breath. It had been a long time without sleep. His heart was racing. Sweat ran down his face.

Donovan turned back to the chopper to locate Sandra Merrall. She was unconscious. He ran to her side. She was bleeding. The head wound didn't appear serious. *I must stop Fajil!* thought Donovan. *Where the hell is he?* He turned around and ran to the far corner of the tower. Slowly, he peered around the wall. He faced the field, the vehicles and the burning gunship. Black smoke and fire rose into the air as rescuers attempted to pull victims to safety near the building.

Where are you Fajil? Donovan was now worried. He had covered three sides of the building. One side remained unchecked. Either Fajil was somewhere behind him or he was around the next corner.

He caught sight of the south wall of the building, every muscle stretched, eyes and ears focused sharp. No one was there.

The blood was pouring from his arm as he saw the chopper blades again rise above the building. Fajil was at the controls. Donovan raised his pistol to fire as the chopper turned and moved away. Firing with no affect, Donovan could only watch as it banked and disappeared over the tree tops and rolling hills to the north.

Inside the MD-80, Kamile stood in the divider between first class and coach covering the Amish family sitting in the forward two rows. Samir was ahead of him in the galley way covering the pilot. The plane was moving east and gaining speed. Two fire trucks, heading across the field, suddenly appeared in front of the cockpit. Captain Holbrook slammed on the brakes, reversed engines, and turned the plane sharp to the left in an attempt to miss the vehicles, forcing everyone forward and to the right.

The plane skidded sideways as the rear wheels smashed into the last truck, shoving it fifteen feet before sending it rolling over. The runaway plane was now moving directly for the burning helicopter and the men attempting to extinguish the flames. The wheels gave way dropping the belly onto the runway; sparks flew into the air. The captain cut power to the engines as the right wing hit the pavement and bent, sending fuel pouring from numerous cracks. Within seconds, the sparks ignited the fuel and the wing burst into a fireball.

Inside the plane, the assassins were knocked to the floor, Kamile between the second and third rows, Samir in the galley area. Holbrook fought to gain some control while waiting to hear the enormous explosion, which would end his life.

As the plane slowed, its nose smashed into a fifteen-ton military truck, throwing blazing fuel into the air and immediately engulfing it with a thick blanket of fire and smoke. The badly wounded MD-80 came to a rest at the north side of the field, in front of the devastated control tower, flames shooting up from its right side.

Gaining his balance, the Amish man leaped upon Kamile and pinned the machine gun to the floor with his body. Holbrook, head and knees bleeding, reached into a side compartment and grabbed a .38 snub-nosed revolver. He then lowered his hand and twisted the latch on the E&E cover, giving it a bang with his fist.

Samir stood, raised his weapon and pointed it at the man lying on the floor against his comrade. Before he could pull the trigger, his head was split open as Holbrook fired three rounds into him.

Kamile rolled over onto the old man and pounded him on the head with his fist, but the man held tight to his arm. Kamile then fired the weapon and the blast split open the man's stomach as he released his grip and went into convulsions.

The plane was quickly filling with a thick dark smoke as the assassin pulled the bloody machine gun to his side and took a few steps back. As his finger tightened on the trigger, he was struck with rapid fire coming from the cockpit.

As Kamile fell sideways, his finger locked to the trigger; stray bullets exploded wildly through the galley and into the cockpit. Kevin Holbrook, kneeling against the lavatory door, was hit in the shoulder, leg, and hand. Other shots slammed into the back of the front seats, wounding a screaming Amish child and a woman next to her.

Sgt. Roberto Dias, stretched out across the pilot's seat, pulled his feet from the E&E hatch and moved through a noxious black cloud, his AK 47 smoking at the barrel. He raced forward, stepping around bodies and brushing past the captain, who was slumped over in shock. Although visibility was rapidly fading, Dias could see the hostages struggling to remove their seat belts as they choked in the dense smoke.

Two men came up quickly behind him as the sergeant went to his right knee at row one, weapon lowered to the rear of the aircraft, providing cover. He motioned behind his back toward the galley door. Within seconds, the door was open and the escape slide deployed. However, intense fire and smoke prevented an exit. Another few seconds and the Amish were sweeping down the left wing slide to the waiting arms of men in black combat uniforms, passing a dozen commandos scampering up the slide ropes and into the plane.

Not far away, a desperate James Donovan boarded the Apache attack helicopter and headed north above the tree tops, gaining altitude, searching for the small chopper. Thirty minutes later, the chopper was found on a small farm south of Reading. Lying next to it, in a chilled pool of blood, was a farmer who tried to prevent his car from being stolen.

Chapter Thirty-Two

1:45 pm, The Situation Room

Barry Dipaula walked into the crowded Situation Room, accompanied by three Secret Service agents. It had been seventeen hours since the president was killed. They had worked under extreme stress during all of those hours. Now they waited for a word from both Kansas and Pennsylvania.

Dipaula moved to his place at the table and remained standing, a weak smile on his face. The three agents who entered with him, stood close by. The chatter stopped as everyone in the room focused on him. They could tell the news was probably good, for a change.

Looking at the agent standing inside the door, Dipaula said with a steady voice, "Ask Bob Caridene, and as many people from the Secret Service Command Room as they can spare, to join us. Ask all the people who are resting down the hall to join us as well."

In less than three minutes, they were crowded into the room. Dipaula spoke slowly, "Ladies and Gentlemen, it's been the longest seventeen hours of our lives, but I am proud . . . relieved, to tell you we have a temporary president and vice president of the United States. We did it! You did it!" He hesitated for effect. Spontaneous shouts filled the room, as if an immense weight had suddenly been lifted from their shoulders. "It's white smoke, Jerry," Dipaula said with a big grin.

"Goddamn', Barry!" shouted Gannon. "Cut the shit! Who the hell did they elect?" The shouts subsided as exhausted men and women turned their eyes back to the national security advisor.

Dipaula smiled again and said, "They elected Gov. Gary Dupree to serve as president."

He waited for the applause and shouts to subside and then Dansie asked, "Well, who's the VP?"

Dipaula took a deep breath and said, "The vice president is . . . well, it's an unworthy guy from Colorado, Barry Dipaula." The shock hit the room bringing a few seconds of absolute silence. Then, Dansie began applauding, which triggered a thunderous outburst in the room. Congratulations came from all corners.

"God, I love this country!" shouted Gassett. "Bipartisan when it really counts." Water filled her eyes. "A Democratic president and a Republican vice president; a brilliant way to show national unity!"

Tears of relief flowed freely throughout the room as tension drained from each man and woman. They knew that even with its terrible wounds the nation remained strong.

During the celebration in the Situation Room, a few miles away at the Hoover Building, Elliot Doering, received a message from his deputy, Edward Clarke, detailing the closing minutes of the situation in Pennsylvania. Doering immediately contacted the Secret Service Command Room at the White House.

Agent Larry Adams notified Dipaula of Doering's message. No one could hear their conversation. "I know this is sort of anticlimatic, Mr. Dipaula," whispered Adams. "But I have some good news and some bad news as well. Two additional assassins were killed while attempting to escape with hostages from the airport in Pennsylvania. The only known assassin remaining has apparently escaped from the area. It was Fajil. He is still at large. It is believed the other major players responsible for the attack on the Capitol have been killed or captured. A number of our people were killed as well."

Dipaula, replied, "Look, Larry, why not let these people celebrate a bit before we fill them in on the details. God knows they deserve it."

"Barry," Donahue interrupted, "I mean, Mr. Vice President, we just received word from Marty Castellano at state, that Israel has backed down from the deadline. At least for the time being, they may resort to negotiations instead of missiles."

Placing his hands into his pants pockets, Dipaula felt an envelope. Instantly he recalled President Bergstrom's letter to Kilpatrick. He removed the letter from the envelope and read the final paragraphs. A smiled eased across his wearied face. He took a deep breath and handing the letter to Craig Donahue he muttered, "This could have saved us some time and trouble."

Donahue began reading the letter, then paused and said, "He sure thought a lot of you, Barry."

"No, I was referring to the final paragraph," answered Dipaula with a grin.

Donahue looked down at the letter and read in a whisper, "In the most unfortunate event that all members of the line of succession, other than yourself, are lost, I recommend you consider an emergency meeting of the National Governors Conference to aid you in the great crisis." He looked at Dipaula and said, "What do you know, we did all right. The man would have been proud."

January 27, Washington DC

Well, past midnight it began to rain, which was a good thing. The water fell shimmering against the orange light of the arc lamps they set up on the site. It was hard, grim work. The recovery teams had brought in listening gear to probe the rubble for survivors. The deadly clicking of Geiger counters was everywhere. The interior of the dome had been an inner and outer shell of solid cast iron; it now lay in jagged shards the size of small houses, steaming from the lingering heat of the blast, piled among the shattered marble. In their protective suits, the men moved slowly across the devastation like pale ghosts among the ruins of some ancient temple. Only this time the ruins were less than ten days old. One fireman tapping for possible signals from buried victims, struck something metallic with his pry bar. It rang differently than the iron, like a bell. Bracing himself, he levered aside a broken slab, kicked away more debris, and stood very still. 'Here she is,' he said over his radio, and then, against all orders, pulled his mask from his face so he could see her more clearly. When they swung the portable light into place, the rest of them could see he had been crying, his eyes red with exhaustion. At his feet, they could see the face and massive length of the goddess of freedom triumphant—Thomas Crawford's great bronze statue that had topped the Capitol since the Civil War. Undamaged as if by a miracle, shining in the harsh spotlight, she smiled serenely up at them in the pouring rain.

A few miles away, in the Hoover Building, Sandra Merrall put down a file and picked up the telephone. "Hello . . . James? Yes . . . I think I've got something . . . Right . . . The files on Bergstrom's enemies, a match with agency records. One enemy in particular, from way back. You'll recognize the name. A little late but might be the break we're looking for . . . No, I'll come over there."

February 1, Dulles International Airport

James Donovan, Sandra Merrall, Gregg Lawrence, Linnet Singleton, and ten members of a special unit of the FBI and CIA boarded a Boeing 747 at Dulles International Airport. They were headed for Vienna and a meeting with a very select group of people, twenty-seven handpicked specialists assigned to the Red Eagle Team. Their primary assignment; capture Fajil and bring him to justice, or . . . neutralize him.

February 7, Central Europe

In a secluded mansion, high on a mountain in Central Europe, Wade Pike sat at his desk looking out the window. Behind him stood Fajil al-Said, waiting in silence. Pike spoke without turning around, "You've done well. You've succeeded in the most daring assassination of all time. You have won your place in history." He looked up to the sky and out to the wide valley stretching before him. After a few seconds, his fingers leisurely slid under the arm of his chair and pressed a small brown button. The silent alarm was sent to an outer chamber.

Pike turned his chair slowly and faced the assassin. Fajil merely stared down at him, his dark eyes fixed on the arrogant smile of his host.

Pike remained seated, clearly enjoying the moment. He returned the deep stare, waiting patiently for the moment when Fajil realized he had been lured into a trap. Pike knew he could not let this man live, he knew too much.

Wade Pike's smile grew wider as he spoke, "Fajil, you're the best. A few months ago, and I wouldn't have given a dime for your chance at success. I honestly thought you would all be killed."

Pike formed a mock prayer position, a steeple with his fingertips pointing toward the assassin. He continued, "Fajil, you're the one man who would forever be my colleague, or my potential antagonist. We are a lot alike, you and I. Both of us are different from the masses, both born to certain greatness. I really wish we could have worked together again someday; there's so much we could accomplish. Unfortunately, however, that would not be possible. I could never trust you and you could not trust me."

Nothing from Fajil. He was motionless; listening to every word.

"Oh, yes. There is something you should know, Fajil. Revenge is important, however, money is more important. Your assignment was really an investment. There's money to be made when one knows of a growth that will occur in the marketplace, but there is also immense wealth to be had if one knows the exact moment of a major disaster. You see, I made a fortune after your brilliant success in Washington. Fajil, revenge is sweet, but money—money is everything."

Fajil didn't move, his eyes remained fixed on Wade Pike's conceited smile. He thought about Kamile and their dead families, their terrible deaths.

Pike looked to the door on his right and said, "Gentlemen, it's time to conclude this extraordinary man's quest." He looked back to Fajil, curious to see how the world's greatest assassin would face his final moments.

No one entered. A few long seconds passed. The silence, the stillness caused Pike's heart to pound, breathing became an effort. His eyes widened as he looked back at the door. Panic gripped him as he yelled, "Now, you idiots! Now!"

Still, no one entered. Pike looked back to Fajil. The realization of his situation hit him like a kick to his groin. His body went limp, his hands dropped to his sides. With an agonized grimace on his face, he asked, "What? How?"

Fajil took a deep breath and moved his head up slightly as four of his men entered the room. Pike knew he was living his last moments on earth. Looking to Fajil, he stiffened his spine as the assassin raised his pistol and blasted a hole in the billionaire's forehead. Pike's body fell backwards, and then jerked forward. In another instant, he fell out of the seat and onto the floor. Blood spurted from his head as he lay there motionless and died.

Fajil stared down at the one man who most symbolized all he hated about the wealth of the world. It disgusted him to think about how the man lying on the floor before him had used money to destroy the powerless of the world. To Fajil, Pike represented the worst of humankind.

The assassin turned and walked past his men, down the stairway, and out the back door. Pike's bodyguards lay scattered inside the house, on the lawn, and along the driveway. The guard dogs lay dead in their cages.

Four cars drove slowly down the winding road, through the iron gates below the hill and headed to the valley below. A gust of wind blew across the manicured lawns, over the guards' bloodstained bodies, swirled around the quiet mansion, then disappeared into the trees.

Five minutes later the cars were moving at forty miles an hour when they entered a hairpin turn with an abrupt, thirty-foot dirt wall on one side and a steep grassy slope on the other. As the lead vehicle made the sharp right turn around the hillside, the driver instantly slammed on his brakes. Tires screeched as the rear of the car skidded to the left, nearly going over the embankment before it came to a stop only fifteen feet from two large trucks blocking the roadway. The drivers behind him reacted quickly, sending smoke flying from their tires as they stood on the breaks with every ounce of pressure they could apply. The third car slammed into the car in front, nearly pushing it into the hillside. Doors sprung open, men whirled out with guns in hand.

Dozens of armed men in black combat uniforms, emerged from behind the trucks. No one knew for certain who fired the first shot, but weapons opened up and bullets filled the air. Men joined in from high on the cliff above and from the slope below. The assassins were being riddled. The driver of the rear car shoved it into reverse, tires spun as the car shot backwards and up the road. Within a hundred yards, it was rammed hard by a heavy-duty military truck coming down the road. The force of the collision sent the car over the edge and rolling down the hill, slamming into a stand of trees.

As the battle raged below him, James Donovan, from his position on the overhang above, caught a glimpse of Fajil escaping from the rear car and heading for the trees, machine pistol in hand. A dozen heavily armed men sprung from the back of the truck and headed over the hill, straight for the damaged vehicle, guns blazing.

Donovan shouted to Gregg Lawrence lying next to him, "It's Fajil!" He leaped up with a short-barreled automatic in his hand and moved quickly, racing across a rise and down a steep embankment. He wouldn't let Fajil get away this time. Not this time! Bullets zipped by him and he dove for cover among small boulders. He had to chance moving around the rocks and down into the forest below.

Crouching low, he sped down the hill, taking fire from the four men now attempting to use a vehicle as cover before their attention was quickly diverted by the soldiers swarming headlong toward them.

Within seconds Donovan entered a thicket; dense trees, large rocks, and thick brush surrounded him. Distant gunfire was almost eliminated as all senses came to focus on capture of the assassin and his own survival. He stopped, heart pounding in his ears, sharply tuned to nearby sounds, went down on one knee and listened. Nothing. He rose and slowly moved forward a few feet, stopped. Down again. Still nothing. Silence. The agent's eyes swiveled about, looking for the slightest out-of-place movement in the bushes around him. Rising up, he moved along a deer trail about twenty yards. Nothing.

It's come down to this, Fajil. You and me, he thought.

Suddenly, he heard a sliding noise, someone loosing control about twenty yards dead ahead. He raced forward, straight for the sound, barrel up, dodging branches, leaping over fallen limbs and trees, then down again on one knee. Listening. Silence.

Donovan fought to slow his breath, kept it shallow, partially to hear better, more to keep from being heard. *My God, I can't see him. Is he looking at me? No, if he was, I'd already be dead. I've got to focus. Focus! Where are you Fajil, you murdering bastard?*

Donovan stood again, moved forward, slowly, setting each step down easy, avoiding any noise. He suddenly bolted at the edge of a small ravine partially concealed by undergrowth. There, down the slope, he could see skid lines cut into the ground, sliding boot marks. *He was here! That's where he slid—what I heard!*

Crouching, Donovan backed away, convinced that if he followed the tracks down the steep incline, it was almost certain the assassin would be waiting for him below. Then, he heard the faint rustle of a moving branch behind him and instantly turned as a blade sliced his left arm. With Fajil's weight crashing against Donovan, the two men went flying over the edge and down the slope, grabbing at each other as they rolled five, ten, fifteen feet before slamming hard against a cluster of moss-covered rocks, handguns flying into the thick brush.

In one uninterrupted move, the men came to their feet, grasping each other, face-to-face, Donovan holding tight to Fajil's wrist, keeping the barbed knife only inches away. The assassin pulled hard and fell backwards, kicking Donovan in the groin. As Fajil's back hit the ground, he raised the agent high into the air and sent him up over, crashing down on his right side. The reactions were fluid, immediate, as both enraged men turned, reaching for the other. They scrambled for control, trying frantically to get to their knees.

Donovan felt the blade whiz past his cheek as the assassin made a hasty thrust, lost his balance, and missed his mark. The agent drove the butt of his right hand up hard against Fajil's chin, jolting his head back, and followed with a solid left jab to the assassin's face, his body rolling over and on top of him. Fajil used Donovan's momentum to keep him rolling and ended up on top. Donovan was stunned and could do nothing, but bring both his hands up to grab anything, to parry the knife, to gouge an eye, anything!

The blade came down hard, piercing Donovan's forearm, just above the wrist, slicing through skin, deflected enough to land in the dirt an inch from his face. Kicking with both feet, Donovan landed a solid blow to Fajil's stomach before the assassin could yank at the embedded knife. He then shot a solid right to the assassin's chin, jarring his head just long enough to roll over and grab the wrist still locked to the knife buried deep in the ground.

With his right hand pinned down and the agent pushing hard against his chest, Fajil reached around with his left hand and sent his fingers digging into Donovan's eyes and nose, pulling back with all his strength.

Donovan felt the sharp, intense ripping pain, as if his eyes were being torn from their sockets. Still holding tight to Fajil's wrist, he jerked his head around trying to shake off the powerful tearing grip. He could no longer resist as the assassin's fingers, inflicted excruciating pain and pulled him away from the buried knife. Releasing his left hand, he jabbed backward with his elbow, breaking the powerful grip, and came down with his mouth, burying his teeth deep into the assassin's wrist.

Fajil held tight as Donovan's teeth dug deeper into his flesh. He pounded on the back of agent's head, but to no avail. Fajil released his grip on the knife and pulled his right hand back. Then both men rolled over each other a half-dozen times before the assassin could get to his knees. Instantly Donovan reacted, rolling away and then leaping to his feet as Fajil flew into him, knocking him back against a fallen tree. Both men grabbing, punching, and kicking, blood covering their hands and faces as they slammed against rocks, branches, trees in a desperate fight for survival.

Donovan lost his balance and fell to the ground, pulling the assassin with him. Fajil got to his knees, reached for a jagged rock and raised it high into the air, a clear path to the agent's face. Donovan didn't hear the shots as the body above him was pounded to the side, down onto the ground and went limp. Getting to his knees, he looked at Fajil who appeared to be unconscious, blood spurting from the left side of his head.

Sandra Merrall had risen from her firing position and was moving toward him, pistol aimed at the assassin; Gregg Lawrence, Linnet Singleton, and four men in combat uniform immediately behind her. As they approached the two men, Donovan fell back to the ground, totally exhausted, face bleeding, and slowly muttered, "Is he dead?"

Lawrence stared at the limp body of Fajil al-Said and leaning down, whispered, "Do you want him to be?"

Donovan, eyes closed, breathing heavy, responded, "No! I want the bastard alive."

As Lawrence and Singleton cuffed the assassin, Sandra opened a white cloth and pressed it gently against Donovan's face, absorbing blood, pressing flesh back into position and said, "We were right about Pike, James. He was involved."

A few seconds and James Donovan, barely audible, said, "You were right, Sandra. You were right."

Chapter Thirty-Three

March 27, The White House

Down the mall from the White House, the cleanup of the Capitol was nearing completion. Plans for its reconstruction were being drawn. A special monument was added to the plans for the new hall, which would be dedicated to those who lost their lives during the State of the Union Address.

On the south lawn of the White House, President Dupree presented special medals for valor to some of the many people who had struggled in secrecy to keep the union safe during the time of its greatest crisis.

Among those present and receiving medals were James Donovan, Sandra Merrall, Gregg Lawrence, Linnet Singleton, Charlie Morrison, Chris Van Meter, Terry Johnson, Edward Clarke, and a now very famous comedian, Bob Caridene. Vice President Barry Dipaula was presented with the Medal of Freedom.

Dupree, had recently returned from New York where he announced his candidacy for president of the United States. The election would take place in November.

Also, in the crowd on the south lawn, noticed only by a few, was a Russian agent named Igmanov. No medals for Igmanov, but he had the personal recognition of a grateful nation and of a good friend, Barry Dipaula.

President Masarov was sent a very special message from the president of the United States and a promise that the design of the new monument at the Capitol would contain a tribute to Masarov, president of Russia. His restraint in crisis was critical.

Obidiov and his cohorts resigned their positions. But Masarov continued his vigilance, for others lurked in the dark recesses of the Kremlin eager to seize control of Russia, and return her to the tyranny of Marxism.

Gen. Jake McCloud was given his own room at the Walter Reed Army Medical Center Department of Psychiatry, a stopover on his way to prison, and Gen. Sanchez became chairman of the Joint Chiefs of Staff.

The individuals involved with the militia groups having participated in the attack were rounded up, charged with conspiracy, and prepared for lengthy trials.

While the Alliance remained a problem and their biological and nuclear capabilities were intact, the United Nations Security Council was successful in removing the immediate threat of a world war. Covert actions by the CIA, creating internal strife among the Alliance nations, kept them from signing agreements.

President Dupree concluded his speech by saying, "President Bergstrom intended to tell us what the state of our union was on the night he was assassinated. He told us in his death and the deaths of our beloved colleagues and fellow citizens, that we can truly be proud of the state of our union. The union is alive and well, and will remain so as long as we have people, like these we honor here today, to keep her safe. They are citizens, like millions more across this country; free men and women determined to remain free. Their courage and dedication demonstrates the secret valor that has made this country the greatest in the history of the world. Secret valor exercised by common, ordinary men and women, no matter what their state in life, working in the shadows for their country without special recognition, praise, or glory, are the true heroes in what has been our nation's highest test of courage and allegiance. Freedom is a delicate treasure, like a fine crystal; if not secured it can shatter in an instant. Freedom is always secured by average, ordinary, ever vigilant people who assume personal responsibility to shield it with their lives and hold it firmly in the palm of their hands."

Following the ceremony, Donovan and Merrall asked Dipaula if he would take a short break with them, away from the crowd. The three walked along the pathway to the outside recreation area, leaving the celebration behind; two protective agents followed a short distance away. They stopped near the outdoor courts and all three instinctively looked up into the azure sky, it was truly a beautiful day, the best since October. Squirrels scampered nearby; a warm breeze blew through the trees, swaying the new leaves casually about.

Dipaula uttered to no one in particular, "My God, what an experience."

Donovan placed his arm around Merrall and she gave him a tender nudge. Dipaula noted the affectionate move and had already accepted that his two friends had become intimately involved. They had shared so much together while he had worked continuously on his new responsibilities.

"What are you going to do now, James?" Dipaula asked.

"Well, I'll be here for a while. I have a few years left before moving on. I'll rest easier once Fajil is put away. Hope to hell he isn't used as a bargaining chip someday."

"No chance!" Dipaula didn't hesitate. "Not a prayer."

"What about you, Sandra?" asked Dipaula.

"Oh, I'll stick around here for a while. Fajil needs to be tried and punished and the militia's still a problem. There's a lot of work to do before this country is on its feet again."

Donovan looked into his friend's eyes and asked, "What about you, Barry? I hear you've been strongly encouraged to make a run for the presidency?"

"Well, the offer's there," he looked up to the birds singing in a nearby tree. Then, with a hesitant voice, added, "I've been thinking about it. But, to be honest with you, the Senate might be a possibility."

"The Senate?" asked Sandra, a frown on her face.

"Yeah," his voice faltered a bit. "Isn't what I'd set out to do with my life, but . . . could be interesting." He wasn't convinced.

"You're a good man to have at the top, Barry," Donovan added. "You could win the big one; right now. A lot of people think so."

"I'm one of them," Merrall quickly affirmed.

"I appreciate that. But I think I've had my fill of this house." They all laughed.

"If I were you," Donovan remarked, "I'd go for it."

"Some very important people want it to happen, Barry," Merrall said. "People who can make it happen. Don't let this opportunity pass you by."

"You've got a lot of political and financial support, Barry," Donovan immediately added. "I agree with Sandra; this is your time. Don't let it get away. By the way," Donovan continued with a smile, "Caridene said he's got your voice down pretty good and, knowing how you hate microphones, could make your radio presentations for you."

Dipaula, grinned, looked back at the crowd a hundred feet away, and noticed a rather large gathering of influential newly appointed republican senators staring in his direction. Thoughtfully, he glanced back to his two friends and after a few seconds, nodded, turned, and walked back toward the White House. He realized this house and its power suited him like a comfortable sweater on a cold winter night and the national spotlight, which he had attempted to avoid over the years, was now surprisingly warm. He would go for it. As he had with the mountains of Colorado, he would go for the top.

April 27, 11:30 AM
ADX Super-Maximum Security Prison
Florence, Colorado

ADX-Florence was tucked securely inside the obscure, stark surroundings of the small town of Florence, Colorado, population four thousand. Once a thriving cattle and coal region not far from Colorado Springs, the city was now home to the worst of the nation's terrorists, murders, and serial killers.

Inside the supermax prison, a weary guard sat in a near stupor outside an isolated cell. A small cockroach scrambled gingerly across the cold concrete floor, its eyes focused on the tiny breadcrumb lying below the guard's metal chair. Corporal Jonathan Bailey had nearly dozed off when the movement on the floor brought him back to life. The guard eased his legs a bit, leaned forward and the chair came slowly and quietly to rest on all four legs.

The roach changed direction, moved a few feet toward Bailey then suddenly stopped. Bailey slowly raised his left foot, anticipating the loud slam about to break the silence in his corridor, to be followed by a familiar grinding, crunching sound. The cockroach froze to its spot, having shifted focus toward the approaching footsteps which now echoed down the long hall. The Corporal's eyes instinctively moved to the prisoner behind the open bars, then to his right where three men in dark blue uniforms were moving toward him.

The officers approached, hard leather boots echoing down the hallway, one carrying a tray of food. "Back away." bellowed one of the officers, as he rapped his stick on the thick metal bars. Bailey sat up straight as a small rectangular door opened at floor level and the tray slid inside the cell.

Fajil ignored the interruption as he lay on a cot, hands behind his head, staring thoughtfully at the ceiling. His mind wandered back through time to that fateful day in 1973. His eyes closed; the image of his wife and child filled his mind.

As the three officers moved down the hall, Corporal Bailey broke into a satisfied smile upon hearing the familiar crunch as he stepped squarely on the stupefied cockroach, grinding it into the cold concrete floor.

Fajil slowly opened his eyes, looked over at the dead cockroach just outside the cell and then at his hand, studying the scar. He felt again the searing pain from that day long ago when he pulled the brass panel from the wall in his destroyed Soviet-built flat in the Qahirah section of Port Said, the home where his wife and daughter had perished. He recalled the panel clearly. It read, *McDonnell Douglas Aircraft Corporation, St. Louis, Missouri.*

The End

Printed in the United States
85987LV00007B/124-141/A